…a dream come true.

…grew up in Wales and now …Hertfordshire market town with her scientist husband, her incredibly imaginative and creative daughter and her adventurous, adorable little boy. In Sophie's world, happy *is* for ever after, everything stops for tea, and there's always time for one more page…

Jo McNally lives in coastal North Carolina with one hundred pounds of dog and two hundred pounds of husband—her slice of the bed is very small. When she's not writing or reading romance novels (or clinging to the edge of the bed), she can often be found on the back porch sipping wine with friends while listening to great music. If the weather is absolutely perfect, Jo might join her husband on the golf course, where she tends to feel far more competitive than her actual skill level would suggest.

She likes writing stories about strong women and the men who love them. She's a true believer that love can conquer all if given just half a chance.

You can follow Jo pretty much anywhere on social media (and she'd love it if you did!), but you can start at her website, jomcnallyromance.com

Also by Sophie Pembroke

Newborn Under the Christmas Tree
Island Fling to Forever
Road Trip with the Best Man
CEO's Marriage Miracle
Carrying Her Millionaire's Baby
Pregnant on the Earl's Doorstep
Slow Dance with the Best Man
Proposal for the Wedding Planner

Also by Jo McNally

A Man You Can Trust
Nora's Guy Next Door
She's Far From Hollywood

Discover more at millsandboon.co.uk

SNOWBOUND WITH THE HEIR

SOPHIE PEMBROKE

IT STARTED AT CHRISTMAS...

JO McNALLY

MILLS & BOON

First Published in Great Britain 2019
by Mills & Boon, an imprint of HarperCollinsPublishers,
1 London Bridge Street, London, SE1 9GF

Snowbound with the Heir © 2019 Sophie Pembroke
It Started at Christmas... © 2019 Jo McNally

ISBN: 978-0-263-27274-1

1219

MIX
Paper from
responsible sources
FSC™ C007454

This book is produced from independently certified FSC™ paper to ensure responsible forest management.

For more information visit: www.harpercollins.co.uk/green

Printed and bound in Spain
by CPI, Barcelona

SNOWBOUND WITH THE HEIR

SOPHIE PEMBROKE

For Laurie, with every possible best wish
for your adventures ahead!
Hope this Christmas is your most magical one yet.

CHAPTER ONE

TORI EDWARDS STARED up at the crenellations and chimneys of Stonebury Hall and wondered which eighteenth-century aristocrat had decided to build a house with battlements in the middle of nowhere, on the north-westerly edge of the North York Moors National Park. Who did they think they were defending themselves from out there anyway?

She supposed the answer was probably in the plastic information file she'd been given on arrival, but her fingers were too frozen to open it and check. The agent who'd welcomed them could probably have told her too, but Tori wasn't here for the guided tour. She was here to judge exactly how Stonebury Hall could be the next link in the Earl of Flaxstone's chain of profitable estates, since apparently he'd bought it without consulting her, his deputy, anyway. The agent could only tell her what the property *had* been. She needed to explore it alone to get a feel for what it *could* be.

That said, maybe she could explore *inside* for a while, on the off chance it was ever so slightly warmer away from the biting wind. She looked up at the crenellations again. The stonework matched the heavy grey of the sky, and the whole building gave off a 'go away' vibe. She had a suspicion that inside would be just as chilly.

Still, she needed to see the rooms too. Get a feel for if this building was itching to be a hotel, or a business centre, or a restaurant and tea room with craft and independent shops around it. Maybe a place for team-building retreats. Or a farm shop and café, if the land around it proved profitable. So many options…and, for once, Tori might actually get to decide what happened to the space next. Her own project, her chance to show the earl how far she'd come in his employ, that she was ready for more—more responsibility, more challenges, more independence. More life.

'This place is smaller than it looked on the agent's website.' A clipped, plummy voice swept in on the cold draught through the windows, before its owner even appeared in the room. Wasn't it just like Jasper, Viscount Darlton, the earl's only son, to assume she'd be there waiting breathlessly to hear him talk? 'Come have a look at the kitchens.'

He disappeared back through the doorway, not even waiting to see if she followed. Typical. Jasper *always* expected women to be at his beck and call—there when he wanted them, and then gone when he didn't. Just like everything else in his privileged life, she assumed.

She *did* follow him, though. Not because of his aristocratic manner, or his dark, handsome looks, or even his air of expectation and confidence. Because it was her *job*.

And because she wanted to see the kitchens. She was definitely leaning towards some sort of culinary enterprise for this place…

'Huh.' She looked around what, in a building without battlements, would have been a nice, average, farmhouse kitchen, with space for a dining table.

'See what I mean?' Jasper ran his hand over the battered wooden table in situ. 'This is more like an over-sized home than a commercial property.'

A place can be both, Tori thought, but didn't say. Just those simple words would give away more of her past than she'd be comfortable with Jasper—or anyone in her new life—knowing. It was the sort of comment that would raise questions. Ones she was far happier not answering.

She'd let Jasper get too close precisely once in her life. It wasn't a mistake she intended to repeat.

'It's cosy,' she admitted instead. 'But I can still see a lot of potential here. I'm going to go check out the other rooms.'

She'd meant alone, but Jasper followed her all the same, adding his own observations about the property. To Tori's irritation, she found they often matched her own—which meant she then went out of her way to find evidence to the contrary. Apparently, five years away from Flaxstone hadn't made the earl's heir any less irritating or persistent. Or maybe she was just oversensitive to it, given the last time they'd seen each other.

Strange to think that for one night she'd honestly thought there might be more to him than the spoilt playboy he portrayed to everyone else. Stupid of her, really.

'This would be a fantastic master bedroom,' Jasper said, once they'd reached the upstairs. He crossed the room to the window—rising from Jasper's waist level almost to the high ceiling, and wide enough to fit a cosy loveseat beneath. 'Look at those views over the moors.'

Tori didn't want to look. Out of that window was just another memory she was working on forgetting. She knew what those moors looked like. She'd grown up there. And she was far happier now she was away from them, she reminded herself, in case nostalgia slipped in again just at the sight of the landscape. Living in the tiny cottage on the earl's estate, just south of York, was far more pleasant. And more than that, a sign of how far she'd come. How right she'd been to leave.

Whatever the consequences had been.

It was important to always remember that. Especially at this time of year, when the temptation to go back was so strong.

'Those clouds look heavy,' Jasper added, squinting up at the grey skies. 'Did they forecast more snow? I know they're even talking about a white Christmas.'

'That'll be good for the Christmas fair at the estate,' Tori replied. That was what this season meant to her now. Revenue and marketing potential. It was better that way.

'I was rather thinking it would be good for snow-ball fights.' Jasper turned away from the window with a wicked grin.

Tori rolled her eyes. 'Your father is hoping for a spectacular event this year.'

Jasper's grin fell away at her mention of the earl. Interesting.

What had brought the errant Viscount Darlton home to Flaxstone, after five long years away? Tori found herself wondering—not for the first time—as they toured the rest of the upstairs of the house, then made their way back to the wide entrance hall. Before he'd left, Jasper had been the quintessential aristocratic playboy. Laid-back, permanently amused by life, and confidently parading a selection of beautiful women through Flaxstone Hall—and never the same one twice.

He'd also been an incurable flirt, and seen Tori as a challenge, she figured, since she couldn't imagine why he'd waste time flirting with her otherwise. Not when he had all those moneyed honeys to seduce.

Since he'd returned to Flaxstone, Jasper was still all those things, but with a darker edge to them somehow, one she didn't quite understand. And it niggled at her, not knowing what had changed.

Not knowing why he'd left in the first place.

If she had more of an ego she'd think he'd left and then returned purely to make her life hell, except she was certain she didn't rank that high in his thinking or priorities. Except for that one night, just before he'd left. He'd been thinking about her then, as he'd kissed his way across her naked body, whispering her name against her skin in the darkness.

But that night was something she *definitely* wasn't thinking about. Ever again. It was another thing that was better left in the past. She'd known better then, and she *absolutely* knew better now.

'I think we've seen all we need to see,' Jasper told the agent, who was loitering in the chilly hallway waiting for them, his hands jammed into his armpits to try and keep warm. 'Right, Tori?'

She tried to think of a reason to disagree, just on principle, but nothing sprang to mind, and it *was* cold, so she gave a short nod of agreement.

'We'll be back in touch to organise our next moves once we've shared our findings and ideas with the earl,' she said, shaking hands with the agent before they left. With the sale in the bag already, he didn't seem particularly bothered by how long that might take, or what they had planned for the place.

'My turn to drive.' Jasper held out his hand for the

keys to the four-by-four as they strode across the gravel driveway to where she'd parked, an hour or more earlier.

Tori's fingers flexed around the keys in her pocket, reluctant to give them up. 'I can drive back.'

'I know you can. You drove here, after all. Which is why it's my turn,' Jasper said, with exaggerated patience.

Tori hesitated, and he sighed.

'What? Are you afraid I'll crash? Or steal you away to some secluded inn in some village and treat you to dinner—I am actually starving, though, so that one might happen.'

Depends on the inn.

But she couldn't tell him that either, so, reluctantly, she handed over the keys.

'Thank you.' Jasper's smile was wide, bright and genuine—the sort of smile only someone raised with advantages rather than disasters could smile.

It just made her resent him more.

'Come on,' she said as she opened the passenger-side door and climbed in. 'I want to get home.'

Home to Flaxstone, that was, where she could put the past firmly behind her again. Not anywhere along the way that might have once held the title of 'home'.

Because maybe once she was safely back in her bright, light and solitary cottage, she'd be able to stop thinking about the one night she'd spent with Jasper, and forget all about a dark, cosy inn out on the moors that she used to call home.

Jasper eased himself into the driver's seat and immediately turned up the car's heating. It was colder than ever out there—chillier even than his father's reception when he'd returned home to Flaxstone a week or so earlier. And Jasper hadn't honestly thought that was possible.

The earl, in all his aristocratic glory, had obviously decided that the rift in the family had to be *Jasper's* fault, rather than a result of his own behaviour. Jasper had had plenty of time to think about it over the past five years, and the only conclusion he'd been able to reach was that his father's life hadn't ever allowed for the possibility of not getting everything he wanted—so he just took it, and to hell with the consequences for everybody else.

Well. One thing he couldn't just take was his son's respect. That had been lost five years ago when he'd discovered the truth about his father—and nothing that had happened since showed any signs of the earl winning it back.

But he was done thinking about his father for the day. He'd done what he came here to do.

Coming back to the UK at all hadn't been his first choice; he was happy with the life he'd forged over in America, with the reputation he'd built up and the portfolio of work he'd created. But then his father had emailed and told him that, given Jasper's absence, he intended to legitimise his *other* son as his heir, too. The title was Jasper's by law, and Flaxstone went with the title, but everything else—the business, the money, the properties—that was the earl's to distribute as he pleased.

And apparently his illegitimate son by the housekeeper was what pleased him most. The son Jasper had only discovered existed by accident, five years ago, and the reason he'd left home in the first place.

His best friend, Felix.

Jasper hadn't come back for the money, or the property, or the business. He'd come back for his reputation and, most of all, for his mother.

And it was his mother that had brought him to Stonebury Hall with Tori.

Stonebury Hall would be the perfect home for his mother, if Jasper couldn't dissuade his father from making a big, public announcement, and the earl went through with his latest, ruinous plan. Jasper wasn't even sure his mother *knew* about Felix, or if his father had any intention of telling her before the rest of the country. His mother, lovely and loving as she was, had never really seemed to inhabit the same world as the rest of them, as far as Jasper could tell. She was perfect for opening church fetes, throwing Christmas parties and keeping their little corner of England the way things had been fifty years ago, when she'd watched her mother run her own home in a fashion that was out of date even then, but she'd never really caught up with the changing times— or shown any desire to.

But the changing times had caught up with them.

Right now, the earl was still sticking his fingers in his ears and humming, metaphorically at least, telling himself that an illegitimate son, brought up in the household, with his mother still working at the house, was nothing in this day and age. That no one would care that the boy Jasper had grown up with, whose birthday was just weeks before his own, was actually his half-brother.

That Jasper's father had been lying to him, and everyone else, his whole life.

People would care, that Jasper was sure of.

Jasper had cared, mightily, the day he'd found out— an accidental glimpse of some paperwork in his father's office that had turned out to be his updated last will and testament, detailing what he left to each of his *sons*.

That plural had nearly destroyed him on its own.

Hearing the details from his own father, and realising that Felix already knew *exactly* who his father was—that was what had driven him away completely.

And now the earl was talking about legitimising Felix, handing responsibility for some of the estates over to him, since, as he put it, 'My other son seems to have disowned us altogether.'

The media was going to have a field day with that. And Jasper wanted to protect his mother from that, even if he couldn't protect himself.

She needed a retreat, a bolthole, somewhere to hide away from the media, the public, and her husband for a while. Or for ever. And Stonebury Hall would be perfect for that.

Now he just needed to convince the earl to let him make it happen. His father might be the one who decided on the estate's investments and built up the property portfolio, but the actual work of transforming these places into whatever it was they believed they could be—and make money as—was delegated to others.

And that work, that sort of huge development project, was exactly what Jasper had spent five years managing overseas. He could take it on, make it everything his mother needed. A home, perhaps with a small business involved to bring in income and give her something else to focus on. Perhaps a teashop. Or a stable yard, if the paddock at the back was large enough. He needed to examine the specifications again.

And then he needed to convince his father. Surely, once the sordid truth about him, about their marriage, was out in the world, the earl would understand that his wife needed an escape, a refuge. He wouldn't begrudge her that, Jasper was almost certain. At least, not when he saw the inevitable backlash and scandal it caused.

It was possible that the whole announcement was just a ploy to get him back in the country, Jasper mused as he eased the car onto another tiny back road that led to another back road, and another, until they finally reached something wide enough for two cars to pass without one of them ending up in a hedge. Maybe it was all a cunning plan to appeal to Jasper's pride, or even his greed, by threatening to give away his inheritance, responsibilities and status to Felix.

Which just showed how little his father knew him. He had plenty of money of his own these days, thanks to a lucrative career and some canny investments with his inheritance from his grandparents. And he took pride in the career and the life he'd forged for himself away from Flaxstone. As for the responsibilities, Felix was welcome to them, too. Living a life free from expectations, except the ones he placed on himself, had a lot going for it.

But he couldn't leave his mother alone here to be humiliated and, worse, hurt. That was a step too far. If his father was going public, Jasper needed to be there when his mother found out the truth, and he needed to protect her, spirit her away from everything that followed. Preferably to Stonebury Hall.

And he was still thinking about his father.

Shaking his head, Jasper forced himself to focus on the road, the snowflakes starting to fall in earnest outside. The woman sitting next to him.

Anything except what had brought him home.

Although, he had to admit, the line in his father's email about Tori had only added to his certainty that he urgently needed to return. He hadn't imagined she'd still even be working for his father after all this time. And just one sentence—a note about how Felix had been working closely with her on estate business—had sent his mind spiralling back to that one night they'd spent together.

The night he'd found his father's will.

The night before he'd confronted his father and learned the full, awful truth.

He'd left the country without speaking to her again, which was, he had to admit, a pretty shoddy move on his part. But then, she'd clearly regretted their night together because she'd got up early and crept out of her own bedroom, in her own cottage, to avoid him the morning after, so it wasn't entirely on him.

'So, shall we take the boring route home or the scenic one?' he asked, grinning with a jollity he really didn't feel.

Tori looked up from her phone, eyes wide. The silent journey so far apparently hadn't bothered her at all—no surprise there, really. Tori Edwards was the most closed-off woman he'd ever met, so unlike all the other women he spent time with. Well, almost all the time…

He allowed himself a real smile at the memory of the one night he'd managed to slip under her defences and find the real woman hiding behind them. Tori had more battlements than Stonebury Hall, Jasper decided, remembering a time before his life had fallen apart, when trying to breach those defences had been a kind of game for him and Felix. A challenge. Something that niggled at him until he couldn't help but strive to get her to react, to show something of her real personality—rather than those closed doors behind her eyes.

It hadn't escaped his notice that the one time he'd succeeded was the night he'd felt more wounded and open than ever before.

Maybe it was all the thinking he'd been doing about his father, or maybe it was the snow and the enclosed space, but suddenly Jasper wanted to see if he could break through those battlements again—even if only for a moment.

'Given the snow, I'd suggest sticking to the main roads,' Tori said, her voice even, uninterested. At least, if a person weren't listening carefully.

Jasper was listening *very* carefully. Which was why he caught the faint tremor underneath her words. She cared, one way or another, and suddenly he wanted to find out which.

He needed a new challenge—a distraction from his disintegrating family. Persuading Tori Edwards to open up a little could be the perfect entertainment for a snowy afternoon.

He smiled, and began his campaign.

'The snow isn't that heavy,' Jasper pointed out, his lazy voice easy with lack of caring. 'And the main roads will be packed with drivers avoiding the more interesting routes. We could cut across the moors and make it home before the real weather rolls in.'

Tori glanced out of the car window. The clouds above definitely suggested that there was a lot more snow to come.

'The weather can be different on the moors.' She bit down on her lower lip to dispel the memories. 'The snow might have already hit there.'

'Or it might miss it entirely.'

That didn't sound likely. But he was irritatingly right

about how busy the main roads would be in this weather. If they *could* make it across the lesser-used moor roads it would be quicker—unless the snow was heavier, or too many other people had the same idea, or there was a rogue tractor or sheep blocking the road…

They were idling now at the crossroads, the junction where Jasper had to choose which path to follow. Any minute now another car would come up behind them and start beeping its horn—not that Jasper seemed bothered about holding other people up. She wasn't sure he'd ever realised that it was human to worry about *anyone* else's feelings.

Normal, empathetic people didn't leave the country for five years after sleeping with a person, and then never mention it again.

'Don't you ever take a risk?' he asked, that wicked grin she remembered too well on his lips.

That grin had got her into trouble before. Well, that grin and half a bottle of gin—stolen from the earl's drinks cabinet, of course—and a bad day that had lowered her defences, if she remembered correctly.

'Unnecessary risk is the height of foolishness.'

Of course she took risks. That was a normal part of doing business. But personal risk? That was another matter. She'd taken enough of those in the past to know what happened when the risk didn't pay off. Okay, she'd taken precisely one. But that had been more than enough to teach her a lesson.

Her single night with Jasper had just been an extra reminder. She'd known better than to get involved, however fleetingly, with someone for whom romance was basically a sport. But she'd put her fears aside and let herself believe that there might be more to him, that he might think more of *her*, only for him to prove quite comprehensively that she was as unimportant to him as she'd always imagined.

She didn't need reminding again.

'This risk is necessary,' Jasper announced. 'I'm starving, and I want to get home for dinner.'

'Your stomach is not an emergency.'

'Maybe not to you.' Jasper pulled on the handbrake and leant closer, looking into her eyes. 'Are you worried about the snow? Because if it's bad we'll turn back. Or find that secluded inn I mentioned and have some dinner while we wait it out…'

Tori tore her gaze away from his. She wasn't even going to imagine what *he* was imagining could happen between them if they did that. Jasper's determined campaign of flirtation had always been distracting, however much she knew better than to let herself fall for it. '*Not* happening. Fine. Just get us home in one piece, okay?'

'Your wish is my command, milady.' Humming a few lines from a Christmas carol, Jasper took off again—heading, of course, for the road that traversed the Yorkshire moors.

Tori hunkered down in her seat. It wasn't the snow she was scared of—not that she planned to let Jasper know that.

She knew those moors. They were her home, her playground, her life, growing up. But she'd avoided so much as driving through them for nearly eight years now. She'd made her whole life away from them—not too far away, but far enough. This was the first time the earl had sent her to look at property practically on them.

And she knew the road that Jasper would take. Knew the tiny villages and hamlets it would wend and wind through, the landmarks and features it would pass. The inn that would be sitting not far from the side of the road that they would speed past without comment, without recognising the part it had played in Tori's life. The valley they'd pass through, without any sign of the car that had crashed into the rocks there, and torn her future apart.

The car crash that had killed Tyler, the man who was supposed to be the love of her life. Even if she'd been every bit as responsible for his death as those rocks he'd crashed into.

All of that was part of the life she'd put firmly behind her for ever.

Tori tugged her coat tighter around her, feeling a chill that the fancy four-by-four's heating system couldn't hope to warm. She couldn't wait for this cursed trip to be over.

CHAPTER TWO

OKAY, THIS WASN'T working at all.

Keeping his main focus firmly on the road ahead, and the swirling snowflakes that grew heavier with every moment, meant that Jasper could only spare the briefest of glances at his travelling companion. But even that was enough to realise that any hopes he'd had of Tori opening up or even relaxing a little as they took the secluded, picturesque road through the moors were doomed. Curled up in her seat, her coat wrapped tightly around her slim body, she looked almost like a child having a sulk.

Maybe that *was* what she was doing. And Jasper had teased Felix out of enough sulks in their childhood to know how to fix that.

Except he wasn't thinking about Felix. Ever.

Think about Tori. And not crashing the car.

Tori Edwards was an enigma. She'd appeared in his life one day and hadn't left, and despite their night together he wasn't sure he knew her any better now than the day she'd arrived.

After his father's revelation about Felix's parentage, Jasper had worried briefly that Tori was another of the earl's illegitimate children, but that fear had been quickly dispelled. And given her colouring—her pale skin, her dark hair, and her bright green eyes—he should have known better anyway. He got his own dark hair from his mother, and his eyes were his father's distinctive golden brown—the same, he realised too late, as Felix's.

Jasper and Felix had both been about to start their third year of university down in Oxford when Tori had shown up that first summer, a year into her own business degree at York, and working for the earl during the holidays. He'd claimed he'd plucked her from obscurity at some roadside inn where her talents were clearly wasted. Tori had never denied the story, but Jasper suspected that his father's desire to appear a patron, a benefactor, to a penniless girl who had just needed the right chances in life had had more to do with harking back to a previous era of aristocracy than anything else.

In truth, Jasper assumed the earl had hired Tori because she was very good at her job, patronage be damned. She'd worked hard all that summer learning the ropes at the Flaxstone estate—dealing with the groups of executives there for team building down in the woods, with the paintballing range and the go-kart track; hosting birthday parties for horse-mad little girls; serving teas and coffees in the farm café and even leading walking tours of the land around Flaxstone, up to the ruins of the old hall that had been crumbling away nicely for the last three hundred years. There had been no job she wouldn't take on, and before long she'd known more about how the estate was run than staff who'd been there for decades.

The earl, for all his many faults, had at least seen the writing on the wall for Britain's landed gentry, and had found a way to diversify the assets the Flaxstone estate gave them, making the best use of their aristocratic inheritance by turning it into a business. And once Flaxstone itself had been running consistently in the black as a commercial enterprise, he'd turned his sights on the many estates in the country that *hadn't* been so prescient—and done the same for them.

And Tori, from what Jasper could gather, had been a big part of that during his absence over the last five years.

But back when she'd first arrived, she'd been nothing more than another girl to flirt with, a challenge when she didn't flirt back, and then a puzzle for him to solve when he couldn't get her to open up at all. He and Felix had spent that whole first summer trying to bash holes in those walls she put up; teasing her, asking every question they could think of, even trying to get her drunk on long summer nights. She'd been just nineteen to their nearly twenty-one, close enough in age that it had seemed natural they'd spent time together, even if she'd lived in the staff quarters with the casual summer staff, and they had been up at the main hall.

She had been there again at Christmas that year, organising stalls for the annual Christmas market, decorating trees and staircases in the hall, and corralling carollers. Jasper had wondered briefly why she hadn't gone home for Christmas, he remembered now. Later, he'd got the feeling that she hadn't had a home to go to.

But she'd made a new one at Flaxstone. By the time she'd graduated, Tori had earned such respect from the earl that he'd given her the gatekeeper's cottage and hired her full time, before she'd even attended graduation.

And two years later, the summer he'd found out the truth about Felix, Jasper had finally broken a small hole in those defences of hers, even if only for one night. Or maybe she'd broken a hole in his.

It had been the night that he'd found his father's will,

read about a potential second son he'd never heard of. His father had been out of town for meetings and Jasper had known it wasn't a conversation he could have over the phone, so he'd resigned himself to waiting until his return the next day for answers.

But patience had never been one of his virtues.

Felix, he remembered now, had been off with some girl he'd fallen for on the summer staff, and not available for drunken oblivion. But Jasper had found Tori hanging bunting on the pop-up coffee stall she'd convinced the earl to install at the start of the garden walk.

'Don't you ever stop working?' he'd asked her, leaning against the nearest tree to watch her work. She'd been methodical, focussed, and the bunting had dipped and hung at precise intervals from the tin roof of the stall.

'When it's all done, yes,' she'd replied without looking at him.

'When it's done, I need something stronger than coffee. Join me?'

She'd turned then, looked him in the eye for a long moment, and then nodded.

He hadn't expected her to say yes, not after so many years of telling him no at every possible opportunity. But maybe she'd seen something desperate in his eyes that evening. Seen that he'd needed her. Or perhaps she'd had her own reasons—if so, she'd never told him what they were.

They'd stolen a bottle of the earl's finest gin from his healthy drinks cupboard, and drunk most of it while talking about nothing at all. But underneath the inconsequential, and in between them, every now and then there had been glimpses, moments when her armour had slipped. Seconds when he'd been able to see that she was hurting too, even if she'd never tell him why.

Then the alcohol had taken over completely, and soon they'd been giggling their way back to her cottage, pausing only to kiss against the trees that lined the path.

And then when he'd woken up the next morning she was already gone.

Did she ever think about the night they'd spent together? She'd certainly never mentioned it again. Not that she'd had much chance. She'd crept out of her own cottage before he was even awake, and avoided him for the next day. He'd confronted his father about the will the moment he'd returned, and his world had imploded. He hadn't been thinking about anything beyond the lies he'd been told his whole life when he'd decided to leave Flaxstone, and in the end he'd left in such a whirlwind he hadn't even seen Tori again. He'd barely said goodbye to his own mother, but that was partly because he couldn't bear to lie to her about Felix, but couldn't hurt her either. She couldn't have known what sort of a man she'd married, he was sure. And if she had...then she'd been lying to him too.

He couldn't face that possibility right then. So he'd run as far and as fast as he could, until the pain had started to recede.

Since he'd returned to Flaxstone, Tori had barely acknowledged his existence, until today, when she couldn't possibly avoid it.

Jasper's gaze darted to the left again to take in her profile, pensive as she stared out at the snow. Then he focussed back on the road again.

One night. Just a few hours. That was the only time he'd ever seen behind the mask. And even now, so many years later, he couldn't help but wish he could see it again. The real Tori Edwards.

Because that flash of the real woman behind the defences had been more potent than the weeks, months or even years he'd spent getting to know anyone else.

Of course, maybe that was just because he'd spent his time getting to know the wrong women—or *not properly* getting to know far too many of them. But after his teenage experiences of love, that was enough for him. He still winced at the memory of Juliet Hawkes, the object of obsession for his teenage heart that could have ruined romance for him for life.

Still might, actually, coupled with the rubbish example his father had set him.

And now he was back to thinking about his father again. Perfect.

'The snow's getting heavier,' Tori said, suddenly sitting up straighter beside him.

Jasper blinked, and let his eyes see the falling snow, rather than blocking it out to concentrate on the road.

It really was getting heavier. A lot heavier.

He'd only picked this road because it was the first thing he'd said all day that had got a real reaction out of her, and that curious, need-to-know nature of his had made him push it forward, to see where it went, in case it led him to a better understanding of Tori Edwards.

Now, looking out at the snow, he was starting to wonder if that was the best choice.

Then he saw the tail lights of the stationary cars ahead, and the blue lights flashing beyond them, and knew that it really, really wasn't.

Tori insisted on being the one to go and find out what was happening.

This was her land, her place, even if Jasper didn't

know it. Despite the swirling snow she knew *exactly* where she was. Recognised the rises, the scars in the land disappearing under that blanket of white. She knew that tree, dead and black her whole life, but now covered in the blossom of snowflakes. She recognised that uneven stone wall, bracketing the road on one side, meandering along in nothing like a straight line.

She knew where that wall led. Knew the land it marked out. If she squinted, she could almost see the building it belonged to, rising out of the snow a little way further along the road.

The Moorside Inn.

Or, home, as she'd always known it.

Tori shivered, looking pointedly away from where she knew the inn sat, and focussing instead on the treacherous and slippery path ahead of her. It was hard by now to see where the road ended and the grass verge began, and the ground seemed to shift and move under her feet as she stepped from one to the other.

Maybe she should have let Jasper investigate instead. But more than anything she'd needed to get out of that car, breathe fresh air, and step away from his curious gaze.

Did he even remember that they'd once slept together? She wasn't sure. He certainly hadn't mentioned it since his return, and there *had* been a significant amount of alcohol involved that night.

She'd never understood what had made that night so different for them both. Well, that wasn't entirely true. She knew why *she'd* felt different that night. An unfortunate clash of an anniversary she'd been trying to forget and too many reminders that wouldn't let her. When he'd looked at her with that lost look, one she'd never thought to see on his confident and assured face, for a moment he'd reminded her of Tyler.

Later though, after much alcohol, as he'd leaned in to kiss her for the first time, she hadn't been thinking about Tyler at all. Only Jasper. Something else to feel guilty about.

Anyway. Whether he remembered or not, it was better for all concerned that they pretend it never happened, so she definitely wasn't going to bring it up.

But that didn't stop her wondering.

Not right now, though. Right now she had to figure out what the hell was going on with this road and get off the moors before Aunt Liz or Uncle Henry came out to see what was happening on the road outside the inn.

With hindsight, she really, really should have stayed in the car. And apparently she wasn't the only one who thought so.

'If you'd get back in your car, please, miss.'

A uniformed police officer approached, looking cold and very fed up. She couldn't blame him, to be honest. She felt much the same and she'd only been out in the snow for a few minutes. 'Someone will be coming along to speak to all drivers in turn.'

'What's happened?' she called out anyway, her voice fighting against the wind and snow.

'The road ahead is blocked,' the policeman responded. 'But please, wait in your car and someone will tell you what to do next.'

I know what to do next, Tori thought as she trudged back towards Jasper and the waiting car. *Get the hell out of here.*

They could turn around. Head back to the main road and take the other route. Yes, it might take for ever, but at least they'd get home tonight. And she'd be far, far away from the Moorside Inn. As long as they got moving now, this didn't have to be a disaster.

But as she reached the four-by-four, she could already see Jasper leaning against the car, his shoulders and hair coated with snow, talking to another police officer.

'Ah, the wanderer returns!' he said as she approached, sounding far too jolly for the circumstances.

'What's happening?' Tori shoved her hands deep into her pockets and wished her smart leather gloves were fleece-lined and warm, rather than just looking good.

'Road ahead is closed. Too much snow and ice building up, and there's a risk of rock slides in the valley from the weight of the snow.'

Tori winced. She knew that valley, almost too well. The road grew narrower as it twisted between the low hills, the sharp edges of the rock rising steeply on either side. Too much fallen snow could send rocks and stones battering down.

That valley was where Tyler had died, on a warm spring night totally unlike this one.

'We'll go back, then,' she said, shaking away the memories. 'Head back to the main road. We should have taken that route in the first place.' She shot a glare at Jasper to remind him whose fault this all was.

'Probably,' the policeman agreed, glumly. 'But it's too late now. There was an accident about half a mile back, probably not long after you passed through. No serious injuries, but the road is closed that way too while it's cleared—in fact, they've closed off this whole section from the main road until it comes out the other side of the moors. Too dangerous in this weather.'

Tori swallowed down the panic rising sharply through

her throat. She couldn't afford to lose it—not here, not now, and definitely not with Jasper watching.

'Then how are we supposed to get out of here?' she asked, forcing her voice to remain even.

'Good news on that front, at least,' Jasper said, grinning even as he blinked away snowflakes from his eyelashes. Those golden-brown eyes of his shone in the light from the headlights and the policeman's torch. 'Apparently there's an inn nearby that's offered to put up all the travellers caught up in this mess. See, I told you I'd take you to a nice secluded pub for dinner!'

He was so busy congratulating himself, telling the police officer how he was a man of his word, and always looked for the silver linings, that he probably didn't even notice Tori's heart sink down out of her feet and bleed into the snow. Or maybe that was just how it felt.

All she knew was that she was trapped. That the past she'd been running from for so long had caught her at last.

And it had brought Jasper, Viscount Darlton, along as well, just for the fun of it.

'Hell,' she muttered into the night. 'I'm in actual hell.'

'I think that would be hotter, miss,' the policeman said, with a confused frown. 'Now, if you'll excuse me.' He disappeared into the night to talk to the next car in the line.

'Shall we?' Jasper asked, crooking his elbow for her to hold. 'I believe it's this way.'

Tori tucked her hands under her arms and stepped forward without him. 'I know the way.'

If she had to face her past, she'd at least do it head-on. She owed Tyler that much.

I'm coming home, Aunt Liz.

* * *

This whole day kept getting more and more interesting.

Okay, so getting stranded in the snow on the moors wasn't exactly in Jasper's original plan for the day, but it wasn't quite the disaster Tori's face suggested it was, either. They had a nice, cosy inn to shelter in and wait out the storm, and it wasn't as if either of them had been caught in a rock slide or car accident.

So why did Tori look as if she would almost rather they had?

'Looks like we'll get that dinner at a secluded inn after all,' he joked again as they trudged their way across a snow-covered field, towards the lights in the distance. Maybe she'd missed it the first time around.

Tori didn't answer.

'Maybe there'll be steak and ale pie on the menu. I love steak and ale pie.'

Still nothing.

'And I could murder a pint of something dark and hoppy. Since it looks like we won't be driving anywhere tonight.'

She flinched at that, although he had no idea why.

Jasper sighed. This was going to be a very long night if Tori refused to talk to him altogether.

Maybe it was time to bring out the big guns. Apologising.

'Look, I'm sorry I brought us along the moors road. You were right, it was too dangerous in the snow, and we should have kept to the main roads. Where we'd probably still be stuck in an epic traffic jam, arguing over which radio station to listen to, instead of heading towards what looks like a really nice inn and hopefully some steak and ale pie. But sorry, anyway.'

He could just about make out the inn through the snow. The sloping roof, the thick stone walls, and the warm yellow lights glowing out into the darkening sky. There was even a giant Christmas tree out front, strung with old-fashioned coloured lantern lights, the sort he remembered from his childhood.

It definitely looked like the sort of place that served steak and ale pie. And now he'd apologised, Tori would stop ignoring him and they could enjoy a nice evening together.

He turned to her, smiling—until he saw the sceptical glare on her face.

'You honestly think that was a good apology, don't you?' she asked.

Jasper blinked away snowflakes, confused. 'I mean, I said I'm sorry. So…yes?'

'You said you were wrong and should have listened to me—and then told me why actually I was wrong and you'd made the right decision even now we're stuck in the snow on the middle of the moors walking towards—' She broke off suddenly, her gaze jerking away.

'A…perfectly nice-looking inn?' Jasper finished for her, more baffled than ever.

Tori sighed, hard enough that he saw her shoulders rise and fall even in her thick, woollen coat. 'The Moorside Inn serves the best steak and ale pie in Yorkshire. Possibly the world. Henry, the cook, he won't share the recipe with anyone. You're going to love it.'

'Great,' Jasper replied. But he couldn't find the enthusiasm for it that his hungry stomach had exhibited just moments earlier.

There was something about her voice. The slow, resigned monotone.

'So, you know this place?' Knew it well, he'd guess, given her words. And her reluctance to re-enter it.

Before he'd left Flaxstone, five years earlier, he'd believed he might actually be getting to know Tori Edwards at last. To see the real girl under the mask she put up for his father and everyone else.

Now, staring at her in the snow, outside a Yorkshire inn, he admitted to himself that he didn't know her at all.

He didn't know where she'd come from, or why. He didn't know what had driven her away from her home the way he'd been driven away from his.

But he had a feeling that this might be the night he finally found out.

Tori didn't answer his question, but then she didn't need to. They were almost there, now, the windows of the inn changing from blurs of light in the distance into a clear vision of the cosy, wooden-beamed rooms inside.

And as they approached the heavy, wooden front door, it flew open, revealing an older woman in a Mrs Christmas apron, her bright red curls pinned back from her face, and a wide smile on her lips.

'Welcome, weary travellers, to the Moorside Inn! I hope we can make your impromptu stop a little more comfor…' Her words faltered mid-sentence, and so did her smile. She peered out into the snow, her gaze fixed on Tori's blank expression. 'Vicky?'

Tori sighed again, but at least managed a small smile this time. 'Hello, Aunt Liz.'

Jasper looked between the two women. Yes, he was *definitely* going to find out more about Tori Edwards tonight. But the realisation only showed him just how very little he'd known about her to start with.

Maybe it was time to fix that.

CHAPTER THREE

THE MOORSIDE WAS just as she remembered it.

As Tori pulled away from the tentative, uncertain hug her aunt gave her, she took in the inn beyond. Same wooden beams. Same gleaming pumps, polished by Uncle Henry every night after he'd finished in the kitchen, ready to serve local ales to visitors. Same battered, rustic oak tables and mismatched chairs. Tyler's paintings still on the walls. Same feeling of shame, guilt and of being a disappointment as she stood there.

'We got snowed in on the road, about quarter of a mile away,' Jasper said, looking with far too much interest between her and Aunt Liz. Tori curled in on herself, as much as she could when wearing so many layers. This place was her past, another life almost. She didn't want to share it with anyone from her new life.

Especially not Jasper.

'Of course, you must be freezing! Come on in.' Aunt Liz ushered them both inside as if they were normal paying customers.

Jasper took the opportunity to raise his eyebrows at her and mouth, 'Vicky?' She ignored him. She supposed it was too much to hope for that he'd missed that use of her old, other nickname.

She was Tori now. That was all that mattered.

The things Vicky had done… She didn't want to be that person any more. The person who'd caused Tyler's death.

But family…they always remembered who you were, even once you'd become someone new. She'd always be Vicky to Aunt Liz and Uncle Henry, even if they weren't actually *blood* family. They were the closest thing she'd had for an awful lot of years now.

They walked into the bar proper, the one she'd only glimpsed through windows in the door, and suddenly Tori noticed something that *was* different about the place.

It was packed. Every table, chair, bar stool and window seat was occupied. Tori was certain she'd never seen so many people within the walls of the Moorside Inn ever before.

'I guess we weren't the only ones to get stranded, then?' Jasper said, and Aunt Liz laughed.

'Not by a long shot! That road out there is treacherous in the snow.' She shot Tori a look. 'I would have thought you would've remembered that, Vicky.'

There it was. That not so subtle reminder of why she'd left. Well, no. Why she'd never come back.

She couldn't bear to look at this place without Tyler in it. Couldn't take the pain and the grief—and most of all the pity. Pity from people who should be hating her, blaming her, and only didn't because she was too cowardly to tell them the whole truth.

Only now it seemed she had no choice but to be there.

'That was my fault,' Jasper jumped in. 'Tori—Vicky—tried to tell me to stick to the main roads, but I didn't listen. Always thinking I know best, that's my problem.'

He sounded so sincere, so disarmingly charming, that

Tori could see Aunt Liz melting in front of her. Did he really believe that about himself? She doubted it. But he had at least taken the heat off her, which she appreciated. And it was worlds better than his first attempt at an apology outside in the snow.

'Well, I hope you'll know better next time,' Aunt Liz said, as if she were letting a small child off the hook for something.

'Definitely,' Jasper agreed, nodding. 'Now, I don't suppose you have any of that steak and ale pie you're famous for around here somewhere?'

Tori rolled her eyes. Thinking with his stomach. Why wasn't she surprised?

'Or perhaps we can help you get everyone here settled and sorted?' she suggested. 'I mean, unless you've changed things a lot around here I can probably still locate enough blankets and pillows for everyone.' The Moorside only had a handful of bedrooms it hired out for guests, so people were definitely going to have to share. But if they set up a dormitory sort of arrangement in the restaurant part of the inn, there should just about be enough room for everyone. They'd done it before, Tori remembered vividly, on nights like tonight when the roads were closed by weather or accidents and people got stranded. Including, once, the national rugby team during a particularly violent storm, when their bus had broken down. If *they'd* all fitted in snugly, so would tonight's guests.

'And Jasper here can help Uncle Henry in the kitchens,' Tori added. 'Since he's so concerned about the menu tonight.'

Of course, her altruistic plan also meant she could escape from close quarters with her family *and* her colleague, something she was sure they'd both noticed. Tori didn't care. She needed some space—and that, she knew, was hard to come by in the community-spirited world of the Moorside Inn.

'That would be very helpful,' Aunt Liz said carefully. 'Although you're here tonight as a guest…'

Tori shook her head. She'd never be a guest at the Moorside. It was too much a part of her. 'I want to help. And so does Jasper.' She nudged him with her elbow until he nodded.

'In that case, if you could set up the dormitory in the restaurant, like we did that time they closed the roads and we had the—'

'England rugby team staying,' Tori said along with her. 'Absolutely.'

As she turned away to go and find blankets and pillows, she could hear Jasper talking as Aunt Liz showed him to the kitchens. 'The England rugby team? Now, that I want to hear more about…'

Tori stepped through to the empty restaurant and breathed in the silence. Perfect.

This was going to be a very long night. She could feel it. And she needed a little personal space before she faced it.

Especially before she had to talk to Uncle Henry.

Tori's Aunt Liz led Jasper through the mass of people gathered in the main bar, behind the bar itself, and through a door that took them along a narrow passageway and down a short set of stairs into the kitchens. Jasper took in everything as they walked, especially the dramatic paintings that lined the walls—all slashes of dark greens and browns and purples, showcasing the land-scape of the moors at its most impressive.

This place felt almost a part of the landscape itself, he realised. As if it had been here as long as the rocks and rises.

He ached to know what could have driven Tori away from it. What secrets she was hiding behind those emotional battlements.

Were they as all-consuming as his own?

And another, niggling question that had been at the back of his mind for five long years, before emerging for re-examination tonight: Did she already *know* his secrets? She and Felix had always been friendly, far more than she had been with him. *Felix* had known. Had he told her?

Jasper had to admit to himself that it seemed unlikely. But Tori was good at keeping secrets, that much was obvious. If she *did* know about Felix, Jasper was sure she was very capable of keeping it from everyone—including him.

'Henry?' Liz called out as they entered the kitchens. 'Brought you some help.'

A large, grey-haired man, broad at the shoulder and his head almost grazing the lower of the ceiling beams, ducked out from a side room that, from what Jasper could see, appeared to be full of freezers and fridges. He was wiping his hands on a clean tea towel.

'Help? Think I'm too old and slow to do this on my own?' He smiled as he said it, though, so Jasper was almost sure it was a joke.

'Not me.' Liz jerked her red curls in Jasper's direction. 'He arrived with Vicky. *She* thought he might be able to give you a hand down here.'

Henry stilled, the tea towel taut between his hands, his white knuckles giving away his reaction to Liz's news even though his expression didn't change. 'Vicky's here?' The words were barely more than a whisper.

'We, uh, got caught up in a road closure on the moors,' Jasper explained. 'A crash behind us and a chance of the snow bringing down rocks on the valley ahead.'

'I know the place.' Henry's words were clipped. 'Police direct you here with all the others, did they?'

'That's right.'

Henry sighed. 'Too much to think she'd come back of her own accord, I suppose. So, what are you, then? Fiancé? Boyfriend?'

'Colleague,' Jasper corrected him quickly. He could just imagine Tori's face if he let her family believe there was anything more between them.

However much he might enjoy remembering the night when there *was*.

'Humph.' Henry sounded faintly disbelieving. Oh, well, that was Tori's problem. He'd told the truth. She hadn't told him *anything*.

'So, what can I do around here? Tori's setting up beds somewhere, I guess.'

'Tori, is it?' Henry asked. 'Well. You can help me pack up these ploughman's boxes for our unexpected guests. Each one gets one of each of the things set out on the table. Should be simple enough.' The words 'even for you' were unspoken, but Jasper couldn't help but hear them anyway. He got the feeling that, arriving in Tori's company, there was nothing he could have done to make a good impression on her uncle.

But that wasn't going to stop him trying, all the same. After all, how else was he going to uncover some of those secrets Tori was still hiding? If there was even a chance she knew his—and even if she didn't yet, she would soon if his father got his way—he wanted to know some of hers too. That was only fair, right?

'I'm sure I can,' he said with a grin, and picked up the first of the plastic boxes and started work.

Each ploughman's box got a hunk of bread, some cheese, a thick slice of ham, a small pot of chutney, an apple and some celery.

'I've got a giant pot of soup heating too,' Henry explained. 'We can take that up and dish it out in cups, to help people warm through. It's not much, but—'

'It's more than any of us would have got stuck out on the roads in this snow,' Jasper interrupted. 'And I'm sure they'll all be as grateful as I am for it.' Even if he still lusted after the steak and ale pie Tori had promised was the best in the county. Maybe he could come back another time and try it. In better weather.

'Humph,' Henry said again, but this time he sounded more mollified. 'So. If you're Vicky's "colleague" what sort of work have the two of you been up to?'

He was in tricky waters here, Jasper realised suddenly. If Tori hadn't been home for who knew who long—maybe since she first showed up at Flaxstone—then her aunt and uncle probably didn't know she was working for the earl. Or that she had stayed so close to home. How much would she forgive him for giving away?

'We were visiting a property that our…boss is looking to invest in, up at the north of the moors.' That was neutral enough, wasn't it? 'Tori didn't mention that she had family so close though, or I'd have suggested we stop by without the snow forcing us on you.'

Henry barked a laugh at that. 'Which is exactly why she wouldn't tell you, I'd wager.'

'She does like to keep her cards very close to her chest.' Jasper watched Henry carefully, looking for the right way in, to get the man to tell him something, *anything*, that would explain the strange feeling that had settled over the place since they'd arrived.

There was so much to this story that he didn't know. And Jasper *hated* not being in full possession of all the facts, always had. Especially since everything had gone down with Juliet, and he'd discovered that everyone else in his world had known a lot of truths about her that he, as her boyfriend, also should have known—but hadn't. How could he possibly make good decisions if he didn't know what he was basing them on? Telling Juliet he loved her, for instance, had been a spectacularly bad one.

Especially since it had turned out *she* had been in love with his friend Fred, and everyone else had known it. At nineteen, it had seemed the worst thing that could possibly happen to a guy.

But right now, he wasn't thinking about the past. He was trying to decide how far he could push Tori to tell him her story. To let him in.

Maybe it was just the residual instinct to push at those walls of hers, that instinct that had plagued him since they were both barely more than teenagers. Or maybe it was something more—the sadness in her eyes that he'd only really noticed since his return. Or the way she bristled whenever he said anything at all…

Whatever it was, he needed to solve the puzzle of Tori Edwards. And here was her uncle, holding the key.

But all Henry said was, 'She has her reasons. Heaven knows the girl has never talked when she doesn't want to.

She'd always run away instead, even as a child. Hide in the strangest of places, until…well, until someone found her. Now, are you done with those boxes?'

Jasper nodded, his mind occupied with Henry's words. And the certainty that he'd been about to say a name there, when he was talking about who usually found her. What had stopped him?

Or rather, who?

'Let's carry these up, then.' Henry hoisted the first, heavy tray of ploughman's lunch into his arms, and Jasper followed suit with the second. 'We'll come back for the soup.'

'If my arms can take it,' Jasper muttered, staggering a little on the stairs. But he knew he'd do whatever Henry told him to, really.

He'd do whatever it took to unravel the mystery of Tori Edwards.

The advantage of being on home turf was that Tori knew all the best hiding places. Add in the associated chaos of having far too many people crammed into the building, all needing something all the time, and keeping busy enough to avoid any difficult discussions with Aunt Liz and Uncle Henry, or questions she didn't want to answer from Jasper, was almost too easy.

Henry had sought her out as she'd laid down bedding in the restaurant. He'd watched her from the doorway for a moment or two, she suspected, before she'd turned around and spotted him. Then, he'd thrown his arms around her and held her tight, whispering into her hair that it was good to have her home.

He'd smelled of spicy vegetable soup and the Moor-side kitchens, and the scent was so familiar she could almost believe that she'd never gone away at all. Then he'd stepped away and headed back to the bar without another word, and suddenly she felt every inch of the gulf between her and her family all over again.

A gulf created by her own secrets, and their shared loss.

It had been eight years. Eight years since Tyler died, eight years since she left. Was it time to tell them the truth about why? Tori knew in her heart she wouldn't. Too many painful memories for them all. The best outcome she could hope for if she *did* tell them about the last few months of Tyler's life was that she'd end up tarnishing their memories of him, as well as giving them more reasons to be angry with her. Nobody won anything that way.

Better to keep all those secrets inside, where they couldn't hurt anyone but her.

At least, with so many people crowded in eating their soup and ploughman's, there was no need for a sit-down family meal and all the awkwardness that would follow—as much as Tori would have loved one of Henry's home-cooked meals. She smiled at the sight of Jasper handing out soup from behind the bar, for all the world like one of the college students Liz and Henry used to hire to help out over the summer, before Tyler and then Tori were old enough to take their place.

There were about nine groups of people staying at the Moorside, she counted, watching over the bar. Mostly families of three or four, although there was one multi-generational set of seven, too. A couple of couples, and two sole business people—and Jasper and Tori.

She hoped they had enough beds.

As one of the children in the family nearest to her

started yawning, then nodding off into her apple slices, Tori crouched down next to them and asked if they'd like to be taken through to get settled in one of the bedrooms. The largest guest room at the front of the inn would just about fit them all, she decided, and it made sense for those with younger kids to have the actual bedrooms.

The parents smiled gratefully and, clearing their dishes to the bar, followed her up the rickety stairs to the guest rooms.

Tori made a point of not looking down the narrow corridor that led to the family rooms as they passed. For all she knew, Liz and Henry might have converted her tiny single room—and Tyler's slightly larger room, for that matter—into more guest accommodation, or even an office for Liz to do paperwork in. She'd never know, because she wasn't going to ask and she definitely wasn't going to go and look.

Too many memories down that corridor.

By the time she made it back downstairs, Liz had already shown most of the other guests to rooms upstairs, or to the makeshift dormitory in the restaurant. Jasper was wiping down the bar, and Henry was pouring himself a pint.

Tori's heart contracted at the familiar sight of her aunt and uncle going about their evening, as if nothing had changed in the last eight years. Or even the last day, as the inn had been invaded by stranded travellers. Even Jasper seemed strangely at home in a place she could never even have imagined seeing him before today.

'Well, I'd better go grab a bedroll in the restaurant before they're all gone,' Tori said, as cheerfully as she could. It was late, they were all tired. Surely no one would call her out on wanting to avoid Awkward Question and Family time right now, would they?

But Liz, glancing up from wiping down tables, gave her an odd look. 'I've kept your old room free for you and Jasper,' she said. 'I know it's not big, but it'll be more private than sleeping with the hordes in the restaurant.'

'Quieter too,' Henry added. 'Some of those kids had a real set of lungs on them.'

Tori had heard. She'd hoped that if she couldn't sleep, as she often couldn't, the sound of the kids' shrieks would at least distract her from her own thoughts.

But now it seemed all she'd have to distract her was Jasper. And she knew from past experience that he could be far too distracting by half.

'Jasper and I are just work colleagues, Aunt Liz,' she said, in case her family had got the wrong idea. Whatever else they'd shared once, briefly, it was long gone. And whatever she thought she'd seen in him that night, she knew now she'd only imagined it. She was pretty certain he'd have spent the last five years flirting with any woman who caught his eye, seducing plenty of them and then moving on. Just as he'd done with her, and plenty of others before her.

Her love life was depressing enough without adding 'fell for Jasper's seduction line and got abandoned *twice*' to her romantic résumé.

'That's what I told them,' Jasper said, with a shrug. 'But to be honest, at this point, a bed is a bed and I'm knackered.' He tossed his towel over the rail on the bar, raised the section of wood to let himself out, then crossed towards her. 'So, lead on, roomie.' He flashed her an obnoxious grin that was both annoying and weirdly reassuring. Everything else felt wrong and out of step tonight, but at least Jasper was still Jasper.

Tori wasn't sure she should find that as comforting as she did.

She just hoped that when Liz and Henry had renovated the room they'd added bunk beds, or something. Otherwise they were in for a very awkward night indeed.

CHAPTER FOUR

'I COULD SLEEP on the floor,' Jasper said, eyeing the bed with annoyance. Was it even a full single? It didn't look it. To be honest, it didn't look all that much more comfortable than the wooden floor beside it, but he supposed at least with shared body heat it might be warmer. The ancient stone walls of the Moorside Inn didn't seem to do much in the way of retaining heat, this far from the fire roaring in the grate downstairs in the bar. Even this tiny bedroom—not much wider than the bed itself, and with space for just a small bookcase and chair at the end, by the door—was icy cold.

'If you freeze to death on my watch your father will fire me,' Tori said, ever practical.

'Nice to know my well-being is of such great personal concern to you,' Jasper replied. At least she was still being snarky. He'd be really worried about her, otherwise.

Oh, who was he kidding? He was worried about her anyway.

Back home at Flaxstone Tori was always aloof but in control. Here, at the Moorside Inn, she seemed…jumpy. As if she was dashing from one thing to the next so she didn't have to stop and look around, take anything in.

Or talk to her family.

Yeah, he could totally get that part of it. It was pretty much exactly what he'd been doing since he came home, too. His father didn't deserve his time or attention. And as for his mother…he just didn't know what to say to her. How much she already knew, or, if she *did* know, how she felt about the discovery that her husband's illegitimate son had been living under her roof since he was born. He needed to have a proper conversation with her, soon, but his mum had always lived stubbornly in her own world, one that was extinct outside her mind, and Jasper knew he had to time it properly.

Which only really left him Tori to talk to at all. Well, Tori and Felix, but one of those two had lied to him for the last decade and a bit, so he was fine with ignoring him too.

But he couldn't exactly ignore Tori. Not when they were sharing a bed the size of a postage stamp for the night.

'I mean it,' he said, not meaning it at all. 'I can take the floor.'

Tori looked over her shoulder at him, halfway through stripping off her suit jacket. 'Look,' she said, with a weary sigh. 'Nothing that has happened since we left Stonebury has been exactly…optimal, but it's where we are. Let's just get through it, get out of here tomorrow, and pretend this whole day never happened, okay? Even the part where we have to share my childhood bed to make sure neither of us catches pneumonia.'

Okay, now he was really worried about her. She wasn't even protesting at the idea of having to share the bed with him. This was not the Tori he knew.

The Tori he knew would have stolen his coat as an extra pillow then shoved him onto the floor.

This was actually getting a bit unnerving now.

Cautiously, Jasper stripped off his jumper, shirt and jeans, leaving his T-shirt and boxers on for Tori's sake. And warmth. In fact, he was reconsidering the jumper; it was absolutely freezing in this room.

'How did you make it through childhood without freezing to death in here?' he asked, turning back to find Tori already tucked up under the covers, holding them close to her chin.

She shrugged, the brightly patterned duvet moving with her shoulders. 'Mum and I didn't move in until I was eight. I guess I was past the delicate stage by then.'

Jasper wasn't sure if she realised it, but that was the most she'd ever told him about her life before Flaxstone.

Rather than draw attention to what she'd said, he slipped under the duvet beside her, tugging it to get her to release enough to actually cover all of him. The bed was an excruciatingly tight fit, and the duvet far too small for two grown adults anyway. Jasper shifted self-consciously to try and get comfortable while still maintaining an acceptable distance between them, forcing himself not to think about the last time he'd been this close to Tori Edwards.

He'd been younger then. Stupider. Lost and unsettled and in need of something real, something grounding. Like Tori.

And she'd been...beautiful. Soft to touch and melting in his arms, under his kisses and— He really needed to *not* be thinking about this. If she got the slightest hint that he was—and his body was more than ready to give that to her if he let it—then he'd be on the floor faster than an avalanche, even if his father *did* fire her for letting him freeze to death.

Which he was pretty sure he wouldn't. He got the impression that, these days, Tori and Felix were more his father's children than he was. Not that he cared.

'Oh, for heaven's sake.' Suddenly, Tori twisted under the duvet, reaching around to grab his hand and pull him close against her back, curved around her body like a question mark.

Jasper took a lot of deep, calming breaths.

'Trust me, there is no other way for two people to get any sleep in this bed together,' she said, her words muffled against the single pillow.

'Speaking from experience?' He wasn't sure he liked the idea of Tori in this bed with another guy, even if she wasn't really there *with* him now.

'I wasn't always eight,' she said, caustically. 'I was eighteen when I left this place.'

Why? The question battered at the inside of Jasper's skull, desperate to get out. But he knew Tori better than that—even if he was realising by the moment that he didn't know her as well as he'd thought. She'd never tell him, and it would only make the whole situation more awkward.

But maybe she'd tell him something else.

'What made you move in here with your aunt and uncle in the first place?' Maybe she'd be more comfortable talking about those long-ago, and hopefully happier, times.

'They're not really my aunt and uncle,' Tori said, her voice blurry with encroaching sleep. 'Liz was my mum's best friend since primary school. When my dad left us… Mum brought us here and Liz and Henry took us in without questions. Mum worked the bar, or the kitchens, whatever they needed. And she baked cakes and things for the local mums' groups in the village who started meeting here for coffees on weekday mornings. She ran a book club, a babysitting circle…she really made this place home.'

It sounded idyllic. But something in Tori's exhausted voice told him the ending wouldn't be quite so happy.

'When she died, Liz and Henry kept me anyway. It was that or foster care, and Liz wouldn't let that happen.'

'How old were you?' His heart hurt at the pain in her voice. He knew she wouldn't be telling him any of this if it weren't for the situation and the lateness—it was always easier to talk in the dark, and this snow-buffeted, muffled night was darker than most.

But he couldn't help but be grateful for this glimpse behind the barricade.

'Fourteen,' Tori said. 'It was a long time ago now. Nearly half my life.'

But Jasper would bet money she still thought about it every day. That it still caused her pain, all the time.

'When was the last time you were here?'

'Eight years ago. Before I came to Flaxstone.' Her voice was slurring, sleep overtaking her. He was almost certain she wouldn't have given him such an easy, honest answer otherwise. She was speaking on autopilot now.

He was about to ask something else, to really push his luck and the power of the moment, but then Tori's breathing changed, and when he peered over in the thin light coming under the door from the corridor outside, he could see her eyes were closed, her mouth a little open as she slept.

The moment was gone. And it was probably just as

well. He didn't want her regretting tonight in the morning—the way she obviously regretted the last night they'd spent together, albeit for different reasons. Even if, at the time, she'd been a more than enthusiastic participant.

He slumped back against the mattress, keeping his careful position around Tori's body, and closed his eyes. He should sleep too. It had been a long day, and who knew how tomorrow would pan out?

But he couldn't stop wondering what could have been so awful it had driven Tori away from the home and the people who had taken her in and loved her when she had no one else.

Tori awoke with her nose and cheeks freezing and the rest of her…pleasantly warm. Cosy, even. Cocooned in blankets and—wait.

Her muscles tensing, she slowly turned her head to look behind her. She'd just pat around with her hands but, if her memory was right, she didn't want to risk finding out what parts of a person her fingers might accidentally come into contact with…

Jasper's aristocratic profile was irritatingly perfect in the blurry, morning light. The sun must still be on its way up over the horizon outside, but the whiteness of the world after the snowstorm made the early light brighter than it would otherwise have been. The whole world felt muted, muffled, as if they were protected away in a cotton-wool landscape where nothing could ever hurt them.

Except she was in her room at the Moorside, in bed with Jasper, so clearly that couldn't possibly be true.

He breathed in, deep and sudden, and Tori realised she was staring. But really, who could blame her? She'd never get away with studying him like this while he was awake. He'd tease her for all eternity about it—or read more into it than there was. He was an attractive man. Those long, dark lashes against his cheek. The fall of his black hair against his forehead. His neck, sloping to meet strong shoulders somewhere under the blanket… not to mention everything else that was covered out of sight, but that she could still feel pressed up against her sleep-heavy body. She was, you know, human. She noticed these things.

Which didn't mean she was going to do anything about it. This time.

Besides, while she was studying him, she wasn't remembering all the secrets she'd given up to this man in the anonymous dark the night before. Wasn't worrying about how he might use those secrets, either.

At least she hadn't told him everything. So, he knew about her mother. Knew about her father, too.

He didn't know about Tyler. That was the important thing.

The only people in the world who knew about Tyler were Aunt Liz, Uncle Henry and herself—and even they didn't know all of it. The most awful, terrible parts. And Tori knew she needed to keep it that way.

She couldn't bear the guilt, otherwise.

Beside her, Jasper stirred, and she quickly snapped back into position facing away from him, before he caught her staring. Now she wasn't focussing on his face, she could hear the inn coming to life below them. She supposed that no one would have slept particularly well, however exhausted they were after a difficult day. Everyone was waiting to move on—for the roads to open, the snow to clear. To return to their real lives.

Just like her. Because none of this—not this place,

not her family, and definitely not sharing a bed with Jasper—felt at all like the Tori she'd become since she walked away from the Moorside and never looked back.

Conscious of Jasper starting to move behind her, Tori slipped out from under the duvet and winced as her bare feet hit the cold floor. Still, frostbite was still less alarming than actually waking up in bed with him again.

Last time that had happened, she'd run before he'd woken up at all. And they'd been in her bed. Finding herself outside, barely dressed and without her phone, purse or keys had been awkward—as had climbing back in through her bathroom window later that day—but still less awkward than sharing a morning after with Viscount Darlton.

Tori wasn't sure what it was exactly about Jasper that rubbed her up the wrong way—*or the right way*, her mind added unhelpfully—but she thought it might have something to do with his eyebrows. The way they twitched up in a quizzical manner whenever she spoke, as if he was trying to find the truth behind her words. As if he was trying to *understand* her.

Only one person had ever really understood Tori, and he hadn't liked what he'd discovered, in the end. She had zero reason to think Jasper would be any different from Tyler, in that regard. And given how badly it had gone last time…being understood was not a phenomenon she wished to repeat in a hurry. Or ever.

Liz and Henry already saw too deep, too much. They knew her, and maybe even what she was capable of. She had no idea how much Tyler had told them, while she was gone. Maybe they already knew everything, after all. Another reason she wasn't exactly keen to extend

the family reunion. She liked her secrets hidden at best,
or at least unspoken.

Time to go.

Wriggling back into her clothes at speed—it was too
damn cold out to risk another half-dressed escape—Tori
kept one eye on Jasper as he stirred again, one arm flung
over his eyes as he flipped to his back and started to
stretch. Definitely waking up.

Grabbing her boots to put on later, Tori slipped out of
the bedroom door, checking the corridor was clear before padding down the stairs. Hopefully, Liz and Henry
would be busy enough with their unexpected guests that
they wouldn't notice her sneaking out.

She was in luck. Dodging a couple of small children
racing out of the restaurant dormitory, she manoeuvred
herself towards the exit and, pulling on her boots, back
into the snow. The knee-high leather boots weren't really suitable for the snow, but neither was the suit she'd
worn to tour Stonebury the day before. But they were
the only clothes she had with her, so they'd have to do.

The guilt landed on her within the first few snow-
crunching steps, but guilt was a feeling so tied into her
connection with the Moorside Inn she found it easy
enough to shrug off. Yes, she should have stayed to help
Liz and Henry serve breakfast to the other stranded travellers, but she had at least left them Jasper as a dogsbody.
And besides, she just couldn't stay there a moment longer, fighting off the memories.

She'd just walk as far as the road, she decided, and
find out what the situation was. If she was really lucky
they'd already have opened it—although she suspected
someone would have been up to the inn to tell them that
already if they had. But perhaps they'd be close to doing

so. Perhaps she'd be able to return to the Moorside with the good news that they'd all soon be free to get on their way again.

But she should have known better than to hope for that sort of luck.

'Can't see them opening it today, to be honest,' the young policeman guarding the police cordon told her. 'There's more snow scheduled this afternoon for a start, and there's already been a mini rock slide in the canyon.'

'What about opening it the other way?' she asked, a little desperate. If they couldn't cross the moors the quick way, surely they could go back the way they'd come and escape to the main roads?

But the policeman shook his head. 'Too much snow. They've closed it that way too, right back at the turn off from the main road, to stop anyone else stupid enough to try and cross the moors in this weather.' He seemed to realise what he'd said a moment too late, as his cheeks turned even pinker than they already were from the cold, but Tori waved away his stuttered apology.

She didn't care what some stranger thought about her plan—or, actually, Jasper's plan—to take this road. The only people alive whose good opinion mattered to her were her business associates, and her aunt and uncle.

And *they* probably weren't thinking lovely thoughts about her for skipping out this morning.

With a sigh, Tori turned away from the road and trudged back to the inn, pulling her phone from her pocket and dialling as she walked.

'Tori? Everything okay?' Felix's voice came sharp over the line as he picked up on the first ring. 'I got your text last night, but it didn't make a lot of sense…'

Probably because she'd said as little in it as possible.

Felix was a friend, a good one. But he didn't know about the Moorside or her family, and she had no intention of telling him now.

'Everything's fine,' she said, calmly. 'Like I said in my text, we got caught in the snow and a road closure, so stayed the night at a local inn.' She took a deep breath. 'And it looks like we might be stuck here a little longer, too. Apparently it could be tomorrow before the roads are clear again.'

'So you and Jasper are stuck in the middle of nowhere together?' Felix barked a laugh. 'Well, try not to kill each other, yeah?'

'No promises,' Tori said dryly. 'Can you let the earl know what's happening?'

'Yeah, of course. Now, while I have you, I had a couple of questions about the set-up for the Christmas market…'

By the time she hung up, the inn was almost in sight again. At least the fresh air had cleared her head a little—and she'd escaped from an awkward morning-after-the-revelations-before moment with Jasper.

She wondered how he was coping with being cooped up at the Moorside with all those families and kids. He'd grown up in Flaxstone Hall, probably with a whole suite of rooms to call his own, and the ballroom to use as a playroom. The Moorside, with its low ceilings and poky rooms—and especially in its current state of overcrowding—wasn't at all what he was used to. Last night it had all still been a game to him. Tori suspected that by this morning he'd be losing patience.

But as the inn came fully into view, so did Jasper, his head visible above the wall that surrounded the grounds of the Moorside. His companions, however, were hidden by the snow-covered stone.

She could hear them, though.

'Jasper! Jasper! Use my scarf for the Mummy snowman!' one of the kids chattering around him called.

'But then your neck will get cold,' Jasper pointed out, taking off his own scarf and wrapping it around the neck of his snow creation.

There was a whole row of them, Tori realised, of varying shapes and sizes. Big snowmen, little snowmen, and something that might have been a snow dog, with a stick in its mouth.

'How long was I gone?' she asked as she reached Jasper's gang, still amazed at the sight of Viscount Darlton playing with a horde of little kids. 'We seem to have been invaded in my absence.'

Jasper looked up at her voice and gave her a careful smile. It hadn't escaped his notice that she'd done a runner this morning again, then.

'The grown-ups are all eating breakfast inside,' he explained. 'But kids eat fast, and it just seemed cruel to keep them all cooped up when there was all this snow out here to play with.'

Tori raised her eyebrows. 'If all the grown-ups are inside, what does that make you?'

He shrugged, and this time his grin felt real. 'Maybe I'm just young at heart.'

Handing a carrot that she imagined he'd filched from the kitchen to the tallest of the children, Jasper moved past the crush to join her by the wall, calming their groans of complaint with a promise that he'd be back to play more soon. 'You went to check the road?'

Tori nodded. 'Still closed. Both ways. The policeman

I spoke to reckons it won't be open until at least tomorrow; there's more snow forecast for this afternoon, but hopefully temperatures might rise after that.'

Jasper looked back over at the kids playing by the snowmen. 'Looks like I'd better come up with some more activities to keep this lot entertained, then.'

Pushing away from the wall, he headed back to his little gang, clapping his hands together and asking, 'Who reckons they can take me in a snowball fight?'

As a dozen hands went up, and Jasper used the distraction to toss the first soft snowball at the nearest kid, Tori laughed, despite herself.

This was *definitely* a side of Jasper she hadn't expected to see this week.

Then she turned to go inside and saw Uncle Henry waiting for her, and her smile disappeared again.

Time to face the music.

CHAPTER FIVE

JASPER'S FINGERS WERE taped together for the thirteenth time. The little girl—Sasha—sitting on his right stifled a giggle as she looped another strip of paper perfectly through the last circle, selected a piece of tape from the edge of the table beside them and taped it in place, another brightly coloured loop in the paper chain.

'Obviously this is a job for little fingers,' Jasper said as he shook off the tape again. But he reached for the next paper strip anyway, and fed it dutifully through the loop and taped it in place.

All around him, Christmas music hummed softly from the speakers hidden behind the ceiling's wooden beams, the sound of jingle bells and children's choirs ringing. A fire crackled and popped cheerily behind a fireguard—and far away from kids with kindling—and an old, skinny greyhound lounged in front of it, clearly happy with its lot. Outside, snow was falling again; big, fat flakes that tumbled onto the already white-covered ground. The sun had already started to dip behind the horizon, and Jasper knew that soon Henry would want to start on dinner, and that he would go and help again, because at least that way he was being useful, he was doing *something* in this world of forced inactivity.

Across the room, Tori's Aunt Liz sat cutting festive wrapping paper into strips to add to their piles, smiling at him approvingly. All around him, industrious kids were adding to the, to quote Sasha, 'most epic paper chain in the history of paper chains'. Jasper suspected it would loop around the whole pub several times over by the time they were done.

The kids' parents sat at the bar, obviously grateful for the ongoing reprieve from having to entertain their children while they were stranded. Tori's news—and the subsequent visit from a policeman who looked about twelve to confirm that the road would be closed until at least tomorrow—hadn't gone down well with anyone. Well, except maybe the kids, who were having a whale of a time. And Jasper.

He hadn't learned enough about this place where Tori had grown up to leave just yet. He hadn't learned enough about *Tori*.

She'd disappeared with her Uncle Henry before he'd been able to have a real conversation with her, then hadn't shown herself at all at lunch, while he and Henry had served up sandwiches and home-made sausage rolls. He'd wanted to go and look for her, take her some food, but Henry had shaken his head and kept him downstairs.

That had been hours ago. Now, making paper chains was the only thing that was distracting his curious mind from driving itself mad wondering where Tori was and what she and Henry had talked about.

What was it about her that made him so desperate to *understand*? He'd been happy enough for all of his life so far letting other people exist in their own little bubble, without having to know what made them tick, what mattered to them or why they did the things that they did. So what had changed?

Well. He knew the answer to that well enough. Discovering the truth about his family—that his father had lied to him his whole life, that his best friend had done the same for years—it had cemented the lesson that his first experience of love had taught him at nineteen: no one was really what they seemed. Any happy, smiling facade could conceal a whole barrage of lies. If the people who claimed to care about him most could lie to his face, day after day, how many more deceptions and untruths could people who didn't care about him hide?

But until now that revelation had only made him keep people at arm's length—so far away that they couldn't get close enough for their lies to impact him at all. He'd learned in business to assume that everyone was, at the very least, massaging the facts. And in an industry where most people *were* that caution had served him well.

For some reason, that same assumption had the opposite effect on him when it came to Tori. He wanted to get closer, to draw her in and discover her lies and her secrets.

Maybe it was because they were stuck there, with nothing else to do. Jasper had never been good at boredom. Except he'd found plenty to do, hadn't he, between the kids and the snowmen and the paper chains and helping Henry serve meals?

Maybe it was that night they'd spent together before he left for America. He'd had plenty of other nights with other women, before and since, but something about that one stayed with him. Not the sex—well, not *just* the sex, although that had been pretty damn memorable too—but the feeling of closeness.

To start with it had been drunken conversation and tipsy kisses. Then it had been desperate and lust-driven, glorious sex. But afterwards…that was when things had changed. The alcohol wearing off, and the memory of the papers he'd glimpsed in his father's office coming back to haunt him. Knowing what he had to face the next day, the conversation he had to have. The same frantic feeling of helplessness and concern had started to settle on his chest again—until Tori had stopped it.

Her head resting against his shoulder, she'd run her fingers over his skin and said, 'You're worrying about something. Want to tell me about it, or want me to distract you?'

She'd known, he realised now. Known exactly how it felt to have a worry or a fear that nothing could be done about. How it ate you up and you couldn't stop it.

'Distract me,' he'd said then, and she had.

She'd talked for ages. Not about her past, of course— but about her future. Things she'd hoped for, wanted for herself. Carefully curated ramblings of gentle possibilities, designed to lull him into calm and even sleep. Which, eventually, they had, his heart rate slowing and his muscles relaxing as he sank into her voice and let her warmth soothe him.

There hadn't been any sign of anyone else featuring in her imaginings, Jasper realised with a start, about five years too late. Not him, of course—it had been one night together, she was hardly about to start imagining their future happiness, and he'd have run a mile if she had. But no mention of anyone else, either. Not a shadowy future partner, or kids, or a family at all.

She'd mentioned maybe getting a dog. One day. When she was more settled.

She hadn't, as far as he knew, got one in the five years since.

He glanced at the greyhound by the fire. Had she been remembering the dogs of her childhood when she'd told him that? And was this place the reason she couldn't settle enough to imagine owning a dog, let alone having a family? He suspected it was. And that made his heart ache for her.

Ever since he'd met her, Tori Edwards had been a mystery. But she was one he finally felt on the verge of solving. And for that reason alone, he couldn't be sorry for spending another night here with her, trapped by the snow.

Maybe tonight he'd finally find the answers he craved.

She was going to have to go back downstairs soon. Lying on her side on her childhood bed, staring out at the falling dusk, Tori knew that she couldn't hide away for ever. As much as she might want to.

'You have to know we don't blame you for what happened to Tyler,' Henry had said that afternoon, his blue eyes sad, the crinkles and wrinkles at the edges making him look older than she'd ever imagined him being.

Eight years she'd been away. Eight birthdays missed, eight Christmases. Eight anniversaries spent standing by a graveside with a bunch of flowers that changed nothing at all.

Of course they blamed her, whatever they said now. And if they didn't, they should. They *would* if they knew the whole story. Even without that knowledge, she remembered the recriminations in Aunt Liz's eyes the day of the funeral. Remembered how Uncle Henry had barely been able to look at her. Even Flash, the greyhound, had whined and turned away from her.

She'd left the Moorside, left Tyler, for university. And Tyler had died because she was gone.

It was as simple and as awful as that. Of course they blamed her.

The pub itself...that told far more truth than Henry had.

Everything was the same. From Tyler's paintings on the walls, to the menu, to the bar towels hanging in the same old place. It was as if the Moorside had stopped, the day that Tyler died.

She'd tried to make herself go into his bedroom, but failed at the door. Instead, she sat on the floor of the landing, staring at the wooden door, imagining how it looked inside. Because she would bet money it was exactly as she'd left it, eight years ago, the day of the funeral. From the paint on the walls to the faded grey and white chevron blanket Tori's mum had crocheted for him at one of her clubs, to his favourite of his paintings hanging on the wall. The glow-in-the-dark constellations still stuck on the ceiling, and the photo of the two of them on the dresser, with her smiling up at him as if he'd hung the moon, while he beamed at the camera—the kind of young, flawless happiness that people could only experience once in their lives. And once it was broken, there was no way to ever get that innocent joy back again.

Nothing had changed.

It was still her fault that Tyler had died. The only man—boy, really—who'd ever known and loved her.

Now, lying on her own bed again, she forced herself to remember that. To remember the way he'd begged her not to leave him to go to university. How he'd raged about long-distance relationships just being a drawn-out way of breaking up—as if York were the other side of the world. The break in his voice as he'd told her he was scared of what he'd do without her.

And then, six months later, the call from Henry telling her exactly what he *had* done.

'It was an accident, Vicky. He'd had too much to drink, took the bend wrong.'

But she'd known it was more than that. It was what he'd done—what he'd been scared he'd do—without her there to keep him on the rails, keep him safe.

'You're my North Star,' he'd always told her. *'You keep me on the right path.'*

A path he couldn't keep to without her.

He'd died because she hadn't been there to stop it. Henry and Liz *should* blame her.

He was their son. She was just some orphan they took in because she had no one else. And because of decisions she had made, now she had no one at all.

No, that wasn't true. She had *herself*, and that was all she needed. She had an employer, and colleagues. She had a career and purpose and a good income and a home. She'd achieved so much since she'd left this place. There was no point looking back now.

Except for the part where she was actually trapped in her own past.

'Stupid snow,' she muttered as she pushed herself off the bed and onto her feet.

Crossing to the window, she watched the thick flakes falling against the pale glow of the setting sun behind the clouds. Hopefully it would ease off again soon, and maybe tomorrow the road back to the main road at least might be open. She didn't want to go the other way—

the Moor Road, past the valley that had claimed Tyler's life—anyway.

Her conversation with Henry buzzed through her mind as she ran a brush through her hair, and splashed her face with water to try and take away some of the blotchiness. The last thing she needed was Jasper asking her why she'd been crying.

Jasper. He seemed to be slipping into life at the inn with astounding speed. Even Henry had commented on how he seemed like a nice young man. Tacit approval for a relationship that didn't exist.

It might have, once, she supposed. That one night they'd spent together…she'd let herself wonder, just for a minute or two, in between the panic, if it might happen again. If it might become something that happened with regularity. Officially, even.

Like a relationship. Not that she wanted or needed such a thing.

But…it had been…nice was the wrong word. But it had been something. Something she hadn't expected to feel again, after Tyler died. A connection. A possibility.

Plus, the sex had been kind of mind-blowing. So much better than her teenage fumblings and experimentation, even if it felt like a betrayal of Tyler to think it.

But then Jasper had left, of course, as she should have known he would. Ever since she'd met him he'd had a parade of girls passing through Flaxstone, none ever staying long enough to make much of an impact. Felix always said it was because he'd been burned by love before, but Tori had her doubts. More likely that Jasper's looks, title and money gave him access to far more adoring women than was good for him, and he didn't even consider that saying no to any of them was a possibility.

She'd thought she had the measure of Jasper, Viscount Darlton, until the evening she'd seen that strange vulnerability in him, and wondered if there might be something more to the man, behind the charm and the confidence. If that one night could have meant something more to him than simply comfort on a bad day.

But then he'd fled the country before she'd even had the chance to stop panicking about having slept with him at all, let alone moved on to actually talking to him about what happened next. Thank God she'd never been stupid enough to fall in love with him. In fact, she'd decided it was probably all for the best, at the time, and that thought had helped her keep that one night firmly at the back of her memory for the last five years. Well, mostly, anyway.

And then he'd come back. He still had that shining brightness he'd had as an entitled, self-confident young man, but there was something more brittle about it now. As if he was trying too hard to be that person again. Tori hadn't been around him enough to even think about why, really, until this week. Or to be reminded of their night together.

But now? Stuck in her childhood home, reliving all the other memories she'd buried for the better part of a decade, and sharing a *bed* with the man?

Yeah. She was thinking about it. She was remembering *everything*.

At least it was more fun than dwelling on Tyler and her many, many mistakes.

With a sigh, Tori decided she was probably about as presentable as she was likely to get, and headed downstairs. Already as she descended she could smell wonderful food scents rising from Henry's kitchen, and wondered what he'd managed to concoct for them for dinner, from whatever he had in the freezers and stores. Having missed lunch, she sincerely hoped it was both hearty and filling. Something to ward off the cold so she didn't feel driven to snuggle quite so close to Jasper tonight.

It would help if he weren't so damn attractive. As much as he could irritate her with that constant bright-side vision, not to mention his entitled, son-of-an-aristocrat presence, she had to admit she sometimes went out of her way to *be* irritated by him. Because if her brain kept telling her how annoying he was, perhaps it would override her body reminding her how damn sexy he was, to boot. That optimist's smile of his was almost impossible not to return, as hard as she tried. And she always knew the instant she failed, because it turned warmer, more heated, as if getting a reaction from her was all just foreplay.

Maybe it was, to him.

Hell, maybe it was to her too.

Because her brain was doing a worse and worse job these days. It had even taken the time to point out how damn cute he was building snowmen with kids, or how non-aristocratic he looked helping Henry dish out dinner last night.

Damn it. She was *not* falling for her boss's son. No way. Not after five years of trying to forget about him.

And definitely not here and now.

But then she walked into the bar and saw Jasper standing on the counter, pinning garishly coloured paper chains to the beams, cheered on by a swarm of grinning children, as Slade blared out of the speakers and she realised that she might already be too late to stop it.

Maybe even five years too late.

* * *

Dinner that night was a delicious sort of everything stew that Henry declined to detail the ingredients of, but Jasper suspected was 'everything I could find in the freezer this morning'. He sat perched at the bar mopping his up with a giant hunk of homemade bread, thankful that it was nearly bedtime at least. The one point in the day where Tori couldn't possibly avoid him any longer.

She'd arrived downstairs that evening just as he'd finished decorating the bar, and he'd almost fallen off his stool at the sight of her. Not because she'd changed into some glamorous new outfit, or done anything different with her hair or make-up, like in some high-school romantic-comedy movie. Because she looked so young, so open, and so scared, in a way he'd never seen before.

What the hell did Henry say to her?

Now, an hour or two later, she surprised him all over again—by hoisting herself up onto the bar stool next to him, as Henry placed a pint of bitter in front of her.

'You drink pints?' Jasper asked, figuring she'd probably clam up again if he asked what he really wanted to know. *Are you okay?*

Tori shrugged and took a sip. 'I grew up in a pub. Henry taught me to appreciate the good stuff—whenever Liz wasn't looking.'

Flashing them both a grin, Henry took himself off to serve someone at the far end of the bar.

Jasper hoped the pub was well enough stocked with kids' juices to get them through the night.

'Is it strange, being back here?' That was neutral enough, right? He wasn't asking why she'd left, or what Henry had said that had made her hide herself away all day.

'Very,' Tori said, with feeling. Her eyes cast around

the place, as though she was cataloguing everything that had changed in her absence.

'I guess it's a lot different. You said you hadn't been back in eight years…'

She looked up at him sharply. 'When did I say that?'

'When we were talking. Last night.' Damn. He should have known she wouldn't remember; she'd barely been conscious when she said it.

'Right.' She stared down at her pint. 'Well, yes. It's been a while.'

Why? He desperately wanted to know, but he also knew that if he asked she'd never tell him. She was contrary that way. It was one of the things he found most intriguing about her.

'But actually I was just thinking about how everything is exactly the same,' she went on, unprompted. Jasper stayed silent, listening intently. He'd take any scrap of a clue she gave him. 'Same paintings on the walls… It's like a time capsule in here. They've kept everything *exactly* the same. Like they never moved on from—' She broke off.

'You leaving?' Jasper guessed.

Tori gave him a half-amused smile and shook her head. 'No, not that.'

Slipping from his bar stool, Jasper moved from painting to painting, taking in the landscapes and colours, the drama and contrast. He was no great art connoisseur, but he'd spent enough time staring at his ancestors' oil portraits in the Long Gallery at Flaxstone to know he much preferred these slashes of paint that somehow encapsulated the wildness and the wonder of the moors.

'They're great paintings,' he said, returning to his seat.

'And perfect for the location. Why would they change them?'

Her smile was sad, this time. 'They wouldn't. Ever.'

Jasper made a mental note to ask Henry about the paintings.

'So. Are we roomies again tonight?' he asked, bringing the moment back to the present.

'I guess so. It's not like there are suddenly fewer people crammed in here.' Tori didn't sound as if she was jumping with joy at the prospect. Really, she was hell on a guy's ego. But then, just when he was about to say something self-deprecating in the hope of making her laugh—he'd take his wins where he could get them, with her—her expression softened in a way he remembered too well, from one night five years ago. 'You were great with the kids today. I don't know what everyone would have done without you here to keep them entertained.'

Jasper shrugged and looked away. 'I mean, I was pretty bored too. They might have been entertaining me, for all you know.'

She laughed at that, bright and surprised, and he was glad she didn't know the truth. That kids were easier for him to interact with because they'd had less time to build up all the secrets and lies.

Maybe that was the real reason he wanted to solve the puzzle of Tori Edwards. If he knew all her secrets, maybe he could let her in, for real, and tell her his. If Felix hadn't already.

Maybe they could have that one night again. And maybe he could get back that feeling he'd had when he was with her. Soothed and relaxed and hopeful. As if the world was shining with possibilities, not tarred and dull with lies and deception.

Maybe if one person, this person, gave up their secrets voluntarily, he could have faith again. Faith that some people could live without secrets, or without deceptions meant to hurt others or protect themselves.

Jasper knew, suddenly, somehow, that if he ever had faith in anyone, it would be Tori Edwards.

And he wanted it so much that it hurt.

CHAPTER SIX

TORI STARED AT the single bed. Somehow, it looked even smaller than it had last night.

'Do you want me to sleep on the floor tonight?' Jasper asked, obviously catching her studious observations of their sleeping place. 'I mean, I *probably* won't freeze to death. Much. And even if I did, I don't reckon my dad would fire you.'

Rolling her eyes, Tori yanked back the covers. 'But after today, Henry and Liz would never forgive me, and I'd have seven kids after my blood if you weren't around to throw snowballs at tomorrow.'

'True.' Jasper flashed her a smug smile. It really shouldn't be as attractive as it was. 'I am easy to love.'

Did she imagine it, or was there a brittleness to his words? As if there might actually be some vulnerability behind the bravado and self-confidence. Something she'd never even really looked for until now.

Tori shook her head. It seemed unlikely.

But then, so did Viscount Darlton sitting on the floor of the Moorside Inn making paper chains with children.

They prepared for bed in silence—at least, *they* were quiet. In the absence of conversation Tori could hear the whole inn settling down for the night. Kids protesting bedtime; adults laughing over one last pint; the faint strains of Christmas hits from yesteryear still playing through the ancient speakers. Downstairs, Henry would be wiping down the bar, and Liz would be fetching the keys, ready to lock up. No need to shoo out the last of the patrons tonight; with the snow still thick on the ground, no one was leaving.

How many nights had she hidden in the shadows on the stairs, watching Henry and Liz put the pub to bed? Feeling so safe, so loved, here at the Moorside?

But that was a long time ago. Before Tyler.

'What are you thinking so hard about?' Jasper asked, softly, as she climbed into the bed beside him.

'Tyler,' she whispered back, without even thinking about what she was saying.

He stilled behind her. 'Henry told me that the paintings we talked about earlier were painted by their son, Tyler. The same one, I assume?'

Tori nodded. She didn't trust herself to answer. But she had nowhere to go and nowhere to hide from this conversation now she'd started it. And maybe she'd spent too many years not talking about Tyler anyway.

Maybe Jasper would understand. Not if she told him everything, of course—then he'd just know the truth. He'd know that Tyler's death was her fault, the same way Henry and Liz knew it, and then she'd never be able to look him in the eye again.

And Jasper had nice eyes. Despite herself, she couldn't deny she liked looking at them. At him.

He touched her shoulder, and she turned to face him. She could barely make out his features in the darkness and the moonlight, but she knew his face well enough to picture it through the gloom. Knew his body too, even after only one night. One night she'd spent a lot of years pretending to forget.

She hadn't forgotten any of it.

'You and Tyler were...together?' Jasper asked. There was a twist of his mouth, even in the dark, that Tori knew was distaste for the idea. Maybe even jealousy.

Something about that warmed her, even though she hated herself for it. There was no point being jealous of a dead man, after all.

'Ever since I was sixteen,' she said. 'Henry and Liz weren't thrilled about it, but...it wasn't like we'd ever been brought up as brother or sister or anything, and we weren't actually related, so there wasn't much they could do. Well, except for Henry's epic "not under my roof" talks.'

'Which I'm sure you ignored.'

'Not for the first year or two,' Tori admitted. 'Although we did decide that the barns at the far edge of the pub lands didn't really count as his roof.'

It had been so exciting, sneaking off together, honestly believing that no one else knew where they were going or what they were doing—although as an adult, Tori realised that they probably all had. No one who had watched them together could have seen anything but young, first love. The infatuated kind. The kind that blinded a person to the whole rest of the world.

Until it didn't, any more.

'So, what happened?' Jasper asked. 'Where is Tyler now?'

Tori shut her eyes. 'He died. While I was away at university.'

She heard his sharp intake of breath, felt the pity in his gaze even if she couldn't see it. His fingers twitched against her hip as if he wanted to hold her close, to take away the pain.

But the pain was eight years old now. Dull and aching like an old injury that only hurt when it snowed. Tyler was with her every minute of every day, a ghost looking over her shoulder.

But if she didn't turn around, didn't look back, at least she didn't have to see the accusation in his eyes. The hate and the blame.

'I'm so sorry,' Jasper said, after a long time.

'Yeah.'

Because what else was there to say? Other than, *It was my fault. I killed him the day I went away.*

Tori turned to face away from him again, holding her hurt tight inside, even when all she really wanted to do was curl into Jasper's body and let him hold her while she cried.

She didn't deserve the tears. Not when she was to blame.

So instead, she tried to sleep. Even though she knew that Tyler would be waiting in her dreams.

He always was on nights like this.

That was what she deserved tonight.

Jasper woke suddenly, unsure of what had disturbed him. He'd been luxuriating in a particularly relaxing dream— one so opposite to his actual life he'd known even as he experienced it that it couldn't be real. In it, he and Tori were walking beside a frozen river, gloved hands clasped together. He looked up to see the strange battlements of Stonebury Hall rising against the winter sky ahead of them, snow coating them like icing sugar on one of Felix's mother's cakes.

They didn't talk at all—which was probably just as

well, as an argument would have ruined the perfect peace of the dream—but Jasper knew he was happy, content, in a way he didn't remember being since he'd discovered the truth about his father and his half-brother.

Of course, it couldn't last.

Jasper blinked into the darkness, trying to put his finger on what had jerked him out of the dream and wondering if he could get back to it if he fell asleep again quickly enough. But then Tori cried out—a sound of such pain and torment it twisted his heart—and he knew that he wasn't going to be sleeping again any time soon.

'Tori? Tori.' He pressed a hand to her shoulder, feeling the heat of her skin burning through her T-shirt despite the chill in the air. 'Wake up.'

She didn't, though. Instead, she sobbed again, and buried her face in his chest, crying in a way he'd never even imagined Victoria Edwards was capable of.

All those battlements were broken, the mask cast aside and the brittle shield she kept up, always, shattered.

Jasper knew she'd never have let him see her this way under any other circumstances. He was pretty sure that the moment it was over Tori would pretend that it had never happened. He couldn't blame her; he wouldn't want her—or anyone—to see him so broken, either. To see deep inside him where the pain lived. Hell, he'd moved continents to avoid it. Staying at Flaxstone with his father and Felix would have made that hurt raw and visible every day—and so he'd left, and only returned when he knew his defences were strong enough to hide it.

But now, holding Tori, he wondered if *any* emotional defences were strong enough to hide behind, in the end. Maybe everything always came out, eventually. Just like secrets and truths.

'Tori, sweetheart.' He whispered the words against her hair, kissing her head softly as her cries lessened. 'Wake up, love.'

And she did.

Lifting her head, she blinked up at him, tears still glistening in the half-light. 'I was dreaming...' She shuddered at the memory.

'About Tyler?' he asked gently. She nodded. 'Would it help to talk about it?'

This time, she shook her head, her hair whipping around in defiance. 'I just want to forget.' She looked up at him again, and there were no tears this time. Just a new fierceness to replace the armour she'd lost. Her body shifted, and suddenly every inch of her seemed to be pressed up against him, tempting and hot and everything he'd never even dreamed of.

That was a lie. He'd dreamed about it. *Often.* Especially since the night they'd spent together.

But he'd never imagined it could actually happen again, not here and now.

She raised her mouth, pressing it firmly to his, her tongue sweeping out across his lower lip, and his whole body shuddered with want and desire as he kissed her back. The kiss was deep and desperate and everything he remembered about their other night together. When she pulled back, just far enough to kiss her way along his jawline, Jasper could barely remember his own name.

'Help me forget?' she murmured against his ear.

And suddenly the heat faded.

Not completely, of course. The lust she'd inspired was still coursing through his blood, and certain parts of his anatomy were *absolutely* on board with her plan—right now, preferably.

But his brain, that frustrating, overthinking part of him—the part that had come up with a dream of a frozen river and this woman's hand in his—had other ideas.

'Tori…' He pulled away, as far as he could without falling out of the narrow single bed. 'Tori, not like this.'

God, he wanted her. But he wanted her to want *him*, too. Not just forgetfulness, not just oblivion. He'd had enough of that sort of relationship himself, when he'd first moved away from Flaxstone. The kind of sex that just blocked out the world for a time, that helped him pass out and sleep without dreaming of the life he'd thought he'd had and the lies that had lurked behind it.

He didn't want that with Tori. Not this time.

Last time had been freeing—for him, at least. She hadn't just helped him to forget his worries, she'd given him new hope for what came next. Hope that had only lasted until the next day, when he'd confronted his father, but still. It hadn't been despair or desperation that had driven him to her, not like it was for her now. Now he wondered again what it had been for Tori that had allowed her to let him in that night.

Whatever that was, he knew that if they were to have that connection again, he needed it to be something more. *Tori* meant something more to him, now. Seeing her at the Moorside these last couple of days had convinced him of that, if nothing else.

She mattered. It might not be love or for ever or any of the other impossible things his dream had seemed to promise him. But it was more than this—more than forgetting who she was in his body for a while.

And he knew, if he took what she was offering right now, he'd never be worthy of anything more.

'Tori. Tori, no. Not like this.' He said it again as gently

as he could, but hurt flashed across her face all the same. He was so close he could see it, pale in the moonlight.

But then she nodded in acceptance. 'I know. I just… it still hurts.'

'I imagine it always will.' He didn't know about this sort of emotional pain, not really. But he understood about having a whole world he thought he knew being snatched away from him.

What sort of a future had Tori imagined with Tyler? How much must she have loved him to have not even been able to come back and see her family because the pain was so great?

Jasper wasn't foolish enough to imagine she might ever love *him* that way—wasn't even sure he'd know what to do with that kind of love if she did. But just for a moment, in the darkness, he wondered how it would feel. To be loved *so much*.

Had his father loved Felix's mother that way? Did his own mother love his father enough that she'd love him still when the truth came out?

He didn't know. He'd run away before he could ask those questions.

But suddenly, holding a silent Tori in his arms, he wondered.

How had they loved each other? And could he forgive them, if it was enough?

Maybe, with the thaw, it would be time to find out.

Tori woke alone, this time. Hardly surprising, given the way she'd behaved the night before. She cringed even to remember it.

But Jasper hadn't mocked her, hadn't been smug or even dismissive. He hadn't even said just *no*.

He'd said, *'No, not like this.'*

And he'd been right.

Of course, the odds were good he'd tease and joke about it this morning, make comments about his ego and her flattery of it being good for the soul or something. But the more time she spent with him on this abortive road trip, the more she came to realise that those jibes and barbs weren't the real Jasper. They were the thorns and brambles he used to keep people away. To stop them from seeing the man inside.

But she'd seen him. Well, glimpsed him, at least. Watching him with the children, or helping Henry. Feeling his arms around her as she cried. And the strain in his voice as he told her no, more telling than his words of how much he was giving up.

She'd felt the real Jasper in his kiss. And she knew for certain now that he was nothing like the entitled, shallow man he pretended to be.

Tori wasn't entirely sure what to do with this information just yet.

Make fun of him, probably. Wasn't that the way their relationship went?

But maybe it didn't have to, any more.

She was still thinking about the possibilities as she headed downstairs thirty minutes later, washed and dressed and as presentable as she was going to get while wearing the same clothes she'd had on for three days now. Not that it could matter all that much; Jasper had seen her at her worst last night, in the grips of a nightmare and covered in sweat, and he'd still wanted her. And Liz and Henry…well, they'd seen her in her teenage Goth phase, so nothing would alarm them now.

Jasper was perched at the bar when she walked in,

surprised to find the place less busy than it had been yesterday. Across in the dining room she could see people folding sheets and packing bags through the open doorway.

'The roads are open?' she guessed.

Jasper nodded. 'Well, the way back to the main road is open. The moors road is still closed, so we'll have to go the long way round. But when you're ready we can head out and go…home.'

There was a slight pause before the last word, as if he realised that Flaxstone could never really be her home, not while the Moorside still stood, not even if she never came back here ever again. She'd had home once. She didn't expect to be so lucky as to find it twice.

Except maybe he was thinking of his own complicated feelings about the place. Tori didn't know what had driven him away from Flaxstone, or what had persuaded him to return, but she knew he hadn't seemed at ease on the estate ever since he'd arrived back in the country.

The time they'd spent at the Moorside Inn might not have been planned, or convenient, or even what she'd have chosen if she'd had any say in the matter at all. But Tori had to admit that it had changed them. It had given them the space to see deeper into each other, behind their defences.

And it had given *her* the chance to be part of a family again.

Walking away from that a second time somehow felt far, far harder than it had been eight years ago, deep in the grip of her grief and guilt over Tyler's death.

'You'll come back and see us soon, won't you, Vicky?' Aunt Liz said, holding her hands tight as Jasper loaded their stuff into the car. They seemed to be leaving with more than they'd arrived with—including two of Uncle Henry's steak and ale pies from the freezer, something that had made Jasper beam. There was something else, too—something wrapped in Christmas paper, that she hadn't been allowed to examine too closely. Tori was fine with that. Christmas presents smacked too much of family, and togetherness, and all the things she needed to say goodbye to again.

She wasn't 'Vicky' any longer. She'd been Tori since the day she walked out. Vicky and her dreams and ambition and selfishness had got Tyler killed. And even that hadn't been enough for her to give them up entirely.

She didn't want to be Vicky again. It hurt too much.

But Aunt Liz looked so hopeful, her grip on Tori's hands so desperate, that she couldn't tell her that. 'Sure. I'll come soon.'

'For Christmas maybe?' Aunt Liz pressed.

'Maybe.' Tori gave a faint smile, and pressed a kiss to Liz's cheek. Her skin felt more papery, older than Tori remembered.

They were all older now. Just not necessarily wiser.

'We'll look forward to it,' Henry said, leaning in for his own hug and kiss. 'Family shouldn't be apart at Christmas.'

Jasper came over to make his last goodbyes and then, suddenly, they were back on the road again.

Tori watched the Moorside Inn grow smaller and smaller in the wing mirror, and blinked away more tears she refused to shed when it disappeared completely.

CHAPTER SEVEN

SNOW STILL COVERED the land around them, inches deep and untouched except for the odd footprint or animal track. The road, however, was that horrible grey mush of snow mixed with salt and earth, churned up by car tyres. Jasper took the drive slowly, carefully, wondering if maybe they should have at least waited until after lunch to set out. But as soon as she'd heard the road was open, Tori had been getting ready to leave and shoving his backpack and laptop towards him.

The Moorside Inn might have been her home once, but she'd been conspicuously eager to leave it.

The memory of Tyler, he supposed, remembering that strange, middle-of-the-night connection between them after her dream. She hadn't mentioned it this morning, unsurprisingly, so neither had he. In fact, she hadn't mentioned much at all, and they'd reached the main road in complete silence. Jasper was starting to think they'd be all the way home at Flaxstone before Tori spoke, if then.

But they couldn't just go back to being the people they'd been before they got snowed in together, could they?

Then, she'd been a challenge to him—and he was pretty sure he'd just been an annoyance to her. They had the memory of their one night together, sure, but that had been five long years ago. They'd both changed since then, right? He knew for certain that he had.

And he'd changed again over the last few days. No, not him, exactly. But his understanding of who Tori was, and his strange compulsion to know her better. He couldn't return to being just colleagues—and acrimonious ones at that.

He wanted more.

He wanted her in his bed again tonight—a bed with enough room to spread out so that when she slept snuggled in his arms he knew it was because she wanted to be there, not just to avoid falling onto the hard floor.

And he wanted her wide awake, not dreaming. Wanted her thinking of him, not a dead lover he could never compete with.

Jasper shook his head and refocussed his attention on the road. What was he doing? Imagining himself in competition with the memory of an eighteen-year-old boy he'd never met?

Tori wasn't his girlfriend, or even his lover. She was barely even a friend.

But somehow, the last few days, she'd seemed so much more.

At the Moorside, in their snow-induced bubble of time, she'd seemed like a partner. Maybe family, even. At the bare minimum, a real friend. One he badly wanted to kiss…

Would he be able to cling onto that seed of a relationship, once they were back at Flaxstone? It felt as if the connection between them were a tiny seedling, poking its head through the snow too early, and the slightest frost could kill it off.

But Jasper was determined to nurture it and help it grow. He'd seen behind Tori's defences now, and he wanted that woman in his life. Not the brittle, argumentative, sarcastic woman he'd seen since he'd returned— well, actually, he wanted her too. He wanted all of her.

Hell. He really was in trouble.

By the time they pulled into Flaxstone Hall it was early afternoon, and Jasper's eyes ached from focussing on the treacherous roads and idiots who didn't know how to drive in the snow. The last thing he wanted to do was deal with his family, especially his father. But Tori had other ideas.

'We should go and check in with the earl and give him our report from Stonebury,' she announced, before he'd even cut the engine.

'Now?' he asked plaintively, as he climbed out of the car. 'Can't we just go back to bed first?'

She arched an eyebrow at him. 'Together?'

'Well, preferably,' he admitted.

With a sigh, Tori opened her own door, got out, and moved to meet him in front of the bonnet. 'Jasper, do you want my list of reasons why that would be a bad idea alphabetically or in order of importance?'

Ouch. 'Why don't you just give me the top three?' Hopefully ones he could counter with a reminder of just how good they could be in bed together. That searing kiss the night before had definitely confirmed for him that five years hadn't stolen any of the passion that they'd shared.

But Tori lifted her hands to tick her points off on her fingers. 'One, we need to talk to your father—like we were supposed to two days ago. He doesn't like waiting.

Two, I've been wearing these clothes for three days and I'm exhausted. And three, you and I both know that you'll be running back off to the States again soon, and I'm not all that interested in being another of the background models in your peacock strut across the estate, thanks.'

'My peacock strut?' He didn't have a strut. But he was pretty sure that number three was the only reason that was really stopping Tori after last night.

'You definitely do. I had the misfortune to witness it for years with every new girl you brought home.' She sighed. 'Look, Jasper, I'm sorry if I gave you the wrong idea last night. I was…upset. But I honestly believe that… giving in to anything between us again would be a bad idea. We were just caught up in the romance of being stranded in the snow.'

'With about thirty other people,' Jasper observed.

What was he missing here? She wouldn't quite look him in the eye, he realised, and her hands were clasped tightly in front of her. Upset or not, he knew that the *attraction* had been real between them last night, which meant that her reasons not to act on it must be stronger.

Was this really because he'd had plenty of girlfriends in the past? Or because she knew he was leaving soon and didn't want a meaningless fling? Both perfectly good reasons, except…they hinted at her wanting something *more*.

Jasper felt suddenly warm inside, despite the icy air all around them.

He'd avoided even a *hint* of more for years. But with Tori…maybe it wasn't impossible?

Or maybe she wasn't giving him the whole reason for her reluctance. Was this to do with *his* romantic past— or *hers*?

Eight years since Tyler died and she still woke up screaming from nightmares of losing him. Maybe *he* was the real reason she wasn't willing to move on, if she knew that what was between them was more than just a fling.

And now his head was starting to hurt with all the possibilities.

Rolling his eyes, he felt his usual arrogant, aristocratic demeanour taking over, the way it always did when he was confused or threatened or embarrassed. It was an automatic defence system, just like Tori's, he supposed, if a little flimsier.

'Fine, you don't want to go to bed with me. But I still think bed should be top of our list of priorities today. I'd happily take going to bed solo over dealing with dear old Dad right now.' In truth, he wanted a little more time to marshal his arguments for making Stonebury an escape for his mother. He *should* have been planning that while he'd been stuck at the Moorside, but he'd been a little… distracted. 'All that entertaining kids and serving meals wears a guy out, you know.'

'Should have known you couldn't handle an honest day's work,' Tori responded tartly.

Neither of them mentioned again the lack of sleep they'd suffered the night before after her nightmares, or the staying up late sharing secrets. Tori had packed that back in its box with her vague apology for 'giving him the wrong idea'. Already, Flaxstone had brought back the people they'd been before the Moorside Inn. He should have expected it, but it hurt all the same.

'Really, though. Can't reporting in wait until tomorrow? Or at least later this afternoon?'

Tori opened the car door and stepped out into the snow. 'Time and earl wait for no man.'

Then she strode towards the imposing doors of the place Jasper used to call home, and he found himself following without deciding to.

Until he doubled back, rescued the steak and ale pies from the boot, and decided to detour past the kitchens to pop them in the fridge for later. See? Totally in control of his own life, really.

They found the earl in his study—well, once they'd stopped by the kitchens. Even Tori couldn't argue with the fact that Henry's pies took priority over almost everything else.

Especially over any more discussion of what had happened between them last night.

She'd been brutally honest with her three reasons for Jasper, but she couldn't deny that she'd held one of them back.

I can't risk falling for you when I know you're leaving.

Already, he felt like someone new. Or rather, someone she'd hoped existed—the Jasper from the night they'd spent together. Maybe that Jasper really was there, underneath all the charm and the confidence. But she couldn't risk letting him out—or letting him into her heart. Even if he drastically changed his playboy ways—which she doubted—he'd be going back to the States after Christmas. And Tori knew better than anyone that long-distance relationships were a tragedy waiting to happen—or at the very least a disaster.

When he'd left last time, she'd been fine, because despite her hopes she'd still known who he was. It hadn't been a surprise that one night together was all they'd had. Leaving the country had seemed a little extreme, but whatever. Her heart had been safe.

This time…this time, he kept making paper chains and helping Uncle Henry and holding her when she cried and it was all far too much. This time, if she let herself fall any further…she feared for her heart when he went away again.

She'd spent eight years protecting her heart—from the hatred Liz and Henry would feel towards her if they knew everything about Tyler's death, from the guilt she felt herself, and from anyone else who might try and damage it even further. She wasn't about to stop now.

Which meant that focussing on work again for the rest of Jasper's visit was by far the best possible plan.

The earl looked up from the papers on his desk and studied them both with that strange, scrutinising stare he'd given Tori the first day they'd met. As if he were in the audience, watching her on the stage, waiting to see what she'd do next. An observer, not involved in her life choices.

How strange that he'd look at his son the same way, she realised suddenly. Jasper must have had his reasons for leaving, after all. She'd just never managed to ask him about them.

The Earl of Flaxstone had been Tori's benefactor since she was eighteen years old. It was a ridiculously old-fashioned term, but then, the earl was an old-fashioned kind of guy, and in the years since Tori had never been able to find a word that better described their relationship.

He'd discovered her not long before she'd left for university, when he'd stopped by the Moorside Inn. She'd been sitting outside at one of the picnic tables, studying the inn's books, trying to find somewhere to save some money. Times and takings had been lean just then, and

Henry and Liz had needed any help they could get—
but Tori just hadn't known enough to be any help at all.

She'd said as much to the earl, when he'd stopped by
to ask what she was doing. She hadn't known who he
was then, of course, but her frustration had leaked out
all the same. When she'd looked up to see exactly who
she was talking to, she'd seen the same considering look
on his face as she saw now. As if he was deciding quite
what to do with her.

Last time, he'd offered a few suggestions—negotiating
down the cost of some of their overheads, and other obvious things that she would have known if she hadn't
been eighteen and ignorant—then given her his card,
with instructions to look him up if ever she needed a job.

She'd left for university a month later, and it had only
been the following spring, after Tyler's death, that she'd
dug out the card, steeled herself, and called him. After
all, by then, she'd known she couldn't go home again. So
she'd do whatever it took to find somewhere else to go.

It had been a good call. The earl had given her more
than a place to go. He'd given her holiday work on the estate that summer—and all the holidays after that, which
suited her perfectly. He'd offered advice and insight when
she'd been deciding her course of study in her second and
third years. Then, once she graduated—top of her business class—he'd offered her a better-paying and more
interesting job than any of the other companies she'd in-
terviewed for, and accommodation to boot. And not the
staff dormitories, filled with sweaty students all summer, and freezing cold in the winter. Her own little cottage on the edge of the estate, to live in as she pleased.

She'd repaid his confidence in her, she thought, working her way up to become his trusted lieutenant, learn-

ing everything she could about the estate's business and developing it further every year. The earl hadn't exactly been a father figure to her, but he'd been a great boss, and she knew she would always owe him for the opportunities he'd given her.

Which was why she felt so damn awkward with him staring at her and Jasper this way.

'So. You've returned from your little adventure, then?' he asked, his gaze still flitting between the two of them. 'Felix filled me in.'

'More an inconvenience than an adventure,' Tori replied, taking her usual seat opposite him as he indicated she should. Jasper stayed standing, ignoring the chair at his own side, and his father's gesture to sit.

Obstinate man.

It hadn't escaped Tori's notice that Jasper seemed reluctant to spend any time at all with his father. In fact, she couldn't remember even seeing them together since he'd returned. Before he'd left, she'd have always said they were quite close. Clearly something fundamental had changed.

Apparently she wasn't the only one keeping family secrets.

'I'd have emailed our initial report on Stonebury Hall to you,' Tori went on, when it became obvious that Jasper had nothing to add to the conversation, 'but the Internet connection at the Moorside has always been spotty.' He was lucky she'd even managed to get a text message out to warn him they'd been delayed. Her call to Felix had only gone through when she was out by the road. Inside the inn calls were practically impossible. She'd seen plenty of the other guests standing up on the snow-covered picnic tables trying to get a signal.

The earl's attention was all on her now, as if Jasper weren't even in the room. 'And how was the old homestead?' he asked casually.

Tori hesitated before answering. She'd never told the earl her reasons for leaving, or for not returning. But now she wondered how much he knew. The Moorside wasn't *that* far from Flaxstone, and who was to say the earl hadn't stopped by there once or twice in the last few years? It was where she'd *met* him, after all. Why had that never occurred to her before?

'It was…fine. A little crowded. There were a number of families taking shelter there. Jasper entertained the kids,' she added, throwing him a smile.

He didn't return it. Neither did the earl.

Right. Maybe it was better to just concentrate on business for a while.

'So, uh, Stonebury Hall.' She handed over her tablet with the photos she'd taken of their visit for the earl to look through while she talked. 'It wasn't quite as spacious as we were hoping, or perhaps that space just isn't being used very well—I think the floor plans and photos from the agent were a little misleading. But there's definite potential for a farm shop and café-style business, and I could see the outbuildings being used for craft stalls, or maybe even a children's soft-play area.'

'I disagree,' Jasper said suddenly. 'It's far too small a property, battlements or not. It would be best used as a home. Perhaps even a family bolthole or escape, should anyone need it.' He stared hard at his father as he spoke, while Tori gave him her own, incredulous stare. Then the pieces started to fall into place.

Of course he wanted to keep the place for himself, the entitled, selfish prat. Had she really thought she'd seen another side to him while they were at the inn? How foolish of her. At heart he was just what he'd always been. A spoilt little rich boy who thought he deserved everything and ran away when he didn't get it.

Thank God she hadn't given in to him.

'I think Stonebury has far greater potential than just another holiday cottage,' she argued. 'The rental on such a place, probably only in season, would be far lower than if we put the whole property to work. Not to mention that *my* plan would make the land and the house available to local people—*all* of them, not just those who could afford to hire the place.'

The earl might be a quintessential aristocrat, with more land and money than anyone had any reason to expect in this world, but he'd always been enthusiastic about sharing it—to a point. The estate lands were generally open to walkers and locals, and they ran many events at the hall and gardens, as well as on the wider lands, throughout the year. Partly, Tori knew, that had begun as a way to keep the estate profitable after his father had almost run it into the ground. But with the earl's hard work, and her help over the last few years, the Flaxstone estate and business interests were more than profitable enough that he could have closed up the metaphorical drawbridge and kept Flaxstone private again. Instead, he'd begun using it for more charitable endeavours instead of paying ones, allowing even more people to make use of the estate.

She'd asked him once why he chose to run things that way. He'd responded that the estates were a part of history, one that belonged to the whole of the British Isles. He was merely their custodian for a time.

She liked that. She liked him. And the idea that his

only son and heir was trying to take the whole family and estate backwards annoyed the hell out of her.

Jasper shot her a glare. 'Perhaps this is something we can discuss in private. *Father*.' The emphasis was obvious, an attempt to stake a higher claim on their boss's attention. And it made Tori's blood boil.

To think she'd been starting to actually *like* the guy. Had confided in him. Found comfort in him.

Kissed him.

Grabbing her tablet and notes, she gave the earl a quick nod. 'By all means. I wouldn't want to come between *family*.'

And then she walked out of the office before she threw something at the Viscount Darlton's far too gorgeous head.

'Well. I think you've got some making up to do there,' Jasper's father said as they both watched Tori stalk out of the office. 'I *was* hoping that some time away together would help you two find some common ground, build a friendship perhaps, but...' He sighed. 'So. Tell me why you think Tori is wrong about Stonebury Hall.'

An uncomfortable feeling settled in Jasper's stomach. 'I don't think she's *wrong* exactly.' But that was what it had sounded like, he realised now. No wonder Tori had stormed off. 'Stonebury *could* be all the things she thinks it could. But at its heart, that house is a home—and I know she felt it too. But she's thinking about your property empire and her job. I'm thinking about our family. And *your* plans to ruin us.'

There was an echo of that desperate, clenching, wrenching feeling in his chest—the same one he'd felt when he'd first read his father's email, thousands of miles and a few weeks away from there.

It's time to be upfront and honest with the world. Felix deserves my acknowledgement as my son.

No consideration about what Jasper deserved and—more importantly—no thought of how it would affect his mother, the earl's dutiful Lady Flaxstone for almost thirty years. His father was just doing whatever *he* thought was best, or simply whatever he wanted. Just as he'd done when he'd had an affair with Felix's mother while engaged to Jasper's.

Other people were the last thing the Earl of Flaxstone thought about.

The earl sighed again. 'You're still against me publicly acknowledging Felix as my son.'

'Yes! Of course I am!'

'I never realised the Flaxstone reputation mattered so much to you, Jasper. I would have thought, if you were so concerned about our legacy and your place in it, you might have stayed to help protect it personally.' There was an edge to his father's words now. One a younger Jasper would have swerved away from, made nice to avoid that sharpness of the earl's temper.

But Jasper wasn't a child any longer. He knew his own mind. And he knew when his father was just plain wrong.

'I am deeply concerned about my mother's well-being. I can't stop you doing this—God knows, no one ever stopped you doing anything you wanted—but if you insist on making our private lives public then at least give Mother somewhere to take solace and refuge from the media chaos that will follow. Buy Stonebury, let her retire there until everything blows over.' Jasper remembered those incongruous battlements and crenellations. That was what she needed. Protection. Defences. She'd never really had any of her own, and so Jasper would have to give her some.

'If there's any decency left in you, don't drag her down with you,' he said. Then he turned and walked out on his father, pushing past Felix as he appeared in the doorway.

'Jasper?' his one-time best friend said, but Jasper ignored him.

Felix's paternity wasn't his fault—Jasper knew that logically. But hiding the truth from him for so many years was. Felix had known the truth ever since his mother died, years before, and not told him. Jasper wasn't ready to forgive that just yet. Not until he knew that his mother was protected.

At least he'd given his father something to think about. And now…now he was rather afraid he had to find Tori and explain himself. Maybe even apologise.

He pulled a face, even though there was no one to see it. He hated apologising.

Perhaps he'd make a stop for one of Henry's pies, first. For the energy. After all, he'd asked Mrs Rawkins, the cook, to put one on to warm for him before they went to meet his father. It would be a shame for it to go to waste, and Tori would probably take a little time to calm down, anyway.

He veered left, down the corridor that led to the kitchens, and took a moment to appreciate the aroma of steak and ale pie, wafting towards him. Yes, this was definitely the right decision.

Then he walked in, and saw Tori lifting a forkful of

his pie to *her* mouth. He froze. She gave him a wicked grin, then ate the mouthful right in front of him.

'Mmm…' she said, licking her lips. 'Delicious. Shame there's hardly any left.'

'Henry gave us two pies.' Jasper shot an accusing look at Mrs Rawkins, who folded her arms across her ample chest.

'Don't you give me that look. Tori told me everything.' Sadly, Mrs Rawkins had known him for his whole life, and any respect she'd had for his title or station had long since faded away in a litany of stolen food, broken plates, and his and Felix's teenage attempts to fix themselves food when returning late from the pub.

'What, exactly, did she tell you?' Jasper asked. And when had Tori got Mrs Rawkins on her side anyway? He shook his head. 'Never mind, I can imagine.' Probably the truth as she saw it, embellished to make him out to be as evil as possible.

Tori deserved to know the real truth—about his family, his father, his half-brother, and why he was acting the way he was. She was stuck in the middle of it all, another pawn in his father's game, and he owed her the full story, however hard it was to tell it.

But more than that, he *wanted* her to know. Because he couldn't bear her looking at him again the way she had when they were in his father's office. Not when she'd finally started to look at him differently, while they were away.

And who knew? Maybe it would even do him some good to have someone to talk to about the whole sordid affair. Although, if his father got his way, soon he'd be able to discuss it with the whole world.

The thought didn't cheer him at all.

He looked at Tori, who was happily cutting herself another piece of pie. 'I don't suppose you're going to share that, are you?'

Tori shook her head as she chewed another mouthful, her expression blissful. 'Nope. But, like you say, there's another one.'

'In the freezer,' Mrs Rawkins added. 'Take hours to cook now, that will.'

Jasper sighed, and sank into the chair opposite Tori to watch her eat his pie.

'Fine,' he said. 'Consider me punished. But when you're finished, perhaps you'll do me the courtesy of letting me explain myself.'

Tori's eyebrow's shot up in obvious surprise. 'Okay,' she said, after a moment of chewing. 'When I'm done.'

'Great.' Jasper sank back in his chair and prepared to endure his punishment.

CHAPTER EIGHT

HENRY'S PIES WERE always delicious, but watching Jasper's pained expression as she ate it in front of him made the whole dining experience even more sublime for Tori.

Eventually, she set her cutlery down on her empty plate, thanked Mrs Rawkins—who had been a dear ally ever since she'd discovered that Tori knew her way around a kitchen and could be a big help when there was an event on and not enough trained hands on deck—and turned to Jasper, her arms folded across her middle.

'Okay. Explain.'

And it had better be something more convincing than, *I'm a poor little rich boy who always got everything I want so I don't know any better.*

'Not here.' Jasper's gaze darted around the kitchen furtively, as if he thought Mrs Rawkins might intervene or take sides—which she'd totally already done, so it seemed a bit pointless. 'Let's go take a walk by the river.'

'Yay. More snow and ice,' Tori replied, letting the sarcasm flow. But, actually, the kitchens were warm and stuffy, and she could do with walking off some of that pie before she fell into a food coma, so she followed him all the same.

They paused in the boot room to grab hats, gloves,

scarves, warm coats and walking boots—all the things Tori wished they'd had with them when they were stranded on the moors. Maybe then they could have escaped to somewhere other than the Moorside Inn. *Anywhere* else would have been ideal.

Not just because of having to see Aunt Liz and Uncle Henry again. If she was honest, having that time with them had been kind of…lovely. Her guilt still sat heavy in her chest, too easily revived by being back in that place where her romance with Tyler had flourished and died. But feeling part of a family again? That part she'd enjoyed.

No, the reason she so bitterly regretted their pit stop in her past was walking beside her, as they strode out from the manor and towards the river that ran along the edge of the woods on the far side of the estate.

Spending time with Jasper had helped her see him in a new light. A more hopeful one. She'd got to know a man she'd thought she could actually *like*. Maybe even care for.

But the minute they'd returned to Flaxstone he'd reverted to type. People didn't really change—she knew that. And trying to make someone into something they weren't never ended well. She'd learnt that with Tyler. Or maybe he'd learnt it from her—the very hard way.

Jasper was what he was: a spoilt only child who went through women as she went through chocolate, and who hadn't ever learned to think about anybody but himself.

'I want to explain exactly what was going on in my father's study earlier,' Jasper said as the river came into view.

'Besides you being a Grade-A tosser?' Tori asked cheerfully. He shot her a glare, and she added, 'If you want to change my mind about that, you really should have started with an apology.'

Jasper sighed. He looked exhausted, she realised suddenly. Probably at least partly because she'd kept him up half the night with her nightmares.

Maybe she owed him a little bit of an apology too. But not unless he said sorry first.

'I apologise,' Jasper said stiffly. He seemed nothing like the joking, carefree guy she'd known when she'd first started at Flaxstone, or the irritating, sarcastic one he'd been since his return. And he definitely wasn't the relaxed, smiling man who'd built snowmen and paper chains with kids at the Moorside. Was she missing something? What exactly was going on here? 'I shouldn't have dismissed your ideas in front of my father like that.'

'So why did you?' Tori asked, feeling an echo of the hurt she'd felt back in the office. But the look of pain that flashed across Jasper's face was far more intense. And intriguing. 'Did you honestly not agree with me?'

'It wasn't that exactly…although I still think Stonebury is better suited as a family home.'

'Except that's not what we're in business for,' Tori pointed out.

'No.' Jasper sighed again, then glanced back over his shoulder as a burst of laughter cut through the air. Over the crest of the rolling hill behind them appeared a group of tourists, being led by Felix, presumably through to the Christmas market taking place around the old stable yard for the whole week before Christmas. The event was well signposted, but every year some visitors arrived at the wrong entrance and got promptly lost. It was obviously Felix's turn to round them up and get them where they needed to be that afternoon.

Jasper grabbed her arm and led her further away, down to the edge of the river, as if he was afraid of being overheard. And remembering his behaviour in the kitchen, Tori realised he *was* afraid of just that.

What on earth was he about to tell her? What could make Viscount Darlton look *that* vulnerable?

The river was frozen, icy white and solid. A robin hopped across the frozen surface, searching for food. With the backdrop of the naked trees and the winter white sky, it looked for all the world like a scene from a Christmas card.

But Tori was too tense now to appreciate the beauty.

'What's going on?' she asked, when it became clear that Jasper wasn't about to talk without prompting.

He stopped beside a bench, looking out over the river to the woods beyond. Brushing a thin layer of powdery snow from the surface, he motioned for her to sit down, then sat beside her, close enough that his gloved hand lay beside hers.

'It's about my father,' he said slowly.

Tori rolled her eyes. 'I'd guessed that much. Is he ill? Is there anything I can do?'

'He's not…that's not what's going on.' Jasper took a deep breath, and swallowed so hard she saw his throat bob. Still staring out at the wintry scene ahead of them, he spoke so seriously, so deliberately that even Tori didn't dare interrupt.

'Five years ago I discovered that my father has another son, by a woman other than my mother. That son is Felix, and now the earl wants to make that knowledge public to the world.'

Tori blinked at him, and wished with all her heart that

Henry had sent them off with a decent bottle of something highly alcoholic, too.

It looked as if they were going to need it.

Jasper wished he could say that telling Tori his family secret lightened the load he felt on his shoulders, but if anything hearing it out loud only made it feel more real. An inescapable hurricane about to rip his family and life apart because his father hadn't been able to keep it in his pants and had a misguided belief about the 'right thing' to do.

Tori stared at him. He stared back, waiting to see which way she was going to jump.

He realised, a little belatedly, that he was putting an awful lot of trust in his beliefs about Tori Edwards. If she wasn't the sort of person he thought she was, then telling her even this much could bring about all the outcomes he'd come home to try and avoid.

He watched the emotions and thoughts flickering behind her eyes, and decided he was comfortable with the risk.

She wouldn't run to the papers. He was pretty much certain of that. Not only would it be detrimental to her own career—because he couldn't imagine the scandal was going to do a huge amount for Flaxstone Enterprises, either—but she wasn't that sort of person.

Exactly when he'd come to know Tori well enough to be sure of that…well, he could pinpoint it quite precisely, as it happened. It was last night, when she'd fallen apart in his arms, then put herself back together again.

'That's why you left,' she said finally. 'I always wondered.'

'I couldn't stay.' Jasper looked back out at the tiny

robin, scratching the ice for food. 'I just… I didn't know how to deal with it. With any of it. My father, Felix, all the lies… I needed to be somewhere where I didn't care if people were lying or telling the truth. I needed to not care for a while.' Because he'd cared so damn much while he was at Flaxstone. All the conflicting emotions he'd experienced on finding out the truth had threatened to burn him up from the inside out, otherwise. 'Felix never told you?'

Tori shook her head. 'I had no idea. How did *you* find out?' He sensed it wasn't the question she *wanted* to ask, which only made him more nervous about what that would turn out to be. He had no doubt that she'd get around to it eventually.

'I came across a copy of my father's updated will on his desk one day. Talking about his two sons and heirs. The earl was away and I couldn't even talk to him about it until the next day.'

'That was the night you came to me,' Tori said, putting it together far quicker than he'd expected. 'I *knew* there was something different about you that night.'

Jasper looked down at his hands. 'I felt like a different person that night.'

'I liked the man I saw that night.' She pressed her gloved hand over his, and he gripped it tightly, grateful for the small show of comfort. 'So, the next day you confronted your father for a full confession?'

'Yeah. Of course. Why wouldn't I?'

Tori shrugged. 'Some people would prefer to pretend they'd never seen that paper, that they never knew the truth. Or save it for a later time when they could use the information.'

Jasper stared at her. He couldn't imagine doing anything other than seeking out the truth at that point. Secrets were bad enough. Why live with them longer than necessary or, worse, add another layer of deception to the whole situation? 'Would *you* have?'

'Probably not.' She gave him a wan smile. 'I just… sometimes the truth can be the worst thing to hear, you know?'

'I know,' he replied darkly. He remembered all too well that feeling, hoping against all the evidence that it would prove to be a mistake, that his father still had just the one child, only to find out that the truth was far worse than he'd even imagined.

His half-sibling wasn't some random stranger, conceived and born before his father had met his mother, or even through some awful affair since.

He was his best friend, the boy he'd grown up with. Felix.

'How did Felix take the news?' Tori asked, as if she'd read his mind. Or maybe his thoughts were just that clear on his face. He didn't hide things well—he knew that much about himself.

Unlike his half-brother.

'Turns out it wasn't quite the surprise for him that it had been for me.'

'He already knew?' Tori, at least, sounded suitably stunned at that revelation. 'When you asked if he'd told me, I assumed you meant *since* you left. But he knew before?'

Jasper nodded. 'I… I went to him first, of course.' It had been so natural. They'd been each other's confidant since they were small boys together. Felix had been there for him through every argument with his father, every incident at school, and Jasper had supported him too, against jibes from school mates about Felix being a scholarship boy—a scholarship funded, Jasper realised now, by their father—all the way to Felix's mother's death when they were seventeen, and the grief and torment that had followed. Felix knew all his secrets and he knew Felix's— or so he'd thought.

'I wanted to talk it all through with Felix before I approached my mother. I figured that he'd be as horrified as I was, that we could work through it together. But when I told him…there was no surprise behind his eyes. He turned pale, and, as I studied him, suddenly I could see all the signs I'd missed for so many years. He has our father's eyes, you know, if not his hair. And a certain look, sometimes, that's so like him…' Jasper shuddered. 'Anyway. I realised almost instantly that he already knew. I demanded to know when he found out, how long he'd been keeping it from me…that was the worst part, in lots of ways. The idea that my father and my best friend, two of the people who mattered most to me in the whole world, had been lying to me for so long. And I'd never even known…'

Tori let go of his hand and gripped the base of the bench, not looking at him as she asked, 'How long had he known?'

'Since his mother died. She knew how ill she was, couldn't leave him without ensuring he knew the truth. I guess she didn't trust my father to tell him, understandably.'

Felix had gone so completely off the rails after his mother's death. At the time, they'd all thought it was just the grief. But once Jasper had found out the truth, it all made so much more sense.

'So he knew for years before you did,' Tori said, thoughtfully. 'I can see how that would have hurt.'

Hurt seemed like such a small word for it. 'It was like I suddenly couldn't trust the whole world around me. Like my senses might be lying to me and up might actually be down. *Nothing* was the way I thought it was. I mean, I idolised my father, and I trusted Felix more than anyone, and suddenly neither of those things were true any longer.'

'What about your mother?'

Jasper stared down at his hands. 'I still don't know how much she actually knows. That's why I came back. Knowing Mum…even if she suspected something she'd pretend she didn't. You know what she's like.' Happy living in her own world, and stubborn enough to refuse to see anything beyond it. Even if hers was a world built entirely on lies and secrets. 'I suspect she'd prefer *not* to know the truth, to be honest.' That was how she'd always been. Jasper had learned young how to deal with her, and he'd stuck to those lessons even when his world had fallen apart.

'So you've never spoken to her about it?'

'No. But I'm going to have to. If my father publicly legitimises Felix the papers will grab that story and run with it—they always do. And then…'

'The whole world will know.' Tori pulled a face. 'Okay, I see why you came home. What I still don't get is why it meant you had to trash my meeting with your father.'

Okay, so one meeting probably wasn't the most important thing in the context of this conversation, but it was the piece of the puzzle Tori still didn't have, and she hated not knowing things that impacted her life and work.

If she'd realised exactly what was going on with Tyler sooner, maybe she'd have been able to stop it. Or maybe she wouldn't. But at least she'd have been working with all the facts. Instead, she'd assumed he was guilt-tripping her, when he'd told her he didn't know what he'd do without her. She'd never imagined that he'd actually meant that, without her there to keep him in check, he'd act out every stupid thing that passed through his head. And by the time she'd realised just how far he'd go, it was far too late.

Her heart ached for Jasper, so betrayed and alone. At the back of her mind she'd always wondered if him leaving had had anything to do with *her*, with that night they'd spent together. Now she knew he'd had far bigger worries than an ill-advised one-night stand. He wouldn't have been thinking about her at all.

Which, oddly, didn't make her feel as better as she'd imagined it would.

'Stonebury Hall,' Jasper said, with a sigh. 'I insisted on coming to look at it with you because I think it would be perfect for Mum. Somewhere she can ride out the media storm, get away from my father, and be safe.'

'All those battlements,' Tori mused. He wasn't wrong. Stonebury Hall was definitely a good place to hide out and take cover. But she couldn't help but think there was a better plan in there somewhere. If they worked together...

'Exactly. I want her safe.'

'But *she* wouldn't like it to look as if she was running and hiding.' Tori didn't know Lady Flaxstone very well, but from the comments she'd heard over the years she knew that her reputation was important to her. She wouldn't want people to think a scandal had driven her into hiding, even if it had.

'I know.' Jasper sounded frustrated. 'But if she's here, facing down the press at the door, or on the phone, the whole circus… We went through that once before, you know. When Father was involved in a business deal with an old friend that turned out to be *incredibly* ill-advised.' Tori knew the deal he meant. 'Ill-advised' might be the understatement of the century.

'How did your mother take it?'

'Badly,' Jasper said, flatly. 'Very badly. It didn't fit her perfect world view that she'd created, but she couldn't ignore it either, so she couldn't cope. She basically took to her bed for months, and that wasn't even personally connected to her, really. This? I'm worried it will break her.'

'So we get her out of here and up to Stonebury,' Tori agreed. 'But how about we give her a reason to be there, and a team to support her?'

Jasper frowned at her. 'How do you mean?'

The idea was coming together in her head now, so quickly Tori wondered how she hadn't seen it straight off. 'You're right that the main house at Stonebury is more like a home. So, you move in there with your mother to start with, get her set up with a trusted manager and assistants. Then when she's settled, you can head back to the States and your real life.' Tori pushed aside the tug on her heart as she mentioned him leaving. She almost wanted to offer to go, look after his mother herself, but she knew that the final decision on staffing, and particularly her assignments, would lie with the earl. 'But she's not just hiding out. The team are developing the barns and outbuildings—not to mention that fantastic old stable block—to provide spaces for craft workshops and stalls, a café, maybe a little farm shop. It can be named after your mother or something, give her a real connection to the place.'

Jasper stared at her in amazement. 'That might…actually work. Why didn't I think of that?'

'Because you were scared, and too focussed on your immediate problem,' Tori replied promptly.

'I wouldn't say scared, exactly…' Jasper rolled his eyes. 'Fine. Maybe a little. Okay, so, we have a plan. How do we convince the earl?'

'We work up a killer proposal,' Tori said. 'Together.'

Suddenly, Jasper seemed very close, although neither of them had moved. Maybe it was the way his eyes seemed to grow warmer, as if he was looking deeper inside her. Or perhaps it was the soft smile that flickered around his lips. 'You think you can stand being stuck with me a little longer, then? While we work on the proposal, I mean.'

That wasn't all he meant. Tori could see the truth in his eyes.

He was thinking about last night. About that kiss.

And she had to admit, so was she.

God, I want to kiss him again.

'I think I could just about bear it,' she said, unable to tear her gaze away from his. Her mouth was dry, her throat too tight, and despite the snow and ice her face felt glowing warm.

'Who knows?' Jasper said, leaning in just a little closer. 'Maybe you'll even come to enjoy it.'

'I suppose miracles do happen,' Tori replied.

Even if she'd never believed in miracles before. Suddenly this one felt inevitable.

CHAPTER NINE

'I CAN'T STARE at this thing any more.' Frustration oozed from Tori's very being.

Jasper put down the latest research he was reading—printed out, because if he had to stare at a screen for another moment his eyes might fall out—and studied her instead. It was a much more attractive prospect, anyway.

Her dark hair tumbled forward over her forehead, curling a little against her cheek, and her grumpy expression somehow served only to make her look more adorable. She looked tired—they were *both* tired—but beautiful, and suddenly Jasper knew that he couldn't waste another moment with her working. Not on such a gorgeous winter's day.

'Let's get out of here,' he said. She gave him a scandalised look. One thing he'd learned from working closely with Tori for the past few days was that she worked too damn hard, and too long. And he'd thought *he* was a workaholic. Apparently he had nothing on Tori.

'It's less than a week before Christmas,' he argued reasonably. 'And a *Saturday*. I think we're allowed a little time off for seasonal cheer.'

'You wanted to present this to your father before Christmas,' Tori pointed out.

'And we will. I mean, we're nearly there with this, right? All we're really doing now is double-checking the figures and making sure the research holds up.' Tori had been adamant that every I had to be dotted and every T crossed before they presented their ideas to the earl. There had to be no gaps, no wiggle room, if they wanted to pull this off.

Jasper totally agreed in principle. In practice, he needed fresh air, a break, and maybe even a cup of mulled wine.

'Come on,' he wheedled. 'We could head down to the Christmas market. It might even give us a stunning idea for that finishing touch you're still hankering for.'

Tori was adamant that there was still something missing from their proposal, something that would set it off perfectly and give them an unbeatable proposal the earl would have to go for.

Right now, Jasper would be happy with just guilting his father into doing the right thing and giving his mother an out. But Tori insisted that it had to be good business sense, too.

Tori considered his suggestion, and Jasper could see in her expression the workaholic warring with the desire for a proper break.

'I'll buy you a mulled wine…' he tempted her, and she broke, tossing her papers down on the desk.

'Oh, fine. Come on, then. But I want a mince pie, too.'

'Have you spoken to your mother yet?' Tori asked as they strolled out through the hall's back door and down through the gardens to the market, out by what used to be farm outbuildings. Much of the Flaxstone land was still farmed by tenant farmers, but the structures they used these days were rather more efficient and well equipped

than the more historic versions. Still, Tori and his father
had found plenty of profitable ways to use the unneeded
buildings, just as they had the rest of the estate.

'I've spoken to her about many things,' Jasper said
evasively. 'Although she still won't tell me what she
wants for Christmas. Apparently I should be able to
surprise her.'

He knew that wasn't really what Tori was asking, but for
just ten minutes it would be nice to forget about his family's issues and enjoy her company. Something he'd found
himself doing more and more over the last week, even
while deep at work on the Stonebury project. He just liked
being with her. Even if she wouldn't let them take their
relationship any further. He wanted her there, with him.

He wasn't thinking too hard about what that meant.

'Jasper,' she said, a warning tone in her voice. 'You
know what I mean. You *promised* me you'd talk to her
about Stonebury before we put this proposal to your father, and you're running out of time. This isn't a decision you can make for her. You have to be sure that this
is what she wants, too.'

'I know.' And he did. Tori was right—something that
seemed to happen irritatingly often. 'I just…haven't found
the right moment yet. I'll do it soon though. I promise.'

'And have you spoken to Felix?' Her tone was softer
this time, and she slipped her arm through his as she
asked. It was funny—but nice funny—the way that, as
they'd grown closer as friends working together, they
seemed to have become closer physically, too. These
days, they always seemed to be finding reasons to touch
each other—for comfort, for support, or just because they
both seemed to need it.

Jasper could hardly imagine the closed-off woman

he'd explored Stonebury with offering him a comforting touch. But that was before the Moorside. Before they shared their secrets.

Now, he wondered how far this casual contact would go. Would she kiss him again? Or let him kiss her?

The anticipation was so delicious he almost didn't want to rush it. Although other parts of him were rather more eager to progress...

He felt like a teenager again, or the much younger man who'd been lucky enough to experience Tori's touch the first time round. He remembered now that curiosity he'd felt towards her, the pull, the fascination he couldn't shake. The challenge she'd presented, with those stone walls up. The way the excitement he had felt building had eclipsed the realisation of his father's betrayal, that night she'd let him see behind her mask, just for a while...

Now, the mask was down. He'd discovered the real woman hiding behind the battlements—seen where she came from and discovered her secrets, her loss. And he liked her so much more for it.

A ridiculous amount more, really. Especially considering he'd be leaving again in the new year, and she wouldn't even kiss him.

'Jasper?' Tori's concerned voice interrupted his consideration of all the other ways he might like her, and he started, jerking his gaze towards her. 'Felix? You spoke with him?'

'No. God, no.' He hadn't been able to look Felix in the eye before he'd left, and the two emails his ex-best friend had sent afterwards, presumably trying to explain himself, had been deleted unread. 'What is there to say?'

Tori gave him a long look. 'Maybe it's more about listening. Hearing his side of the story at last. Seeing if the two of you can find a way back to being friends again. I mean, I remember how close you used to be. Mrs Rawkins used to despair of the two of you. Even the night we…' She blushed, and Jasper found himself enchanted all over again. 'Well, when you came home with me, you had to text Felix to tell him where you'd be first.'

'That was mostly for bragging rights,' Jasper said absently. Then, off her eye roll, added, 'because I was an idiot. Obviously.'

'Oh, I never doubted that,' Tori replied. But there was a fondness to her tone that wouldn't have been there a couple of weeks ago, and it made him smile. 'Come on, speed up. It's cold and I want that mulled wine before we have to get back to work.'

She lengthened her stride and he matched it easily, keeping her hand tucked through his arm as they headed across the estate towards the festive strains of sleigh bells and carols.

It had been five long years since Jasper had visited the Flaxstone Christmas market, and it was clear that things had progressed a long way in his absence. When he'd left, the event had been a few small craft stalls, a poorly decorated tree, and the local junior-school choir singing Christmas carols. Now, the whole market wouldn't have looked out of place somewhere in one of Europe's capital cities. There was a small group of singers dressed in Victorian outfits performing under the oversized tree, which was strung with delicate, glowing white lights. A vintage-looking carousel took up one corner, with a queue of children and adults waiting to ride, and a full-on hog roast was on offer under one of the wooden shelters. The whole place was packed, and everyone Jasper saw was smiling—bar a small child who seemed to be scared of either Father Christmas, his real-life reindeer, or both.

A lot of that, he suspected, was to do with Tori. As they strolled through the Scandi-style wooden stalls, all stocking handmade decorations, gifts and edibles, many of the stallholders stopped to thank Tori for her assistance and support, and several handed over freebie treats in gratitude.

'Looks like you've been busy while I've been gone,' he observed, as another stallholder called them over and placed a paper bag in Tori's palm, with gushing thanks.

'There's still more I want to do.' She fished around in the bag and smiled at its contents. 'Ooh, apple and cranberry mince pies! These are so good. Anyway. Next year, I want to do a light display on the walk through the woods to get to the market, and maybe even look at siting the Santa's grotto in there too, with extra elves to help families find the way.'

'When have you had time to be working on the market?' Jasper asked as Tori handed him a pie from the bag. 'I mean, we've been working flat out on the proposal for days, and before that we were snowbound at the Moorside.'

Tori shrugged, wiping crumbs from around her mouth. 'Most of this was set up months ago. I always start working on Christmas in summer—and so do these guys. They need to know their plans so they can build stock, plan sales, schedule staff and so on. Christmas starts *long* before you think it does, you know. Sometimes I think it's actually an all-year event…' She trailed off, her eyes suddenly wide.

'What?' Jasper asked cautiously. That kind of look made him nervous.

'I've figured out what the proposal needs.' Tori beamed, and reached up to place her palms on either side of his face. Then, without any more warning, she stretched up on tiptoe and planted a firm kiss against his lips.

Jasper's body reacted with a jolt, and he forgot all about food and Christmas and Stonebury as he let himself luxuriate in the kiss. Then his brain caught up, and he wrapped his arms around her waist to hold her closer, and deepened their embrace.

Someone, somewhere, whooped appreciatively, and Tori pulled back, her cheeks bright pink. She stepped out of his arms, then grabbed his hand. 'Come on. We need to get back to work.'

We need to talk about that kiss. And do it again. Very soon.

But Jasper knew Tori. There'd be no discussion about what had just happened—or what could happen—between them until after she'd got this new idea down on paper.

After that, though, Jasper had plans.

'The proposal certainly looks interesting.' The earl put down the printout he'd been reading, lifted his glasses from his nose, and looked up at them. Tori forced her feet to stay planted on the centuries-old carpet. Shuffling from foot to foot wasn't good for her professional appearance *or* the flooring. 'And I must say I'm glad to see the two of you working together so well. That gives me hope for our future.'

He was looking at Jasper as he said it, Tori realised. Jasper, of course, was looking studiously out of the window over his father's left shoulder. It was pitch black outside, so she had no idea what he was even pretending to look at.

She muffled a sigh. She understood Jasper's anger and upset, of course she did. He had every right to be furious with his father for his actions, and maybe even angry with Felix for lying to him for so long. But she couldn't help but wish he was even a *little* willing to move beyond the events of the past and consider the future.

Of course, she wasn't sure if she'd have even had that thought if it hadn't been for two days at the Moorside Inn, revisiting her own past. And it wasn't as if she were rushing back there either, so who was she to judge? Sometimes the past was just too painful to live in—and too hard to leave behind. Jasper had run away, exactly the same as she had. He'd only come back to help his mother, and she'd only gone back to the Moorside because the snow had left her no other choice. Neither of them were exactly poster children for healthy forward momentum away from their issues. They just took their baggage with them when they ran.

And that would be fine. Except Liz and Henry were expecting her for Christmas now. And if Jasper couldn't move on from what his father had done…then he wouldn't be staying in the country much longer. He'd see his mother settled at Stonebury, if their plan worked. But beyond that? Tori had already made herself face up to the unwelcome truth that he'd be returning to his life in the States in the new year.

Another entry on a lengthy list of reasons why she mustn't let herself grow too attached to the Viscount Darlton. Right after the fact that 'Viscount' was his actual title. Not her world, not her people. She was staff, not family.

And she'd given up the only family she had left to achieve even that.

Plus there was his unfortunate habit of never sticking

with the same girl for more than a night or two, something that didn't seem to have changed while he'd been away, given that he was still single.

Not that she'd exactly been pursuing romance and true love since Tyler had died, either. Her one night with Jasper had been a one-off.

Except now she'd kissed him. Again. And that was definitely the sort of action that could lead to it being *more* than a one-off, if she let it.

Well. That was a very distracting line of thought. Tori forced herself to abandon it until later as the earl continued speaking.

'Which one of you came up with the idea for the Christmas tree farm?'

Tori snuck a look at Jasper, who returned it with a hint of a smile—the first she'd seen since they entered the office.

'It was very much a collaborative project, my lord,' she said, diplomatically. In truth, after that kiss she definitely wasn't thinking about, she'd dragged Jasper back from the Christmas market to the side sitting room they'd been using as their office and declared that they were going to create Christmas every day at Stonebury!

Jasper had looked at her as if she were crazy, until she'd explained.

'It's perfect for it. We set up a permanent Christmas village, smaller than the market here, but with crafts for sale and—this is the important part—workshops so people can make their own wreaths, decorations, gifts etc. in the months running up to Christmas. We could do other seasonal workshops too—Valentine's Day, Easter, that sort of thing. But the key would be Christmas, all year round. It's the novelty of it that will draw people in.'

Jasper had looked thoughtful. 'There was a small copse of fir trees behind the house, did you see? Apparently a previous owner had considered setting up a Christmas tree farm, but had to sell before it came to fruition. We could revive it, supplement it with bought-in trees until our own grew up enough...'

'And we could keep reindeer!' Tori had said excitedly.

Jasper had laughed and shaken his head. But Dasher, Dancer and their friends had made it into the proposal.

'Well, I like the work you've done, and the figures and research included. Obviously I imagine the farm shop and catering facilities would be subsidising the more... interesting parts of the project for a while. But if word gets around, it could become a novelty feature for tourists, one of those "must see if you're passing through" places. The location is good for that...'

'And there's a lot of local craftspeople always looking for new places to display and sell their wares. With more "buy local" initiatives springing up all the time, it would be good to be at the heart of that,' Jasper added, the first time he'd spoken directly to his father since the meeting had started.

'But you still want the house for...well, to be a personal dwelling, rather than part of the business?' the earl asked Jasper.

Tori bit her lip and waited to see how he'd answer. Would he even want his father to know that he'd told her everything?

'I want Mother to have somewhere to retreat to, that's all,' Jasper said. 'You owe her that much.'

If the earl was surprised at his candour in front of Tori, he didn't show it. Instead, he sighed, and said, 'Very well. Let me think it over. I'll let you know my decision in good time.'

Tori turned to leave, Jasper close behind her, his hand at the small of her back. It felt warm and protective—and absurdly sexy, given the smallness of the gesture.

'But, son?' the earl called suddenly, and she felt Jasper stiffen behind her. 'I suggest you talk to your mother. While I'm considering.'

'Told you so,' Tori whispered as she was hurried out of the room.

'Yeah, yeah,' Jasper muttered back. 'Come on.'

'Where are we going now?'

'*We* are going for a drink. And *I* am going to celebrate by eating the last of Henry's pies.'

'So you're not going to *share* the pie?' Tori's voice was plaintive as she stared at his loaded plate across the kitchen table.

'Nope.' Jasper gave her a gleeful smile, and tucked in.

Mrs Rawkins had rolled her eyes when the two of them had bowled in and Tori had raided the wine cellar, while he'd retrieved the pie he'd dug out of the freezer earlier to defrost. She'd declared she was done for the night so, as long as they cleared up after themselves, she didn't care what they got up to.

'But my kitchen better be exactly as I left it,' she'd warned as she'd put on her coat. 'I've got staff coming in from everywhere to prepare for the party tomorrow night—and don't you touch *any* of the food we've got prepped in the fridges. Okay?' Tori and Jasper had nodded, mutely. Jasper had felt about sixteen again as she'd given them one last glare before sweeping out.

Mrs Rawkins needn't have worried. Jasper's priorities

for the evening were quite simple. Eat this pie—while making Tori watch. Share a bottle of wine with a beautiful woman. And hopefully get her to talk about and maybe repeat that kiss.

After that, all he wanted to do was fall into bed—even if he was alone. Although he wouldn't say no to company if Tori offered... The last few days of extreme work hours were catching up with him, and Mrs Rawkins wasn't the only one who needed to prepare for tomorrow night's party. As the heir to the Flaxstone estate, he knew there'd be expectations placed on him—even if he'd successfully avoided them for the past five years.

And he needed to talk to his mother. Tori was right; he couldn't put that off any longer.

'A decent man would at least let me try a bite,' Tori tried again.

'A decent woman wouldn't have stolen fifty per cent of my pies,' Jasper pointed out, between mouthfuls. 'Although I guess I could always go back to the Moorside and ask Henry for more...'

The teasing look disappeared from Tori's face at that, and she reached for the bottle of red wine they'd opened and topped up both their glasses.

'Or you could bring me some when you go back for Christmas,' he pushed.

'What's the point?' Tori asked. 'You'll be heading back to the States as soon as your mother is settled at Stonebury, assuming the earl agrees to our plan.'

'I'd come back for this pie,' Jasper said appreciatively, taking another mouthful. Then he caught sight of Tori's expression. 'Unless you don't want me to leave?'

They hadn't talked about this. Hadn't talked about the future. Hadn't even talked about them as a thing that was edging ever closer to happening. Jasper was almost certain she felt it as much as he did, but, apart from that excited kiss at the Christmas market, there'd been no sign that Tori was willing to move any further, and so Jasper had waited.

Until now.

'You need to live your life wherever makes you happiest,' she said, with a shrug. She didn't meet his gaze though. 'And I can't see that being here once your father makes his big announcement about Felix.'

'Well, no, probably not,' Jasper admitted.

Maybe he was wrong about the wider public's appetite for aristocratic scandal, but he doubted it. And even if he was, *local* society would definitely care. That was the society Lady Flaxstone cared about most.

He'd take his mother away with him to the States if he could, but her fear of flying verged on the phobic, and she'd be miserable away from her own country. He hadn't really thought beyond getting her settled at Stonebury, but if Tori took on the project personally, he could definitely see himself visiting regularly...

'So I only have to put up with you and your cruel pie eating for another few weeks, I figure,' she said, staring longingly at his pie.

Rolling his eyes, Jasper loaded up the fork again and held it out across the table to her.

'Really?' she asked, eyes suddenly bright. From the excitement on her face a person couldn't have been blamed for thinking he'd just offered her the crown jewels, or a sparkly engagement ring.

'Go on,' he said indulgently.

Tori's eyes fluttered closed as she wrapped her mouth around the fork. 'So, so good,' she muttered as she chewed.

Jasper had to agree. If it meant he could see that look

of bliss on her face every day, he'd start shipping in Henry's pies by the dozen.

Or maybe he'd just concentrate on finding some other things he could do for her that made her look that way…

Tori swallowed, opened her eyes and smiled at him. 'Thank you. I know how hard it is for you to share.'

'Is that another not so subtle hint that I should talk to my mother and/or half-brother?' Tori hadn't exactly been restrained on the subject until now. Despite her comment, he trusted that she knew him well enough that the issue of going from only child to youngest son wasn't the problem here. According to the will he'd found, his father intended to split the inheritance fairly equally between them, with Flaxstone going to Jasper, and as the only *legitimate* son the title was his by law anyway, whatever his father did.

'Yes,' Tori admitted. 'But not tonight.'

That surprised him. 'No? How did I earn this reprieve? By giving you pie?'

'Basically.' She gave him an impish grin. One that reminded him of the first night they'd ever spent together— before all the secrets that had torn his life apart. 'But mostly, I want you to finish this bottle of wine with me.'

Something in her smile gave him hope. 'And then?'

'Then…maybe you'll walk me home?'

'I can do that. It's only gentlemanly, after all.' Then he reached behind him, grabbed another knife and fork from the drawer, and handed them over. Pushing his plate to the centre of the table, he waited for Tori to help herself to his pie before taking his own mouthful.

Maybe he could get good at sharing after all.

CHAPTER TEN

FLAXSTONE HALL WAS silent as they let themselves out of the back door, and followed the darkened path towards Tori's gatehouse cottage. Tori wasn't sure if it was the wine or the sneaking around that made her want to giggle so badly. But she and Jasper were both grown adults, and it wasn't as if they hadn't done this before, anyway.

Memories of the last time they'd snuck down to her cottage only made her feel warmer despite the chill of the night.

God, what was she doing? Was she really going to invite Jasper in for a nightcap—and more?

Well, yes. Yes, she was.

Because he might be leaving soon, but that was probably a good thing. The Jasper she'd got to know over the last week or two was far too tempting, too risky. Given long enough she knew she could fall for him—and fall hard.

It was, she could admit now—to herself, anyway— exactly what she'd been afraid of five years ago. He was so gorgeous, so charming, and had a way of making her feel as if she were the only person in the world when he flirted with her. If she'd let her defences down for a second she could have found herself in love with him, and ripe for having her heart broken like all the others girls he'd paraded through Flaxstone.

That was why she'd run away, after their night together. She'd had to protect her heart. And if he'd woken up, sober, in her bed and still wanted her, still smiled at her the same way he had the night before, she'd have been a goner. And if he hadn't…well, Tori wasn't entirely sure that wouldn't have been worse.

But now, now she was older, wiser, and she knew this thing had a time limit. She could risk one more night with Jasper, as long as her head and her heart both understood that was all it could be.

Because even if he stayed, she wasn't looking for love, not again. And she *definitely* wasn't looking for a long-distance relationship. She'd tried that with Tyler and— she wasn't thinking about Tyler tonight.

She wasn't thinking about the past *or* the future tonight.

She was thinking about right now, and how good Jasper's arm felt around her waist as they stumbled down the path, and how much she wanted to kiss him again.

Stay in the moment, Tori.

The security light Felix had helped her install, after a fox started getting into her bins, flared to life as they crossed the threshold into its sensors. Jasper jumped, making Tori laugh, until he wrapped her up in his arms and suddenly she didn't have the breath for laughter.

'So, I've walked you home,' he said, his forehead resting against hers as he looked down into her eyes. 'This is the part where you have to decide if you want to invite me in or not.'

And even though she'd already made that decision, the moment she'd asked him to walk down to her cottage with her, Tori hesitated.

'Do you *want* to come in?' she asked.

'More than anything.' She could hear the sincerity in his voice. 'God, Tori, you have to know I've been thinking of practically nothing but kissing you again ever since—' He broke off.

'The other day at the Christmas market?' she guessed, but Jasper shook his head.

'Since you kissed me at the Moorside,' he admitted. 'Even though I knew that wasn't about me, that it didn't mean what I hoped it might mean, I couldn't stop thinking about how incredible it felt to have you in my arms. And imagining all the things I'd do if I got the opportunity again, when the timing was better.'

He'd been thinking about her since then? Even when they'd been clashing in his father's study, or when she'd been working for too many hours straight on the proposal and had rubbed her eyes until her mascara had smudged into black rings around her lashes and she hadn't noticed until she'd got home?

He'd been thinking about her. The same way she'd been thinking about him.

Imagining him.

'The timing seems pretty much perfect right now,' she said, the words coming out breathier than she'd intended.

'That's exactly what I thought.'

He met her gaze head-on as he lowered his lips to hers, obviously watching for a sign that she wanted him to stop, or take things slower. But she didn't, so she raised herself up on her tiptoes to meet him halfway, falling into a kiss that seemed to have been years in the making.

It hadn't been like this the last time they were here, Tori realised. She hadn't known him then the way she did now—hell, he wasn't even the same person, really. Too much had happened in the last five years.

But in a way, she was glad he'd left, after that one night they'd spent together.

Because it meant they could be the people they were now, and they could have this perfect, mind-blowing kiss.

After long, long, blissful moments, Jasper pulled back, putting just enough distance between them to whisper. 'So. Are you going to invite me in?'

Tori smirked. 'Invite? I think I'm going to have to insist on it.'

Jasper grinned back at her, his eyes bright and alive like she remembered from before he'd left Flaxstone.

'Works for me,' he said.

This time, when Jasper woke up in Tori's bed in her cosy gatehouse cottage, she was still beside him, gloriously naked and tangled in sheets and blankets and his arms.

Just another reason why this time had been so much better than the last. Add in five years of maturity, experience—and a far deeper understanding of each other—and the night had been, well, glorious. So much more than he'd expected, even yesterday.

'You okay?' Tori mumbled, turning over and looking blearily up at him. 'I mean, was everything…okay?'

'More than.' He pressed a kiss against her bare shoulder, then moved his lips up towards her ear. 'Better than the best steak and ale pie in the country,' he whispered, and she laughed.

God, he loved that sound. Loved seeing her, hearing her, free from secrets and the past and inhibitions. They'd told each other everything now. She knew about Felix and his dad, and he knew about the boyfriend who died, who'd made her close herself off to the world.

He'd looked behind the battlements and discovered

the real Tori Edwards. And he didn't think he'd ever stop being grateful that she'd let him.

'Do you think you can get me some more of those pies, though, when you go back for Christmas Day?' he asked.

She rolled her eyes. 'If I go. And if you're still here when I get back.'

'You might not go?' Jasper frowned. He'd thought she'd made her peace with Liz and Henry, found some closure. He didn't like the idea of her being all alone in the world again once he returned to the States. Not when that meant the only family she had was his dysfunctional one.

Tori sighed. 'I'm not sure it would be a good idea. And besides, they gave me my Christmas present already, remember? Wrapped and packed in the car when I wasn't supposed to be looking.'

'You don't think they're expecting you to show up either,' Jasper said, piecing it together. 'But why not? Because of Tyler?'

At that, Tori tumbled out of bed, keeping one of the blankets tucked around her, and flashed him a quick smile. 'Let's not worry about this now. We have the party to look forward to tonight. I need to survive that before I can even *think* about Christmas Day.'

She was deflecting, he realised. Leading him away from the question.

Suddenly he wondered if she *had* told him everything about why she'd left the Moorside, after all. And if she would even tell him if he asked.

More secrets. Great.

The happy, relaxed and sated feeling he'd woken up with started to ebb away, leaving him tense and awkward again. He sat up, as Tori gathered his clothes together from where they'd been scattered on the floor, and handed them to him.

'You can use the shower first, if you like,' she said, with a false brightness. 'After all, you need to go talk to your mother this morning. But I'll see you tonight for the party.'

Then she disappeared towards the kitchen, and he heard the kettle flick on.

Brilliant.

Jasper swung his legs over the side of the bed. Given how quickly his perfect morning had deteriorated, he supposed he'd better go have that conversation with his mother before things got any worse.

Tori heard the cottage's front door close quietly behind Jasper, and let out a sigh of relief. Then, she tipped the coffee she'd made him down the sink, and took her own cup to the tiny kitchen table where she could look out of the window at Flaxstone in the snow and think. Something she'd apparently been doing too little of lately.

The euphoria and hope of the night before had worn off quickly in the early morning light. It had felt so right, so easy, waking up beside him. The peace of a snowy winter's day outside her window, and the warmth of his arms around her. Like the Moorside again, only better.

As if it was where they were meant to be.

What *had* she been thinking, bringing Jasper back here last night? Well, she knew the answer to that. She'd been thinking that he was gorgeous, she was insanely attracted to him, still, and she wanted him in her bed again. And she'd *also* been thinking that he was leaving soon. That he'd disappear back to the States and leave her and her mess of a history behind without another thought.

Because the truth was, as much as she hated the

thought of Flaxstone without him again, it would probably be the best thing for both of them.

He was too invested, too deep into her personal life
already. Tori had always kept that side of her—Vicky's
side, as she thought of it—walled off, for a very good
reason. Because of the pain of the memories, of course,
and because of the guilt. Because of the way Jasper—or
anyone—would look at her if they knew how she was responsible for Tyler's death. But mostly because she knew
it could all too easily happen again.

She *wanted* things. She wanted success, she wanted
a career, she wanted to go places and see things and do
stuff that her mother could only have dreamed of. Even
if, so far, she hadn't quite made it out of Yorkshire. It
was that selfishness that had killed Tyler.

And it hadn't changed.

She'd tried—really she had. Straight after his death,
she'd vowed she'd never put her personal ambition above
what her loved ones wanted again. But that wasn't who
she was. She was Victoria Edwards and she *wanted*. No
amount of love could change that, and eight years definitely hadn't.

Which was why it wasn't fair to get involved with
people, not when she knew that she'd always choose her
own ambition over them, and only end up getting them
hurt. Or dead, in Tyler's case.

He'd told her, to her face, that if she left for university
bad things would happen. That he wouldn't cope without
her. And he'd been right.

But she'd gone anyway.

A better life for her meant a worse life for other people. But she was such a terrible person that she *still*
couldn't stop wanting.

She'd wanted Jasper. But this morning, hearing him

ask about Henry and Liz and Christmas at the Moorside, she'd realised what a mistake that was.

Jasper couldn't be an anonymous one-night stand. Even last time he'd been a risk, but she'd wanted so badly she'd taken it anyway, and lucked out when he'd left without seeing her again. He'd always been too desperate to break through her walls—through curiosity more than anything, she suspected. Jasper hated anyone having secrets he didn't know and understand—just look at his reaction to the news about Felix.

What would he do if she told him hers? Explained exactly why this couldn't happen again?

Tori had a horrible feeling she was going to find out, and soon. Certainly before he left for America again. Because Jasper never let secrets stay hidden.

Jasper found his mother exactly where he expected to find her: settled on the loveseat in her small sitting room, looking out over the gardens, a tea tray at her side and a murder mystery novel in her hands. Mornings were sacred to Lady Flaxstone. In the afternoons, she'd busy about with local events, estate business, fundraising, visits and so on. But the mornings were entirely hers and not to be disturbed.

'I'm not a morning person,' he remembered her saying once, when he'd asked her about it. 'I don't even like my own company in the mornings. Why would I enjoy anyone else's?'

Perhaps, with hindsight, he should have waited until this afternoon to broach the subject of Felix's legitimisation with her, but now he was here, all he wanted to do was get it over with.

'Mother?'

Lady Flaxstone looked up, obviously surprised at

being interrupted. 'Jasper? What's happened? Is something the matter?'

He forced a smile onto his face, and took the small armchair opposite her. He always felt as if this sitting room had been designed for a race of humans about three quarters the size of the average. He was a giant in this space.

Or maybe his mother had just wanted to make it uncomfortable for other people, so she wouldn't be disturbed. He wouldn't put it past her. She always did create her own world, her own reality, exactly the way she wanted to believe it could be.

'I wanted to talk to you about Father,' he said, not entirely sure where to start. 'And…and Felix.'

'Ah.' His mother put down her book and gave him her full attention. 'I was rather wondering when you would. You've been back three weeks now, after all. But I suppose you've been rather preoccupied with our Tori, haven't you?'

Jasper blinked. Perhaps his mother's shaping of reality didn't mean she was *completely* oblivious to the real world after all. He frowned, as the thought tickled another at the back of his brain. One he couldn't quite put his finger on, just yet.

'Dad has spoken to you about it, then, I assume? What he plans to do? And about, well, Felix's parentage.' He'd always assumed that his father would have been forced to tell her *something* about why he'd left home so abruptly. He'd hoped it would be the truth, although he had no idea how his mother would take the news.

'Of course.' His mother sounded surprised he even had to ask. 'We discussed it at length before he emailed to tell you. I wanted to ensure that your inheritance was still secure—of Flaxstone, and the title. As much as I love

Felix, and agree it's only fair he gets a decent share of the rest of the money and land, Flaxstone really *is* yours by rights.' She gave him a sideways look. 'Although I rather think your father feels that Felix has done more for it over the last five years, and not without reason.'

A strange cold feeling ran through Jasper's veins. 'You…agree with Father?'

'Of course. You didn't think he'd have decided to do this without consulting me, did you?' Her eyes widened as she took in his expression. 'Oh, you did.'

'You know what Father's like,' Jasper replied, thinking his way through the thought process that had led him here. 'He just decides a thing and goes for it. No consultation, no consideration of others.'

'That's how he *used* to be,' Lady Flaxstone agreed. 'But, Jasper, you have to understand that your leaving changed him. Maybe not as much as you'd like, but it *did* change him. And me, for that matter. Have you really not noticed since your return?'

'No.'

Because I've been avoiding him as much as possible, just as Tori said.

Lady Flaxstone's expression turned harder. 'You leaving us… I'm not saying I don't understand why you felt you needed to get away, but I *do* wish you'd at least talked to us—to me, or even to Felix—before you went.'

'I—I didn't want to drag you into the whole sordid mess. I knew Father would have to tell you everything once I'd gone, but I hoped that he'd find a way to keep you protected from the worst of it. Which was why I was so furious when he emailed with his plans to tell the world.'

'Jasper…' His mother sighed. 'Flaxstone has been my whole world, ever since I came here as a bride. Do you honestly believe I wouldn't be aware and alert to everything that happens under its roof?'

'I…no.' And there it was. That niggling thought slotted right into place and something stabbed Jasper around chest level. 'Wait. Are you saying you *always* knew about Felix?'

'Probably before your father did. Anna, Felix's mother, and I were always close, and I have four younger siblings—I knew the signs of a pregnancy better than most, even if I hadn't been going through it myself by then.'

'You knew.' She'd known who Felix was his whole life and had never told *either* of them. *So many secrets…* 'Did Father know that you knew?'

'Not at first. When he first brought me here as his bride…it wasn't entirely a love match, you realise. Oh, we liked each other well enough, and I had faith that we could *grow* to love one another, but beyond that… It was the fact that I had money, you see, and Flaxstone categorically didn't.'

He'd known all this, Jasper realised, somewhere at the back of his mind, somewhere he'd never examined it properly. Because from the earliest time he could remember, his parents had been a team, his father doting, his mother supportive. It felt too strange to imagine a time before that.

'But when Anna started to show I sat him down, told him I knew the baby had to be his. There had been plenty of hints, you see—whispered conversations I wasn't meant to hear, Anna's tears and her refusal to talk to me about it. I knew. And when he realised that…he crumpled. He really did care for her, you know, but not more than he cared for Flaxstone.'

'But he let them stay? Knowing that *you* knew that she was his mistress and Felix his child?'

'*I* let them stay,' Lady Flaxstone corrected him. 'In fact, I insisted on it.'

'Why?' he asked. But even as he said the word, he realised he already knew. She'd shaped reality to fit how she believed the world of Flaxstone ought to be. He'd thought she'd been avoiding the real world. In fact, she'd been working it like a blacksmith with a hammer, beating it into the weapon she needed to defend her version of reality.

'The relationship was over the day we got married, and I never saw a hint that it started up again afterwards. Anna even married, briefly, although it didn't work out. I didn't see why she should be punished for something your father was equally responsible for. And Felix *is* his son, whether he's publicly acknowledged or not. How could I ask your father to cast him out to the world and never see him again? And once you and Felix grew to be so close… I was sure I'd made the right decision. Until you left.'

For the first time in the conversation, his mother looked uncertain—and Jasper had no way to reassure her. Had she made the right choice? He couldn't know.

But one thing he did know for sure: everyone else had known the truth about his family except him. Everyone he cared about had been lying to him, in some cases for his entire life.

And he wasn't sure if he could ever forgive them for that.

'You should have told me,' he said numbly, stumbling to his feet as he headed for the door. 'You should have told me.'

CHAPTER ELEVEN

TORI BUSIED HERSELF with her usual work around the estate that day. It might be three days before Christmas, but in lots of ways that just meant there was more work to be done. The Christmas market would be packing down that afternoon, and the ballroom was being set up for the traditional Flaxstone Christmas party that evening. Yes, the estate staff and contractors had everything perfectly under control, but that didn't mean she shouldn't check in on them all once or twice. Or every half hour.

Eventually, she'd annoyed everyone enough that she needed to find something new to do, so she joined Mrs Rawkins' team in the kitchens, where she was relegated to assembling some of the easier canapés on lemongrass skewers. And that was where the earl found her.

'Oh, I adore these ones!' He cheerfully popped a canapé into his mouth, then grabbed a spare napkin and filled it with a few more. 'For later,' he explained with a wink.

'Can I help you, Your Lordship?' Mrs Rawkins's words were scrupulously polite, but her expression and tone made her disapproval perfectly clear. Tori hid a smile behind a napkin.

'Actually, I just wanted to borrow Tori, if you can spare her.'

Mrs Rawkins brightened. 'By all means!' she said, leading Tori to conclude she hadn't been as much help as she'd thought here, either.

She followed the earl back up to his office. He munched his way through his pilfered canapés as they walked, making it impossible for her to start a conversation. Once they were seated on either side of the desk, the door closed, however, the earl didn't beat around the bush.

'I've considered your proposal, and there's much to approve of in it, as always.'

'Thank you, Your Lordship.' A niggling feeling of guilt made her add, 'But if we're going to talk about the Stonebury proposal, Jasper really should be here too.'

'I'll talk to Jasper separately. Later.' The earl looked uncomfortable. 'I believe he spoke to his mother this morning and then took himself off for a walk. We assume he'll be returning this time, but...' He shrugged, and the niggle in her stomach only grew worse.

Of course he was coming back. Wasn't he?

'I think there's a lot of merit in the Christmas craft farm, and I even agree that the main house might be best kept as a personal dwelling. And Lady Flaxstone has expressed some interest lately in getting more involved with wider estate projects, so this might well win her approval. And if she wants to go and stay at the hall for a while, for whatever reason, I won't stop her. But Lady Flaxstone does not have the necessary business knowhow to get the place up and running and making a profit, even with a good manager there. In fact, it's clear to me that if this new venture is to be a success, it must have a talented, enthusiastic and dedicated leader on site to run it.' He leant over the desk a little towards her, before adding in a whisper, 'That's you, by the way.'

Tori blinked. 'Me?'

'Yes, you, Tori Edwards. As much as I'd like to keep you here making my life run smoothly for the rest of my years, you're far too talented for that. It's time for you to spread your wings and start running your *own* business ventures—or at least running one of mine for me to start with. Later, we'll see what sort of deal can be done, if you want it. Otherwise it will be good experience—and lucrative enough, I hope—for you to take flight and set up on your own, if you decide to.'

Her own business. Control and autonomy and the ability to really make a success of something she believed in. Wasn't this why she had left the Moorside Inn in the first place? She'd worked hard for the earl, and it was paying off with everything she'd ever dreamed of.

'I do have one or two conditions, however,' he added, and the hope that had sprung into her heart started to fade, just a little.

'Of course. And they are?'

'I want you to take Felix with you. You'll need a right-hand man and he's worked hard at learning the farming side of the business.'

'And that's the one part of it I haven't got much experience in.' Practically and business-wise, it made sense. Except for one thing. 'But if the point of the exercise is to get Lady Flaxstone away from any potential scandal—' She broke off as the earl raised his eyebrows.

They'd never actually said that in the proposal. They'd hinted at it, sure, and Jasper had implied it in his tone and expression, but they'd never said it. Jasper had never even confirmed that he'd told Tori the whole sordid story.

'I think my son will find that his mother is stronger than he thinks. My *other* son, however...' He sighed. 'Felix has never had to experience that kind of media scrutiny before. And I'm fairly sure he has no desire to now. For his sake, I'd like him somewhere less…obvious for a while. Besides which, I want him to get to know all the corners of our estate business. After all, if Jasper refuses to come home for good…' He shrugged, but he'd said enough.

The earl was grooming Felix to take Jasper's place if Jasper refused it.

And he wanted her to help. He was offering her the best opportunity of her professional career and, oh, but she wanted it.

But she knew Jasper would never forgive her if she took it. For taking his father's side over his. Choosing Felix's well-being over Jasper's. For ruining the plan they'd worked so hard to develop together.

And as evidenced, Jasper wasn't the forgiving kind.

But then, Jasper wouldn't be here much longer. Would he?

'I need…may I take a little time to think about it?'

The earl gave her an amused look and she suspected that he somehow knew exactly what the situation was between her and Jasper. Knew exactly what he was asking her to do.

Damn him.

'Of course,' he said. 'Enjoy the party tonight, but let me know your decision before you leave—for the Moorside, I understand? We can call it my Christmas present.'

The whole downstairs of Flaxstone Hall was a hive of activity. Jasper weaved his way through caterers, waiting staff, event planners moving decorated trees taller than him, and a few family members who'd arrived early and would stay for the duration.

He needed to find Tori.

She'd been weirdly absent all afternoon—finally Mrs Rawkins had told him that the earl had dragged her off to his office, but after that it seemed no one had seen her at all. She hadn't been at her cottage when he'd knocked, either.

But she *must* be back there by now, surely, if she had any hope of being ready for the party on time.

Jasper was already dressed in his dinner jacket and bow tie, ready for the festivities. And for a drink, actually. But first, Tori.

'Jasper?' The voice caught him just as he was about to exit the front door, and it made him wince. He turned slowly, to face the half-brother he'd been pretending didn't exist for five long years, even since his return.

'Felix.'

His search for Tori—including a long ramble through the woods in case she'd gone for a walk—had given him plenty of time to think. About Tori, about his parents—and about Felix.

He'd thought about Tori, and how she'd stayed away from the Moorside, from her family, for so long after Tyler's death, because it hurt too much to be there. Was that why *he'd* stayed away? He'd concluded it was only part of it.

Mostly, he'd stayed away because he'd been too angry not to.

But after his conversation with his mother that morning, some of that anger had started to ebb away. Not all of it, not by a long way. And he still wanted to protect his mother, and the family reputation, from any media fallout after his father's announcement.

The only real thing that had changed was that he knew

now he couldn't go on blaming Felix for something that had happened before his birth, or for not sharing a secret he knew could blow up their whole lives.

What would I have done in his place?

That was the question that had made him think the most. Would he have done things differently in Felix's place? In fact, in Felix's place, discovering his whole life had been a lie, would he have thought about how his friend was affected at all? Probably not.

Maybe the real problem was that he didn't know where to direct his anger, now he knew the real story behind it all.

'Mrs Rawkins said you were looking for Tori?' Felix asked, eyeing Jasper cautiously, as if waiting for him to explode. Jasper couldn't entirely blame him.

He really needed to talk to Felix. Maybe see if there was anything left of their friendship they could salvage.

But after he'd talked to Tori.

'Yes. Have you seen her?'

'Your mother gave her a room in the main house for the night, to get ready for the party. She's up in the Yellow Room, if you want her.'

Felix turned to go away, and Jasper found himself suddenly eager to make him stay.

'Thank you,' he called belatedly.

Felix looked back, a bemused smile on his face. 'You're welcome.'

Civility. That was a start, right? It was something.

And now he needed to talk to Tori.

He needed to know why she'd closed herself off to him again that morning. Whether she honestly expected him to just leave again like last time, as if their time together had never happened.

Because he couldn't.

Not now, not when he knew her. Not when he'd finally got her to lower those walls the whole way and let him in. Not when he knew, at last, how spectacular the woman waiting behind them was.

Because he'd realised something else out on his walk.

Flaxstone was where he belonged. And maybe, just maybe, Tori might belong there with him.

He just had to find a way to tell her that, to convince her of it, without her throwing those defensive walls back up again.

Tori reached behind her to tug up the zip of her evening dress, and failed to get it past about halfway. Wriggling the dress up a little, she stretched further, until her shoulder popped, trying to see the tiny silver zipper in the mirror, her head twisted almost all the way around.

Still no dice.

Sighing, she allowed her body to return to its more normal position and concluded that this was simply not a dress for one person. She'd have to sneak down to the kitchens with a wrap over her and find someone there to help her with it, once she'd finished perfecting her hair and make-up.

Or not. A knock at the door let her reconsider, and when she opened it a crack to see Jasper on the other side, looking handsome and irresistible in his dinner jacket, her heart thumped against her chest.

This was perfect. He could help her do up her dress— or undo it first, if he liked. There was still time, right? As long as she kept protecting her heart, made it clear this was just a festive fling, just sex and nothing more, what harm could one more night do?

But even as she smiled at him and opened the door, another part of her brain was already arguing back.

I can't lead him on. I can't let him think there's something between us—even if it is just sex—not without telling him about his father's offer. Not without admitting I'm thinking about taking it.

'You look beautiful,' he said, his gaze scanning her dress, her heels, her dark hair pinned back from her face before falling around her shoulders. He'd never seen her so dressed up, she realised.

'You scrub up reasonably well too, I suppose,' she replied, with a smirk. She needed to keep things light, familiar. He was already looking a little wary—not that she could blame him after the way she'd hurried him out of her cottage, and her bed, that morning.

Tori knew she was being unfair, inconsistent, not letting him know where he stood. And she hated it, probably as much as he did. But she didn't *know* where either of them stood.

Or where they'd be if she took the job his father had just offered her.

Would he leave without another word, as he'd done last time? Or would he argue with her, the way Tyler had when she'd made the decision to leave the Moorside, trying to wear her down with threats and promises and accusations?

She couldn't think about it now.

Focus on tonight. Focus on the party. Worry about tomorrow tomorrow. It'll be here soon enough.

'I could do with your help, actually.' She turned her bare back towards him, motioning towards the zip, but he made no move to fasten it.

In fact, his hands slipped between the material and her

skin, skimming up over her ribs and cupping her breasts as he bent in to kiss her neck.

Tori leaned into his touch, the tingles he was sending through her body happily distracting her from the moral dilemma buzzing around her head.

She needed to make a decision soon, she knew that. But maybe not *right* now. Maybe she could have this with Jasper just once more, just one more perfect night in his arms, before she had to ruin it all.

Tori turned and kissed him, and let him blot out all her thoughts for a while.

Whatever weirdness had been between him and Tori that morning faded away the moment Jasper touched her. Whatever she'd been hiding from, she wasn't running any more.

At least, until afterwards.

'A guy could get a complex, you know,' he said, as she slipped out of bed and pulled that damn dress back on. 'The way you're always so keen to get *out* of bed with me, I mean.'

The smile she flashed him didn't quite reach her eyes. 'We don't want to be late for the party.'

That's not why you're running.

Trouble was, he didn't know the real why. What was Tori hiding now? Too many secrets, all over again. And just when he thought he might have uncovered the last of his family's secrets.

'I suppose you're right.' Jasper sat up, lounging against the bedhead for a moment to watch her dress. If she wanted to pretend that everything was fine, he could do that. But he knew it wasn't just her clothes that were going back on.

Her mask was in place too. Her defences, her armour.

She was hiding again. Even this morning, she hadn't pulled the drawbridge up so completely.

So what's changed since then?

'I haven't seen you all day,' he observed as she shimmied the dress over her hips. He forced himself not to get too distracted by the motion, or the bare skin on display, but he couldn't stop himself looking. 'What have you been up to?'

Tori shrugged her bare shoulders. 'You know. Work. Lots to do for the party tonight.'

Except she hadn't been anywhere around the hall when he was looking for her, and, as far as he knew, the party had been almost entirely organised by his mother's event planner, same as every other year.

Tori backed up to the bed, that same zip dangling. This time, he did it up. Putting temptation out of reach, and completing her retreat into her armour all over again.

'What about you?' she asked, crossing again to the dressing table. He watched her reflection in the mirror as she threaded long silver earrings through her lobes.

Like chain mail.

Was everything about this woman armour? 'Did you talk to your mother?'

The question jerked him out of his reverie. 'I did, actually.'

'And?'

And she's been lying to me my whole life. Just like you're lying to me right now.

'And it turns out there was more to the story than I realised. She knew all along that Felix was the earl's son.'

Tori spun round to face him, her eyebrows high. '*Really?* And she still let them stay?'

'It was her idea, apparently.' Jasper swung his legs off the bed and reached for his trousers. 'She forgave him the affair, and didn't want Felix to suffer.'

'Huh.'

Jasper looked up to see her brow creased in a frown. 'What?'

'She forgave him. Like, properly. I didn't see that coming.'

'What were you expecting?' Jasper tilted his head to the side to watch her as she considered her answer. Maybe her mask wasn't quite as complete as it usually was— or perhaps he'd simply learned to see through it, somewhat—because her thoughts were almost telegraphed across her expression. Confusion, doubt, and something Jasper couldn't quite put his finger on. Something that might even have been…hope?

'I don't know. Maybe that kind of grudging forgiveness where people say they understand because it's too late to say anything else. I mean, what difference could it make now, being angry, when the misdeed is almost thirty years in the past and nothing can change it? But she forgave him *then*, right when it happened. I… I just didn't expect that.'

'Neither did I,' Jasper admitted.

What did it say about them that neither had considered that sort of unconditional forgiveness as even a possibility?

'So…does she not want to go to Stonebury?' Tori asked.

Jasper shrugged. 'To be honest, I didn't get the chance to ask her. I think it's definitely worth keeping it as an option, though. I mean, it's hard to predict what the media reaction will be. These days, a child out of wedlock isn't nearly so much of a big deal. But keeping it a secret for so many years…'

'There's a story there, and they'll want to tell it.'

'Exactly.'

'How are you…how are you feeling?' Tori asked, after a moment, and Jasper couldn't shake the sensation that there was something more than concern behind the question. As if she was trying to get a read on a business competitor or something.

Either way, he didn't know how to answer.

'I… I don't know yet. It took me five years to come back here after I found out about Felix. And now learning that my mother knew all along, that she's not going to stop my father making it public… I haven't processed it all yet. I spoke to Felix earlier—for the first time in five years. I guess that maybe I'm coming to terms with the facts of it all, and that Felix, at least, wasn't to blame for what happened. But it's the lying and the secrets I can't move past. You know?'

'I know.' Tori's voice sounded raw, more than just an agreement. But before he could ask if *she* was okay, she pasted on a smile and held a hand out to him. 'Come on. We've got a party to get to. There'll be plenty of time for introspection and misery later.'

Her words were light, joking. But somehow they still sounded like a prediction.

And more than ever, Jasper felt the festive party spirit slipping away from him.

CHAPTER TWELVE

DOWNSTAIRS, THE PARTY was in full swing. The air hummed with classic Christmas tunes from the band, the singer a glamorous redhead who made everything sound sultry, and the waiters circulating with trays of champagne were being kept very busy. The Flaxstone Christmas party was always a highlight of the local social calendar—and normally of Tori's too. In a room full of people, she could forget that she was alone for Christmas, usually.

But not this year. This year, she felt more alone than she had since she'd left the Moorside, eight years ago. Because this year, she had someone to lose.

And she knew in her heart that she'd already lost him.

Jasper, returning son and heir, had been swept away by family, friends and acquaintances who hadn't seen him for five long years. He'd tried to keep her on his arm to start with, but she'd shaken her head and slipped away, indicating that she was heading for the canapés.

Mostly, she'd just needed to escape.

She needed to get everything straight in her head. A project list, the same way she always began any new project the earl delegated to her. Before she could start work, she needed to know the parameters.

Mentally, she ran through her usual checklist. After

all, business was what she knew best—far more than people or relationships. And in the end, weren't they more
or less the same thing? Interactions and negotiations and
compromises—only on life choices and personal futures,
rather than business proposals and property.

So, first up: what did she already know?

That was easy. She ticked them off in her head, half
wishing she'd brought her notebook with her to write
them down.

One. She knew that she felt more for Jasper than she'd
felt for anyone since Tyler. A lot more. However much
she'd tried to pretend to herself otherwise. She wouldn't
be feeling this mixed up about the earl's offer otherwise.

Two. She knew that Jasper would be leaving for the
States again in the new year. And she knew that she couldn't
risk another long-distance relationship, not after Tyler.

Three. She knew that Jasper struggled to forgive even
those he loved most. The man definitely knew how to
hold a grudge.

Four. She knew that Jasper would feel betrayed if she
left Flaxstone to run Stonebury with Felix. She couldn't
fall in love with him, give him everything he needed, *and*
go after what she needed too. She'd tried that before with
Tyler, with disastrous results. This time, a relationship
with Jasper—assuming that was even what he wanted—
would mean either her leaving Flaxstone and the opportunity at Stonebury to be with him or…what? Asking
him not to go back to a life he'd established overseas?
To overlook the fact she was working with, supporting
and hiding his half-brother—using the very plan she'd
developed with him for protecting his mother? None of
those options seemed likely.

So. Not a pretty picture so far. But there was one more

thing she knew, too. She pulled a face as she made herself add it.

Five. She knew she wanted the job at Stonebury. She knew she was the best person for it, that it would rocket her career forward, and, most of all, she knew that she'd *earned* it.

Okay. They were the known factors. So, what *didn't* she know?

One. She didn't know how Jasper felt about her. Oh, she knew that he *wanted* her, that much was obvious. But beyond that? She got the impression he was just as confused by it all as she was.

Was that it? If that was the only thing she didn't know—and, really, since Jasper was leaving anyway did it really matter how he felt?—then surely she should be able to make a decision on the information she had?

In fact, Tori knew deep down that she'd already made her choice. She'd felt it in the way she'd kept Jasper at arm's length—emotionally, if not physically—and she'd felt it sink in when he'd looked so confused by his mother's ability to forgive his father.

She wanted this job, this chance, and she couldn't give it up for someone who wasn't even staying around. And even if Jasper *could* forgive that, she wasn't going to even consider the idea of a long-distance relationship—not after what had happened the last time she'd tried it. In the end, the mistrust and the distance had destroyed not only her relationship with Tyler, but Tyler himself.

She needed to move on; she knew that now. The guilt was too heavy to hold onto for ever. But her heart ached too much to put it down. She didn't even know who she would be without it, after so long.

No. Better to end this thing with Jasper now, and move

on with her solitary life. Box up the last couple of weeks and store them away in her heart with all the other painful memories, until she was strong enough to look at them again. One day.

With one last look to check that Jasper was still busy entertaining the guests, Tori slipped away to find the earl and tell him her decision.

And then she would go back to her cottage to pack.

She had a feeling that when Jasper found out, she'd be more welcome at the Moorside Inn than at Flaxstone, anyway.

The party was so busy, so loud, that it took Jasper some time to realise that Tori wasn't there any longer. He searched all the usual places—the buffet table, the dance floor, the quiet areas his mother set aside for conversation and flirtation—no sign of her. He even lingered outside the incredibly swanky portable bathrooms set up in the quad in case she was in there—although since she had access to a bedroom with its own bathroom upstairs it seemed unlikely. No Tori.

'Jasper!' His father's voice boomed out as he re-entered the ballroom where the main party was taking place. 'Let me introduce you to—'

'Have you seen Tori?' Jasper interrupted. 'I need to find her.' He *knew* there was something weird going on with her tonight. Why had he even let her out of his sight?

Because I'm not her boss. I have no control over where she goes or what she does. I'm not even her boyfriend; I don't even have the right to ask, *really.*

He should have talked to her earlier. Told her all the things he'd realised during his walk. Told her he was thinking of moving back home. That he didn't want to be without her any longer. More talking and less seduction might have meant that their positions were clearer and she might even have shared whatever was going on with her. But she'd displayed that long, slender back, naked under her dress, and he'd lost his mind over her. Again.

'Not since she told me the good news!' the earl said, raising his champagne glass in a happy mock toast.

Jasper froze. 'Good news?' All his instincts were screaming that whatever the news was, it wasn't going to be good for him. Otherwise she'd have told him first.

'Yes! That she's taking the job at Stonebury with Felix.' The earl's eyes widened a fraction. 'I assumed she'd spoken to you about it first…'

'Well, she hadn't,' Jasper snapped. Around them, awkward partygoers were starting to sidle away, but he didn't care. Suddenly, things were falling into place. *This* was why she'd been distant upstairs, earlier. She'd already made her decision to leave, without even talking to him about it. He'd thought their lovemaking had been the start of something. But apparently Tori had been saying goodbye.

'When she said she needed time to consider, I interpreted that as a conversation between the two of you. I mean, it was obvious that you two were, well, fond of each other, and with you staying here at Flaxstone now—'

'I never said I was staying.' But he wanted to. He wanted to stay here with Tori. Or at Stonebury with her. Except she'd be there with Felix, apparently. The half-brother he hadn't even managed a full and unstilted conversation with, yet. The one she'd chosen over him all the same.

This wasn't a steak and ale pie she was stealing. She'd

taken their whole plan, the project they'd designed for his mother, and handed it over to Felix instead, without even considering him.

'Well, maybe that's why Tori didn't talk to you about it, then,' the earl said, far too reasonably for Jasper's liking. 'If you're not here what does it matter where she goes?'

'You *know* why it matters.' Anger was rising through him now, red hot as it burned through his chest, up his throat and out of his mouth. 'We planned Stonebury as an escape for Mother, you know that. And now you're taking whatever you want and screwing it all up again, just like you did nearly thirty years ago. You always want everything, don't you? To have your cake and eat it. You wanted to marry Mother for her money, and you wanted your mistress on the side. You wanted your legal heir and your illegitimate son growing up together, even if neither of them knew the truth. And now you want to tell the world that Felix is your son and damn the consequences for anyone else, and even if it means stealing away the woman I'm falling in love with from me.'

It was the gasps—those sharp intakes of breath that spoke of total shock—that made Jasper realise he was shouting. And the instant chatter that followed that alerted him to what he'd actually said.

Oh, God. He was in love with Tori Edwards. When the hell had *that* happened?

The minute she kissed you, you idiot, his brain retorted.

But it wasn't until he turned and saw Felix and Tori standing in the open doorway, their eyes wide with horror, that he realised what it all meant.

'Well, son,' his father said softly. 'I think you've out-done me this time, don't you?'

Jasper blinked, and Tori and Felix were gone, probably running away, but he couldn't even blame them. Who told a woman they loved her in front of an entire party while yelling at their father and spilling family secrets? Although, in fairness, he hadn't known he was going to say it until it was out there.

He hadn't even known he felt it. But now, looking back at their meandering relationship…it seemed impossible that he'd ever *not* known. When he'd returned to Flax-stone, he'd thought Tori was just unfinished business—one night that could have been more but never got the chance to be.

But now he knew better. He knew she was his future. Or she could have been.

'Yes, Dad,' he said, his voice faint. 'This time it's all me.'

And he wasn't even sure he deserved forgiveness.

Tori hoisted her overnight bag onto her shoulder as she stormed down the path to her cottage, Felix hurrying after her.

'Are you this furious with him on my behalf or on your own?' Felix asked as she fumbled with the key in her lock. 'Because, you know, this wasn't exactly how I wanted the news to come out, for sure. But he said he loved you.'

'Because he's trying to make me feel guilty about taking the job. Or manipulate me into turning it down, one or the other. I've been here before.'

She knew how this went. She'd been exactly here with

Tyler, and she wasn't going to let herself get caught up in it again.

'Or because…he really means it?' Felix suggested, eyebrows raised.

Tori sighed. She liked Felix, really she did. But considering his birth and upbringing he had a surprisingly uncomplicated view of the world. Opening her front door, she tried to find the familiar sensation of home. Of security.

It wasn't there.

She stepped inside anyway, turning back to stop Felix on the threshold.

'Look, I appreciate you trying to help, but unless you want to do my packing for me you might as well go back to the party.' She caught the uncomfortable look on his face and realised: he couldn't go back either. Everyone would be talking about him and him being there wouldn't stop that. If anything, it would make it worse.

Yeah, maybe Felix *was* having a worse night than her.

Fumbling with her key ring, she removed a silver key and pressed it into his palm. 'Sneak in through the locked garage entrance, and head up to the Yellow Room,' she suggested. 'I'm not going to be using it again tonight.'

'Are you sure?'

'Very.' She wasn't going back to Flaxstone Hall tonight. Or possibly at all, until she was sure that Jasper was safely on another continent. 'Wait!' She took another key from the ring and handed it to him.

'Why do I need your cottage key?'

'Just…in case,' she said. She didn't know in case of what—or didn't want to think about it. *In case I never come back.* 'And maybe you could water my Christmas tree while I'm gone?'

Felix rolled his eyes, but took the key and left. As she shed her dress and changed into normal clothes, grabbing her overnight bag, Tori felt a pang of guilt for leaving Felix to weather this night on his own, but she had to get moving fast, before Jasper—

A hammering on the door interrupted the thought.

Too late.

Taking a deep, steadying breath, Tori opened the door, grateful at least that she'd changed out of her evening dress and into a more professional, and comfortable, pair of black trousers and sweater. She had made a work decision. And that was what this conversation needed to be about.

'Tori. I… Can I come in?'

With a short nod, she stepped aside to let him enter. 'But I don't have long,' she said, turning her back on him as she returned to her packing. 'I want to get to the Moorside before last orders.'

For so many years, the thought of the inn had driven her away. But suddenly, it was the only place she wanted to be.

'You're going? Really? I thought— Is this because of the job, or because of what I said?'

'Both, to be honest.' She just needed to get away. Why couldn't he understand that?

She'd rather take the pain in Uncle Henry's eyes than the anger she expected to see in Jasper's.

'Look, I know I shouldn't have blurted out what I said that way. It's no excuse, but my father told me about the job offer at Stonebury—you running the place with Felix—and I guess I was hurt that you didn't talk to me about it first—'

'Why would I?' she interrupted.

She couldn't let him say too much, or she risked him saying all the things that could sway her, change her mind, as Tyler had tried to do.

I love you. I can't do it without you. It'll all be your fault if you go and leave me.

'It was a work decision, but not one I had an obligation to discuss with you as a colleague. Especially as a colleague who will also be leaving soon.'

Jasper looked as if she'd slapped him in the face. 'What if I wasn't? Leaving, I mean?'

He was planning on staying? Tori shook her head. It didn't change anything. It *couldn't* change anything. The physical distance between them was only one problem. The emotional gulf was far bigger.

She hadn't moved on from Tyler's death, and *neither* of them knew how to forgive—others or themselves. How could they start a relationship there?

She had to end this, now, before her heart broke too much. 'Then you'll stay and be furious at your family and at me for all time, and I'm sure that will be just brilliant for all of us, but I'll be at Stonebury helping the brother you just exposed to the world keep out of the limelight for a while.'

That stopped him. '*That's* why you took the job? Because you wanted to help Felix?'

'I took the job because I wanted the job. Because I deserved the job.'

'And you didn't care how I felt about it.' Jasper's expression hardened.

Of course she cared. But she couldn't let him see how much. 'Jasper, we've slept together twice. Three times if you count five years ago. It's hardly a lasting relationship. You can't expect me to make decisions about my career and my future based on it.' Not the way Tyler had. Expecting her to give up all her hopes for her future, her ambition, for a teenage relationship she couldn't even be sure would last. Now Jasper was asking her to do the same, but it was different this time.

She hadn't made Jasper any promises. Hadn't told him she loved him. And Jasper...he was stronger than Tyler had been. He'd be fine without her.

It was her own heart she was worried about.

'Maybe not,' he admitted. 'But as a friend I would expect you to talk to me before running away.'

'Like you did to Felix five years ago?' she shot back.

Jasper swore under his breath, raking his hands through his hair as he visibly tried to calm himself. That was no good. She didn't want him calm. She wanted him gone, so she could run far away and let her heart break in peace.

He wasn't offering her for ever. He was offering her exactly what Tyler had—a possibility of love as long as she did what he wanted. And she wasn't going to take that risk.

Still, when Jasper spoke again, his voice was softer, calmer. 'Look, Tori, I should have told you I was planning on staying at Flaxstone. I meant to, tonight. And I'm going to work on my relationship with my family, really I am.'

'But will you ever forgive them? Would you ever forgive me, if I went to Stonebury with Felix?' Because that was what it all came down to. Forgiveness. She couldn't forgive Tyler for what he'd done, and she couldn't forgive herself for letting him. And Jasper couldn't forgive the lies and betrayal that had driven him away from his home in the first place.

How could they start any kind of a relationship when they were both so filled with resentment? Maybe they weren't good people like Lady Flaxstone. Maybe they weren't meant to forgive.

But that just meant that one day they'd do something to each other that couldn't be forgiven either. Far better to cut this off now and avoid that pain later.

'I'm… I'm trying, Tori. I… I said I love you. Isn't that enough? Enough for you to stay and work this out with me?'

'You love me?' She shook her head. 'Jasper, you don't even know me. If you did, you'd know that love isn't ever enough. Love just forces us down roads we don't want to walk, and makes us feel guilty for wanting the things we want. I've been here before, and I know how this ends. I've had enough of love, thanks.'

With that, she turned away and walked into her bedroom to finish packing. And tried to pretend that her heart wasn't breaking. Because for once, just once, she wished that love really *could* be enough.

CHAPTER THIRTEEN

'YOU REALISE THIS isn't at all healthy, right?' Felix's voice cut through the quiet of the snowy countryside three days later, and Jasper looked up suddenly from his seat on the bench outside Tori's cottage.

'I'm enjoying the miracle of a white Christmas in Britain. Besides, it's quiet here,' he said defensively. 'There's a seat, no one bothers me, and it's not like Tori's here to object.' He had a lot of thinking to do, and he found he thought best somewhere he couldn't hear his father's voice.

Although at least the earl's jolly tones drowned out the sound of Tori tearing down everything he'd hoped for, playing on a loop inside his head. But Jasper couldn't shake the feeling that he deserved to hear it. That if he replayed that moment enough, he'd find the key to fixing it. Something she'd said, something he'd missed.

So far, however, he was mostly just depressing himself.

'Tori not being here is exactly why it's getting kind of creepy, you sitting outside her empty cottage every day.'

'Not every day,' Jasper lied. Felix raised his eyebrows at him, and he sighed. 'Fine. Every day. I just… I can't think straight up at the hall.'

'I know the feeling.'

Jasper winced as Felix brushed the snow off the bench and sat down beside him. Jasper just had to contend with his father's pointed comments about his loyal deputy's absence. Felix had to cope with the media on the phone, the Internet covering every aspect of his life so far, and all sorts of acquaintances he barely knew popping out of the woodwork to get in his good graces, now he was set to inherit a significant portion of the Flaxstone estate and bank accounts.

'Did I mention I'm sorry for outing you at the party?'

'Yes,' Felix said. 'Many times. But do feel free to mention it again. You can throw in a bonus apology for running away five years ago too, if you like.'

'Sorry,' Jasper said again. He seemed to be saying it a lot. But he also seemed to be rebuilding bridges he'd thought were damaged beyond repair. Maybe he and Felix wouldn't ever be best friends the way they had been once, but perhaps instead they'd be something more.

Brothers, even.

It was weird, in a way, to go from the man who couldn't forgive the lies he'd been told, to the one who needed to ask for forgiveness. But maybe that was the lesson he'd been meant to learn all along: that forgiving and asking forgiveness were two sides of the same coin, and everyone needed to do both from time to time.

He wished he could ask Tori for forgiveness, even if he wasn't entirely sure what he'd done wrong. Wished he could forgive her for leaving, but he wasn't there yet, however much he was learning.

He didn't *understand*. How could he forgive what didn't make any sense?

He hadn't understood how his parents could lie to

him for so long, or how Felix could keep the truth from him after he'd found out, but he was starting to, now. When love and family and everything was so fragile, people did what they had to in order to keep it together. He wouldn't have understood that at seventeen, when Felix learned the truth.

But he didn't think he would ever understand how Tori could walk away from the connection between them, when he was offering to change his whole life, his whole existence for her. How she could hear him say he loved her, and have it mean nothing.

Maybe he should have told her about the last time he'd said that to a woman, only to have her turn round and humiliate him. Maybe then she'd realise how much it meant to him.

Or maybe not. His first love had ended in embarrassment. Hers had ended in death. She wasn't likely to cut him much slack for that.

And anyway, *she* was the one who had left. Maybe she should be running back and begging *him* for forgiveness.

'You *could* go after her, you realise,' Felix said after a moment. 'It's not like you don't know where she is.'

'It's also not as if she gave me any indication at all that she wanted me to follow her,' Jasper pointed out. 'I told her I loved her—'

'No, you told a party full of strangers you loved her, mostly to make our father feel guilty.'

Our father. That still sounded strange.

'It doesn't matter. She said love isn't enough.' But it was all he had to give.

The realisation had been a slow one, creeping in between snow falls and frozen rivers, silent in the muffled winter landscape. Eight years ago when they'd met, she'd been a challenge. Five years ago, when they'd first spent the night together, she'd been a refuge. Two weeks ago, when they'd been stranded together at the Moorside, she'd still been a mystery—but one he was piecing together the clues to make sense of. By the time she'd kissed him at the Christmas market, she'd been all he could think about. She'd become a friend, then something more, something deeper, something he was scared to name unless it escaped again.

He'd barely known he was falling until he was all in. Like slipping on ice.

Yes, that was a perfect description for how falling in love with Tori Edwards felt. As if his feet had gone from under him and he was flat on his back on the hard, icy ground wondering what the hell just happened.

'She said something else, before you got to the cottage. Something that made about as much sense as all of that did.' Felix's brows knitted together as he obviously tried to remember it word for word. 'She said she'd been here before. That you were just saying you loved her to try and get her to stay, or make her feel guilty or something.'

'She thought I was only proclaiming love in the most embarrassing way possible to make her feel bad?' Jasper's brain caught up with the rest of what Felix had said. 'Wait. She said she'd been here before?'

'That's what she said.'

Yes. She'd said that to him, too, but he hadn't realised the significance of it until now. He'd assumed she was talking about the first time they'd slept together, just before he'd left the country. But what if she wasn't?

Because she *hadn't* been here with him before. This was all different, this time. He'd definitely never told her he loved her before. And, given what else he knew about her love life and relationship history, that left him only one possible candidate.

'Tyler.'

'Who?' Felix asked.

'Her ex-boyfriend. The son of her sort-of foster parents. He died, before she came here. But I'm starting to think there was more to that story than she told me.' He'd known that—or sensed it at least—before. But he hadn't imagined it could be something big enough to derail everything between them.

'Isn't there always?'

'Maybe I just wasn't asking the right questions.' And maybe he needed to.

No more secrets. That was what he'd promised himself when he came back here. He just hadn't anticipated the challenge that was Tori Edwards and her defensive walls.

Jasper sprang to his feet, and Felix followed. 'You're going to go see her?'

'I'm going to go see her.'

'Hang on, then.' Felix fished a key from his pocket and let himself into Tori's cottage.

'Wait, why do you have a key to her cottage?' Jasper called from the doorstep, reluctant to go inside without Tori's permission even though she wasn't there.

'She wanted me to water her Christmas tree,' Felix yelled back.

'Of course she did.'

Felix re-emerged moments later with a parcel wrapped in Christmas paper; one Jasper recognised. It was the one Henry had given him for Tori when they'd left the Moorside, just a couple of weeks ago now.

'It's Christmas Day. She'll want this,' Felix said.

Jasper nodded, and took the parcel from him. 'I'll

deliver it. Make my excuses with the parents for Christmas dinner?'

'Of course. Just be careful on the roads,' Felix said. 'There's more snow forecast. And I don't want to lose a brother when I only just got him back.'

'Neither do I.' Jasper flashed him a grin, then ran for his four-by-four, parked up in the garage by the house.

It was time to put an end to all the secrets. It was time to bring Tori home again.

Tori stared at the door in front of her, willing herself to open it.

She'd been back at the Moorside for three days now. It was time.

She just still didn't quite feel ready.

Aunt Liz and Uncle Henry had looked about as surprised as she'd expected when she'd appeared on their doorstep three nights ago. For all they'd asked her to come back for Christmas, it was clear they hadn't actually expected that she *would*. Still, Liz had made up her room for her, and Henry had fed her dinner—'Anything but pie?' she'd asked, at which question he'd given her a knowing look—and she'd settled back into life at the Moorside as if she'd never left.

Well, almost.

'Are you going to go in?' Henry's voice behind her made her jump. 'Only, our turkey will be ready in six hours, and I'd hate for you to miss it because you're busy staring at a door.'

Not just any door. Tyler's door.

Henry sank down against the wall to sit beside her on the floor, their legs stretched out across the hallway ahead of them. The pub was still open, for all that it was Christmas Day, but all the lunches were cooked and being served. Another couple of hours and all that would be left was mopping up the last of the drinkers before sending them home to their families and having their own, very late, Christmas dinner.

'He loved you so much, you know,' Henry said. 'He'd want you to move on and be happy, if that's what this is about.'

'It's not.' Tori considered. 'Well, not entirely.'

Yes, she felt guilty about moving on and leaving Tyler behind, but then, she'd been feeling that guilt since long before he'd died. Weirdly, she didn't feel as if she was betraying Tyler with Jasper. If anything, she felt she was betraying Jasper, by clinging onto Tyler's memory.

She'd done a lot of thinking over the last three days, and one thing was crystal clear to her. If she wanted to move on—with Jasper, or with anyone—she needed to put Tyler's ghost to rest.

And the only way she'd been able to come up with to do that was by telling the truth.

'Did he ever talk to you, about me leaving for university?' Tori asked. She'd never spoken with Tyler's parents about what had happened before she'd left, or after. But suddenly, she wondered if they knew anyway. They'd loved their son deeply, but they'd never claimed he was perfect. None of them were.

All of them needed forgiveness, she realised now. But the dead couldn't give it.

'He didn't want you to go, I know that,' Henry admitted. 'But I told him then, if you truly love her, son, you have to let her go. She has great things in her and she has to go and achieve them. She'll come back when she's ready, but not if we hold on too tight.'

Tori looked away from the door and stared at the man who had chosen to be her uncle, even when blood didn't make him one. 'You told him that?'

'Yep. Bet he didn't listen though.' He shook his head. 'I loved that boy more than my own life, and it kills me every day that he's gone. But he never listened to a word of advice his whole life.'

'He…he begged me not to go. Told me if I truly loved him, I'd stay. That leaving would break him. He said…he said he was scared he'd do something stupid if I wasn't there.' Henry's expression hardened at her words, but she pressed on. She needed to say this. Needed to get it all out, at last. No more secrets. 'I told him I had to go— that if I gave up this opportunity I'd never forgive myself. I thought we could carry on together anyway; you remember, I came back every weekend that first term to see him.'

'I remember.' Henry's voice was dark. He already knew how the story ended, of course. 'Liz was worried. She thought you should be spending more time making new friends at university.'

'Every time I came back it got harder. Tyler…he seemed more and more unstable. Accusing me of cheating on him. Of laughing at him, when I was away. He kept telling me that if I went back to university without him he didn't know what he'd do. That he wouldn't be responsible for what happened.' The implication had been clear. Whatever stupid thing Tyler did without her there to stop him would be her fault. Her responsibility.

'And then he went out, got drunk, and tried to drive home.' Henry rubbed a hand across his wrinkled brow, looking older and more tired than Tori had ever imagined he could look. Then he stretched out his arm and wrapped it around her shoulder, pulling her close against him as they both stared at Tyler's bedroom door, and remembered the boy they had lost.

'He was an idiot,' Henry said after a moment. 'And that wasn't your fault, not for a moment. I... I'm angry with him now, and I'd have been furious with him then if I'd known what was going on. But at least I know now. And I can tell you what happened to Tyler wasn't your fault. Not in any way, shape or form.'

'But if I hadn't gone—'

'Then maybe it would have happened later, or differently, or not at all. But it still wouldn't have been your fault. He made his choices and some of them were terrible ones, and he paid the price for that. He should never have tried to make you carry that blame.'

'We both made choices,' Tori pointed out. 'I chose to leave him behind, even though I knew it could be the end of our relationship.' It hurt to admit that; that she'd chosen her own ambition and future over the boy who was supposed to be the love of her life.

'You were only eighteen,' Henry replied. 'And you made the right choice. You couldn't mortgage your whole future for a teenage relationship that probably wouldn't last anyway. And if it was meant to be, it would have been. If it was meant to be he would have supported you every step of the way. I'm ashamed that he didn't.'

Tori lowered her head as she shook it, too overcome to find words, her eyes burning with unshed tears.

'This is why you didn't come back here after the funeral, isn't it?' Henry said. 'Why you stayed away so long. I always wondered... Liz said it probably just hurt too much to be here with all the memories, but I suspected it must have been something more.'

'I thought you'd blame me, if you knew the truth. *I* blamed me.' She took a shuddering breath. 'I thought you'd hate me, and it hurt so much I couldn't face it.'

In all honesty, it *still* hurt. Maybe her first visit back to the Moorside in the snow and the dark had started to soothe some of the pain, but the guilt still hung on.

'You're our family, every bit as much as Tyler was, even if it is by love, not blood.' Henry hugged her tighter. 'We could never do anything but love you, the same way we'll always love Tyler, even if we don't agree with his choices. But in *your* case, you made the right choice going. Staying away…that choice I'm less keen on.'

'So you *are* mad at me?'

'No. I *missed* you.' Henry sighed. 'Maybe I'm not saying this right. What I mean is… Vicky, Liz and I will always forgive you and always love you, even if we don't agree with you. You're family and you will always have a home here.'

That was all it took to send her over the edge. The tears cascaded over her cheeks as she buried her head against Henry's chest, her body shaking with sobs as he held her. As if the guilt and the self-loathing were leaving her in the flood of tears. Washing her soul clean.

She was truly home again, at last.

It took a while for her to regain her composure. But when she did, she wiped her eyes, kissed Henry on the cheek, and straightened her back as she stood again, ready to enter Tyler's room at last.

It was time to say goodbye, for the last time.

And then she had a new life to say hello to, she hoped.

CHAPTER FOURTEEN

FELIX HADN'T BEEN kidding about the snow.

Thick, heavy flakes landed on his windscreen faster than his wipers could clear them, and Jasper peered through the glass at a world turning whiter by the moment. The air swirled and rushed with snow, whipped up by a wild wind that whistled down the valleys and around the rocks of the moors.

Somewhere up ahead was the Moorside Inn and the woman he loved.

Now he just had to get to her. And not crash on the way.

A shiver went through him at the thought. From what she'd said, he knew he couldn't be far from where Tyler had died. The last thing Tori needed was another man to mourn.

He slowed the car to a crawl. Maybe it would take him longer, but he'd get there in one piece, at least.

He was just picking out the landmarks that he knew led to the Moorside Inn when he saw the blue flashing lights. Easing onto the brakes, he slowed a good distance away from them, glad that the date—Christmas Day—meant the roads were mostly clear. Unfastening his seat belt, he pulled the hood of his coat over his head and ducked out of the car to find out what was happening.

'Tree down in the road, sir.' Was that the same young policeman who'd visited the Moorside last time? Jasper had a feeling it might be. The last few weeks seemed to be coming full circle. Squinting through the snow, he could see the heavy, old tree trunk spanning the whole width of the road. A set of headlights on the other side showed that his wasn't the only Christmas Day not going to plan.

'Going to be closed until they clear it,' the police officer continued. 'You might want to turn round and go back the way you came, if you can make it through the snow.'

Jasper looked back down the road he'd just travelled, and saw the weather closing in behind him. But more than that, he saw all the distance and pain and anger that had filled his last five years. The lack of forgiveness, the burning sense of injustice eating away at him.

He didn't want to go that way.

'I'll park up and keep going on foot,' he said.

'I know an inn you can shelter at for the night. If you like.'

He knew that voice. He loved that voice.

Jasper spun to find Tori leaning against the fallen tree, a bright red hat pulled down low over her dark hair, and a hopeful smile on her face.

He'd never seen anything so beautiful.

'That would be wonderful,' he said, stepping closer. 'Any chance it serves steak and ale pie?' He could almost take her in his arms, but he still wasn't completely sure that was what she wanted. Although the fact that she was here, in the snow, on this road…had she been trying to reach him, too? He hoped so. But either way, the next move had to be hers.

'It might. But it's Christmas Day so, mostly turkey and trimmings, I think.' She took a step too, and suddenly she was so close he could see the snowflakes landing on her eyelashes. She blinked them away, and met his gaze, and he knew.

He knew that he had to convince this woman to give him a chance. Maybe she'd never be able to love him, and he'd have to let her go. But if there was any chance she might want to stay in his life for always…he had to try.

'Tori, I… I'm sorry. For everything. I've learned a lot about forgiveness recently—most of it from you, in a roundabout way. You were right, about so many things. I've talked a lot with Felix, and with my parents, especially since you left. And while I'm still not all the way there, I'm trying, really, I am. And I hope that you—'

He broke off as she placed an icy hand against his cheek. Then she stretched up on tiptoe and pressed her cold lips to his. 'Yes,' she murmured, barely pulling away at all. 'Yes to all of it. Now come on. Let's get out of the cold.'

Henry and Liz barely even looked surprised at all this time when she turned up with Jasper in tow, his car parked out of the way on the side of the road to worry about later. They had more important things to deal with now.

'Here for the turkey, I suppose?' Henry asked Jasper, holding out a hand for him to shake.

'Not just the turkey,' Jasper replied, smiling down at her. Tori tried not to blush, but from Liz's soppy smile she was pretty sure she'd failed.

She'd talked to her aunt, too, after she'd made her peace with Tyler, talking to him as if he'd never left his childhood bedroom. Maybe he hadn't, in essence. But when she'd closed the door behind her for the last time, she knew she, at least, had pulled whatever part of her heart that had stayed in the past with him fully into the future. Liz had hugged her tight and told her that she should listen to her uncle. Tori was family, and that was the end of the matter.

And now, as she sat around the best table in the inn, all the other patrons gone, with Jasper at her side and Liz and Henry across from her, Tori started to truly believe that maybe she *could* be part of a family again. That she could forgive herself and start over.

And it started here, now, this Christmas Day, somewhere she'd never expected to be again with someone she'd never imagined she could like, let alone love.

But she did—love Jasper. She hadn't told him yet, and she hugged the truth of it deep inside her. She had a feeling this would be one secret he wouldn't object to. Maybe it could even be her Christmas present to him.

She couldn't pinpoint the moment she'd fallen in love with him, but maybe she didn't have to. He'd crept under her defences, finding holes she hadn't known existed while she'd been trying desperately to build the walls higher so he couldn't climb them. However he'd got inside her heart, he'd helped to crowd out the old feelings that had filled it, and brought in fresh, new ones.

Like hope.

They still had a long way to go, and many, many walls to climb. But this time, she had hope that they could do it together.

She wanted to get Jasper alone. She wanted to tell him everything, to listen to everything he had to say. But it was Christmas Day—her first Christmas Day with her family in eight long years—and there were traditions to be followed at the Moorside Inn. Ones even love couldn't delay.

Christmas dinner was everything she remembered from her childhood: crackers and terrible jokes and stupid hats and the most delicious dinner anyone ever ate because Henry saved all the best bits for them. The tree lights twinkled in the corner, and festive tunes played softly from the speaker system. It was nothing at all like the fancy Christmas party at Flaxstone Hall, but it felt more magical to Tori.

'Your parents don't mind you joining us for Christmas dinner?' Liz asked as they all tucked in.

Jasper shook his head as he chewed a mouthful of turkey. 'I asked my…my brother to explain to them why I had to go. I think they'll understand.' He shot Tori a look that made her mouth dry, and had her reaching for her wine glass. In fact, she was so distracted it took her a whole swallow to realise that he'd called Felix his brother.

Seemed he really had made progress while she was gone.

But finally, *finally*, dinner was over. Liz and Henry shooed off their offers of help to clear up, and suddenly they were upstairs in her old bedroom, staring at each other across that damn single bed again.

At least we won't mind cosying up nearly so much this time…

'I'm sorry I ran away from Flaxstone,' Tori started, when Jasper seemed content to just look at her, his eyes warm and wanting. 'Away from you. I just… I told you about Tyler. How he died when I went away to university. But I never told you everything and… I think it's time that I did.'

Jasper blinked, then reached out a hand to take hers and sat them down beside each other on the bed. 'Tell me everything.'

And she did. Everything she'd told Henry, everything she'd been keeping trapped inside her for eight long years.

'In the end, I just knew it was my fault that he'd died,' she said, once she'd explained the whole story. 'I'd chosen my ambition and my future over my relationship with him, and he'd done something stupid, just like he'd warned me he would. That's why I couldn't come back here, couldn't move on, couldn't find love again. Because I knew my choices had killed him and—worse still—I knew I'd make the same choices again if I had to.'

Jasper shook his head. 'No. *His* choices led him to that car accident. He chose to drive after drinking—you didn't make him do that. And if he really loved you, he wouldn't have tried to scare and threaten you out of going after your dreams. He'd have lifted you up to help you chase them.'

'I'm starting to see that now,' Tori admitted. 'But when I thought you were leaving the country again, I knew I couldn't risk my heart on a long-distance relationship, which meant I couldn't risk falling for you at all. And then when your father offered me the job at Stonebury… I knew I was about to do the same thing that I'd done to Tyler all over again. Take the opportunity I wanted so badly, even though I knew it would hurt you. And I was so damned scared that it seemed better to run away before you could talk me out of it. Before anyone got hurt.'

'It wasn't the same,' Jasper said. 'But…but I wish you'd felt you could talk to me about it. That we could discuss it and come up with an answer together.'

'I just couldn't. I still had Tyler's ghost in my head. Until I laid that to rest, anything between us was impossible.'

'But you have done that now?' Jasper asked.

'I...hope so. I suspect these things are a work in progress.' She had to be honest, now most of all. Even if the answer wasn't the one she really wanted to give.

'Like rebuilding a family riddled with secrets, lies and abandonment.' Jasper gave her a half-smile. 'And I get it. I understand why you couldn't talk to me—even without Tyler's ghost whispering lies at you. I hadn't exactly shown myself to be the most understanding and forgiving of boyfriends, anyway.'

'Boyfriends?'

He shrugged. 'Well, if you'll have me.'

Tori tilted her head and considered him. He was gorgeous, rich, he made her whole body hum with wanting him, and he made paper chains with bored kids.

'I suppose I could do worse. I have conditions, though.'

'Why am I not surprised?' Leaning back against the bedhead, he pulled her up into his arms, and she twisted so she could still see his face. It was less comfortable than just nuzzling up to him, but Tori knew they had to look each other in the eye as they made these decisions together.

No more secrets between them, now. And not ever.

'Go on, then,' he said.

'No running away when things get tough—and, yes, I know that one goes for me too,' she said, before he could even open his mouth the whole way. 'We talk about things instead of, well, our usual way of doing things.'

'Holding grudges and feeling guilty? Yeah, I guess talking *does* sound a more sensible plan.' He gave her a gentle smile and kissed the top of her head. Tori leaned into his shoulder, feeling stronger just from the touch of him.

'And we forgive when we mess things up,' Jasper added. 'That's my condition. Because we're not going to get things right all the time, either of us. *Especially* us. But you're right. We don't run. And we forgive—each other and ourselves.'

For him, she knew the first would be a challenge. For her, it would probably be the second. But she figured that together they might even balance each other out.

'Okay,' she agreed. 'Number one rule: forgive, always.' She placed a kiss just where his shirt collar sat open, and let herself rest her head for a moment.

'And please…' He placed a finger under her chin and tilted it so she was looking at him again. 'Don't pull up that drawbridge again? I spent so long trying to get behind those battlements…when you put all your defences back up on me that night at the party, I honestly thought that was it. That I was back out in the cold for good.'

'I'm sorry. I just—'

'I understand why you did it,' he interrupted her. 'I'm not asking for apologies. I just need you to know…you don't have to do that any more. Not with me. There's nothing you need to hide from me, and no need for the armour. I'm all in, Tori. I didn't expect to be—I came home thinking I'd be leaving again, and quick. But instead I got snowed in with you and my whole world changed. Because I saw behind your armour and I realised that was all I wanted to do. Solve the puzzle of Tori Edwards. And now I know I could happily spend the rest of my life doing just that, if you'll let me.'

His eyes were so serious, so sincere, that Tori's heart

rose until she had to swallow it back down. 'Let's start with figuring out the puzzle of fitting both of us in this bed, shall we?' She smiled gently, letting him know she wasn't turning down everything he was offering. 'Take it one day—or night—at a time.'

He returned her smile. 'Yeah. One day at a time.' Then his grin turned wicked. 'And I definitely have some ideas about the bed-sharing thing…'

He wrapped an arm around her waist and tipped her flat on her back, smothering her squeal with a kiss. And Tori knew that if they could just keep talking, and forgiving, everything was going to be just fine.

Better than fine. Life was going to be wonderful again.

EPILOGUE

STONEBURY HALL LOOKED at its best in the snow, Jasper decided.

All spring and summer they'd worked on getting the estate into shape; setting up the barns for the craft stalls and workshops, getting the tea room ready for its first customers—not to mention doing up the house itself.

But now that Christmas was almost here again, a full year since he and Tori had first walked the grounds of this strange, crenellated hall in the snow, it felt as if *this* was how the place was always meant to be.

'Did you imagine for a moment, a year ago, that we'd be here now?' he asked as he and Tori stood, gloved hand in gloved hand, looking up at the battlements and stone walls of their new home.

Tori gave him her usual 'are you crazy?' look. He was actually surprisingly fond of it these days.

'Me? Absolutely. I figured I'd be here making a huge success of the business. You? Not so much.'

Rolling his eyes, Jasper nudged her in the ribs, wondering if she even felt it through all the layers of coat and clothes between them. She squirmed out of the way and laughed, all the same.

'Okay, fine, I hadn't exactly anticipated us living here

together, spending *Christmas* here. But then, I didn't imagine spending last Christmas at the Moorside, either.'

'Last Christmas was perfect.' Maybe it hadn't started out that way, but by the end it had been everything he'd ever wanted—even if he hadn't known until that very moment that he wanted it. Tori had given him a chance to spend the rest of his life learning her, loving her. And they hadn't gone into it with more secrets, more hidden expectations. They'd gone in openly, knowing what they needed from each other—and from themselves.

Which wasn't to say it had all been plain sailing. They'd still had to navigate the revelations of Felix's parentage—which society and the gossip magazines had enjoyed as much as Jasper had feared. But Felix had gone with Tori to Stonebury as their father had planned, and managed to stay out of the limelight, until things had at least started to blow over.

Jasper, meanwhile, had been required to go back to the States and tidy up his affairs there before he could move back to Britain full time. Neither he nor Tori had been happy about the idea of a long-distance relationship, especially given Tori's previous experiences, but they'd made it work.

Well, actually they'd been miserable, and bickered for a lot of it. But they'd visited when they could, forgiven each other when things got too much, and they'd made it through.

And now they were here, about to spend their first Christmas at Stonebury. The Christmas village had been doing a roaring trade for months, and even in the summer some of the festive workshops had proved popular. There was still a lot of work to do to make the place a long-standing success, but Jasper had faith that Tori could do it. This project was her baby, after all.

And he…well, he'd be getting back to working with his father in the new year, and with Felix. The earl had announced, rather impatiently upon Jasper's return, that he *did* want to retire one day, and his sons needed to be ready to take over his empire.

So they were all working together. Which would be *interesting*. But with Tori to come home to every night, and a promise that there were no more secrets to worry about, Jasper had faith that it could work. Hopefully.

'I'm just glad that Henry's coming to cook us Christmas dinner,' Tori said, shivering a little beside him. Her aunt and uncle had taken the unprecedented step of actually closing the Moorside Inn in order to join them for Christmas. Jasper hoped that was a sign of how far Tori's relationship with them had come in the last twelve months.

'Do you think steak and ale pie could be considered a traditional Christmas dish?' he asked hopefully.

Laughing, Tori shook her head. 'Not even a little bit. But when they get here, you might want to put your Christmas present in the fridge straight away. Henry has a soft spot for you, I think.'

Jasper beamed. 'Christmas with the woman I love, and my family, in my new home, and with steak and ale pie. I can only think of one more thing that would make this the absolutely perfect Christmas.'

'More than steak and ale pie?' Tori asked, eyebrows raised.

'Yep.' Jasper reached into his coat pocket and pulled out the ring box his mother had given him, last time he'd seen her at Flaxstone. He handed it to Tori, who opened it with a gasp. 'Marry me? I can't promise it will always be easy, but I *can* promise I'll make it worth it. Because I love you, and I want to spend my whole life showing you that.'

Tori looked up at him, tears at the corners of her eyes. 'Of course I'll marry you.'

'Really?'

'Absolutely. Because I love you too, and the last year has shown me that love isn't what I thought it was. That *I'm* not who I thought I was.' She gave him a wicked grin. 'Besides, if we're married, half your steak and ale pies become mine, so—'

She shrieked as he wrapped his arms around her middle, lifting her to kiss her thoroughly. And then he did it again for good measure.

Because he'd solved the first part of the puzzle of Tori Edwards; who she was now and what she needed.

And he knew he'd spend the rest of his live figuring out how to keep her as happy as he was right now.

Even if it meant sharing his steak and ale pies.

* * * * *

IT STARTED AT CHRISTMAS…

JO McNALLY

This book is dedicated to my smart,
talented, funny agent, Veronica Park,
for never giving up on this story of my heart.

Prelude

Three days after Christmas...

*B*ig fat snowflakes swirled through the air at the cemetery, making everything look fuzzy three days after the worst Christmas ever. Zachary watched the people walk back to their cars. Big piles of flowers surrounded his mother's grave.

"Do you think Mom sent the snow?"

"What?" Uncle Blake looked down at Zachary and frowned.

"Maybe...maybe Mom sent the snow. Like a message or something. She taught me how to catch snowflakes on my tongue, like this..." Zachary stuck his tongue out. A white flake landed, melting in a quick, cold burst. Uncle Blake's face screwed up like he'd just stepped on a Lego, but Zach rushed on. "Remember how much she loved Christmas, Uncle Blake? Maybe she's still here, but you can't see her... like the ghost of Christmas future in that story—"

"No." His uncle's voice sounded rough and scratchy. "She's not here, Zach. Your mom isn't a ghost. She's just... gone."

He meant Mom was dead. Zach wasn't stupid. He knew what dead meant. What he didn't get was, why wouldn't people just say it?

Uncle Blake looked up at the snow for a minute. "She loved Christmas so much because it's for little kids, and she never stopped... She never really grew up." He knelt in front of Zach, one knee in the snow. "I know this was *a lousy holiday, and I'm sorry. I miss her, too. But you're going to have to be a man now. You need to leave make-believe for the little kids, okay?"*

Zach straightened his shoulders. He missed his mom. She was funny, and she gave the best hugs ever. Hugs that made him feel safe, even in the middle of another move or if she was changing boyfriends again. And now he'd never have another hug from her. He blinked his eyes. Would any-one ever hug him like that? Probably not. Hugs were like Christmas—for little kids only. He looked into his uncle's eyes and nodded.

He wasn't really sure how to be a man, but if that's what his uncle wanted, he'd try.

Chapter One

"This has got to be the stupidest thing I've ever done."

"What? The shopping or the job?"

Amanda Lowery juggled the bags in her hand, laughing at her cousin's question.

"Both, I guess. There's no way I'll get the job after Mr. Randall meets me tomorrow, which means I won't be able to pay for any of this stuff."

The two women stood on the sidewalk in Gallant Lake, New York. Like so many upstate villages, a lot of the brick or clapboard storefronts were empty. There were still a few businesses left, and they'd managed to shop in every one of them. There was just a hint of color starting to show in the mountains surrounding the lake, which glittered in the afternoon sun. Labor Day was just over a week away. Soon those trees would be ablaze in the reds and golds of autumn. Amanda and Mel were standing in front of a colorful coffee shop directly across the road from a tiny park overlooking the lake.

"Hey, you got this final interview fair and square..." Mel grimaced. "Well, not exactly *fair*, but you know what I mean. You're the one who came up with the plans the guy liked."

"Yes, but he thinks those plans came from *David*, not me. He's expecting a *man* to show up tomorrow morning. Like I said—stupid." She looked up at the bright orange coffee shop door. "Come on, let's get a cappuccino before we head back to the resort."

After ordering, they settled in at a table by the window.

The café was small, but there weren't many people inside, so Amanda didn't have to worry about her personal space. Their table was bright blue. The chairs were each a different color. Nothing in the place matched, creating a chaotic, but energetic, atmosphere. As a designer, Amanda would describe the look as bohemian eclectic. Local artwork on the brick walls displayed widely varying degrees of talent. The place smelled of roasted coffee beans, cinnamon and sawdust. The latter was courtesy of the woodworking shop next door.

"Amanda, once this Randall guy meets you and hears that you specialize in historic homes and how many projects you've already managed, he'll forget all about that little 'mix-up' and hire you on the spot." Mel smiled and pushed her dark hair behind an ear. Two older men sitting near the counter were openly staring at her, but Mel was used to it. She had cheekbones most women would kill for. And legs that went on forever. And violet eyes that evoked memories of Elizabeth Taylor. Amanda sighed, glancing down at her short legs and...um...curvy figure. Genetics were tricky. That's why Mel was a former supermodel, while women like Amanda ended up working behind the scenes with furniture and fabric.

"It wasn't a mix-up, Mel. It was *intentional*. I'm a *deceiver*." She was so desperate for this job that she'd resorted to unethical business practices. That was *so* not who she was. But a woman had to eat, right?

Mel waved off her concerns—easy to do when you were rich and famous. "I wonder what these signs are about? I've been seeing them all over town."

Mel pointed at a cardboard sign in the window with the word *casino* across the front in black, and a giant red circle and diagonal line over it. Amanda hadn't noticed, too occupied with worrying about tomorrow.

The café's owner brought their cappuccinos to the table.

She was an older woman, with long salt-and-pepper hair and a heavy skirt that doubled as a floor sweeper. There was no doubt where the hippie vibe of the coffee shop came from.

"Here you go, honeys. My name's Cathy. Anything else I can getcha?"

Mel pointed to the sign. "What's the story with that?"

Cathy's smile faded. "Bad news for Gallant Lake." She shook her head, lips pressed together. "Some big-shot developer bought the old resort a couple years ago, and instead of fixing it up like we'd hoped, he wants to tear it down and build a damned casino. A *casino*! I mean, what is this, New Jersey? Are we going to be living in one of those De Niro movies now?" Cathy's face twisted in disgust. "We're fighting him, though. No way do we want some giant sign of a neon bimbo here in our town, kicking her leg at the sky."

Mel smirked, and Amanda knew what she was thinking. Clearly, someone hadn't been to Vegas lately. Not all casinos were gaudy and gauche. On a more selfish note, Amanda wondered if they'd hired a decorator yet.

"The Gallant Lake Resort?" Mel said. "That's where we're staying. It seems nice." The sprawling four-story stone-and-timber hotel hugged the shoreline of the lake. The decor might be kitschy and straight out of the sixties, but the place was clean and the views were wonderful.

"Yeah, the family that used to own it always took good care of the place. But they could never afford to remodel. Still, there's no need to tear it down."

Amanda looked out the window at Main Street, dotted with puddles from last night's rain. She saw several boarded-up storefronts. "Wouldn't a casino bring in more jobs and tourists?"

Cathy shrugged. "But at what cost? That resort's history is a part of us. Old Blue Eyes himself used to sing there!

The whole Rat Pack did. Streisand sang for the governor's birthday party once. People would come up here from the city and boy, would they spend money!" Cathy brushed some dust off the windowsill with the corner of her apron. "The old resorts are being torn down all over the Catskills, and we don't want to lose ours." She perched on the edge of a nearby table. Mel smiled, as if enjoying the small-town lack of pretense. "We think if it was spruced up and advertised more, it would bring vacationers back to Gallant Lake again. Maybe the old ski resort would reopen. And the golf course. Business would pick up for everyone."

"But wouldn't a nice new casino do the same thing?" Amanda couldn't stand to be in a casino herself, with people pressing in from everywhere. Just thinking about it made her palms sweat. But if it would bring business to the obviously struggling town…

"Ha! The operative word is *nice*. Mr. Hotshot wants to build some ugly ten-story high-rise on our beautiful lake. Main Street will be nothing more than a thoroughfare from the highway to his casino. That won't help *my* business. He's buying up houses just to turn them into parking lots. Parking lots!" Cathy laughed and winked. "Of course, we stopped him from turning *one* of them into a parking lot. We had his big old house declared a landmark and now he's stuck with it! That boy picked the wrong little town to mess with."

Cathy was still cackling when she walked away. Mel gave a low whistle. "Whoever that guy is, I hope he doesn't buy his coffee here. I'm pretty sure Cathy would spit in it."

Amanda giggled, then reached over to squeeze her cousin's hand.

"Thanks for coming with me this weekend, Mel. Whatever happens with the job interview tomorrow, it'll be easier to handle the fallout with you here." She was pretty sure she knew exactly what was going to happen. She was going to be sent packing. Her stomach clenched. It would be exactly what she deserved.

"You'll do great, kid," Mel said. "No matter who he's *expecting*, he liked the plans you sent, and he's going to like you, too."

Her cousin had no idea how close Amanda was to giving up and going home to her mother's house in Nowheresville, Kansas, with her tail tucked between her legs—a failure.

"I hope so. If I can get a showcase job like this, it might be enough to start my own solo business." It would also save her from slinking back home in disgrace after once again trusting the wrong guy. "We should get back to the resort."

"Yeah, I want to look at that purse you found at the antiques shop. I still say that little key was for a really fancy chastity belt."

Amanda smiled. Despite her budget woes, she'd found something she couldn't resist buying. She'd fallen in love with the vintage beaded evening bag from the 1920s. To her delight, she'd discovered a tiny ornate key tucked inside. She and Mel had made up some hysterical possibilities for what that key might unlock.

They grabbed their bags and headed to the rental car parked across the street. Mel was giving another lecture on how Amanda was worrying too much about things. Amanda did her best to tune it out because discussing her worry didn't make her worry any less.

Mel grabbed Amanda's arm with a cry as she stepped off the sidewalk. An enormous black SUV sped by, too close to the curb. It hit a puddle, and before Amanda could react, she was drenched. The jerk barely slowed down before speeding off around the corner.

"Son of a bitch!" Amanda jumped back and turned to Mel, who, of course, was perfectly dry. She was also doubled over with laughter.

Amanda looked down. Her pink sweater clung to her,

and water dripped off her fingertips. She wanted to be mad. She *was* mad. But when she looked up and found Mel still giggling, wiping tears from her eyes, Amanda couldn't help but join her. If there was an edge of hysteria to her laughter, who could blame her?

They were still laughing when they got back to the resort. Mel insisted that they walk right through the lobby with all their packages, despite Amanda's soggy footprints.

"Cathy said they're tearing the place down anyway, so what difference does it make?"

"Nathan, are you kidding me?" Blake Randall pressed harder on the gas and sent his SUV roaring up the country road approaching Gallant Lake. "You took our nephew to school a week early so you could take your girls on vacation *without* him? Who the hell *does* that to a ten-year-old kid?"

Blake floored it past farms, double-wides and large Victorian homes. His hands gripped the wheel so tight he was surprised it didn't snap.

"I've had Zachary all summer, Blake," his brother whined over the speakerphone. "Michaela wanted some time with *our* family."

"He *is* your damned family!" He and Nathan were the only family Zach had left. Their father wouldn't even acknowledge the boy's existence, so that left him and Nathan to give Zach a sense of family. Even if it was a thoroughly dysfunctional one.

"You know what I mean." He could hear Nathan taking a deep breath. His older brother always did that when he was trying to find the balls to challenge Blake. "Look, *you're* his guardian. We took him for the summer, but it wasn't a permanent thing."

"But you already have a family." Nathan was a father. A questionable one, perhaps, but still. At least he wasn't as clueless about kids as Blake was. "Why can't you add one more?"

"Not happening, Blake. Tiffany named you in her will. Not me."

"Only because she and Michaela hated each other." Tiffany used to refer to Nathan's wife as Butt Stick. Blake's lips twitched at the memory of him and his sister laughing over that name.

"And yet you think Michaela should raise Tiffany's kid. What *sense* does that make?"

Nathan had a point. Blake had qualms about Michaela raising her *own* children. As if Blake was some kind of expert.

"He shouldn't be at Beakman Academy by himself, a week ahead of the other kids."

"The upperclassmen are there this week," Nathan sighed. "The headmaster said he'd be fine."

Blake slowed to pass a farm tractor driving up the road. Was that thing even legal? He stepped on the gas after he passed it, going too fast for being this close to the village. Sheriff Adams must have been busy somewhere else because Blake didn't see any flashing lights. Benefits of a one-cop town.

"So Zach's at school with a bunch of kids *four grades* ahead of him? That's perfect, genius. What could *possibly* go wrong?"

"Jesus, Blake, I'm not an idiot. He's not in the dorm— he's staying with the headmaster and his family for the week. Feel free to drive over and get him if you don't like it."

Blake chewed his lip. Zach was ten years old. He'd lost his mother less than a year ago. Blake had a feeling *everything* was a big deal to the poor kid. But still…being at school gave him more structure than he'd have with Blake, or even Nathan and Butt Stick.

"Can you guys at least take him for the holiday break?" Tiffany had died at Christmas. Zach deserved a much happier holiday this year.

"No way. We're taking the girls on a cruise for Christmas, and Michaela already said—"

"Yeah, yeah. I can imagine what Michaela said." Blake let off the gas pedal and hung up on his brother. He reached for his coffee and bit out a curse when some spilled on his pants. What a perfect freakin' day. He saw a flash of pink when he looked up and swore again. A petite blonde stepped off the sidewalk, directly into his path.

Blake swerved. The engine on the big vehicle roared. He'd drifted pretty damned close to the curb, scaring the daylights out of himself and no doubt her. After he passed, he glanced in the rearview mirror and winced. He'd hit a puddle and sent a tidal wave of water over her. She was stomping her feet and gesturing to the taller woman behind her, pushing long, wet hair out of her face.

A nice person would have stopped and apologized. But Blake had learned the hard way that being nice in Gallant Lake got him nowhere. He was not popular, and he'd only attract an angry mob if anyone saw him stopped in the middle of town. He felt bad about ruining the woman's afternoon, though. Driving away without stopping made him feel uncomfortably similar to the ogre some of the locals painted him as. He didn't like it.

Speaking of angry mobs, there were five or six picketers just setting up at the entrance to his resort. The small Gallant Lake Preservation Society liked to show up with their handwritten signs, especially if they knew Blake was in town. They loved telling him, loudly and often, that they "weren't giving up the fight" when it came to his plans for the casino. They didn't seem to realize the town had given up on itself years before. That had nothing to do with him. Their signs proclaimed the same old mantra.

Save Gallant Lake!
No Casino!
Leave Our Lake Alone!
They were usually well behaved and didn't interfere
with resort traffic. But guests would be asking questions.
He saw a scruffy pair of guys at the edge of the group.
They didn't fit in with the generally older protesters, but it
wasn't the first time he'd seen them hanging around. The
two always looked ready to take up torches and pitchforks
rather than neatly lettered signs. Their anger simmered a
little closer to the surface, like it was personal, but Blake
had no idea who they were.

The group recognized his vehicle and pressed closer
to the entrance, forcing him to slow down to avoid hitting
them. He could call the sheriff, but that wouldn't do any
good. The protestors always stayed back off his property
lines when the guy they affectionately called "Sheriff Dan"
was around. Blake had a sneaking suspicion the sheriff supported the locals more than him when it came down to it.

Once past the entrance, he parked in the employee lot
and came in the side door. The old place had character,
along with a stellar view. The previous owners had main-
tained the resort well, even if the interior needed updating
everywhere. Those updates would be pointless now since it
was slated for demolition as soon as the state senate gave its
blessing to the casino plans. He was only a few votes away.

When he'd made the purchase originally, sight unseen,
he'd assumed the resort was one of those tired old Catskills
resorts whose glory days ended with the *Dirty Dancing* era.
It was a pleasant surprise to see the place actually making a
little money with a modest marketing campaign, which took
some of the sting out of waiting for those last few votes.

It was smaller than his other hotels, but he ran it with
the same attention to detail. He was known for his No Surprises approach to business, and the employees here had

been quick to catch on—they took care of little problems *before* they became big ones.

He saw the muddy footprints as soon as he entered the lobby on his way to the front desk. *What the hell?* The sun was shining outside, but this looked like someone had walked through here after swimming in a ditch somewhere. He caught a glimpse of pink ahead, stepping inside the elevator. Well, he'd be damned. The blonde he'd almost mowed down in town was a guest at the resort.

It seemed she'd rewarded his behavior with a trail of mud across the lobby carpet, almost as if she knew it was his place. Blake couldn't help the smile that tugged at his mouth. It served him right for not stopping to apologize.

Chapter Two

Amanda paused by the lobby windows to settle her nerves. The resort's lawn swept down to the lakeshore. A morning mist rose from the water still in the shadows of the mountain. Resting the palm of her hand against her stomach, she focused her energy on pulling air in and letting it out. *In with the good air, out with the bad.* She'd hardly slept all night, and her nerves were jangling so much she could practically hear them rattling in her head.

She held a cup of coffee in her other hand—one last boost of caffeinated courage. Counterintuitive to her attempt to calm down? Maybe. But she needed to be sharp. It was almost time for her to meet Blake Randall and inform him that he'd been corresponding with someone other than her ex-boss. That he'd sent blueprints for his historic mansion to *her*, not David Franklin. His request for proposals asked for suggestions on how to put the building to use, preferably as a commercial space, with no indication where it was actually located or what the exterior looked like. It was all very mysterious. When she "accidentally" intercepted the RFP and *intentionally* responded, she'd provided plans for *residential* use instead. She loved period architecture and felt the home should be used for its original purpose.

Randall had liked her plans enough to request a meeting to discuss them. Her shoulders straightened. They were *her* ideas, and they were good ones. What did it matter who they came from? She tried to dismiss the panic fluttering in her chest. She could do this. She *had* to do this. This

job was the key to her being able to start her own design
firm. One where she didn't have to rely on lying, cheating
bosses who preyed on their employees.

Her summer had been almost laughable in its horrid-
ness. The panic attacks were happening more frequently.
Nightmares left her afraid to go to sleep. She jumped at
every little thing. No wonder her nerves were on a razor's
edge. She felt like a canvas left out in the sun too long—
stretched and dry and brittle.

She turned away from the windows and nearly collided
with a guy in a Gallant Lake T-shirt and shorts. The twenty-
something came out of nowhere, arguing loudly on the
phone with someone about a canceled flight and a job he
needed to get back to. Even though he'd nearly knocked
her on her ass, the guy barely mumbled an apology before
he continued on his way.

The brief, but forceful, male contact set off all kinds
of alarms for Amanda. Black spots swirled at the edge of
her vision.

A panic attack, her all-too-familiar companion these
days, was prowling just under her skin, like a shark smell-
ing blood. *Crap.* This was the last thing she needed this
morning, but ignoring it would only give it more power.
She set down her coffee and closed her eyes, trying to relax
her muscles one group at a time, from her toes to her head,
the way her therapist, Dr. Jackson, taught her.

In with the good air, out with the bad.

Shake off the negative while embracing the positive. So
very much easier said than done. But she worked at it, picturing clean, fresh, strong air filling her lungs. She wiggled
her fingers and rolled her shoulders. The monster quieted.
It was time for her to get going.

Randall's cryptic instructions said to ask for directions
to "Halcyon" at the front desk. She was surprised to get
walking directions to a place right next door to the resort.

She headed outside and up the clearly marked path into the woods and through a gate in an old iron fence. A few minutes later, she stepped into a clearing and froze. Set high on a hill to her right was a *castle*. An honest-to-goodness castle, right there in the Catskills.

Her mouth fell open. She blinked. Then blinked again, as if she expected the sight to vanish. Another strange emotion swirled through her amazement, creating a wave of goose bumps across her skin. She couldn't believe what she was looking at. And yet…it felt as if she'd been here before. That was crazy. Randall had kept the location a deep dark secret in his proposal request. All she'd seen was the first floor blueprint.

The sense of déjà vu was overwhelming. The big house called to her so strongly that she could feel it in her bones, drawing her in like a siren call.

Pink granite walls rose from the ground as if the structure had just grown there. It seemed a natural part of the landscape, in spite of its soft color. It was at least three stories tall, with a sharply angled slate roof dotted with dormers. Two round towers anchored the lakeside corners, complete with pointed roofs like upside-down ice cream cones. There appeared to be another larger tower in the front of the house. A stone veranda stretched across the back, with five sets of French doors opening onto it.

The floor plans hadn't done this place justice. Halcyon was breathtaking. Amanda walked around to the front, noting signs of decades of neglect—overgrown shrubbery, dusty windows with no drapes and a general air of abandonment. The driveway circled around a long-forgotten and empty fountain. She walked up the stone stairs to the covered porch. The scale of everything made her feel like Alice in Wonderland, especially as she approached a massive wooden door. There wasn't a doorbell. She smiled to herself. The only appropriate doorbell for this place would be one you rang by pulling on a long velvet cord.

Amanda knocked, but there was no answer. She looked to the driveway. There weren't any cars there. She knocked again, using the side of her fist this time. Still nothing. She walked back around to the lake side of the house, looking for any signs of life. It had to be the right place, but why wasn't anyone here?

Up on the veranda, she paused to take in the view. The huge yard was surrounded by trees all the way to the water, and the only sound was that of the wind and the birds. It gave the feeling of being far removed from the world. When she turned to face the house, she noticed one of the doors stood ajar. Her skin prickled.

Maybe Mr. Randall was running late, and left the door open for her? Or maybe this was an elaborate ruse for someone to get a defenseless woman into an abandoned house, the monster whispered. Her pulse ratcheted up another notch.

No. She'd been corresponding as David Franklin, so no one was expecting a female. As long as she was here, and the door was open, why not explore? If Randall didn't show up, she'd head back to the resort and consider the missed appointment as karmic retribution for all of her lies.

Her footsteps left prints in the dust on the floor. She crouched down to wipe the dust away. The floors were honey-colored marble. The high coffered ceilings were made from mahogany. The walls bore some truly hideous Victorian wallpaper with flowers and gazebos and birds and…just way too much stuff. The massive fireplace was topped with a wooden mantel that stretched to the ceiling with an ornate carved scene of Saint George slaying a dragon. There were only a few pieces of furniture in the large room, and they were covered with drop cloths.

She wanted to see more of the house, and she *had* been

invited—sort of—but she still felt like she was trespassing. She caught a glimpse of massive iron chandeliers in the large room in the center of the house. Maybe just one quick look.

This house was sensory overload for a designer like her. Light flooded through tall leaded windows in the center hall. Twin iron chandeliers hung above her, with their curving black metal forms arching over the hall like protective birds of prey. The fireplace here was more subdued than in the other room, covered in the same golden marble as the floor and carved with a rose motif. She traced her fingers along the mantel, wondering what stories it could tell.

That's why she loved old homes so much—each one held a unique story. New homes had "potential," but she preferred a house with *history*. Someone had spared no expense a hundred years ago to create this beautiful space. And now it stood empty and smelled of dust and disuse. She absently patted her hand on the roses carved in marble, feeling sympathy for the sad old house.

She heard something that sounded as if it came from inside the house. Footsteps?

"Hello? Mr. Randall?"

There was only silence in reply. It must have been the wind she heard. Or perhaps it was just her overactive imagination kicking into high gear. She shrugged it off and continued exploring. Next to the front door, a stairway wound its way up the inside of the large tower. On the far side of the room, a semicircular glass atrium stretched across the end of the house. The glass was cloudy with age and neglect, and the mosaic floor covered with long-undisturbed dirt, but the atrium had been spectacular at one time.

The sketches she'd sent with her proposal were in black and white, created in a software program specifically for that purpose. They were filled with structural and furniture dimensions, accompanied with detailed lists of required supplies. They were accurate. But she knew now they weren't enough. Not for this house. Plans for this house needed color and emotion.

Amanda rested her hand on the paneled wall near the atrium, then closed her eyes and tried to get a feel for what the house might have looked like originally. It was a trick she'd used before to get a sense of the older apartments in the city she'd been hired to decorate. If only walls actually *could* talk. She pictured the atrium sparkling with candle-light, the metalwork along the roof painted bright white and the colorful floors restored. Exotic rugs scattered across the floor of the salon, creating cozy sitting areas by the fireplace and in front of the library. Lush but comfortable furniture filled this room and the living room. Everything she pictured reflected a sense of family and love.

None of that had been reflected in her proposal to Blake Randall. She pulled her ever-present sketchbook out of her bag, along with a fistful of colored pencils. She didn't have a lot of time, but she had to try to capture the personality of this home.

She lost herself in the drawing process, letting her creative muse take over. Flipping the pages hurriedly, she sketched the salon, then the dining room, which she'd envisioned as a home office. Eventually she went back to the living room, imagining it with touches of modern technology mixed with classic colors and…oh, wouldn't sailcloth curtains be perfect in here!

She heard another noise, and stopped her frantic sketching. She was sure it came from *inside* the house. Was it from upstairs, or the room next door? She tucked her sketchbook back into her bag and headed for the open door to the veranda, ready to flee if needed. Her pulse pounded in her ears. Was that a footstep behind her?

"Hey!" The loud male voice stopped her in her tracks. Panic slammed her heart against her ribs, and her vision blurred. Before she could force her feet to move, a large hand gripped her upper arm and a deep voice growled at her.

"What the hell are you doing in my house?"

Sometimes her panic manifested itself as rage, and she was thankful for that rage right now. It was the only thing keeping her on her feet. Instead of fainting dead away, she yanked her arm free and turned to face the man who'd just sent her panic levels into the stratosphere. Her knees threatened to buckle. Breathing felt like a battle between her lungs and the air she needed.

"Don't *touch* me!" she said with a hiss.

He released her immediately, but he was now blocking her exit. He was older than her—maybe midthirties—and tall. She was wearing heels, and still her head barely reached his shoulders. His features were sharp and his jaw strong. His eyes were the color of espresso, and thick black hair curled down the nape of his neck. He was dressed casually, as if he'd been working outside and just walked in.

She swallowed hard and tried to control her pounding pulse. She'd read once that the tiniest animal, when cornered, could become ferocious beyond its physical size. She drew herself to her full height, ignoring the barest hint of a smile that flickered across the man's face when she pointed her finger and started lecturing.

"You'd better get out of here while you still have the chance, because Blake Randall will be here any minute now to meet me!"

His right brow arched sharply, but instead of leaving, he leaned back against the door frame and folded his arms on his chest, a wide smile on his face.

"Is that right? Blake Randall? Well, that's interesting. Because *my* appointment is with a gentleman, not a nosy, trespassing woman."

Amanda's mouth fell open. *This* was Blake Randall. And

she was an idiot. She'd just blown any possibility of getting the job that was her last hope. The thought of crawling back to Kansas in defeat made her skin tight and clammy. She stepped back and bumped against the door, stumbling when it swung further open behind her. She hated this feeling of her feet being encased in cement every time she panicked, leaving her clumsy and slow.

"Jesus, relax." His voice lost some of its growl. "I'm just sick of people trying to sneak into this place like it's some shrine instead of being private property. What do you want?"

Amanda's lungs were rapidly constricting. *In with the good air, out with the bad.* She was having a hard time envisioning anything good in this situation. He ran long fingers through his hair, clearly running out of patience. She blew out another breath and her vision cleared. Her voice only trembled a little.

"You're Blake Randall?" She did her best not to grimace when he nodded once in reply. "The door was open, Mr. Randall. I assumed you were inside. I'm your ten o'clock appointment." She knew she should hold her hand out, but her aversion to touch made her avoid handshakes at all costs. Maybe he wouldn't notice. "I'm Amanda Lowery."

He barked out a laugh. "Do you think I don't know who my appointment is with? It's with—"

"David Franklin of Franklin Interiors. Yes, I know. I used to work with David. I was an associate at the firm. I'm the one who responded to your email." Someone at the office had taken a little too long closing her email account after she'd left. Randall's email had seemed like a gift—an answer to her prayers—when it showed up in her inbox a month ago.

"You responded *as* David Franklin."

"I responded as a representative of the firm." What she'd done was beyond unprofessional. Probably illegal. But she'd been desperate. She hadn't actually signed David's name to the emails, but she hadn't signed hers, either. She'd deceived this man. But what choice did she have after David smeared her reputation and left her unemployable?

"So you're here representing Franklin Interiors and their proposal?"

"Well…um…no. It was *my* proposal."

"So you work for another firm now, and you're trying to poach me from Franklin?"

"Not exactly. I'm…um…self-employed."

Panic started whispering more loudly in her head. This was a mistake. What if he called David? What if he called the police?

Instead, he just laughed. "Wow—you lost your job at Franklin Interiors." His gaze sharpened. "Fired or quit?"

"A little of both, I guess." When she'd confronted David for taking credit for her work, he'd slandered her with their clients. He and she had basically raced to get the words out after a client told her what he'd said. She was pretty sure her "I quit" beat his "you're fired" by a few seconds.

"And now you're bluffing your way into an interview for the renovation of a million-dollar mansion? You look like you're barely out of college." He stared at her for a long moment, and she just stared back, unsure if she should flee in embarrassment or stand and fight for the seemingly hopeless chance of getting this job. She pictured herself back in rural Kansas and straightened. She *had* to fight.

"I'm twenty-eight. I worked at Franklin for four years. I created the proposal that got your attention and led to this appointment. This house is magnificent, and I really ne—*want* this job."

He snorted. "Magnificent? This pile of rocks is a pain right in my ass."

Her panic was briefly forgotten. He had to be joking. This house was… She looked around and wondered once again at the connection she felt to the dusty, neglected structure. This house…was where she needed to be. She *had* to get this job. He hadn't thrown her out yet *or* called the cops, so that was something. He looked around the room as if trying to see what she saw.

"Everyone in town forced me to keep this place standing, but…"

Something clicked in her brain.

"Wait—is this the historic landmark they were talking about saving?"

"*Who* was talking?"

"The lady who owns the coffee shop was telling my cousin and me about it. She said some idiot wants to destroy the resort and a bunch of houses so he can build some awful casino. Everyone in town hates the idea, and hates the guy trying to…" Her voice faded off as she watched a variety of emotions cross his face, from amusement to anger to…regret? Her cheeks flamed. "And that guy would be *you*, right? You own the resort, too?"

He gave her a mock bow. "Blake Randall, the villain of Gallant Lake, at your service. But don't believe Cathy when she says *everyone* hates the idea. The casino will provide a lot of jobs for people around here if I can ever get approval from Albany." He frowned. "Cathy and her friends in the Gallant Lake Preservation Society managed to have Halcyon declared a landmark, so I have to put it to use, which is why I asked you…well, not *you*, apparently… to give me a proposal. Another firm suggested converting this into an office building, and leasing out whatever space we don't use."

"Using this house for offices would be criminal." She might have been having the worst summer ever, but she knew her stuff when it came to vintage homes like this. It was her specialty, and her knowledge gave her a spark of courage. "This was a family home once, full of love and laughter. It could be that kind of home again."

He looked at her as if she'd suddenly started speaking a foreign language. There was a spark of interest in his expression, but then he drew back and shook his head.

"Look, it took some guts to worm your way into an appointment under false pretenses, and I admire your ambition. But—"

"You liked my proposal just fine when you thought it came from Franklin Interiors. Have you suddenly stopped liking it?"

He shook his head. "Your proposal was the best one I received for residential use, but I'm not convinced a twelve-bedroom castle can ever really be a home." He looked around the dusty living room. "Even if I was, don't you think this project is a little over your head?"

"Why? Because I'm a woman?"

"No. Because you're young, you're alone and you can't possibly have the experience or the resources for a job like this."

His arms went wide, gesturing around the room, and she stepped back, rattled by the sudden movement. He wasn't going to hire her. There was no sense in begging. This had been her last hope, and she wasn't going to get the job. Tears gathered in the corners of her eyes. She'd have to go home to Kansas, where all her nightmares began.

She should get out of here now, while she still had some shred of dignity. She raised her chin, determined not to show him what a blow he was dealing her.

"It's clear your mind is made up. Excuse me." She moved toward the door, praying he'd just let her pass without coming any closer.

His brow arched high.

"That's it? You're not going to fight for the job after going through that elaborate ruse to get yourself here?"

This was nothing more than a game to him. He thought she was some nice young girl pretending to be a *real* designer. Wasn't that what David had called her? As much as she wanted to prove them both wrong, she had to leave. Now. There was a panic attack barreling down on her like a freight train, and she didn't want any witnesses. Especially one who already thought she was a poser.

She started to walk past him and out the door, but her feet refused to cooperate with her bravado, and she stumbled. *Damn it!* Out of the corner of her eye she saw him reaching for her. No!

Her arms flew out. He grabbed at her. *Shit!* She tried to push him away and break her fall at the same time, but she ended up on the stone floor, looking up at him as he gripped her shoulders.

"Careful! Are you o—" Their eyes met. "Miss Lowery? Amanda? Can you hear me?"

His hands were on her. His hands were *on* her! She couldn't speak. Couldn't move. Couldn't breathe. Her body trembled, making her head rattle against the marble floor. Her vision faded. The pain in her chest was so overwhelming she wondered if she was dying. She must have said as much, because a deep voice answered from much too close.

"You're not dying. You just need to breathe. Hold my hand and squeeze. Try to breathe."

"Can't…hurts… Panic attack…" Strong arms gathered her up.

No! But she didn't have the strength to struggle. Every ounce of energy was spent trying to pull oxygen into her lungs.

"Tell me how to help you." She could hear fear in his voice, and it raised her panic level even higher. She heard a keening wail of pain and realized it was her. Her lungs were on fire, and she could barely form words.

"Don't…touch me…"

A gruff burst of air blew across her cheek. "That's not an option."

She was moving, flying. Being carried. He was shifting her around and fishing for something in his pocket. Her breathing came in short, shallow gasps. She wasn't getting enough oxygen to hold on to consciousness.

From far away, she heard a disembodied voice and snippets of conversation.

"Julie?…yes, Amanda Lowery…staying at the resort… panic attack…at the house…" Amanda rested her head on a solid shoulder. It was almost a relief to give up her fight against the inevitable darkness. The last thing she heard were soft words against her cheek.

"You're okay. I've got you."

There was a fairy-tale princess sleeping in his bed, right down to the flowing locks of golden hair. She had the face of an angel. An angel princess. Blake scrubbed his hand down his face, leaning back in the tall chair.

"You keep doing that and you won't have any skin left on your face."

He glanced over his shoulder at Amanda Lowery's cousin standing behind him. He gave a soft, humorless laugh.

"It's been one hell of a morning, Mel."

The tall brunette leaned her hip against the back of his chair. "For all of us. The doctor said she's okay, though. He gave her a pill. She's just sleeping."

Sure, she was sleeping *now*. But an hour ago, she'd taken ten years off his life. The panic had consumed her like wildfire, and there hadn't been a damned thing he could do to stop it.

He'd carried her up to his room in Halcyon while calling Julie, the assistant manager of the resort. Within minutes, a pissed-off brunette charged into his upstairs suite, ready to rescue Amanda and accusing him of all kinds of things. Fortunately, Julie had been just a few minutes behind Mel, along with a doctor staying at the resort. Julie convinced Mel that Blake wasn't an ax murderer, and was actually the guy Amanda had an appointment with. Once Mel calmed down, she confirmed what Amanda had tried to tell him—that it had been a panic attack.

"Why were you so insistent on keeping her here?" Mel asked. "After you knew she'd tricked you into interviewing her?"

Mel sat carefully on the edge of the bed, looking first at Amanda and then at him. It had been no surprise when she'd reluctantly confirmed to Julie that she was the famous fashion model known as Mellie Low. Every move this dark-haired woman made was intentionally graceful, as if there was always a camera on her. If he was in the market for a relationship, she was far more his usual type than Amanda—tall, elegant and coolly confident. But he wasn't in the market. That wall he'd constructed around his heart after losing Tiffany was high and solid. Completely impenetrable. He relaxed back into the chair and met her questioning eyes calmly.

"I'm not a *monster*, Mel. She just about had a heart attack in my house, and nearly gave me one in the process." He dropped his voice. "I keep a few furnished rooms here for when I'm in town, so it made sense to bring her up here." He looked up and noted her skepticism. "At least it made sense at the time."

Mel studied him hard for a minute, and he felt sorry for anyone who got on the wrong side of this woman. Her eyes were sharp as razors. If she ever decided to be a cop, that violet glare would have suspects confessing their guts all over the place. She was trying to protect her cousin, and he respected that. It wasn't the kind of family *he'd* grown up in, but it was the way families were supposed to be.

"She's safe here, I promise."

Mel's shoulders relaxed a bit at his comment, raising a red flag in his mind.

"That hasn't always been the case, has it? She hasn't always been safe?"

"No." She hesitated a moment and glanced at Amanda before answering in a hushed voice. "She's had a tough summer. Lost her job. About to lose her share of a shared apartment. And she was…" Mel straightened as if she realized she was speaking out of turn.

"Someone hurt her," he said softly.

She pressed her lips together and shook her head, but Blake could see the truth in her eyes. Someone had put their hands on the pretty princess sleeping in his bed. That's why she told him not to touch her. Was it a boyfriend? A stranger? His fingers curled into fists against his legs.

"And the panic attacks?" Blake was trying hard not to care, but he couldn't stop asking questions.

"You've seen firsthand how bad they can be."

He nodded. When she'd first landed on the living room floor, he'd thought she was having a seizure. Then their eyes had met and he'd known she was trapped in some nightmare he had no part of. The glassy terror in her eyes would haunt him for a long time to come.

She'd been skittish before that, but he'd figured she was just feeling guilty about the little game she was playing. When she'd stumbled and he'd reached for her, there was nothing funny about the way she couldn't breathe, couldn't speak. She'd scared the hell out of him, that's for damned sure. He was *still* afraid. He couldn't shake it for some reason.

"How often does that happen?"

Mel shrugged. "It's a fairly new development, so I'm not sure."

"Is she getting help for it?"

She started to nod, then caught herself. "That's none of your business."

Amanda *was* getting help. That was good. But Mel was right. It wasn't his concern.

Amanda moved, and he and Mel froze, waiting until she settled on her side with a soft sigh, curled up like a child. Her hand lay on top of the blankets. He had the strangest urge to reach over and take her fingers in his, but he suspected Mel would disapprove. Besides, he'd never been much of a hand holder, except with his young nephew.

"The two of you are close."

Mel smiled. "There are actually four cousins all together, and we Lowery women are more like sisters. I just happened to be the closest to Gallant Lake this week, visiting a designer in New York. I thought her plan was so crazy it might just work, but if it didn't, I wanted to be here for her." She looked at him. "*Did* it work?"

Good question. "Well, she pulled off getting the appointment, but…"

"She's good, Blake. You'd be damned lucky to have her." He glanced at the woman in his bed, and Mel frowned. "As your interior designer, I mean. Did she show you her portfolio? It should be in her bag…" Mel got up and searched through Amanda's leather bag, pulling out a spiral-bound notebook. "I think her photos of other projects are on her tablet, but here's her sketchbook." She handed it to him.

He opened the notebook absently. Hiring Lowery would be a colossally bad idea. He prided himself on making shrewd business decisions, and she couldn't possibly handle this… He blinked. He was looking at a drawing of Halcyon. But not the Halcyon he knew. Not even the Halcyon he saw in her original proposal. This Halcyon had life to it. And color. The living room had a sectional sofa facing the fireplace, with a flat screen on the wall. And a gaming console in the far corner. In a castle. Could he really do that? He flipped the page. This was the room that had intrigued him the most about her original proposal—the one he thought came from David Franklin. She wanted to turn the dining room into a huge home office. He'd need that if he ever decided to live here.

He'd never been one for settling down in one spot, but now that his nephew was going to be a part of his life, maybe it was time. And maybe this was the place. Amanda's drawings made the old castle look like a home.

Chapter Three

Amanda was having the weirdest medieval dream. She was in a massive, heavily carved mahogany bed. The room was large and round, with a marble fireplace. Ribbed cathedral ceilings arched so high that she couldn't see the top of them in the shadows. Tall windows were set into the walls, framed with heavy damask curtains.

A wingback chair was pulled up close to the bed, and a man was sitting there with his feet propped up on the mattress, watching silently. But this was no knight of the round table. Unless knights wore jeans and a T-shirt. Black hair curled down over his forehead.

Blake Randall.

This was no dream.

She sat up with a gasp, pulling the blanket with her. Peeking under it, she was relieved to see she was still fully clothed, sans shoes. Blake didn't react, watching as if he thought she might bolt. And she was seriously considering it. Her memory came back in fragments—collapsing in the living room, being carried up a winding staircase. She couldn't quite make sense of it all, but she didn't feel in danger.

"Where am I?"

Blake sat up and dropped his feet to the floor. Leaning forward, he rested his elbows on his knees, clasping his hands in front of him. His voice was soft and deep.

"You're in my suite at Halcyon."

"What time is it?"

"One o'clock."

"Does my cousin know I'm here, Mr. Randall? Does anyone?"

His mouth quirked into a smile.

"I didn't kidnap you. Mel just left to get some lunch." His smile deepened. "And I think we've been through enough together to be on a first-name basis. Call me Blake."

"Oh, my God—did you *carry* me up here?" she all but squeaked.

"It wasn't a big deal. There aren't that many furnished rooms in this place, so this was the logical choice."

Dr. Jackson kept telling her she had to deal with the past in order to move on, but they needed to rethink that plan if it was going to lead to impossible situations like this, with her waking up in some stranger's bed. Blake must think she was some pathetic, weak little creature, and that wasn't who she was. She wouldn't let it be.

"There's almost smoke coming from your ears from all that worrying you're doing. Relax."

"I should go…"

"Mel will be back soon. Get some more rest, and after lunch I promise I'll release you."

Her eyes narrowed at those last words, but his smile said he was joking. She settled back against the headboard, doing her best to ignore her burning humiliation and impending homelessness. Back to Kansas. Goodbye career.

"Hey…" Blake moved to sit on the edge of the bed. "What's wrong?" To her shock, he reached toward her face. She froze. He gently brushed her cheek with his thumb to sweep away a tear she hadn't realized she'd shed.

"What's *wrong*? I made a fool of myself today. I lied to get an interview with you, and then I had a panic attack in the middle of it. It's ridiculous. *I'm* ridiculous." She forced herself to stop talking. If she couldn't get her emotions under control, she deserved to go home to Mom. Maybe she'd find some nice job in a furniture store selling people plaid sofas.

"Come on, you had a panic attack. That's a physical condition that's out of your control." His hand dropped to rest on the mattress next to hers. "I'm just glad you're okay."

"Clearly, I'm a long way from okay. You've been kind, but I've taken enough of your time. I need to go."

"Stay..." His hand rested on hers, and he stared at it as if he was as surprised as she was.

They both heard Mel's footsteps, and quickly pulled their hands away from each other before she walked in. She looked back and forth between the two of them suspiciously before fixing her gaze on Amanda, who was wiping the last of the tears from her face.

"What happened?"

"I'm fine." Amanda's hands were shaking. She tucked them under her arms and tipped her head toward the box Mel carried. "I'm also starving."

Her cousin stared hard at her, then shrugged. "If you're up to it, there's plenty of food."

They ate together at the kitchen island, Blake and the two women. Mel was staring at him with sharp skepticism. And Amanda wouldn't look at him at all. He set her sketchbook on the marble counter.

"I looked at your drawings."

Amanda straightened. "You went through my *bag*? While I was unconscious?"

Mel started to stammer. "N-no, honey. I did. I wanted him to see your portfolio and the sketchbook was there, so..."

"Those were just dash-offs, not something I'd ever show to a client, Mel."

Blake spoke before Mel could respond.

"Amanda, you were right this morning. I *did* like your

original proposal. That's why I set up an appointment with someone who turned out to be you." He smiled at the flush of color on her cheeks. "And these sketches really make your ideas come to life." He opened the book. "I mean, a sectional in the living room? With a wide-screen TV? You seriously think that can work in a castle?"

"Sure. Victorian is all wrong for this place, and for you, I'm guessing." He grunted in agreement. He hated all the pink and green wallpaper. She nodded with a smile. "Halcyon's architecture is solid enough to support whatever style you want. I'd stick with the classics but give it a modern twist with some pops of color and fun accent pieces." She was in her element now. She might be young, but she knew her stuff. Her proposal had been highly detailed and professional. Even those dashed-off drawings were compelling.

"You really think this can be done?" He gestured to her sketch of the office.

"Of course. It's mostly cosmetic work. There's no actual construction, other than the bookcases in the office. The only reason the budget is so high is because of the sheer size of the place and massive amount of horrible wallpaper you have to remove."

"I need it completed before Christmas. Is that doable?" Nathan clearly had no interest in giving Zach a family Christmas, so it was going to be up to Blake. His chest grew tight. He'd never bought a Christmas decoration in his life, but he had to do *something* for the boy. Amanda was staring at him with wide eyes.

"What are you saying?"

"I'm saying you're hired." He set her sketchbook on the counter. He didn't believe in impulsive decisions, but this just felt right. "You've sold me on your vision. So tell me how long."

"Aaand this just turned into a business meeting," Mel laughed, "which is my cue to leave. I might still make my spa appointment after all." She gave Amanda a quick hug. "I knew you could do it, sweetie." Mel looked at Blake. "You've made a good decision."

"I haven't accepted the job yet." Amanda's chin jutted out in defiance.

Interesting. A few hours ago she'd been begging for it.

Mel laughed again. "You two don't need me to figure that out. Just don't overdo it after this morning. Got it?" That last question was for him.

"Got it." Satisfied, she left them alone.

Amanda looked a little shell-shocked, and he wanted to give her time to absorb her new job. But her silence dragged on so long he started having doubts. He flipped through the sketchbook again.

"Are you suggesting painting the wrought-iron chandeliers *orange*? That's not a pop of color, it's… I don't know… an explosion?"

"It's not orange, it's paprika." She sounded prim and defensive. "It's a spice color. It brings a touch of fun and whimsy to the space. This should be a home where you feel free to kick off your shoes and relax without feeling guilty about it."

"I doubt *fun* and *whimsical* are words people normally associate with me."

"So surprise them."

He looked back at the drawings. "*You've* surprised *me*. Are you taking the job?"

She hesitated. "Don't hire me out of pity, Blake. I don't want your charity."

He gave her a steely glare that usually had his employees quaking in their shoes. She blinked, but didn't look away when he spoke. "I run a billion-dollar business. I don't make decisions based on pity. You're a designer out of work. I'm looking to hire a designer. Do you want the job or not?"

Her willingness to walk away from a job she needed

and obviously wanted surprised him. Finally she sighed
and pushed her plate away. "Let's take another look together and discuss it."

"I promised Mel we wouldn't over—"

"I'm not talking about taking a grand tour. But this
kitchen is too modern—it's an add-on, right?" He nodded. The 1990s kitchen was efficient, but generic. Amanda
grimaced. "I can't feel the house in here."

Blake had no clue what that meant, but he followed her
into the main hall. She rested her hand on the mantel and
smiled a secret little smile that made his pulse quicken.

"This was once a home so full of love." She looked up
at him through long lashes. "Do you know its history?"

"Yes. The stories are full of romance and tragedy—"

"Tell me the stories." Her gentle smile wasn't a secret
this time. It was aimed at *him*, and it caused him to stutter.

"T-tell you what?"

"Tell me the stories of Halcyon. Knowing the history of
a home helps me get a feel for its personality."

He shook his head. He wasn't a storyteller. No one had
read him fairy tales as a kid. No one had read him anything. Even the nannies were too busy for such frivolity.
He wondered if Zach liked stories. Had Tiffany used to
read to her son? "There are plenty of people around who
know the history better than I do. I just wanted the land,
not the legend."

"There's a *legend*? Now you have to tell me!"

He leaned against the mantel and racked his brain for
the history of Halcyon. He'd been disgusted with the whole
stupid story right up until the moment Amanda Lowery
fell in love with it.

"The house was built in the late 1800s by a wealthy
banker from New York named Otis Pendleton. His young
wife, Madeleine, fell ill, and they thought the country air
might cure her. She got better, and apparently Otis had

money to burn, so he built her a castle here. He stayed in the city during the week and came here on weekends to see her and the kids."

Amanda walked over to the ebony staircase and sat on the steps. He followed her.

"Are you tired? We can do this another time…"

She waved her hand in dismissal. "I'm fine, just taking it all in. Finish the story." He stared at her, and she gestured for him to get going. She was a bossy little thing when she wasn't a nervous wreck. He sat on the stairs below her, stretching his legs out in front of him.

"Pendleton lost everything in the stock market crash in the twenties. He took his own life, jumping out the window of his twentieth-floor Manhattan office." Amanda gasped. "Some people insist his brother pushed him. I guess there was bad blood there. The children were sure Otis never would have left Madeleine alone, because they were so much in love."

Amanda sighed wistfully, looking around the empty hall. He had a sneaking suspicion she wasn't seeing an empty room. She was picturing it as the Pendletons' home. He wasn't surprised she was a romantic. He was only surprised that he suddenly felt a bit of a romantic himself just telling her.

"Madeleine was grief stricken and took to her bed upstairs. She died before they could evict her and auction off the house. Supposedly she haunts the place."

"It's *haunted*? Have you seen her?"

He rolled his eyes. "Have I seen Madeleine Pendleton walking around Halcyon? Uh, no."

Amanda looked over her shoulder and up the winding staircase. He knew she was hoping to see some ghostly apparition, but there was nothing to suggest the place was actually haunted. Well…nothing other than some creaky stairs at night and the odd scent of roses in the solarium.

"What happened after Madeleine died?"

"Halcyon's been a little of everything—a boardinghouse, a motel…rumor has it, it was a brothel for a few years. It was deserted for a long time. A young couple with more money than good sense bought it back in the nineties and poured their penny stock fortune into it, trying to make it into a bed-and-breakfast." He glanced up. She was hanging on every word. "They're the ones that added the kitchen and the elevator. But there wasn't enough income to cover all the work they did. They closed it up ten years ago, and I bought it last year." It was surprising how comfortable it was to sit here and talk with her. He looked up at the wood ceilings, feeling more affection for the house than he'd felt since he'd bought it. "Most buildings fall into disrepair very quickly when empty, especially old ones, but this one held up surprisingly well."

"You've told me the stories, but what's the legend?"

He groaned. "Legend has it that Madeleine won't be happy until the place is a private home again, and that's why no business has survived here. I guess that means you're right. It wouldn't be a good idea to put offices in here."

She smiled, but it faded quickly at his next question.

"Are you taking the job?"

"I don't know, Blake. It's a bit overwhelming."

"You don't think you're capable of a project like this?"

She sat up sharply. "Of *course* I'm capable. I specialize in period homes. I can handle this." She gestured around her.

Blake gave her a triumphant grin.

"You *are* taking the job. And you can do it by Christmas?" It was suddenly imperative that he give Zach a happy Christmas this year to erase the memory of the last one.

"It's a lot of work to get done in a few months."

"You've convinced me this place can be a home, and I happen to need one. By Christmas."

Her forehead furrowed. "You don't have a home?"

"I use the owner suites at whatever resort I'm at."

"How many resorts do you own?"

He shrugged. "Five. You still haven't answered my question. Can you have it done by the holidays?"

"Some of the furniture will need to be ordered and may not be here in time…" Amanda looked around, and he could tell she was calculating in her head. It was a hot look on her. *Damn it.* He stood and moved away. Where the hell did *that* thought come from?

Her face scrunched, then relaxed, as if coming to a conclusion she approved of. "With enough skilled people, I could probably get most of the work done in time. I'll need a place to live…"

"If you want to commute from the city, I can send a car for you."

"Umm… I'm actually…between apartments right now. It would be easier to find a rental here in town."

He kicked himself. He forgot Mel had told him Amanda was losing her apartment.

"Stay here at the house."

He probably should have thought that idea through before saying it out loud.

"What?" She stood, her gaze darting around the empty hall. "Here? No."

"Look, it's a big place. There's a nice suite upstairs with a balcony. I'm leaving for Hawaii and Bali in mid-September—I won't even be here part of the time. I'd give you a room down at the resort, but September's probably booked solid for leaf season." He could tell she was considering it. "You can order your meals from the resort, of course. We'll configure lodging and meals as part of the package. I'll have Julie make all the arrangements. Her brother's a contractor, and he's done good work at the resort and around town. Bobby can handle what you're planning to do, and he can find workers locally. And don't worry about being alone here. The security system is excellent…" He was practically begging, and he had no clue why. He just knew he wanted her to say yes. She stared at him for a long moment, then nodded, all business.

"I'll need a week or two to pack my things and get settled. I'll need to meet with the contractor as soon as possible so we can set up a schedule."

"I'll call Bobby in the morning to set up a meeting."

He wasn't prepared for her next question.

"You don't even like this place, so why spend the money? Why the rush to be ready for Christmas?"

He started to answer, but emotion tangled up his words and kept them from coming out. He looked up at the high ceilings and blew out a deep breath.

"I have a nephew. He's my responsibility now that my sister is dead." He ignored her small sound of sympathy. "Being a nomad worked for me before, but that needs to change. I'd never considered this place an option before you showed up. It's close enough to the city to be workable for me. And Zach…well, a boy should like living in a castle, right?"

She started to laugh, then apparently realized he was serious. Yeah, he was damned serious. He had no clue what a ten-year-old boy liked.

"Blake, every child in the world would *love* to live in a castle." She patted his arm affectionately. "I'll make sure he loves this one when I'm done with it."

They exchanged business cards and cell phone numbers, then Blake called the resort and had someone pick her up so she wouldn't have to walk. He watched her go down the front steps. Her long blond curls swayed in counter rhythm to her hips. Damn, she was the real deal. Talented. Creative. And drop-dead sexy.

She was working for him now. Her voice and face

changed when she talked about design work. She lost her nervousness. And she'd be living in his house. He closed his eyes and grimaced. What the hell had he just done? He may have just created his very own hell here at Halcyon.

The sooner he was off to Hawaii, the better.

Chapter Four

When Amanda walked into the restaurant at the Gallant Lake Resort two weeks later, she could barely stay on her feet. Every muscle ached from packing up the apartment she'd shared with two other women. Doubts about her decision to take this job—to *move* here—kept her awake every night. Most of her belongings were now packed into a storage unit in the city. It was depressing to see how little space her entire life took up. And now she had to meet her general contractor tonight over dinner.

She'd settled into Halcyon that morning, unpacking her clothes and the handful of personal things she'd brought with her. The sunny yellow suite on the third floor would be her home for the next few months. An odd flutter of déjà vu had tickled up her spine when she stepped out onto the long stone balcony outside her room. But she hadn't felt afraid. If anything, the familiarity of it all made her feel more relaxed. And the room did have a spectacular view.

At first, she'd wondered why Blake Randall put her in the room right next to his. But after walking through the house, she realized there weren't many options, since so few of the rooms were furnished. The entire second floor was vacant. And the other tower room on the third floor clearly belonged to the young nephew he'd mentioned, since the bed was covered with teddy bears. A key to the house had been delivered to her apartment a few days ago, along with a cryptic handwritten note.

I won't be there to help you get settled, but two of
my employees from the resort will be waiting at the
house on Wednesday to assist with the move. I have
a meeting in Vegas, but I should be back Wednesday
night. Julie and Bobby will expect you to meet them
for dinner at seven at Galantè to discuss logistics.
Blake.

It was hard to believe the note had been written by the
same guy who'd brushed a tear from her cheek, but maybe
that version of Blake Randall was the exception, not the
rule. He was now her client, so it made sense he wanted
to keep things professional. And yet he chose to put her in
the suite next to his. She was too tired to sort out her feelings about that.

Galantè was the formal dining venue at the resort, with
a wall of windows overlooking Gallant Lake. It was mid-
September, and the lake was ablaze with the reflected colors from the trees surrounding it as the sun set. Amanda
glanced down at her tailored navy blue dress and matching pumps, thankful for the wardrobe she'd acquired back
when she was earning a steady paycheck. She was here
for a business dinner, and she could do this. Her exhaustion rolled off her shoulders as her adrenaline amped up.
The renovation at Halcyon would be the perfect project to
begin her own design firm.

Julie Brown, the assistant manager, waved from a table
near the windows. Julie and her brother, Bobby, weren't
twins, but they could have been with the similarities in their
looks and personalities. Both had thick brown hair, hazel
eyes, and warm smiles. Julie's hair was cut short in a lay-
ered bob. Bobby's hair was longer than his sister's, sweeping across his forehead and brushing his shoulders. They
had the same teasing sense of humor, and they laughed
often and easily.

Amanda leaned back in her seat after dinner, feeling satisfied. Not just about the food, but also about the design project. Bobby was more than qualified to tackle what needed to be done at Halcyon. He'd just finished building a custom home for a client, and he didn't have another job lined up, so his crew could start immediately.

Julie cleared her throat and folded her napkin carefully on her empty dessert plate. "Mr. Randall told me you're staying at Halcyon, even while he's gone." Julie shook her head. "You're braver than me, that's for sure. Anyway, I've made arrangements for housekeeping to go up there daily to take care of the living quarters and you can eat all your meals here at the resort."

"I don't need housekeeping, Julie. I can clean up after myself, and there's an old washer and dryer there I can use for my laundry. And I actually love to cook, so I'll feed myself…" Her voice faded when she saw Julie's smile disappear.

"Mr. Randall insisted on the housekeeping and meals. I don't think he'll be happy if you don't accept it."

Amanda rolled her eyes. She didn't want Julie to be in trouble with Blake. "Fine. Send housekeeping up twice a week to do the general stuff. But I'm washing my own clothes and I want to be able to cook. Is there a grocery store near here?"

"There's one on the other side of the village, but our chef can order whatever you want from his suppliers. Mr. Randall won't want you paying for groceries."

"Well, Mr. Randall isn't always going to get what he wants." The last thing Amanda needed was some man trying to take over her life. It was time to take on that role for herself. "I'm more self-sufficient than you might think based on seeing me pass out a couple weeks ago." Julie probably thought of Amanda as some frail thing. But she was certainly capable of driving to the store. Except for one problem. Keeping a car in New York City was ridiculously expensive, so she'd given hers up years ago. "Is there a vehicle I can use until I figure out my car situation?"

"The resort has a minivan…"

"Nonsense." Blake Randall's deep voice made Amanda sit straighter. He slid into the seat next to her. "Amanda can drive one of my cars or use the limo."

Julie slipped immediately into her professional persona. "Of course, Mr. Randall."

Amanda tried to picture herself going to the little grocery store in Gallant Lake in a limousine. Hopefully he had a vehicle she'd feel comfortable driving, because the limo idea wasn't going to work.

He shook Bobby's hand. "I'm sorry I couldn't be here for dinner. Have you made all the arrangements you need?"

Bobby's head nodded in acknowledgment. "Yes, Mr. Randall. I'll start ordering supplies tomorrow, and we'll set up next week to start stripping the walls. I grew up in Gallant Lake and I've always wanted to get inside that old house, so I'm really excited about this job."

They talked about the plans for Halcyon over coffee. Blake hardly looked Amanda's way as he walked her back to the castle when they were done. His stride was quick and tense, and she had to scramble in her heels to keep up. They'd hardly spoken since agreeing to this arrangement, and she wondered if he was having regrets now that she was here. Or maybe he was always this uptight. She tried not to sound out of breath.

"Is there anything you want to discuss?"

"No. Why?" He didn't even glance at her, and her discomfort grew.

"You seem…um…tense. If you'd be more comfortable with me staying somewhere else…"

"Do you *want* to stay somewhere else? Are you nervous about staying at Halcyon?"

"No, not at all." They walked up the back steps to the veranda, and the house glowed in the soft twilight. Nothing scared her about this house. "But I don't want to intrude on your life here."

He looked out to the lake, shoving his hands in his pockets. "I don't have a life here, Amanda. I'm a very busy man, and you're about to be a very busy woman with this project, so we won't be bothering each other much."

"I just don't want to be one of those annoying houseguests who gets underfoot."

His brows lowered. "You're not a houseguest. We're not roommates. You're an employee who happens to be using a room in a property I own. You're on your own here. You said you'd be okay with that."

"I *am* fine with it."

"Good."

"Fine."

He turned toward the house, effectively dismissing her. She'd upheaved her entire life to come here, and the exhaustion and uncertainty caught up with her, coming out of her mouth in annoyance.

"You know, for someone in the hospitality business, you can be downright *in*hospitable, Blake."

He stopped, then slowly turned back to face her. His dark eyes narrowed, and she braced herself. He was already having regrets, and now he was going to fire her. Where the hell would she go?

His glower lasted another moment, then he shook his head and…laughed. It was a soft chuckle, more at himself than anything. He squinted and looked at the darkening lake behind her, then met her eyes and smiled. Holy hotness, he had a great smile.

"I've never thought of it that way, but you're right. I *was* being pretty inhospitable, wasn't I? Good for you for calling me out on it. Most people don't." He rolled his shoulders and rubbed the back of his neck. "I'm sorry. It was a long flight from Vegas, capped off with another phone argument with my father. I didn't mean to take it out on you."

"You don't get along with your dad?"

He shrugged and frowned. "Never have. Did you get settled in your suite today? Do you need anything?"

She recognized the rapid subject change as deflection. She was good at that, too, and she decided to let him get away with it. He didn't owe her any explanations about his family life.

"The room is lovely, and I'm all unpacked. I'm going to head back into the city tomorrow to check out some design centers and look at furniture. If I can snag a few floor samples, I can save us some time on the remodel." She figured she could ask Julie to drop her off at the train station two towns over.

He shrugged absently. His mind wasn't on the remodel. Maybe he was still dwelling on the fight with his father. Or his nephew. Whom she hadn't met yet.

"Where is your nephew living?" she asked. "With your father?"

Blake snorted. "Definitely not. Zachary was with my brother's family for the summer, but he's at boarding school now."

"Boarding school? How old is he?" She didn't even know boarding school was still a thing, and there were teddy bears in the boy's bedroom.

"He just turned ten."

"*Ten?* And you're sending him off to boarding school? Why can't he go to school here in Gallant Lake?"

He laughed again, but there was no warmth to it. "To public school? I don't think so. Beakman Academy is in Connecticut, so he's not that far away. With my travel schedule, it's the best place for him."

"You make it sound like you're boarding a dog, not a little boy."

His face hardened. "Do you always speak your mind about things that don't concern you?"

She gulped hard, but stood her ground. "Just a minute ago you were praising my ability to call you out."

His brow arched, and her heart skipped. "You called me out on my treatment of *you*. My nephew's education has nothing to do with you." He glanced at his watch. "I have a conference call in a few minutes with the West Coast. I'll take it in my room. Good night, Amanda."

And this time, he really did dismiss her, walking into the house without another glance. She blew out the breath she didn't know she'd been holding and looked toward the lake. They were going to have to figure out how to live under the same roof and maintain personal boundaries. She'd obviously crossed his. His nephew, poor kid, was off-limits for conversation. Duly noted.

After spending Thursday furniture shopping in the city, Amanda met Julie for breakfast Friday morning. Blake seemed to spend most of his time in his office at the resort, getting ready for his trip to his other resorts. Julie introduced Amanda to the resort's chef. Dario Manzetti was short, round and energetic, and she liked him immediately. The charming Italian man referred to her as his little *bambolina* and kissed both her cheeks when they met. He had a machine-gun laugh that filled the large kitchen, and she couldn't help but laugh right along with him. His hands flew through the air in wild gestures with every word he spoke, and she wondered how he was able to cook and talk if his hands were this integral to communicating.

She worried he might be offended that she preferred to do her own cooking, but Dario was delighted. He agreed to order whatever supplies she needed, and smiled in approval when she wrote out her list of basic staples for the Halcyon kitchen.

That night, Blake surprised her with Chinese takeout from the village to share for dinner. They sat at the kitchen island and shared a bottle of wine as she outlined her and Bobby's revised plans for the house from their meeting that afternoon. The conversation was strictly business, but oddly comfortable. There was something about Blake, when he wasn't distracted and cranky, that calmed her perpetual undercurrent of tension.

The scaffolding went up the following week, with the marble floors covered with heavy canvas drop cloths. Halcyon was officially a construction zone. Blake left for the city early that morning, so he'd missed most of the noise and chaos. The surprise on his face when he returned that evening told her that, like many clients, he hadn't grasped how all-consuming this project was going to be. She bit back a grin as he walked carefully around the ladders and supplies. It was a good thing he'd be gone for a while on that business trip because it was only going to get worse.

She poured two glasses of wine and walked out to meet him in the main hall. He was staring up at the scaffolding with a frown.

"Every good project starts like this, Blake." She handed him a glass. "I know it seems overwhelming, but I promise I know what I'm doing."

"I'm sure you do." His words were more confident than his expression.

"Look, I know you're leaving Friday…" Saying those words out loud stung more than she expected. They hadn't spent a lot of time together. They'd shared a few meals, although there was never any cooking involved—he ordered food from the resort's restaurant or got takeout. For breakfast, he'd just grab a bagel and leave her lingering over her much-needed morning coffee. They'd never discussed anything too personal but still, the conversations flowed easily enough. She cleared her throat and smiled up at him.

"I'd like to treat you to a home-cooked dinner here tomorrow night. No takeout." His eyes widened in surprise, so she rushed to explain. "I want to do something to show my appreciation for…well, for everything. The job, certainly, but also for…being so generous. You know…after I lied and fainted and all that…"

He shook his head. "That's not necessary, Amanda."

"It is for me."

He finally shrugged, looking away to take in the construction site again.

"Will we be dining on a table made from plywood and scaffolding?"

"No!" She laughed and he glanced back at her, smiling warmly. That smile caused her to stutter a little. Must. Stay. Professional. "The—the solarium is dusty, but it's clutter-free right now, and there's a small table out there. I think I can make it work for dinner. Is six okay?"

"You really don't have to—"

"I want to, Blake. It's just dinner."

If it was just dinner, why did it feel like it might be something more? She shook herself mentally as Blake walked away. It *was* just dinner. It had to be. He was her client and she was a complete professional.

Blake stared at the reports spread across the desk in his office Thursday afternoon. He'd just finished a conference call with the construction crew in Bali. It was a good thing he'd be there soon, because things were moving far too slowly.

As usual, his thoughts drifted to Amanda. He couldn't seem to escape her this week. For a petite little package, that woman managed to be *everywhere*. He saw her in the mornings, all sleepy eyed and husky voiced until she had her second cup of coffee. He'd watched her with Bobby and the workers. She kept her distance physically, but she was smart and in charge, and they knew it. She got along well with Bobby, and they spent a lot of time discussing plans. Blake frowned. A *lot* of time.

He couldn't even escape her at the resort, where she and Julie had lunch together every day. He was glad the two women were friends so Amanda wouldn't be alone while he was traveling. But to turn around in the middle of the day and see her leaning against the front desk, her blond hair falling over her shoulder, laughing with Julie over some girlie thing...well, it made something twist in his gut.

He was doing his best to keep things strictly business with her. He tried not to allow their conversations to drift to anything other than the Halcyon project. Or, at most, to safe topics like movies and stuff. Nothing personal. It was the only way for him to keep that fortress around his heart standing solid. He did not want to get involved with her. Well, he *did* want to, but he wasn't going to. It was bound to end just as badly as every other relationship he'd ever had, and she was working for him. That was a level of messiness he wanted nothing to do with.

He frowned at the investment report he was supposed to be reviewing, then tossed it down and stood, and walked to the windows overlooking the lake. His mind went back to Amanda laughing with Bobby this morning. Bobby was single. He seemed like a good guy. His sister was Amanda's new best friend. Was Bobby interested in Amanda? Would he ask her out while Blake was traveling? Would she say yes? Would he come back home in a month to find that he'd lost her?

He cursed out loud in the empty office.

She wasn't his to lose! He tried to remember that, but it got tougher every day he spent with her at Halcyon. Maybe he should have left for Hawaii on Monday. He picked up

the report, then threw it down on the desk a second time.
Maybe he should walk up to Halcyon to see what she was
doing.

He found her in the living room. Talking with Bobby.
His jaw tightened. She gestured animatedly at the wall
of windows and doors facing the veranda. When Bobby
glanced in his direction, she turned midsentence to face
him. And nearly gave him a heart attack. She was wearing
skintight jeans and a snug blue top that matched her eyes,
with her hair pulled up in a long ponytail that swung as she
moved. Her clothes were dusty and a sheen of sweat glis-
tened on her forehead. She wore no makeup, and she had
a smudge of dirt on one cheek. He didn't think he'd ever
seen anything more beautiful.

He barely registered that there were two other men in
the room besides Bobby, up on ladders doing…something.
He walked straight to her as if she was pulling him in. She
was relaxed. Happy. Was it the job giving her more confidence? The house? Or was she finally becoming comfortable with him?

"Bobby and I were just discussing the window treat-
ments. There's a company that makes draperies out of
sails—they're actual used sails from boats. They're stitched
together and sometimes there's a random big number or
letter on them. They're so cool, and they'd be perfect for
this wall, with the water in the background. When the windows are open they'll move with the breeze. The look will
be so—" She stopped and sighed. "You can't picture it at
all, can you?"

No. He couldn't. But he loved that she could. "You're
the one with the vision."

"You'll love it. I promise."

A long ringlet of blond hair fell across her face. Without thinking, Blake reached out to push it behind her ear.
Her teasing smile faded and her eyes grew wide. He forgot

what they were talking about. He forgot that anyone else was in the room. He forgot everything except how beautiful she was. She swallowed hard and stepped back. He realized then that his fingertips had been resting on the side of her neck, just behind her ear. He cleared his throat and dropped his hand.

Her mouth quirked up into a half grin, then it faded. She was nervous. "Dinner's at six. I need to start getting ready."

With that, she walked away. Her jeans were tight, and her top was tighter. And something on him was a little tighter than normal, too.

He turned to look at the lake, trying to figure out how the hell he was going to be able to have dinner alone with her tonight. This wasn't take-out food at the kitchen island. It was a sit-down meal together. He wasn't sure he could come up with enough questions about the renovation to fill an entire dinner with business talk, and over the past week or so they'd covered every movie of the past century. Maybe he should invent some excuse to skip it. But the meal was already cooking—he could smell it. He was just going to have to control his attraction to his interior designer. Surely he was man enough to manage that.

Chapter Five

Amanda stepped back to admire her work. The beat-up old table was pretty now that it was covered with a crisp white tablecloth she'd borrowed from the resort. Blake mentioned one night over Chinese food that he hardly ever went into the solarium, and she wanted to show him how lovely the room could be as a casual dining and conversation area. The curved walls were lined with windows, with ornate white iron accents tracing up the high ceiling that radiated out from the stone walls of the main house. Tiny blue, green, yellow and white tiles covered the floor in a mosaic design. The room was in desperate need of cleaning and a coat of paint, but it was cozy and always seemed to smell of roses.

The kitchen was boring, but large and nice to work in. Sure, the oven was temperamental and utensils were sparse, but she enjoyed the challenge. She'd plugged her phone into a minispeaker, and her playlist was at full volume. She'd showered and changed earlier, and her long blue skirt swirled around her ankles as she moved. The pork chops were almost done, and a freshly made blueberry cobbler sat on the counter. If there was one thing she'd learned growing up in the heart of the Midwest, it was how to cook.

Bruno Mars was singing about all that funk. She tore up a head of fresh romaine for a Caesar salad, humming along to the music and dancing her way around the island. She was still singing when she grabbed the salad bowl to take to the table. She spun around and let out a squeal of surprise.

Blake was leaning against the doorway to the kitchen, arms crossed, watching her with obvious amusement. The glass bowl bobbled in her arms, and he jumped forward and took it from her.

"You were having such a good time that I didn't want to interrupt your performance." He was flashing her that smile that always melted her. "Are you planning on being my singing waitress tonight? If so, I'm not sure Mr. Mars is period authentic for Halcyon."

"A singing *chef* would be more accurate, I think. And I like Bruno." She turned to the oven to check the meal, ignoring his snort of laughter behind her. She opened the oven door and started muttering. "Damn it. This thing just doesn't want to stay lit." She turned the knobs back and forth a few times, and the pilot light started clicking before the oven came back on with a soft whooshing sound. "There we go."

When she turned back to Blake, he was staring at her with some combination of amazement and confusion.

"You're cooking dinner?"

"Yes." She spoke to him as if she was talking to a small child.

"You cooked it from scratch? It's not Dario's food?"

She straightened. Did he think she wasn't capable of cooking a meal?

"Well, I didn't go out and kill the pig, but yes, I cooked everything from scratch. Including dessert." She gestured to the blueberry cobbler sitting on the marble counter. "It's not that unusual for women to know how to cook, you know."

He looked at the dessert as if he'd just discovered a Rembrandt masterpiece sitting in his kitchen.

"I've never had a woman cook dinner for me before."

Her mouth dropped open. "Never? Not even your mother?"

He snorted and shook his head. "*Especially* not my mother. No woman has cooked for me unless she was paid to. My parents had staff, and now I always stay at my resorts, where *I* have staff. And the ladies in my life have all been firm supporters of restaurants and room service."

Her cheeks flamed. He was rich and handsome, and probably had plenty of "ladies" available to him. But she didn't need to hear about them.

He was still holding the salad bowl. "What would you like me to do with this?"

She rolled her eyes. Was he really this inept at having a simple meal at home?

"Unless you're planning to eat straight from the bowl, I'd suggest you set it on the dining table." His eyes narrowed at her sarcasm. "We're eating out in the solarium, if I can keep this damned stove running. Do you think you can handle pouring two glasses of wine for us? I've already opened it, so you don't have to be nervous about learning any other new skills." She nodded toward the bottle at the end of the island.

"You may want to stow that sharp tongue of yours, young lady. I'm not usually fond of being mocked." He was grinning again, playing along. She hadn't seen much of the playful side of Blake Randall. She liked it.

He walked out of the kitchen with the salad, then came back to pour the wine while she removed dinner from the oven. He watched in apparent fascination as she arranged the food on their plates and turned toward the solarium. She lifted her chin toward the wineglasses, and he obediently picked them up and followed to the table.

Conversation flowed easily over dinner. They talked about the legends surrounding Halcyon and his fight with the locals over his plans to demolish the building and the neighboring resort. She whispered a quiet prayer of thanks to the devoted citizens of Gallant Lake who weren't afraid to stand up to Blake and his wealth. They'd saved this wonderful house.

Blake's deep voice interrupted her rambling thoughts. "Hey, where'd you go?"

"Hmm? Oh, sorry." She pushed her empty dessert plate away. "You may not want to hear this, but I'm glad the house was saved."

His eyes went wide. "Are you saying you're happy I lost in court?"

"Yes, actually, I am. They preserved an important part of Gallant Lake's history."

"And do you support their fight against my casino, as well?"

She couldn't lie to the man.

"Yes."

He sat back in his chair and stared at her. "You continually manage to surprise me, Amanda. Your honesty is refreshing." The corner of his mouth twitched. "Even when it's irritating."

"Yeah, well, my therapist says honesty is always—" she held her fingers up in air quotes "—the 'fastest way through a problem' and I'm trying to follow her lead." She frowned. She couldn't believe she just quoted Dr. Jackson to him. She never talked about her therapy. She ran her fingers up and down the stem of her wineglass absently, wondering if it was the alcohol or the company that had her talking so freely.

"Tell me about what happened to you this summer."

Her head snapped up and she stared at Blake in surprise. "Wh-what do you mean?"

They stared at each other in silence. He reached for the wine bottle and refilled her glass. And waited. Damn Mel and her chatty morning with Blake the day Amanda fainted. She must have spilled more than she'd admitted to. Amanda took a deep breath and ignored her pounding pulse.

"It all started when I lost my job in May." The memory still galled her. She never should have trusted David. "It was one of the hottest new firms in Manhattan, and I was thrilled to be part of it." Until she'd discovered what David had done. How he'd used her. She did her best to appear nonchalant. "And then everything went to hell."

"Were you and David Franklin *together*?"

"Ew. No." Her face twisted. "But not for lack of trying on his part. He was more interested in my design ideas than me, though. He was taking credit for my work with the clients." David stole the one thing from her that she truly loved—her work. "He used photos of my work in his personal portfolio. Not as an associate's work, but as his own. I found out he'd done the same thing with other designers. Hadn't had an original idea for years. Instead of walking away, I confronted him."

"Good for you." Blake's voice was warm with admiration.

"Well, it didn't turn out very good. I'd been writing a proposal for a new client—a huge apartment in a historic building, overlooking Central Park. After I told David I knew what he was doing, he told my client I'd been caught overbilling another account. She refused to work with me." Amanda took a deep breath, still feeling the burning shame of that afternoon. "I went back to the office and found my things in a box. But they forgot to lock me out of the email server. That's how I managed to see your RFP for Halcyon." He smiled at that, and she couldn't help but return it. That rare burst of unethical behavior had worked out pretty well for her. And it served David right. "I had a small nest egg saved, but not enough to last long in New York. David started spreading all kinds of lies to destroy my credibility, just in case I decided to tell someone what he'd done. I couldn't get hired." Her eyes fell to where her fingers toyed with her wineglass. She hadn't taken a sip since he refilled it.

She didn't intend to tell Blake about what came next.

She really didn't. He'd never know the difference. What she'd already told him was surely bad enough to qualify as a Truly Terrible Summer.

He cleared his throat and she looked up as he started to speak.

"Franklin is a jackass. I'm sor—"

"I'm not finished." She inhaled sharply after she said that. Of course she was finished. She wasn't going to tell him about that night. *Stop talking!*

"I went out with some former coworkers in July." Oh, hell, that was *her* mouth that just blurted out those words. Blake's eyes widened, but he didn't speak. "It was late and I decided to walk home so I could think things through. And I was...attacked."

Blake had started to raise the wineglass to his lips, but now he set it back down on the table very slowly, as if he was afraid of shattering it. His eyes grew dark and intense as he listened.

"I was so deep in my own self-pity that I forgot to pay attention to my surroundings. A guy grabbed me from behind and forced me into a narrow alley. He reeked of cigarette smoke..." Her entire body shuddered at the memory. For the second time in her life she'd been helpless against an attacker. "He shoved me up against the wall and grabbed..." Her voice trailed off and Blake spoke, his voice gruff with emotion.

"You don't have to tell me any more."

She waved her hand at him in dismissal. "There's not much more to tell. I struggled. He put a knife to my throat and told me he'd kill me if I didn't do what he said."

Blake blinked, then blinked again. Son. Of. A. *Bitch.*

Amanda took a ragged breath and finished quickly. "A short-order cook stepped into the alley right then to smoke a cigarette, and he came running at the guy when he saw what was happening. The man took off. That cook saved my life." She tried to grin again, but couldn't hold it. "I guess my terrible summer could have been worse. It could have been my *last* summer."

She lifted her glass in a mock toast, but he didn't touch his. He couldn't shake the image of her body thrown against an alley wall. Thank God for that cook. This all happened in the past few months, and she was still standing strong. This woman was tough as nails.

"I'm sorry you had to go through any of that." They stared at each other in silence. The color that had drained from her face when she spoke about the assault returned now, turning her cheeks bright pink.

He could see her sweeping it all away in her mind. Tucking it in some safe dark place so she could go on with her life. She finally pulled her shoulders back and met his gaze. Yep. Tough as nails.

"I've made it to September—almost October now. Hopefully this job will be the start of a much better autumn. I'm looking forward to bringing Halcyon back to life." She stood and started picking up the dishes. "Now come help me clean up."

She needed to close the door on the conversation, and he was more than happy to help her do that. But cleaning up?

"I have staff for that, Amanda."

She rolled her eyes. She did that a lot. Then she laughed. At him. She seemed to do that a lot, too. And damned if he didn't like the way it made him feel.

"Oh, for God's sake, Blake, pick up the dishes and help me clean the kitchen. Housekeeping is only coming up twice a week, and I'm not leaving them my dirty dishes. Of course, if the dishwasher is as reliable as the stove, we may both end up with dishpan hands." She looked over her shoulder at him with a bright smile. And like an obedient little puppy, he found himself piling dirty dishes together and following her into the kitchen.

He set a stack of dishes and glasses on top of the cooking pan in the sink when Amanda reached out to stop him.

"What are you doing? You can't wash that fine crystal with the pots and pans! Have you *really* never washed dishes before?"

He stared at her in consternation. It never occurred to him that dish washing was a critical life skill he was lacking. Why did he feel embarrassed to admit to her that he was absolutely clueless in the kitchen?

"Um... I...didn't know..."

Her blue eyes went wide, sparkling with humor.

"Wow. I honestly thought you were exaggerating about no one ever cooking for you. But you really don't know anything about how a kitchen operates, do you?" She quickly pulled the greasy cooking pans out of the sink, replacing them with the dinner dishes. She set the crystal glasses aside while she filled the sink with soap and water. "You were born into a wealthy family?"

He turned and took a towel from the oven door. Surely he could dry a few dishes without embarrassing himself. When he turned back to face her, his breath caught in his chest. Her hair was falling loose tonight, curls rolling down her back. Her sweater matched her eyes. They were standing close enough that he could smell her spicy perfume. She looked up at him expectantly, but he was too busy getting lost in those eyes.

"Blake?"

"Hmm? What?" He took a step back in an attempt to regain his equilibrium.

"You came from a wealthy family?"

He grimaced. Talking about his family was a surefire way to cool his libido.

"Wealthy? Yes—the proverbial silver spoon. My father

comes from a long line of successful investors. My mother's Texas family made, then lost, a ton of oil money. She married my father because he could keep her in the lifestyle she felt entitled to. Mother thought manual labor was vulgar."

And then she'd decided motherhood was equally vulgar, but he didn't say that out loud. He glanced at Amanda, up to her elbows in soapsuds, and grinned. She was nothing at all like his mother. "No offense," he added.

She snorted. "None taken. My middle-class Midwestern family felt manual labor was somewhere akin to godliness. I've been washing dishes since I was five."

"I guess you had the quintessential perfect childhood, eh?"

Her mouth trembled slightly. "Not exactly perfect."

"Let me guess—you lived in a pretty little house on a tree-lined street with sidewalks and picket fences. Your happy mom and dad had two-point-four children and a dog. You were an all-American girl with long blond pigtails. I bet you were even a cheerleader in high school, the one all the boys chased."

A dinner plate started to slip from her hands, but she caught it before it hit the side of the sink.

"Amanda?"

The color drained from her face. He forced himself to stand still, cursing under his breath when he noticed how badly her hands were trembling. What just happened? He wanted to reach for her, but he had a feeling touching her would be the wrong thing to do.

She took a deep breath, putting that artificial smile on her face. Her overly musical voice sounded forced. "You only got the neighborhood right. I'm an only child. My father died at Christmas when I was six. My stepdad didn't allow pets, so there was no dog. And I *hated* high school." The last words were said with unusual force.

They fell into an awkward silence. The atmosphere in

the room snapped with electricity. Amanda worked at a frantic pace and flinched every time he brushed against her. He felt responsible for making her this way, but he didn't know what the hell he'd done. His jaw tightened. He didn't like problems he couldn't fix. He had to figure out how to fix this.

She hadn't been this uptight when she'd talked about everything that happened all summer. Why was she freaking out *now*, talking about her childhood? There were a lot of possible answers to that question, and none of them were good. She reached past him for a large roasting pan. It slipped out of her fingers and dropped with a loud clatter against the stone counter. She let out a squeal of fright.

Okay, enough was enough. The woman was going to give herself a heart attack at this rate. He set his hands lightly on her shoulders, being careful not to hold her too tightly, just enough to stop her perpetual motion. She stared, frozen, her breathing quick and shallow.

"Take a deep breath, Amanda. In and out, nice and slow. You're okay."

She did as he asked, closing her eyes and breathing deeply and evenly. Her body trembled under his fingers. *Damn it*. This was his fault.

"Amanda, I didn't mean to upset you. I don't ever want to do anything that scares you."

She sucked in a deep, ragged breath, looking so terribly lost and sad. Her eyelids fluttered open. She stared straight ahead, talking to his chest.

"You don't understand, Blake. There are days when… when everything scares me." Her voice was barely above a whisper. His heart jumped. He thought of that first day, when she ended up unconscious in his arms.

Everything scares me.

She'd kicked her shoes off earlier, and in her bare feet

the top of her head barely reached his shoulders. He put his fingers under her chin and gently tipped her head back.

He wanted to kiss this woman.

Wait. *What?*

No. That would be crazy. He couldn't kiss her. Shouldn't. But how could he not?

Her hair tumbled off her shoulders and down her back in golden curls. Before he knew it, his free hand was slowly twisting into those curls. She didn't pull away. Didn't look away. He lowered his head until his face was just above hers. He felt her breath on his skin. She smelled like citrus and spice and blueberries and red wine. Her lips parted and she stared at him with her enormous eyes.

"I swear I don't want to scare you, Amanda. But...may I kiss you?" His voice was a raw whisper. "Please let me kiss you."

His words came out as a plea. He'd never begged for anything before in his life. But here he was, begging this sweet thing for a kiss. Ready to drop to his knees if that's what it took. He heard his father's voice in his head, mocking his weakness. That's when he started to straighten, coming to his senses. Then he heard her whispered answer.

"Yes."

Was there any sweeter word in the world? Adrenaline surged through his body, and his hand tightened in her hair. His eyes opened to meet those two oceans of blue. Dangerous blue. Deep enough to drown in.

She was frightened, but she was trusting him. And that realization scared *him* to death. He raised his hand to cradle the back of her head as his lips brushed back and forth against hers. She shuddered in his arms and his mouth pressed to hers.

She stiffened for a heartbeat as his tongue ran along her lips. He slid one hand down her back and pulled her into him. He groaned, trying to be careful with her. But he wanted this so bad. A soft sound rose from her throat and, wonder of wonders, she opened her mouth to him. He was almost afraid to go further, but his body had a mind of its own. He tried to hold back, to take it easy, but there was just no damned way to do that. Her hands fluttered nervously at her sides, then moved up to clutch his shoulders. And her tongue…her tongue was pushing into his mouth now. He growled and pulled her closer. He didn't want to let her go. Ever.

When she finally pulled back, she looked up at him in amazement. *Right there with you, sweetheart.* Her knees wobbled, and he wrapped his arm around her lower back to support her.

He dropped his mouth to hers again and she moaned. Her hands slid from his shoulders to the back of his head; her fingers tightened in his hair. She stood on her tiptoes to press up against him. With a jolt, Blake knew he had to stop this before they went too far. Before she pulled him over the edge of the abyss. Just one more swipe around her marvelous mouth…

He set her back and raised his head, trying to gather his bearings. He held her upper arms until she steadied on her feet. They stared at each other in stunned silence.

She lifted her trembling fingers to her lips, which were beautifully swollen now. He could see the struggle in her eyes. The uncertainty. Then she raised those fingers to the side of his face, holding the palm of her hand there against his cheek. He leaned into it. The atmosphere changed in a heartbeat from electric to serene. It was the most intimate moment he could recall in his life.

"I—I—I should go…" She was whispering, stammering. She pulled away and he watched in silence as she left the kitchen. He rested his hands on the edge of the counter and dropped his head, trying to regroup, listening to her footsteps climbing the stairs.

This was bad. And not just because she worked for him. She was vulnerable, and Blake was beginning to realize that he was, as well. He suspected neither of them could handle one more failure, one more heartbreak.

He wouldn't be able to help Amanda any more than he'd been able to help his sister, and he'd adored Tiffany. Losing her had shattered him. That's when he'd built that sturdy wall around his heart. But that carefully constructed wall suffered some major structural damage just now when he'd held Amanda in his arms and kissed her. Something was fluttering and flickering to life inside a heart he thought had broken forever in December.

The earth had just shifted beneath his feet, and he had no idea what the hell was going to happen next.

Chapter Six

Amanda stood on the balcony outside her room and watched the sun come up over the mountains that surrounded Gallant Lake. The untouched mug of coffee in her hand was growing cool. She was still reliving last night. Still reliving that kiss. Trying to figure out what it meant, and what was next.

Intimacy, if a kiss could be considered intimacy, was something she only did reluctantly, because a date expected it. Never because it did anything for her. She thought that part of her—the woman part—had died forever on an October night in Kansas twelve years ago. She'd tried—she wasn't a virgin, for heaven's sake. But those few awkward encounters in college, and some fumbling attempts in recent years, had convinced her she was simply no longer wired to enjoy things like kissing and sex.

But last night… Blake's touch hadn't frightened her. When his lips had touched hers, something inside her had risen up like a phoenix from the ashes of her shattered past. The fire had started in her chest, then spread to every nerve ending in her body. She'd been burning for more. More kisses. More Blake.

And *that's* what frightened her.

She was dressed and ready for the day, but she was standing out here, afraid to face him. She was making herself crazy. She leaned back against the stone wall and sighed. This long, narrow balcony felt like a safe place.

A soft knock on her door made her flinch.

"Amanda? May I come in?" Blake sounded uncharacteristically tentative.

"Yes. I'm outside." She couldn't bring herself to walk in and open the door, and instead listened to his slow footsteps.

He looked away from her as soon as their eyes met. He had regrets. *Damn it.* She looked out over the lake in silence, waiting for him to speak because she couldn't.

"I'm leaving in a few hours." He glanced at her and frowned. "I think I owe you an apol—"

"Don't! Don't you dare apologize." His eyes went wide at the vehemence in her voice. She took a deep breath and continued. "It doesn't ever have to happen again…it shouldn't…it *won't*. But please…don't tell me you're sorry."

He walked to where she stood and stared at her in silence, tilting his head as if trying to read her thoughts.

"I don't regret kissing you, Amanda. I just didn't know how you felt…if I overstepped some boundary." He cleared his throat, put his hands on her shoulders and gave her a boyish grin. "But I am damned sure *not* sorry I kissed you. In fact, I'd very much like to kiss you again."

She put her hand on his chest to keep him from coming closer. Again? Could she stay here if he kissed her again? Would she ever be able to leave?

"Blake, you may do this sort of thing a lot, but I don't. I've never felt what I felt last night, and if it means something different to you, something less than what it was to me, then I can't…"

Her words stopped when his lips touched hers. The kiss was demanding at first, as if he were trying to prove something to her, or to himself. Then he softened his movements and tenderly moved his tongue against hers. He raised his head, then lowered it again and kissed her some more. She couldn't seem to move her body, but her mouth responded, and a low moan rose up from her chest. Her hands finally grabbed on to his shirt and she twisted the fabric beneath her fingers. He growled in return.

He pressed her back against the wall. As soon as her shoulders hit stone, she panicked and started pushing against him. He quickly stepped back and released her.

"I can't...oh, God..." She wrapped her arms tightly across her body, gasping for air. He touched her shoulder, but she shrugged him off. "I'm too much of a mess right now." She gave a short laugh. "Who am I kidding? I've been a hot mess for years. I'm sorry. I'm not capable of doing—"

"Stop." His voice was gentle, and he brushed her cheek with his knuckles. "You're scared. I get it. I pushed too hard. But damn it, Amanda, you make me lose my head." The next words were barely a whisper. "You just make me lose my head."

Her eyes closed at his touch. Her heart was racing. "I still don't understand what any of this means, Blake."

"Neither do I." He took a step back and her skin burned from the loss of his touch. "To be honest, the last thing I want or need is any kind of relationship. I'm no good at them. I don't have the time. But you..." He cleared his throat, and the shutters came down in his eyes. Business Blake was back. "Let's just take it a step at a time, okay? And the next step is me leaving for a while, so we'll both have plenty of time to think it through." He shook his head. "Come have breakfast with me. Oh, and there's a delivery team coming this afternoon with appliances for the kitchen."

She raised an eyebrow at him and he lifted a shoulder in return.

"I'd rather you didn't blow the place up now that I'm spending all this money on it," he teased. "I spoke with Dario last night and he called a restaurant supply friend of his in the city."

Amanda just shook her head. He was back in control of the world around him, which is where he liked to be.

Three hours later, she was standing on the front porch saying goodbye to him.

The delivery team was installing new stainless steel appliances. She stepped aside as three men wheeled in an enormous Sub-Zero refrigerator.

"Hey," Blake said, "I have to go." She looked up at him. Her palms started to sweat. As many times as she'd panicked over a man touching her, she'd *never* felt this burst of fear over one walking away. "I'm not sure how long I'll be gone, but probably close to a month. There's a conference in Honolulu, and then I have to get the Bali project back up to speed." He looked up at the castle behind her. "This is why I gave up on having a home base before now. I'm never in one place for very long. But it's time to settle somewhere. If you have any issues or questions, don't hesitate to reach out. And please don't forget Jamal."

She'd met with Jamal Brickman, the head of security for Gallant Lake Resort, a few days ago. The former marine had worked to put her mind at ease, explaining all of the security measures and cameras. Jamal told her it was all part of Blake's No Surprises Lifestyle. He wanted his security team to *prevent* bad things from happening, not just respond after the fact.

"If anything or anyone bothers you, you contact him immediately, understand?"

She rolled her eyes. "Yes, Dad..."

There was a glimmer of amusement in his eyes. "Never mind your smart mouth." His eyes dropped to her lips. For one brief moment, she thought he was going to kiss her again, and she wanted him to. He raised his hand and gently ran his fingers across her cheek instead.

"I've never hated to leave home before. But here I am, standing like an idiot, just staring at you."

Did he like what he felt, or was he appalled by it? She finally just smiled up at him, saying what needed to be said.

"You'll miss your flight if you don't get going. I'll be fine here. Halcyon likes me." She looked fondly up at the rose-colored tower next to the entrance. "And you're going to like Halcyon when I'm done with it. But you already told me you don't like chaos, and that's all there's going to be for a few weeks. Wait until they start sanding the walls. The place will be an absolute mess."

"It's not the chaos in the house I'm worried about. It's what's going on in your head." He tapped her forehead playfully with his knuckles. "Don't work yourself into knots over this…whatever it is…that's going on with us. Maybe it won't be there when I get back. If it is, we'll figure it out then. But in the meantime, no regrets and no overthinking. We both have jobs to do. Right?"

"Right. Have a safe trip, Blake. I'll keep you posted on the progress."

"Oh, I almost forgot," he said, reaching into his pocket. "Here's the key to the Cadillac. And the remote for the garage." They both looked up the hill to the carriage house.

"Don't worry, I won't put a scratch on your fancy car. Now go, or you really will miss your flight."

They looked at each other silently, then he turned and walked to the waiting limousine without glancing back. She watched the car move around the circular drive and down the hill. It was just her and Halcyon now.

Chapter Seven

A little over a week later, she was seriously questioning her relationship with the old house. She stood in the center of the main hall and sighed. She was hot, dirty and exhausted. The house was a complete disaster zone. They were at that most miserable stage of a renovation, where you had to make things look horrible before you could start making them beautiful. Halcyon had officially reached the apex of horrible.

Dust covered every surface. Strips of stubborn wallpaper still hung from some of the walls, while other walls were paper-free and sanded, ready for paint. But the crew couldn't start painting until *all* the sanding was done. The mingling of all the chemicals and dust had given her a permanent headache. The volume of work still to be done made that headache worse. The huge iron chandeliers were down. Bobby had a friend with a body shop who was going to paint them with a high-gloss auto paint.

In a moment of insanity last week, she'd decided to surprise Blake by redecorating the master suite while he was gone, so the upstairs was a mess, too. Bobby's crew of workers were friendly enough, but it was stressful for her to have a crowd of men she didn't really know in the house day after day. Bobby made sure no one bothered her, but she'd still had a few flutters of panic in the beginning. She'd managed to hide it well. She lifted her camera and started taking more pictures. She couldn't let her panic attacks derail this job. Exhausting as it was, this project would be the foundation of her portfolio so she could start her own design firm, and she needed to document every messy step of the process.

She and Blake had spoken a few times, and texted almost daily, but he seemed to be firmly in business mode while on his trip. He said his days were filled with meetings. Their conversations had been about the house and decisions that had to be made. And that was okay. It proved the kiss they'd shared was an aberration, and it was better for both of them if they just moved on.

"Happy Monday!" Bobby's cheerful voice echoed in the main hall as he came in with five of his men.

"Hi, Bobby. Ready for another week of destruction and mayhem?"

He laughed. "We only have a few more days of stripping and sanding down here, then we'll start painting. Are you ready to have those chandeliers painted? My buddy can pick them up today."

"Yep. Paprika it is. I want the highest gloss possible. It will bring just the right touch of fun to the hall."

Bobby shook his head and smiled. "I still can't picture Mr. Randall liking orange chandeliers, but you're the boss." His workers started filtering in and getting to work. The marble floors were scheduled to be polished next week, so they were going to have to remove all the scaffolding before then. With a little luck, they'd make Blake's Christmas deadline. Bobby looked over her shoulder to the door.

"Hey, little dude. You lost?"

Amanda spun around. A young boy stood in the doorway. Shaggy black hair hung over his chocolate-colored eyes. He looked both defiant and frightened.

"Is my uncle here?" he asked.

Amanda's mouth dropped open. Was this Blake's nephew? The one sent to boarding school?

"Are you Zachary?" The boy nodded cautiously. She stepped toward him. "Hi, my name is Amanda, and I work for your uncle Blake. He's not here. Did he know you were coming?"

Zachary shook his head. "No." He squared his shoulders, his eyes narrowing as if bracing for a confrontation.

She glanced at Bobby, who looked even more baffled than she was. The workers were watching with interest. She could see Blake in the boy's wide brown eyes, and smiled.

"Hi, Zachary. Your uncle told me about you. You're ten, right?" He barely nodded. "Why don't you come in and tell me how you got here."

He stared at her. "Call me Zach. I rode a bus."

Her mouth dropped open. "You took a bus *alone*? Zach, that was so dangerous!"

Zach shrugged. "I know. But I got here."

She was stuck somewhere between shock and laughter. Not only did he have Blake's looks, he had Blake's attitude, too. She stepped aside and he walked into the hall, looking at the renovation with interest.

"Zach, you were lucky. *So* lucky. But yes, you're here. Now tell me why."

"I didn't want to be in school anymore. They were mean to me. So I ran away." His feet shifted. "I won't go back there." His voice got stronger. "I *won't*…"

"Zach," Amanda said, raising her hands to stop him. He watched her carefully. She hoped he could see how sincere she was. "You don't have to go back. Not right now." His small shoulders relaxed. "Have you been to Halcyon before?"

He nodded. "Once. Last winter. After my mom died. Didn't look like this, though."

This poor child had been through a lot. "I'm sorry about your mom, Zach. I'm going to call your uncle and let him know you're here, okay? Are you hungry?"

He hesitated, and Bobby stepped forward. "I'll take him down to the resort for something to eat while you call

Mr. Randall." He smiled at Zach. "My name's Bobby, and I'm a friend of Miss Amanda's. Let's go grab some food, then you can help us work on this old place, okay?"

Zach gave Bobby that calm, much-older-than-ten gaze, then slowly followed Bobby out the door.

Amanda reached for her phone, glancing at her watch. It was eleven o'clock. In Hawaii it was, what…five in the morning? He was probably asleep, but he needed to know. She sent a quick text.

Zachary is at Halcyon.

Her phone rang almost immediately. She hadn't heard his voice in a while, and she'd never heard him this furious.

"What the hell? He's supposed to be at Beakman Academy. What happened?"

"Zach ran away. He said they were mean to him."

Blake gave a heavy sigh. "Yeah, well, Zach inherited his mother's flair for drama. How the hell did he get there?"

"Believe it or not, he took a bus."

"Excuse me?"

"He took a bus. Alone."

"A *bus*. From Connecticut."

"When I pointed out how dangerous it was, he basically said, 'I got here, didn't I?'"

Blake barked out a laugh.

"I know it's not funny, but damn, that kid's gonna kill me yet. Let me talk to him."

"He's down at the resort with Bobby. I figured he was hungry."

He paused. "Right. Okay, I'll call Beakman and see what happened. In the meantime, I'll see if my sister-in-law will come get him."

Amanda didn't hesitate. "He can stay here. I'll watch him."

There was something about the kid—maybe the loneliness in his eyes, or the defiance—that touched her heart.

Blake sounded stunned. "You? You're running a major renovation project. Now you want to be my nephew's nanny, too?" She was being impulsive, which wasn't her usual style. But she felt strongly that Zach belonged here. Blake blew out a long breath. "You've seriously blown my mind with this call. Zach's there now, so…sure, if you don't mind, keep him with you for a couple days. I'll call the academy to smooth things over."

"I'm happy to take care of him. But please reconsider the academy, Blake. Something happened there. And he's so young."

"He's had a rough year, Amanda. The school gives him the structure he needs."

"But—"

"This is a family matter, and I'll handle it. Just watch him for a couple of days until I can make some calls. Okay?"

"Fine."

"Thank you. I'll be in touch."

And he was gone. She was now responsible for the safety and well-being of a ten-year-old boy she'd just met.

Life here at Gallant Lake just kept getting more and more interesting.

Chapter Eight

Zach lay down on the old chaise in the living room after he and Bobby returned and fell fast asleep, even with all the work going on around him. When he finally woke, he joined Bobby in sanding the walls. He was reserved, but by the time the workers left, he'd started to relax. He must have started to trust Amanda's promise that he really was going to stay at Halcyon. At least for now.

They talked a little over dinner, and he told her how some of the boys in his class had started bullying him, hassling him about having a mom who was a "druggie." It went from verbal to physical, and *Zach* was the one who got in trouble when he'd fought back. When it had happened again, he'd decided to leave.

"My mom told me it was wrong to get mad and fight. She said people should get along. But…" He took another big bite of the brownies she'd baked. "That didn't work. Uncle Blake said he was here if I needed him, and I figured I did. I knew there was a bus that came this way, and the old lady at the station helped me. I told her my grandma was sick. She had me sit with her until the bus came, then she yelled at the driver to let me sit behind him."

Amanda closed her eyes, sending a silent prayer of thanks that a kindhearted stranger made sure Zach stayed safe on his foolhardy journey. She could see he was still tired, so they went upstairs shortly after dinner. She checked the dresser in his room, relieved to find a few clothes that looked like they'd still fit him. Zach's face fell when he looked at the bed, covered with teddy bears.

She smiled. "I bet Bobby and I can make this room look a little more grown-up for you. Maybe paint it in the color of a sports team you like?"

His face brightened. "Can we do pinstripes? For my favorite baseball team?"

"I'm sure we can come up with something like that." The suite was the mirror image of Blake's, with a circular sitting area and fireplace. She looked at the door that opened to the small balcony. A third-floor balcony was a bad idea for a child's room. She walked over and tried to turn the knob, but the door didn't even jiggle, as if it was sealed shut.

Thanks, Madeleine.

She didn't *actually* believe in ghosts, but she'd started blaming, or thanking, the legendary ghost of Halcyon for anything she couldn't explain in the house—from strange noises at night to curtains that seemed to move without a breeze. Old houses were full of mysteries like that. Like sealed balcony doors.

"Are you and Uncle Blake going to get married?"

Amanda started coughing violently, caught off guard by Zach's unexpected question.

"No! No." She caught her breath. "No, Zach. We're… friends. I work for your uncle."

"But you live here."

"That's only temporary, while I oversee the remodeling." The idea of leaving Gallant Lake made her sad. The fact that she had no idea where she'd live or what she'd do made her anxious. But at least she had some company while she was here—it had been lonely since Blake had left. She grinned at Zach.

"And now *you* live here, too. Temporarily, at least."

Zach jumped to his feet. "I won't go back to Beakman! If you try to make me go, I'll run away again."

"*Why*, Zach?"

"I hate it there." He dropped his head. "Last week was

parents' weekend, and no one came. That's when the other boys started teasing me."

"Oh, Zach, I'm so sorry. Your uncle was in Hawaii, so he couldn't possibly..." It only took one accusing glare from the boy to silence her defense of Blake. Because leaving this kid on his own at a boarding school was indefensible. What was *wrong* with Blake and his family? Why weren't they taking better care of Zach?

"Let's take things one day at a time, okay, Zach? For now, you're here with me, and you can help Bobby and me with the house until we figure out the school situation. Maybe you can go to school in Gallant Lake..." She never should have said that aloud, but Zach jumped on it.

"You mean *stay* here? For real? Could I ride the school bus? I've never ridden a school bus! Would I be here for Christmas?"

She pulled some pajamas from the dresser. "That's up to your uncle." She tossed the pajamas on the bed and gestured toward it. "It's time for bed. And, Zach?"

He looked at her with cautious brown eyes. "Yeah?"

"I promise I'll talk to your uncle about school, but I want *you* to promise you won't run away from here. From me. You're going to have to trust me, okay? And *stay*?"

It was either that or she'd have to sleep outside his door every night to make sure he stayed put. But he nodded.

"I promise. But I'm *not* going back."

He was asleep within minutes. Amanda sent a text message to Blake from her room.

Please don't send him back to Beakman.

Blake didn't respond, so she waited. A full day passed, and no reply. She texted again.

We need to talk. Zach can't go to Beakman.

Nothing.

After a few days of awkward and often one-sided conversations between Zach and her, Zach seemed to have decided that Amanda was not only *okay*, but was also his guardian angel. Probably because she hadn't sent him away. He'd hugged her for the first time the day after his arrival. Once she'd recovered from her surprise, she'd hugged him back.

He seemed to crave human contact. She wasn't normally a hugger, but she made an exception for Zach. Especially after he told her one night that his mom used to hug him all the time. If he needed her to be a surrogate mom, that was okay with her. For one thing, it meant he was less likely to try to run away. And for another…she found *she* was getting as much from those hugs as he was.

They established their ground rules quickly. He had to be sure she always knew where he was. If he went down to the resort, he had to obey Miss Julie and Mr. Jamal. Zach followed Bobby around Halcyon all day, so Bobby put him to work pulling off wallpaper and sanding walls.

His uncle seemed to have just forgotten about him, but Zach should be in school somewhere. It felt as if no one in the Randall family wanted to give any thought to this lonely little boy. She wondered how his mother died, but she didn't want to ask him to talk about it. Her own father had died at Christmastime when she was young. Was he seeing a counselor? Did anyone think to get help for him? Her fretfulness over Zach's well-being shook her to the core. She wanted to look after him the way that no one had when she was young.

When Blake ignored her third text in three days *and* a voice mail, she angrily decided to take matters into her own hands. She cared about Zach, even if no one else did. She talked to Julie, who had friends at the local elementary school. Amanda took Zach to the school and they met Bruce

Hoffman, a fourth-grade teacher. The principal, Elizabeth Cantore, sat in on the meeting. Zach liked Mr. Hoffman, and Amanda did, too. The teacher's dark hair was pulled back into a low ponytail. Dressed in chinos and a chambray shirt with Birkenstocks on his bare feet, his eyes were kind and he seemed genuine. An hour later, it was all arranged.

Zach would attend school as Zachary Lowery to protect his identity. The Randall name was well-known in Gallant Lake, and not in a good way. Even Bruce admitted taking part in protests against the casino, but he vowed he'd never saddle Zach with that. Zach was more excited about riding the school bus than anything else.

She finally heard from Blake that evening. She was just settling into bed when her phone chirped with a text message.

I talked to the headmaster at Beakman. They've agreed to give him another chance. They'll send a car for him.

Her response was almost as swift as the rush of anger she felt.

That's a bad decision. Really bad. The worst.

Her phone rang in her hand. Blake. Finally. He didn't wait for her greeting, just started right in. "Not that it's any of your business, but why is it a bad decision?"

"Well, for one thing, you haven't even asked *why* he ran away. They bullied him, Blake. And when he reported it to the headmaster, they didn't believe him. That's why I've been trying to reach you. He can't go back there. Please..." Her emotions overwhelmed her, and her voice broke. Blake was quiet for a moment, and was much calmer when he spoke again.

"I didn't know that."

"Of course not, because you never returned my messages. Do you know *why* it got so bad? Because none of your family went to the parents' weekend. He was the only one with no family there, Blake, and the kids picked on him."

"Shit. I meant to ask Nathan to go." He sighed. "I can never seem to do the right thing for him. I don't know *how* to do the right thing. I have no idea why Tiffany left him to *me* of all people…"

She couldn't argue that he was making a mess of being Zach's guardian, but she also felt a stab of pity for him. He sounded lost. "It's okay, Blake. He's fine now, and he likes it here in Gallant Lake. I've enrolled him in the local school…"

"Public school is not the answer, Amanda. A good private school will give Zach what he needs. I'll talk to Beakman and make sure they keep an eye on things, but Randalls don't go to public schools—"

"But he wants to go to school here, and he's really excited about it. Please, Blake…"

"Of course he *wants* to. But you can't just let children do whatever they want. He doesn't get to make this type of decision for himself. The answer is no." His voice was firm and businesslike. "I'm headed to Bali tomorrow, so communication will be sketchy, but I'll have Beakman contact you to let you know when they'll pick him up. He'll be fine. Tell him he can come back to Halcyon for Christmas."

"But, Blake…"

"Amanda, I have a meeting to get to. I'm sorry you got caught up in this family mess, and I really am grateful for what you've done for the boy. I'll pay you for your time and trouble. I know he can be difficult."

"This isn't about money!" She didn't give a damn about his money. "He is *not* difficult! He's a kind, loving little boy. He needs a stable home that makes him feel safe. He loves it here at Halcyon. He wants to ride the bus to school with the kids in Gallant Lake..."

"That is not going to happen. He'll be fine. I'll be in touch." And he was gone.

She leaned back against the headboard of her bed. What Blake didn't know wouldn't hurt him, right? She was going to send Zach to school tomorrow in Gallant Lake as planned, and she'd deal with the Beakman situation somehow. She'd fibbed to get this job, so what was one more little lie? She wasn't going to let Zach sit home while Blake wasted his time messing about.

A week later, her cousin's silence on the other end of the phone call spoke volumes.

"Say *something*, Nora." Amanda stared out at the blue waters of the lake from her balcony. It was early October and days were turning cooler, but today the sun was shining bright and warm. Her cousin's unexpected call seemed like a sign from the universe that she needed to tell *someone* about the mess she'd gotten herself into. Zach had been going to the local school, and he loved it. But it wouldn't be long before Blake learned she'd told the headmaster at Beakman Academy that plans had changed and they no longer needed to send a car for Zachary. And once Blake knew, everything was going to come crashing down. She was trapped between doing what was right for Zach and being fair to Blake.

"Nora?"

"I don't even know where to start, Mandy. You kissed this guy, and you actually *liked* it, then he left, you tore his house apart, and now you're taking care of his nephew? Alone? The school let you enroll him without being his guardian?"

"I talked really fast, and Julie may have suggested to the principal that I was his legal guardian before I even got there." Julie was the only other person who knew she'd lied to allow Zach to stay. Everyone else thought it was Blake's idea.

"You're turning into quite the little grifter, honey. I should be appalled, but I'm honestly impressed." Amanda wasn't sure how she felt about this new dishonest side of herself, either. Nora's Southern accent deepened as her worry did. "But, honey, what happens when Blake finds out? Mel said he's pretty intense. Doesn't sound like the type to be amused by any of this. You're getting attached to this boy, and he could be snatched away from you in the blink of an eye. Are you ready for that? Is Zach? Did you really think this through?" Every word hit home for Amanda because she asked herself the very same questions every night.

"Clearly not. But I'm in it now. Blake doesn't see Zach as anything but a burden right now. Maybe when he gets back... I don't know." She shook her head and leaned back against the wall of Halcyon, which felt oddly warm on this chilly evening. "The kid is just so lost and lonely." Amanda closed her eyes and rubbed the bridge of her nose. "I know this could end up being an absolute disaster for everyone. I just have to hope that it's not."

"Have you been talking to Dr. Jackson?"

Amanda blinked a few times in surprise. "Once. We had a phone session a few weeks ago."

Dr. Jackson had been supportive of Amanda taking on the design project at Halcyon, and was thrilled to hear she and Blake had shared a few kisses with no panic attacks. The doctor had been encouraging her for months be more spontaneous, and she, like Nora, thought Gallant Lake was inspiring Amanda's impulsive side. But Dr. Jackson knew nothing about Zach's arrival. She may have taken the idea of being spontaneous a little too far.

Nora broke the silence. "You're taking a lot of chances, and I worry about all the things that could go wrong. You were already having panic attacks..." Her voice drifted off.

Tension simmered under Amanda's skin. Yes, exhaustion was catching up to her. Worrying about Zach, and Blake's reaction to what she'd done, along with the construction chaos and worrying the protestors might show up at the entrance to Halcyon and hassle Zach—it was all wearing on her.

"I'm okay." She had to say it, even if she didn't believe it. "Really, I am. I appreciate you calling me, Nora." She stood shakily and brushed away the tears she didn't realize she'd started to shed. "I have to go. Zach will be home any minute, and he likes it when I meet the bus. Keep me in your prayers, coz."

"Every day, girl. Every day."

She did her best to put up a brave front for Zach, but the strain wore at her as the days passed. Two nights later, he found her sitting on the floor in the solarium, weeping uncontrollably. He'd curled up at her side, hugged her tight and told her not to cry. Which, of course, made her cry more.

And nightmares…well, the nightmares were back with a vengeance. The workers were making her edgy, and Bobby had to fire one that week for wearing a T-shirt with a vulgarity on it referring to the casino plans. Bobby told the guy to go change and the man started yelling about "free speech" and how Blake Randall was "killing Gallant Lake." Bobby fired him on the spot. Did the other workers feel the same hatred for Blake and the resort? The confrontation sent her spiraling into a persistent state of anxiety. Her nerves were frayed. Every passing day added to the amount of trouble she'd be in when Blake discovered Zach was still at Halcyon.

Maybe it was selfish, but she needed Zach as much as he needed her. Halcyon was different since he'd arrived. Warmer. Brighter. So she pushed herself through each day with a smile and tried to ignore the firestorm that was surely headed her way.

Chapter Nine

Blake shook with anger as he marched through the airport in Sydney, Australia. Ten days ago, he'd called Amanda about sending Zach to Beakman. Ten *freakin'* days.

She'd begged him to put the boy in public school, but that was a nonstarter. He slowed his pace a bit as he headed for his gate. His sister, of course, would have loved the idea of her little boy being the first Randall to break the private school tradition. But as much as he'd adored Tiffany, she'd thrown her life away, and now it was up to Blake to make sure Zachary had a proper upbringing.

Amanda finally assured him that she would have Zach ready to go when Beakman sent someone. He'd checked his nephew off on his mental to-do list days ago and focused on getting construction on the new resort back up to speed. The Blake Randall No Surprises Lifestyle was firmly back in place. Until yesterday.

Yesterday was when he got a call from the headmaster, wondering where to send Zach's things, since he wasn't returning. Blake thought he was going to burst a blood vessel right there on the spot.

There wasn't a doubt in his mind that Zachary was riding a school bus to the tired little school in Gallant Lake, getting who knows what for an education. And Amanda *lied* about it. She lied to *him*. About his *family*. He gave the headmaster some excuse about a "miscommunication" and booked his flight home.

The outright gall of the woman, to openly defy him over a family issue that had nothing to do with her! Apparently he'd badly misjudged her common sense. She had to know she'd be finished as soon as he discovered what she'd done.

He walked down the gangway to the plane and frowned. He should have known about Zach before now, of course. He should have checked on his nephew. It rankled him that he wouldn't have known anything was amiss if the school hadn't called him. He would have shown up in Gallant Lake in a week or two and…what?

He fell into his first-class seat with a sigh and shook his head. That woman had big brass ones, all right. She probably figured she was safe because he hadn't communicated with her much while he was traveling. That silence had been very intentional. Every time he heard Amanda's sweet voice, his longing for her increased. He needed his focus, and she messed with that just by breathing a few words into the phone from thousands of miles away.

It started when she sent him that picture a few weeks ago of herself on the ladder in her tight jeans and ball cap, ponytail dangling down her back, laughing at the camera. When he saw the photo on his phone, it took every ounce of strength not to leave the meeting he was in and jump on the next flight to be with her. The woman was bad for business. She was bad for him.

She knew he was going to find out about Zach eventually. She was probably sweating bullets over it right now. What kind of crazy plan did she have? He shook his head grimly and pulled out his phone. It was time to make her squirm. He tapped out a text.

How's the house coming? Any problems getting Zach to go back to school?

He waited so long he thought he was going to have to turn off the phone before she answered. The jet's doors were just closing when his phone finally chirped.

House is great. Furniture arriving. Zach loves school.

He laughed out loud, ignoring the looks from his fellow passengers. She didn't quite lie, did she? She didn't say *which* school. Did she think she could get away with dancing that fine line for long? He'd be in Gallant Lake tomorrow, and he couldn't wait to see her face when he arrived. He sent her a quick reply just as the flight attendant asked him to shut off the phone.

Glad to hear it. See you in a couple weeks.

It was a long twenty-four-hour journey with very little sleep, and he was simmering with angry anticipation when he finally arrived at JFK. Amanda had single-handedly blown his No Surprises plan right out of the water. He had the evidence to throw in her face, which was exactly what he'd do when he saw her.

He leaned back against the seat. Why didn't he feel better about it?

Amanda paced the main hall at Halcyon restlessly. The house was empty and quiet. Bobby's crew was off today, working on a charity home-build down in White Plains. Zach was in school. She walked into the living room and looked at the freshly painted walls. She frowned when she saw a few uneven spots near the ceiling, above the doorway. She sighed. It was going to bother her until she fixed it.

The painting crew's twelve-foot stepladder was nearby, along with paint and an assortment of brushes. She glanced down at her clothes. These old jeans and sweatshirt were perfect for painting. The job would help keep her mind off Blake.

She was standing on the ladder with her back to it, leaning forward to reach a spot above the doorway to the main hall. Humming to herself, she gently smoothed the uneven lines with a small angled brush. She never heard the limo pull up in front of the big house. Didn't hear footsteps cross the stone porch. But she certainly heard the front door fly open with a crash. The sound nearly upended her, and she leaned back against the shaking ladder to steady herself.

"Amanda!"

How on earth could Blake be *here*? He'd just sent a text from Bali yesterday. Her heart dropped. The day she'd been dreading had arrived earlier than expected. He knew Zach wasn't at boarding school. And he'd flown halfway around the world to confront her in person. He shouted her name up the staircase.

His jaw was set, his brows drawn together, and his body was tight and tense. Dressed for the islands in linen slacks and a white cotton shirt, he looked even more handsome than she remembered. When he spun in her direction and spotted her up on the ladder, his eyes were blazing. There was a flicker of surprise, perhaps even concern, as he registered that she was at least ten feet above the floor. Her palms started to sweat.

"What are you doing up there?" He started marching in her direction.

"Um...painting..." Her voice sounded like a squeak in her own ears. *Steady, girl, steady.*

"The idea was not for you to actually *do* the work, Amanda. Come down before you fall."

He had a right to be angry. She'd caused this mess. She studied his stony face, then shook her head. "I think I'll stay right here."

She moved another step up on the ladder, so her bottom was sitting on the very top. The ladder shuddered, and she reached down to grab either side of her seat. His hands shot out to steady the ladder from below.

"For God's sake, Amanda, I have no intention of snatching you off this thing."

The gleaming marble floor was a long way down. It was bad enough that Blake was about to break her heart. Falling off this ladder wasn't going to help matters. She carefully slid down so that she was sitting on the second step from the top. Once she was settled, she raised one brow and gave him her most calm and collected expression. She knew she was about to be fired. Might as well go out with attitude, right?

"So…you wanted to talk?"

If the moment wasn't so serious, she would have laughed out loud at the way he sputtered at her bravado. Then he slowly shook his head and leveled a glare at her. Now that he was no longer worried, he'd found his anger again.

"Do you have any idea how stupid I felt when the headmaster called to ask where to send Zach's things? How furious I was when I realized you must have enrolled him in a *public* school after I told you not to?" He ran an agitated hand through his hair as she watched, wide-eyed and silent. His voice rose to a bellow, echoing off the walls. "Just who the *hell* do you think you are, Amanda Lowery? You're not Zach's guardian. You're not even his family! You're just an employee who can't follow simple instructions."

She stiffened. "Just an employee, huh? Well, that doesn't say much for your parenting skills, does it? Because when your nephew needed you, you pawned him off on this 'employee' you barely know." She struck her chest with her hand. She thought about her own childhood, when her stepfather ignored her at her darkest hour. "You just kept working on your big important hotel projects halfway around the world. You didn't even call to see how he was doing. It took you all this time to realize he wasn't at Beakman. As long as you could stay uninvolved in his problems and send him away again, you were happy as a clam, weren't you?"

He took a step backward, looking stunned by her fierce words. She was just getting started.

"He's a little boy, Blake! A little boy with no parents, and a family who clearly views him as some annoying burden. Do you think he doesn't see how unimportant he is to all of you?"

"He's *not* unimportant. I'm spending a hell of a lot of money on his education..."

She threw her hands up. The motion made the ladder shake, and Blake reached out to grab it again as she spat her words down at him.

"Money! That's all you care about!"

She gestured wildly, and Blake cursed as he held the ladder.

"Come down here, goddamn it, before you fall."

She ignored him. She'd been nursing her rage for days now, and she wasn't about to hold back. Not anymore.

"I don't know what's going on with your family, Blake, but you are all seriously screwed up. This child—and he is a *child*—lost his mother, and is unwanted by anyone in his own family. You farm him out to private schools when he's only *ten years old*. My God, he's a scared, lonely little boy who just wants to have a childhood. What is wrong with you people?"

Blake's eyes narrowed again, and a muscle twitched in his cheek. He was pissed off. Well, good. So was she. His voice was raw with emotion when he finally responded.

"How *dare* you suggest that I don't care about Zachary! He's my sister's son. I don't want Zach to be weak like his mother was. He needs discipline and structure. Beakman is not a prison. It's a school, where he'll be safe and will have someone directing him..."

She shook her head sadly, tears burning at her eyes. She wasn't sure who she felt sorrier for—Zach or Blake. "He's not weak. He's terrified. He's lonely. He doesn't need direction. He needs *love*." Blake rolled his eyes and groaned.

"Oh, yeah, that's right. Love solves everything. Let me know how that works out for you in that Pollyanna world you seem to be living in. Because here in the real world, it's hard work and education that pave the way to success. Love is a ridiculous, frivolous emotion. My sister was chasing love when she died. My mother was chasing love when she abandoned her children. And aren't you chasing it right now by pretending to be Zach's mother?"

His words hit her heart like a box cutter blade—sharp, straight and deep. Blake pointed at her, not done yet.

"Love is like fool's gold, Amanda. Love is an illusion. A trick. A flicker of a moment that's not worth the resulting trouble."

She stared at Blake's hard face, trying to process his words. Did he really believe that? What hope was there for Zachary if he did? What hope was there for her? Deflated, she started moving slowly down the ladder. She stopped on that last step and looked at him sadly.

"Zach is a little boy who is full of love. And he has no one to give it to. How exactly is that going to work out for *him*, Blake?"

He blinked and looked away from her. His voice sounded hollow. "Little boys grow up. He just has to do it a little sooner than most. He'll survive. I did."

"At what cost?"

She whispered the words, but he flinched as if she'd slapped him. Before he could speak, she stepped off the ladder and moved to brush past him. Her heart was a cold, leaden weight in her chest. "I may just be an employee who disobeyed orders. But your nephew is happy at the Gallant Lake school. He's making friends. He does his homework every night. He's a really good kid, Blake. He deserves more than what you had."

He put his hand on her arm and spun her around. She had no choice but to meet his angry stare. "More? *More?* You don't know what you're talking about. I had everything. I was raised in a life of privilege, just like Zach will be. He'll make his mark in the world, just as every generation of Randalls has done. That's what's expected…" His voice trailed off as if he suddenly doubted his own words. As if he were reciting a family mantra that had been force-fed to him.

Her anger flared afresh. "And how has that worked out for *you*, Blake? You were given 'everything'…" She raised her fingers to make air quotes. "How much 'everything' do you need to be satisfied? Is this house enough?" She gestured to the grand staircase. "Or maybe you should defy the courts and tear this down along with all the other properties to build your big casino. Will that be enough? Will ruining an entire community be enough for you?" Her voice hardened even as her tears spilled over. She was ending whatever hope they had for a future. Those wonderful kisses were nothing more than a bittersweet memory. "And what will be enough for Zach? Will he have to be richer than you to have 'everything'? Own more properties? Have more success? Isn't that what already broke his mother?"

His hand tightened on her arm.

"Don't you talk about his mother! Don't you *dare* talk about Tiffany like you knew her. You didn't know her at all. You don't know me. You don't know a damned thing, Amanda. Do you hear me?"

His voice rose with every sentence until he was shouting. She blanched in the face of his fury. His grip wasn't painful, but she felt panic rising in her chest. Or was it heartbreak? Tears poured down her face and she raised her hands to push him away. He was too close. It was too much.

"Let her go!"

Zachary stood in the doorway. Her heart dropped. How

much had he heard? Zach ran in from the main hall and launched himself at Blake's back, pummeling his uncle's broad shoulders with small fists.

"Let her go, Uncle Blake! Don't you hurt her! Let her go!"

Chapter Ten

Blake had no choice but to release Amanda so he could deflect Zach's blows. He turned to focus on his nephew, catching Zach's arms gently in his hands and dropping to his knees.

"Zachary, stop!" Blake's voice was firm but calm. "I would never hurt her…" Over Zach's shoulder, he saw Amanda run up the stairs. He felt a searing flash of guilt. He'd put his hands on her in anger. The thought made him sick.

"I saw you! She's the only person who's been nice to me and you made her cry! She cries so much…" Zach's brown eyes were wide and overflowing with tears. Appalled, Blake pulled the little boy into his arms.

Wait. What had he said? Blake held Zach out at arm's length again.

"What do you mean 'she cries so much'? Why does Amanda cry, Zach?"

Zach shrugged, sniffling at his tears. Blake handed him a handkerchief and sat back on his heels while Zach blew his nose and dried his eyes.

"She was crying in the sunny room last week. And she has nightmares…"

"Nightmares?"

Zach nodded solemnly. "She screams really loud."

A chill settled over Blake's heart. Nightmares. Alone in this big house. The thought was so disturbing he barely noticed Zach was speaking again.

"She won't let me in there, Uncle Blake. She locked her

door after the first time. She said she's afraid she'll hurt me, but she'd never do that."

Blake dropped his head into his hands and groaned. What the hell had been happening in this house while he was intentionally avoiding them? While he was too far away to know or care that a frightened woman and his lonely nephew were barely holding each other together here without him. The same way he'd left Zach alone with Tiffany while she fought her demons. The kid was only ten years old. Was there any relationship Blake *couldn't* screw up?

"A bad man scared her."

Blake looked up sharply at those words. Staring straight into those brown eyes that reminded him so much of his sister's, Blake forced his voice to sound light and unconcerned. He didn't want to show the panic that Zach's words incited in him.

"Tell me what you mean by that, Zach. What bad man?" He thought of those sleazy guys hanging out with the protestors. Did someone harass her?

"She said it was a long time ago. Sometimes she sees the guy in her sleep and has nightmares."

A long time ago? She got upset when he asked her about her childhood. What the hell had happened to her? His face burned with shame, thinking how he'd just grabbed her like an angry brute.

"Zach, do you know where Amanda went?"

His nephew frowned. "Probably to the balcony in her room. She likes it up there." Zach fixed him with a stern look. "Don't hurt her."

"I won't. I promise." He swallowed hard, hating that his nephew thought him capable of hurting Amanda. "I'm going to apologize for scaring her. Why don't you do your homework while I do that, okay?"

Zach studied him solemnly, then nodded. "Can I use the living room?"

"Of course. And, Zach?" Blake caught Zach's hand as the boy started to turn away. "I want you to know that I would *never* intentionally hurt Amanda. Hurting girls is a very bad thing to do. You know that, right?"

Zach stared back, wide-eyed. He looked so much like his mother, with that intriguing blend of innocence and wisdom.

Blake sighed. "Do you like your school?"

The boy's eyes lit up. "Yeah! Mr. Hoffman is cool, and the kids are nice. And I get to ride the school bus!"

Blake gave the boy a quick, awkward hug. Things hadn't been easy for Zach, and Blake really didn't know what to do for the kid. He winced at the realization that he'd basically done nothing at all. Amanda was right. He just kept sending him away. She was probably the first person to show Zach any true affection since his mother died.

"I'm glad you like it. Now go do your homework. We'll all go down to the resort for dinner in a while." Zach dashed into the living room with his backpack. Blake took the stairs two at a time. Would Amanda forgive him?

Could he forgive himself?

She was sitting on the stone railing of the balcony, her feet dangling on either side of the waist-high wall. Her back was braced against the tower, but it was still a precarious position far above the stone veranda. Blake had never been fond of heights, but apparently Amanda had no such fear, scampering up ladders and sitting on balcony walls.

God, she was beautiful, even more so than he remembered. Her hair was pulled up into a ponytail high on her head, showing off her long neck and pretty face. She'd put everything she had—her only job and her only home—on the line for his nephew. She had bravely gone to work picking up the pieces of the little boy's shattered life.

She quickly wiped tears from her cheeks with the back of her hand when she noticed him there. She raised her chin defiantly, gazing out over Gallant Lake before turning to slide off her perch. Still avoiding his face, she started to push past him.

"I'll start packing my things…"

His arm slipped around her waist to stop her forward motion. They stood like that in silence, side by side, facing opposite directions, with only his arm connecting them. He slowly pulled her closer, and she inhaled sharply when their bodies came in contact. He reached across and cupped her chin in his hand, turning her face toward his. He gazed into her wide eyes, which were glistening with unshed tears. Neither of them appeared to breathe.

"Let me go…" Stress and exhaustion were etched on her face. There were dark shadows under her brilliant eyes. She'd been shouldering far too much in his absence. His chest tightened. He was such an idiot.

"Damn it, Amanda…" The words came out on a breath, soft and ragged. He dropped his head and rested it against hers. "Sit with me so we can talk. I'm sorry, okay? I never meant to frighten you. As angry as I was, I never wanted to do that." He pressed a chaste kiss on her forehead. "And please, no more talk about packing. I don't want you to go."

He released her, and for a terrifying moment he thought she was leaving. But she only walked as far as one of the wicker chairs, where she sat with a sigh. He pulled another chair close and sat facing her, their knees nearly touching. She stared out at the lake.

"Look at me, Amanda."

Her eyelashes swept up and her blue eyes locked on his. Time had done nothing to cool the attraction between them. Those eyes still managed to leave him breathless. He cleared his throat and tried to focus, running his hand through his hair in frustration.

"I'm sorry for what happened downstairs, more than you can know. If I hurt you…or scared you… There's no excuse for putting my hands on you that way, and I swear to God I'll never do it again."

She stared at him as if she was trying to gauge his sincerity. For once in his life, he wanted someone to see his pain. He wanted her to know how much anguish he was feeling over what he'd done.

She finally nodded. "We were both pretty heated, weren't we? I… I know I overstepped my bounds with Zach. I *do* know that…"

"You did. But that doesn't excuse my behavior. Please forgive me, Amanda." Here he was, begging again. They looked at each other in silence.

"I forgive you." His entire body relaxed. Her forgiveness shouldn't mean so much, but it did. Apparently, it meant everything.

Her forehead wrinkled in concern.

"I shouldn't have said what I did about your family. About you and Zach."

"I'm pretty angry about that." He rushed to explain when her face paled. "But only because it's so true. My family *is* totally screwed up, Amanda. I know it. I just don't like hearing it. It's one of those things where I can bitch about them, but no one else can. My family is a train wreck. My mother is a gold-digging shrew. My father is a cold, unemotional son of a bitch. My sister was a drug addict. And my brother is a spineless coward controlled by his wife and his father."

"I didn't tell you the truth about Zach and school."

"No, you didn't." He waited for her to explain.

"I know it wasn't my decision to make. He was so upset, and I couldn't get you to listen to me. I felt like I was the only person protecting Zach." He winced at the truth in her words. She blinked back tears, but a couple escaped and rolled down her cheek. He reached out and wiped them away with his fingertips while she kept talking. "And he's so much happier now…he loves Gallant Lake…"

"He said he likes the school and his teacher."

Her eyes went wide and a smile danced across those crazy beautiful lips of hers. "He really does love it. He's doing great."

"Randalls aren't exactly popular in this town. Some of the protesters are more aggressive than the others. I don't think anything will happen, but they're…unpredictable." He thought again of those angry younger men mingling with the usual picketers. "There's no protection for him at that school."

"Bruce and the principal are the only ones who know who Zach is."

"Bruce?"

"His teacher. Bruce Hoffman. I enrolled Zach under my last name. Bruce watches out for him and keeps a close eye on him when the kids are outdoors. Bruce also makes sure Zach gets on the bus without a problem."

Blake was torn between appreciation for Amanda's handling of the situation, and a slow-burning rage every time she said the word "Bruce" the way she did. Like they were friends. Like they were close.

"Sounds like you and *Bruce* have spent some time talking about this."

She shrugged. "We had dinner at the resort and I explained the situation to him. He's with Zach all day, and I felt he should know what to watch for, between security and everything Zach's dealing with emotionally…"

"You had dinner…" Blake swallowed an illogical rush of anger and tried to focus on the matter at hand. "I have to say, Amanda, I was afraid you were taking Zach's situation too lightly, but you covered all the bases. Except for telling me what you were doing." He raked his fingers through his hair. "I can't imagine what my family will say about him going to public school, but it's my decision to make."

"He just wants to have a home with you."

He dropped his head and shook it. "I don't know how to raise a boy."

Why the hell had Tiffany trusted *him* with her son? What did she see in him that he didn't see in himself? And here he was screwing it all up.

Amanda looked at him curiously. "How did that happen? How did the single guy end up as Zach's guardian when your brother is married and has children?"

He shrugged. That was the question of the hour, wasn't it? "Tiffany stipulated me as Zachary's guardian in her will. She and I were close as kids. She was only a year younger than me. Mother always said the back-to-back pregnancies ruined her body or something, and blamed Tiffany specifically, since she was unplanned. I always tried to protect her. Clearly, I failed in the end..."

"Blake..." Amanda reached out and put her small hand over his. He huffed out a soft laugh, looking out over the lake.

"You know, I can still see Tiffie as a little girl at our place on Long Island." He could picture her as clearly as if she was right there in front of him. Her long dark hair whipping around her face, running in the sand, challenging the boys to race into the waves. He looked back to Amanda and smiled. "She was an undeniable force of energy. Very artistic—she loved creating things. Her favorite time of year was Christmas. She was always laughing, always plotting some practical joke, always getting into trouble with our father. I tried to deflect Dad's anger from her, but that just made it worse. He'd punish her more harshly for 'lowering' me to her level of irresponsibility. And responsibility is the gold standard in the Randall household. That and *winning*. Tiffany never cared about any of that." He paused, realizing it had been a long time since he'd talked about his sister. "She was the kid who would be leading the race but turn back to help someone who stumbled. She actually did that once, and Dad grounded her for a month for being 'stupid.'"

"Poor Tiffany." Amanda squeezed his hand. All of his childhood memories, even the good ones, inevitably lead to pain.

"Mother left us for some Italian race car driver when Tiff was around seven, and we stayed with Dad. When Tiffany realized she'd never win either parent's love or approval, she turned to a different crowd of friends, and got into drugs. I was away at school. By the time I saw it, it was too late. She was out of control. If she ever knew who Zach's father was, she never admitted it. At least she knew enough to stop that shit while she was pregnant, but by his first birthday she was right back with her old crowd and old ways. The rest of the family eventually disowned her." He looked down at his feet and sighed. "I tried to help her. I really did. I'd send her to rehab, and she'd be fine for a while, then she'd slide right back. Street drugs, prescription drugs, booze…anything she could use to make herself numb. I paid to keep Zach in private schools so he didn't have to face the reality of her addiction, but of course, he knew something was wrong."

Blake looked up at Amanda. He could see his own pain reflected in her eyes. But no one could help him bear his guilt. "I really thought the last facility was the charm. She came out after three months in great spirits, looking better than ever. I put her up in a nice apartment in New York and enrolled her in art school. I even moved Zach to a school near the city so he could stay with her on weekends, and they seemed to be doing really well together. I was in Barbados when she called. Zach was skiing in Vermont with the family of one of his school friends, so she was alone.

She started crying about the mess she'd made of her life. Her voice was slurred. I could barely understand her. She sounded drunk, or high. Probably both." He scrubbed his hand down his face. The last thing he wanted to do was relive that night, but Amanda deserved the truth. "I was so frustrated that she'd relapsed *again*. Life was just a never-ending roller-coaster ride with her, and I was fed up with it. I didn't want to listen to her self-pity or her apologies."

He'd never told anyone about that phone call. "All I could think about while she rambled on was that we'd have to get Zach into a new school and find another rehab center for her. Finally, I told her to go sleep it off. She started crying harder. I told her I didn't want to hear it, and then I hung up on her." He stopped, swallowing the sadness. "The cleaning staff found her body the next day, sprawled across the bed with a pile of empty pill bottles on the nightstand and an empty bottle of vodka on the floor. The girl who loved Christmas died at Christmastime. They ruled it accidental, but I think she was saying 'goodbye,' and I was too selfish and stupid to realize it."

Amanda made a strangled sound of pity. "You couldn't have known that, Blake. Poor Zach…that's why you want him to have a good Christmas this year."

He gave her a halfhearted grin. "I have to try. She loved him more than anything in the world. Tiffany was like a child herself so he adored her." Blake closed his eyes, and he could hear her laughter. "All she ever wanted was for the people around her to be happy. She wanted to be loved."

He stopped, realizing that's exactly what Amanda has said about Zach. He wanted to be loved. Was that why Tiffany had named Blake as guardian? Because she thought he'd understand?

"The next thing I know, the lawyers are telling me I'm responsible for a little boy. I tried to get my brother to take Zach, but my sister-in-law, Michaela, didn't want him living with her precious little girls, as if Tiffany's problems were contagious. They agreed to keep him this summer because I was traveling, but no longer than that. My father won't even acknowledge his existence. So here I am, arguing with you over a kid I barely know. And it's my fault that I don't know him. I haven't even tried. Goddamn it, I failed them both."

He blew out a long, tortured breath. Unshed tears stung his eyes. Now Amanda knew what a complete loser he was. A man who couldn't love his own sister enough to save her. She was silent, then finally just shook her head.

"You didn't fail Tiffany. Your sister was an addict. You can't *make* an addict quit. You can't *wish* them sober. You gave Tiffany the tools, but she didn't use them. You were raised to think kindness was a sign of failure, and in spite of that you were still kind to Tiffany. You tried to protect her and Zachary. And you took care of Zach when she couldn't. That's not failure. That's love."

That's love.

His heart pounded hard against his chest. He didn't believe in love anymore. Did he? He could hear Tiffany's laughter in the air again, and he closed his eyes. It was crazy, but he could smell the ocean, hear her giggles as she ran ahead of him. He always let her win those races, just to see her joy. Amanda squeezed his hands again, and he looked up at the woman who was doing far more than rebuilding his house. She was redesigning his entire life.

"I loved my sister." The words felt heavy and warm on his lips.

"Yes, and you'll love Zach, too. You know how I know?"

He looked into her bright blue eyes and shook his head, unable to speak.

"Blake, the person you just described to me *is* Zachary. He has his mother's sense of fun and adventure. And he really cares about people. He's been so kind to me…" Her voice drifted off. Blake remembered Zach's words. *She cries so much… She has nightmares.* Zach had been taking care of Amanda. Just like Tiffany would have.

He stood, pulling Amanda to her feet in front of him. He put his hands gently on either side of her face. She stared up at him, looking uncertain.

"It's still there, isn't it?" he whispered. How was that possible? "This thing between us, even after all this. It's still there."

She nodded, suddenly solemn. He slowly dropped his head and brushed his lips against hers. He didn't go further until he felt her hands sliding into his hair. With that unspoken invitation, he pressed into her and tasted everything he'd been missing for these desperately long days. Sweet Jesus, it was even better than he remembered. She was warm and intoxicating, sweet and dangerous. He wrapped his arms around her waist and pulled her up off her feet without moving his mouth from hers, wanting to consume her. All the emotion of the past few hours ignited in this kiss. When he finally set her down, it was with a groan of frustration. Kisses were no longer going to be enough with this woman.

Chapter Eleven

Amanda couldn't think. Blood pounded through her veins and a hot flush spread across her skin. Her entire body trembled like a tuning fork.

Blake stared down at her, looking just as ravaged as she felt. His hair was mussed from where she'd had her fingers in it. His dark eyes were nearly black now. She knew her eyes reflected the same desire, so she closed them, terrified of what he might see. This wasn't her. Her chest tightened. Blake was turning her into a different person, and she was so far out of her carefully constructed comfort zone that she couldn't think straight. She shuddered.

"Amanda…" His voice was soft and deep, and her heart raced at the sound of it. "It's okay. Take a deep breath and relax. We'll figure this out together."

"I can't…" She backed out of his arms and away from the heady scent of him so she could think. "I don't know how to do this. I don't even know what 'this' is. It's too much…" The stress of the past few weeks crashed over her like an icy wave, and she felt new tears spilling from her eyes.

Blake brushed the teardrops from her cheeks. She wanted to shove him away, and she wanted to bury her fingers in his hair again and kiss him long and deep. The corner of his mouth twitched up into a crooked grin as if he could read her mind. Then he grew serious.

"You're exhausted." He shook his head. "And it's my fault. I should have come home as soon as I knew Zach was here. But I was afraid of being here with you." He grinned at her surprise. "That's right, sweetheart, you're not the only one who's confused by all of this energy between us. I'm the guy who doesn't believe in romance, and you're the girl who's terrified to try it. I don't know if that makes us the perfect couple or a recipe for disaster." His hands rested lightly on her shoulders. "We'll slow things down a bit, okay? I'm willing to try if that's what you need. Can you help me get to know my nephew better? I really need your help with that."

Her panic faded as she stared into his coffee-colored eyes. He'd opened his heart to her, and she had a feeling that didn't happen very often. Slowly, she returned his smile.

"Friends is a good place to start." She broke the gaze and looked out over the water. She could hear music. She frowned. It was loud rock music.

"Speaking of your nephew, where is he?"

He shrugged. "He's doing his homework."

"That's *what* he's doing. I asked *where* he was."

"He asked to use the living room. Why?"

Amanda started to laugh. "Oh, you've got a lot to learn about little boys. Of course he asked to use the living room. Because he knows that *I* wouldn't have allowed it. Hear that?" She tilted her head toward the sounds rising from the room two stories below them.

"The music?"

"Your living room is now home to two flat-screen televisions, Blake. And the music system. And the game consoles. That sounds like *Guitar Gods* to me. *Not* homework." She tapped her finger lightly on the tip of his nose and giggled when his eyes went wide. "You just got played by a ten-year-old, Uncle Blake." She spun on her heel and headed for the stairs.

Blake helped her put away the painting supplies and ladder after they got Zachary settled in the solarium to do his homework away from the temptation of any state-of-the-art electronics. Once they made sure he had his books open, she gave Blake a tour of the work that had been accomplished while he was gone.

She was proud of how the magnificent old house looked, but Blake was quiet as she showed him around. His only display of emotion was a crooked smile when he saw the iron chandeliers sporting their fresh coat of shiny paprika paint. Three Persian silk rugs divided the large main hall into a trio of distinct spaces, with the formal dining table occupying one end, a sitting area in front of the fireplace, and another near the library.

Blake's future office was still very much a construction zone, with floor-to-ceiling bookshelves and cabinets being constructed the length of one long wall.

The living room was almost completely furnished. She'd managed to snag an enormous leather sectional off the floor of a design center. Several low-slung chairs sat by the windows, with a game table and chairs on the opposite end of the room. That's where the second flat screen was hanging, set up for video games and movies.

Blake still had nothing to say. He hated it. She was sure he hated all of it.

He stopped abruptly in the doorway of his suite upstairs. The massive bed was now washed with a cream-colored finish. All of the formerly dark wood trim in the room was painted to match the bed. The walls were soft blue, reflecting the lake outside. Blake stood in the middle of the room in stunned silence.

"Say *something*, Blake. You're killing me."

"You painted the bed…" He put his hand on it, then turned with a perplexed look on his face. "I couldn't envision this. But you did."

He went to one of the windows looking out over the lake and ran his hand down the knobby raw silk drapes. Elegant but natural. Rich and rough. Like him. That's why she'd selected the material, but she'd never tell him that. She was still holding her breath when he turned to look at her.

"It's amazing. *You're* amazing."

She almost laughed out loud in relief. "I'm so glad you like it."

He gave her a strange look, then shook his head. "Don't take this the wrong way, Amanda. I knew you had talent, but what you've accomplished here in basically a month is mind-boggling. I should stay here and send *you* to Bali to manage the resort opening. You clearly know how to get things done. And your taste is flawless." He walked over to her and put his hands on her shoulders. Her skin tingled at his touch. "When this house is done, I want to talk to you about doing some redecorating at some of the resorts."

Her mind started to spin. Stay in Gallant Lake and work for Blake. Stay here with Zach. Wasn't that what she wanted? But that kiss…

"We can talk about that later." She needed time to process everything. "Right now, Zach needs dinner so we can get him to bed. It's a school night."

"Yes, Mom."

She swatted at him and he ducked, laughing. He spun her by the shoulders and nudged her toward the door.

Chapter Twelve

Amanda leaned against one of the two stone pillars flanking the driveway, wishing she'd grabbed a jacket before coming down to meet Zach's bus. It was almost November, and the air was chilly and damp.

Blake had been back at Halcyon for a couple weeks now, and they were settling into a comfortable routine. They kept their relationship professional during the day, and carefully platonic outside of work hours. They made it work by making Zach their priority. It took a while for uncle and nephew to really warm up to each other. Zach resented his uncle's arrival. Not only because of the argument he'd witnessed, but because he felt Blake betrayed Zach by sending him away, first to Blake's brother, then to boarding school. At least, that's what Zach told the school counselor. The counselor recommended Blake give Zach time to start trusting. That Blake would have to earn it.

It was sports that had finally broken the ice a few days earlier. When Amanda showed them Zach's redecorated room, complete with pinstripes and life-size decals of his favorite athletes on the wall, Blake was almost as excited as Zach was. Amanda tried explaining her paint and curtain choices, and realized they weren't even listening. They were busy studying a poster of the home football team, debating their chances in the play-offs this year.

During dinner in the solarium that night, the two moved on from football to discover more things they had in common. They liked the same computer games. They liked *Star Wars* and *Star Trek* and anything else that started with *star*.

And they both loved her dark chocolate cake. Zach was still wary of Blake, but at least they were talking.

Blake worked from his office at the resort every day while Zach was in school and Amanda was supervising the work at Halcyon. Then he'd help his nephew with homework while Amanda prepared dinner. The three of them would gather in the living room after the meal for television, a movie, video games or a hotly contested game of cards.

Once Zach was in bed, Amanda and Blake would watch television or read before retiring to their rooms. Conversation was usually at a minimum when they were alone together, but their time was still comfortable and relaxed, except for that pesky sexual tension that always made her heart race in his presence.

There was still some work to be done at Halcyon, but it was on hold while the cherry wood needed for Blake's office was on back order. In the meantime, Bobby's crew was working on the outside of the house, ripping up the overgrown shrubbery and beginning repairs to the old fountain. Today they were up the hill, working on the old carriage house, now a garage.

She was glad to have them out of the house for a while. Especially that one guy, Russ. He put her on edge. It felt like he was *watching* her all the time. No one was allowed to smoke inside, but the room always reeked of cigarettes when he was in there. Maybe that's why she took such a dislike to the man—he reminded her of the guy who'd assaulted her in the city. She shook off that train of thought with a shudder.

She was still fighting off little panic attacks, although she'd been better since Blake's return. The nightmares were less frequent, but not gone. With all this stress, starting any kind of relationship with Blake right now would have been a bad idea. Besides, Zachary needed a stable home, free from drama. That was why she'd begged Blake to dial it back. It was the right thing to do.

He wasn't making it easy to ignore the sizzling energy between them, though, making a habit of appearing at odd times throughout the day. She'd turn around from cleaning the grout in the solarium, and find him standing in the doorway, watching her with that crooked grin. She and Bobby would spread the plans for the office on the dining table to determine what to do next, and suddenly Blake would be leaning over the table with them, discussing the options. He'd stand so close she could feel the heat from his body, but he was careful not to touch her. She'd be sipping her morning coffee on the veranda, and there he'd be, steaming mug in hand, joining her silently to watch the autumn sun rise above Gallant Lake. She wasn't sure if he was testing *her* willpower or his own, but she had no doubt the seemingly casual appearances were very intentional.

The rumble of the school bus broke her reverie. When Zach saw her standing there, he started waving before the bus even stopped. He jumped off with a football clutched tightly in his hands. Several boys shouted goodbyes to him as the bus pulled away.

"Miss Amanda! Look, Kyle gave me his old football so I can practice with it!" Zach held it up for her to admire, which she did while giving him a quick hug. He squirmed away, but not until she'd held him for a few seconds.

"A football? That's awesome, Zach!"

"You wanna see how I can throw?"

She laughed at his eager expression. "Sure! I'll run up the driveway and you throw me the ball!"

She caught his first pass with ease. She tossed it back and ran farther up the driveway as he followed. Rain from earlier in the week left the center of the circular drive wet near the fountain, with a huge puddle of standing water at the edge of the paving stones.

When Zach threw the next pass, it veered to the side. All those childhood memories of playing touch football with the neighborhood kids came flooding back to her. She kept her eye on the ball and leaped for it. Her fingers wrapped around the ball and brought it down, but she lost her footing.

And landed with a splash in the midst of the muddy water.

Blake was chatting casually with Jamal in the surveillance room as they reviewed some of the new camera locations at Halcyon that had been added to the resort's security feed. Jamal cleared his throat and grew serious.

"I was talking to Julie yesterday, and she said some of the employees are being harassed around town."

He stiffened. *"What?"*

"Julie had some guy ask her if she worked here. When she said yes, he spat at her feet and called her a money whore, then took off."

"Jesus…"

"Yeah. A few other employees have reported incidents, too. And in the past couple of weeks, we've had some cars vandalized in the employee lot. Key scratches and crap like that."

"And you're looking into it?" Jamal gave a sharp nod.

"I've got Tim doing some recon around town to see if he can ID the guys. Julie didn't recognize him. We brought the deputy sheriff into the loop, and he's on it, too."

"Oh, great." Sheriff Dan, who grew up in Gallant Lake, wasn't a fan of his casino plans.

"Dan's good people, Blake. He doesn't want this kind of trouble in town." Blake looked at the camera feeds coming from Halcyon, and Jamal rushed to reassure him. "The so-called preservation society swears it's not one of theirs. We're keeping a tight eye on the house. The new cameras will help."

On one of the monitors, Blake saw Zach jump off the school bus, running toward Amanda. Their quick, tight embrace was such a simple thing. Such a moment of very normal, everyday joy for a little boy. Blake had never in his life ridden on a school bus. He'd never been greeted at home like that. Amanda was right. Zach needed this. It was everything Tiffany wanted for her boy.

Amanda took off running and disappeared from the view of the gate camera. Then Zach threw the football. Jamal was watching the same action, and he tapped a few keys to switch the view to the feed from the cameras on the front of Halcyon, looking down the driveway.

Amanda was running, her eyes firmly on a well-thrown football. He could see what was going to happen, but there was nothing he could do to warn her. She leaped for the ball and fell into about five inches of muddy water. He held his breath until she sat up, unhurt, her ponytail hanging down her back in a soggy mess. And clutching the football in her hands. He couldn't stop from laughing out loud, and Jamal chuckled, too.

Zach was running up to Amanda now, and even without sound it was easy to see he was laughing hysterically. He dropped to the driveway and howled with glee, arms wrapped around his stomach as Amanda sat there in the water eyeing him. She held out her hand for Zach to help her up. He stood and walked over.

"Don't do it, Zach!" Blake and Jamal both called out at the same time. Even from that distance, they could read Amanda's expression and body language.

Zach couldn't leave her there. He couldn't see this damsel in distress was plotting revenge. As soon as she clasped Zach's hand, Amanda yanked him into the puddle alongside her. Water and mud went flying when he landed on his hands and knees. He sat up and looked like he was sputtering. Not satisfied, Amanda smacked the heel of her hand onto the water and splashed Zach. They were both laughing now, and Zach splashed her back. Amanda tackled him into the thick mud at the edge of the water. He grabbed a handful of mud and rubbed it into her face. Blake winced and laughed out loud again.

Those two were having too much fun. In a mud puddle. Something else Blake had never done. A memory of Tiffany came back to him in a rush, which had been happening a lot these past few weeks. Tiffany was about Zach's age in this particular memory, and she was dancing on the back terrace of their house on Long Island in the pouring rain. Her long dark hair clung to her skin, her clothes were drenched, and still…she danced. He could hear her laughing voice, begging him to join her. But he didn't. He was too afraid of what his father would have said.

There wasn't a doubt in his mind that his vivacious sister would have been right there in the mud today with Amanda and Zach. He watched as they scrambled for the now slimy football. Eventually they both got to their feet, still laughing and wrestling with each other. That's when Blake identified one of the emotions coursing through him. He was envious.

He was envious of these two people finding that much joy in a mud puddle. He was envious of Zach being able to hear Amanda's pealing laughter while Blake watched a silent monitor. He was envious of Amanda planting a big, muddy kiss on Zach's face. He was even more envious of Zach for receiving that kiss. He stood abruptly and left the room without saying a word to Jamal.

He needed to get to Halcyon.

Chapter Thirteen

Amanda and Zach climbed the stone stairway laughing and gasping for breath. She couldn't remember the last time she'd laughed this hard. It wasn't until they reached the door that she realized they had a dilemma.

They were covered in mud and dripping wet. They couldn't go inside like this. Not across those newly polished marble floors and hand-knotted silk rugs. Amanda pressed her lips together. That's what she got for cavorting in the mud like a teenager. She looked at Zach.

"Okay. We need to get you into a bathtub, but I don't want to bring this mess in the house. Take off your shoes and socks and leave them out here. I'll run and get some towels from the laundry room and I'll be right back to wrap you up and get you upstairs. Okay?"

Zach nodded with a shiver. She should have been more practical and kept him out of the puddle. She toed off her muddy sneakers and rolled up her jeans.

"I'll be right back—stand close to the building to stay out of the wind, okay?"

"I'm cold, Miss Amanda."

"I know—I'll hurry." Amanda wrung the water out of her ponytail—she must have looked a sight—and dashed into the house. She ran to the laundry room next to the kitchen, grabbed two big towels and ran back into the main hall. She slid to a stop when Blake walked through the front door with Zach in his arms. *Uh-oh.* Surely Randall men didn't believe in playing in the mud. She braced herself for a scolding.

But wait—he was grinning. He winked at her as he walked by. *Winked!*

"I'll take care of this little mud puppy. You get yourself into a hot shower, Miss Amanda."

"But your clothes…" He was holding the filthy little boy against his white dress shirt and gray pants. The shirt was surely ruined. Zach looked up at Blake mischievously and slapped his hand against Blake's cheek, leaving a perfect muddy handprint. Amanda couldn't hold back her giggle.

"Nice," Blake said with resignation. "It's a little late to worry about clothes at this point. You both need to get clean, warm and dry. Upstairs. Now." His words were demanding, but his brown eyes were twinkling with humor. She threw a towel around Zach and draped the other around herself to catch the dripping water as she followed them upstairs.

Steam wrapped around her in the shower and she sighed as her body warmed up again. When she stepped out to dry herself, she could hear Blake and Zachary laughing in Zach's room next door. She could only imagine what *that* bathroom was going to look like when they were done. The deep timbre of Blake's laughter made her skin tingle as she pulled on a fresh pair of jeans and a sweater. He stopped by her room and called through the door that he and Zach were headed down to the living room, and he was going to light a fire. She told him she'd join them shortly.

But first, Zach's bathroom.

She got on her hands and knees by the bathtub and scrubbed the remaining dirt from the sides. Blake may have cleaned the boy, but he was predictably blind to the mess he left behind. She reached across to wipe down the far side before rinsing it one last time.

There was a sharp intake of breath behind her. Blake stood in the doorway. His clean shirt was still unbuttoned, leaving a wide swath of chest exposed. She forced her eyes away from that sight to make eye contact. But *his* eyes were focused elsewhere. They were fixed on her behind, which, from his angle, must have been quite a sight with her in this position. She blushed and sat back on her heels quickly. His eyes flickered to hers.

"Hey, you just ruined my view." He grinned and tipped his head toward the door. "Come down and enjoy the heat from the fireplace. We have staff to clean bathrooms. Although I may rethink that after the sight I just had…"

She threw the sponge at him playfully and turned on the water to rinse the soap away.

"You're such a diva, Blake. How did you ever become so successful in the hotel business when you can't even clean up after yourself?" She held out her hand for him to help her up. He ignored her question and asked one of his own.

"Isn't this how Zach met his fate outside? Helping you to your feet?"

He read her confusion and laughed as he pulled her up to stand directly in front of him.

"Security cameras. I was in the surveillance room."

"They're watching us from the resort?" She knew there were cameras, but it never occurred to her that someone was sitting around watching her.

"Relax. Exterior views only—the entrances and the gate. Today's episode of *Life at Halcyon* was highly entertaining." He was looking at her intensely now, a look that didn't match the playfulness of his voice. The air evaporated from her lungs when he slid his arm around her back and pulled her close, brushing her damp hair away from her face with his other hand. His fingers lingered on her cheek. "Actually, I find everything you do to be highly entertaining."

Since his return, they'd carefully avoided touching each other. It was all a wonderfully played performance. But now they were too close. He smelled like soap and something intoxicating. She found herself leaning into him rather than pulling away. Unbidden, her hands rested on his forearms, then slowly slid up past his shoulders, stopping with her fingers behind his broad neck. He stared at her silently, waiting for her to decide what would happen next. With a groan of surrender she pulled him down to her mouth. She wanted this. She needed it. Right now.

He let out his breath with a growl and his mouth fell on hers hungrily. Their tongues met and danced and twisted, and she was every bit as aggressive as he was. He pulled her hips into his. She not only allowed it to happen, she ground her lower body against his and felt a thrill when he hardened against her. She'd lost control of herself, and for once in her life, she didn't care. He pulled his mouth away from hers, dropping quick kisses on her cheeks, her eyelids, her hair, her chin. Then he took her mouth again and she clung to his shoulders. She felt like she was falling, and she was. She was falling for him. This was uncharted territory, and a surge of panic rose.

He sensed it immediately and pulled away, leaving his hands on her hips to keep her upright. She had no doubt that if he let go of her, she'd crumple at his feet in a boneless heap. They stood there, panting, staring at each other. Every kiss seemed to leave them in this same position. His hooded eyes were deepest dark mahogany, his voice gruff and tight.

"I won't apologize for how much I want you, Amanda."

Instead of the normal dread that thought should invoke, she realized she wanted him, too. She wanted to defeat *all* of her demons and she wanted this man to help her do it.

He gave her one last gentle kiss on the lips. "We should go. The fire's lit, Zach's waiting to beat us both at *Guitar Gods*, and I ordered a pizza from the village."

Amanda followed him in thoughtful silence. Is this what life could be like at Halcyon? Or was it just a teasing glimpse of something she'd never be a part of?

* * *

Blake looked down at Amanda sleeping in the big chair. He'd pulled the chair closer to the fire earlier, and she'd read a book there while he and Zach played a video game. It had been a lovely family evening. Another first for Blake.

There'd been no pizza nights in his childhood. No mud fights. No women cleaning bathtubs in snug jeans that made their ass look like a perfect heart. He didn't realize how much he'd been missing until right this very moment.

Zach had gone up to bed, and was probably fast asleep already. Blake dropped to his knees in front of Amanda's reclining form and brushed a golden curl away from her face. She stirred and opened her eyes dreamily. Stretching like a cat, she sighed and smiled at him. It was a smile of contentment and security. Of innocence and anticipation. More than anything else in the world, he wanted to see that smile on her face every day for the rest of his life. The thought was unfamiliar and sobering, but truer than anything he'd felt before. This woman made him think about forever. That wall around his heart was shattering, leaving him frighteningly vulnerable.

She sat up and grew more serious. Was she worrying about that bathroom kiss? She stood and they faced each other, not touching, tension filling the space between them.

He bit back a frustrated curse and put his hands on her shoulders. Then he did what he thought he had to do. He lied.

"Nothing has changed, Amanda." He didn't know about her, but *everything* had changed for him. Still, he told her what she needed to hear. "We'll take things at your pace. It won't be easy after that kiss, but we're adults, and we can handle this." He pressed his lips against her forehead and felt her body tense. He was missing a piece of her story. This reaction of hers was from more than being mugged. He lifted his head and waited quietly until she raised her eyes to his. "What is it, baby? What happened to make you so frightened? Who hurt you?"

She shook her head quickly, pulling away from him. Her clear eyes grew cloudy with tension. Then she drew her shoulders back and gave him that brave, but false, smile. She was burying her fears again.

He tried one more time. "Tell me what it is. Let me help you…"

"I'm fine. I'm good. Just tired. Good night, Blake." Without another word, she turned and headed up the staircase. He followed in silence, watching her close the door to her room without looking back at him once.

He stood in front of his bedroom windows for a long time. Gallant Lake was bathed in the soft light of a nearly full moon, but he had no appreciation for the view. All he could think of was the troubled woman getting ready for bed next door. He distracted himself by checking his email and responding to a few questions from his resort managers in various locations. Work was his comfort zone, somewhere he felt sure of himself and in control. Two things he never felt when he was in Amanda Lowery's presence.

He finally stood and stretched, ready to attempt sleep at last. Walking over to the fireplace, he stared at an old painting of Halcyon on the mantel as he unbuttoned his shirt. He couldn't shake the feeling that something was wrong in this house tonight. He was sitting on the edge of the bed removing his shoes when he heard the first scream.

She has nightmares…

Amanda!

He ran into the hallway, wearing nothing but his jeans. Zach was just coming out of his room at the opposite end of the hall with wide eyes. Blake ran to her door and grabbed the knob. Locked. Another terror-filled scream shuddered through the hallway. He didn't hesitate. A well-placed kick splintered the wood next to the lock and the door flew open.

She was thrashing under the sheets, her face soaked with tears.

"Get off me! Stop!"

"Amanda! Wake up, it's just a dream." Blake grabbed her shoulders. She tried to hit him so he took both of her hands and held them over her head with one of his. His upper body was over hers, pinning her down. "Open your eyes! Look at me!"

Her eyes flashed open at his demand. So much stark fear staring back at him. As she began to focus, her breathing slowed, but she was still shaking all over. She tried to move her hands, but he had them captured above her. Her face paled.

"Please don't…that's how he…"

He released her immediately and slid off her. He held one of her hands in his and sat on the edge of the bed. She took in a ragged breath. "Zach?"

Blake turned and saw Zach frozen in the doorway.

"Go back to bed, buddy. It was just a bad dream. I'll take care of Miss Amanda."

Zach looked from Blake to Amanda, and she gave him a nod of reassurance. He hesitated, then turned away. When they heard his bedroom door close, Blake let out a long breath.

"Jesus, Amanda." He brushed a strand of hair away from her face. "Why didn't you tell me this was happening?" He felt a stab of guilt for not asking her about them before now. She was right—he dealt with problems he didn't know how to solve by ignoring them.

She pushed herself up, and he quickly propped pillows behind her so she could lean back against the headboard, curls tumbling around her shoulders. Her pale blue cotton nightgown was damp with her sweat and clung to her. Her breathing was rough and uneven, her cheeks wet with tears. What was left of that wall around his heart came tumbling down with a thundering crash. Finally exposed, he could actually feel his heart breaking for her.

"You broke my door." She sounded so forlorn.

"Yes, I did. And I'll do it again. No more locks."

She shook her head emphatically, but he caught and cupped her chin in his hand. "No more nightmares behind locked doors, Amanda."

He turned so he could lean against the headboard next to her, then pulled her close. Her arms wrapped tightly around his torso, and she felt soft and sweet in his embrace. He kissed her hair as she rested her head on his chest. She was so quiet he thought she'd fallen asleep.

"I was sixteen." When she spoke, a chill fell over the room. He held his breath, wondering if she'd continue. Maybe she was talking in her sleep.

"I was sixteen," she started again with a stronger voice, definitely awake. "And you were right, I *was* a high school cheerleader. Jimmy Waldron was our quarterback. The team was undefeated that season, and Jimmy was the hero of Jenner, Kansas. He was a senior. So handsome. So popular. And he asked *me* to the homecoming dance. I couldn't believe it. I wore my first long dress...it was yellow. I'd always been a tomboy, you know, climbing trees and playing softball, but that night I felt like a princess."

He pulled the blanket up and wrapped it around her. He imagined her as a teenager, dressed in a sun-colored gown, with her wavy blond hair falling down her back. As pretty as the image was, he already knew this story was not going to have a happy ending.

"Jimmy said he had a surprise for me after the dance. He drove me out to the river in his truck. There was a full moon that night." Her voice was flat, and she paused after each sentence as if she was summoning the courage to say the next one. "I thought that's why he took me there. To see the moon over the water. He kissed me. My first kiss.

But then…" She stopped talking for so long that he thought she might not continue. He wasn't about to push her. "He… grabbed at me. I got scared, and he got rough. He pushed me to the ground and I just lay there staring up at him. I didn't run away. I didn't even try to. I was so stupid…"

"Don't say that. It wasn't your fault." Blake's throat was tight. "You did nothing wrong."

She kept talking, as if she couldn't stop herself from reciting the story she'd been reliving in nightmares. "He tore my dress. Everything he did hurt me…"

His stomach churned.

"You don't have to tell me…"

But apparently she did.

"He held my hands over my head and…" Blake closed his eyes tightly, trying to block the image of what she was describing. "I thought I was going to die. I begged him to stop. There was a stone under my left shoulder. A really sharp stone. I still have a little scar where it cut into me while he…while he…" She took a deep breath. "He kept saying I *wanted* it. But I didn't. I *didn't!* I finally just focused on that stone cutting into my back. I didn't think about anything but that damned stone…"

"Amanda…" His voice broke.

"By the time he dropped me off at home, I was numb."

"You were in shock, baby," Blake whispered into her hair. "He's in prison now?"

She shook her head against his chest. "Last I heard, he was selling used cars in Wichita."

"He wasn't charged?" How could that bastard be walking around free after raping her?

"It was…complicated. That's the word my stepfather used. You see, Jimmy's father was the mayor of our little town. He also owned the car dealership. My stepdad, Mitch, worked for him. My mom *wanted* to call the police, but Mitch didn't want me to cause any trouble…"

"And your mom dropped it, just like that?"

"She'd come hold me when I had nightmares, but she wouldn't go against Mitch, not even for me. I hated her for that weakness. He left her a few years after that for some woman he sold a car to."

Blake squeezed her tightly. He tried to imagine a young girl coming home torn and bloodied and in shock. What kind of man could see her like that and not call the police? But he knew. He knew his own father probably would have reacted the same way. Don't cause trouble. Don't damage the family reputation. Don't look weak.

She gave a short, mirthless laugh. "You know what Mitch was worried about? He said if I caused trouble for Jimmy while the football team was headed for the state championship, the whole town would hate us. And they *did* win the state championship. I always thought that trophy should have been mine. They wouldn't have had it without me staying quiet."

He swallowed hard, not knowing what to say to that. "Did you at least change schools?"

"We would have had to move, and Mitch wouldn't do that. He let me stay home until the bruises healed, and then I had to go back to class. It was just pure luck that I didn't end up pregnant or infected with something. But the girl I was died that day. The guys on the football team snickered when I walked by. The whole school was talking. By Christmas, I'd dropped my friends, or they'd dropped me—I don't really know which. I didn't trust anyone or anything." She fidgeted in his arms, restless and tense. "I couldn't stand to be touched after that. So much worse than I am now. Every man's touch felt like his hands."

Blake ran his hand slowly up and down her arm, stunned into silence. He kissed the top of her head again, then tipped her chin up so he could look at her face. Her eyes were sad and bright with tears, and the sight made his heart tighten.

"You've been having nightmares this bad all these years?"

"No. I locked it all away for a long time once I left Kansas. I had some counseling in college to deal with my fear of being touched. I built my career. I even dated a little. But being touched…like that…has always been a problem." He felt her tremble. "I went back to counseling a year ago. Dr. Jackson insisted I talk about the rape in session, which brought it all back, and that's when the nightmares and panic attacks started up again. She said it's healthy in a way, because I'm finally confronting my past. When I'm stressed, it's so much worse."

"But Dr. Jackson thinks you'll work through it?"

"God, I hope so." She smiled for the first time, and Blake kissed her forehead in relief. It was amazing anyone could smile after what she'd gone through. "She said I pushed the whole thing so deeply into denial for so long that I'm paying the price now, by having this hyperreaction to it. But she insists I have to confront my past before I can move on. Being raped ended my childhood. But I can't let it be the end of me."

Her voice faded at the end of the sentence, as if she wasn't quite convinced. He thought back to that first day they'd met. How she'd tried to keep him from touching her. When she'd landed on the hard stone floor and he'd been above her, she'd passed out from terror. Now he knew why. He couldn't imagine the toll that would take on a person as years passed. He looked down at her.

"Thank you, Amanda."

Her forehead crinkled. "For what?"

"For telling me. That couldn't have been easy."

She rested back against his chest. He put his hand protectively on the back of her head, cradling her, ready to fight off the whole damned world for her.

"It just came out. I've only talked to my cousins about it.

And Dr. Jackson, of course. Did I tell you that in my dreams, I always fight back? The doctor says that's important—something about reclaiming my power. She keeps encouraging me to talk about it more. She says it will help me accept it so I can move forward. But it's…hard to talk about. It takes a lot out of me… I get so tired…"

And just like that, her breathing changed, and Blake knew she'd fallen into a deep sleep. He carefully slid down onto the bed with her and held her against him, watching her face as she slept.

Some deep, unnamed emotion began to blossom in his heart as he watched her breathe in and out softly. He didn't know what it was, and it frightened him. He placed his lips softly on her forehead, then pulled her closer as he closed his eyes.

Chapter Fourteen

Blake slipped out of Amanda's room before she woke. Leaving her soft, warm body was more difficult than he'd expected, and he almost crawled right back under the covers. He stood next to the bed for a long time, watching how the early morning light kissed her face, with her hair fanned across the pillow.

He wanted to make sure she never had another sad moment in her life. *Ever.* And that realization was what propelled him out of her room. These roiling, unfamiliar emotions scared the hell out of him.

He was a coward for showering and leaving for the resort before she came downstairs for breakfast, but he didn't know what to do. He'd never felt this way about a woman in his entire life. In his world, women chased after *him*, and for all the wrong reasons. They wanted his lifestyle, his wealth and, yes, he supposed they liked his looks, too. But none of them really knew who he was.

His whole life was just one unending example of how relationships never worked. His parents. His brother and Michaela. He and the few women he'd tried getting serious with. Tiffany and every loser she'd brought home. The Randall family seemed genetically incapable of long-term relationships.

He stopped pacing his office and headed down to the lobby, restless inside and out. Amanda knew what Tiffany's death had done to him. She knew his fears about Zachary, and she loved his nephew fiercely. She knew his secrets, and after last night, he knew hers. Did that mean they had a relationship? Did he want that? Did *she*? Would theirs be just as doomed as every other relationship he'd had?

His attraction to her made no sense at all. She was petite and blonde, while he generally preferred tall and exotic. She was vulnerable, and he'd never liked weakness of any kind. She challenged him, and he generally had no patience for people who did that.

But she had ocean-blue eyes he could easily drown in. Curves that whispered his name every time she came near him. Lips softer than velvet. He scrubbed both hands down his face with a groan. He was driving himself crazy.

"What was that, Mr. Randall?" Julie's question jolted him back to awareness. He'd been so lost in his thoughts he hadn't even noticed she'd walked over to join him near the center of the lobby.

"Nothing, Julie. I'm just tired."

She tipped her head thoughtfully. "Yes, you've been busy since your return to Gallant Lake. Is everything all right?" Then she came right out and asked it. "Are you happy with everything Amanda did at Halcyon?"

He gave her a hard look. She was asking about more than the renovation of the house. Amanda hadn't had many champions in her life, and he was glad Julie was one of them. The corner of his mouth lifted in a crooked grin.

"Yes, Julie, I'm happy with *everything* Amanda has done at Halcyon."

Her shoulders visibly relaxed. "Good. She's working so hard to make that place a home. Zach's a great kid. We'd all miss him if he had to leave. And Amanda—"

"Neither of them will be leaving." Not if he had anything to do with it.

"Oh! Well, that's good news."

She saw something she didn't like near the front door and frowned at one of the doormen. He caught her expression and jumped to attention, looking around frantically for the infraction. He finally saw the crumpled piece of discarded paper on the floor and scooped it up, disposing of it. He glanced back for Julie's approval. Blake bit back a smile. When the general manager retired that coming winter as planned, Blake couldn't imagine anyone other than Julie taking the job. She ran a tight ship.

A silver Rolls-Royce came to a stop in front of the front doors, which were propped open on this crisp but sunny morning.

"Is it just me," Blake asked, "or are there an unusual number of very expensive cars rolling up to the resort this morning?"

Julie nodded, glancing at the two clerks manning the busy reception desk. "Yes. The entire west wing is booked with guests for the Fitzgerald wedding tomorrow. Very upscale. A lot of guests are arriving today from the city."

"How'd we land something that big?" Blake watched a silver-haired woman stride through the front doors draped in a fur cape, carrying a tiny dog in her arms. "And when did we start allowing *pets*?"

"Remember that *Times* bridal magazine ad you thought would be a waste of money? Too expensive for a one-time deal?" Julie's voice stayed cool while she kept a sharp eye on the doorman carrying Dog Lady's Louis Vuitton luggage. Blake gave Julie a sharp look and caught the barely perceptible shrug she gave him. "We ran it, and the phones have been busy ever since."

No wonder Julie and Amanda had become friends. They were both smart, sassy women who had no problem challenging him. "We started allowing dogs weighing less than fifteen pounds in August as an experiment. Manhattan socialites love to take their little fashion-accessory doggies everywhere. We only allow them in certain rooms, and guests pay a very large, nonrefundable deposit for the privilege."

There was a time when he would have been furious to find out about these policy changes after the fact. No Surprises Lifestyle and all that. It must be the lack of sleep that was making him so complacent.

"Sounds like you've got everything under control here, Julie. Nice work."

He didn't miss her self-satisfied smile, gone as fast as it had appeared. "Thank you, Mr. Randall. Now, if you'll excuse me, I think I should step in and help at the desk."

"No problem." She started to turn away, but stopped when he rested his hand on her arm. "Julie...thank you for being there for Amanda and Zachary while I was gone."

There was an awkward silence. It was unlike him to be so personal with his employees. Then she patted his hand softly.

"Mr. Randall, it was my pleasure. You're a lucky man to have both of them in your life."

He watched her walk away. There was a time not long ago when he made sure there was a very clear line between his all-consuming business life and barely existent personal life. That line had become increasingly blurred lately.

Amanda busied herself with dinner that evening, trying to determine how she felt about everything that had happened in the last twenty-four hours. The kiss in Zach's bathroom. Blake asking questions about her past she couldn't answer. And then the nightmare, which answered all those questions anyway.

She placed a pot of water on the stove. She'd woken during the night and watched him sleeping next to her. She'd reached out and touched the dark, curling hair on his chest with her fingertips, then pulled away when he moaned and rolled onto his side. He'd wrapped his arm around her and drew her close, and she'd let him. No panic. No fear. His arms felt like a safe place to be. She felt oddly bereft when she woke later and realized he'd left her, and she hadn't seen or heard from him all day. She wasn't even sure he'd show up for the ravioli dinner she was cooking right now.

Did he feel differently now that he knew her past? Would things be weird between them? She chuckled to herself. How much weirder could they be? The two of them continued to dance around each other, pretending to be no more than friends, walking on eggshells unless, of course, they were kissing. When they kissed, they couldn't get enough of each other.

But something was. Ever since the work started in Blake's office, she'd felt this sense of impending...*something*. It wasn't the protesters, although Blake said there'd been a few acts of minor vandalism recently. It wasn't her usual panic-driven imagination. It was deeper than that. For all the joy of watching Blake and Zachary become a family, and whatever was blossoming between her and Blake, it still felt like there was trouble simmering in this house. The kind of trouble that couldn't be blamed on an imaginary ghost.

She was dumping the pasta into the boiling water when her skin warmed and her pulse quickened. She turned to find Blake leaning against the door frame in virtually the same pose he'd used weeks ago when she'd cooked that first meal for him. His eyes sparkled with knowing humor. "I have some very fond memories of this kitchen." He pushed away from the doorway and moved deliberately in her direction. She had a wooden spoon in her hand and ended up holding it between them as if to ward him off. He didn't stop until the spoon was resting lightly against his chest.

"I have to go into the city tomorrow morning for a meeting. I'll be back in time for dinner, but you're not cooking. I'm taking you to Galantè. Just the two of us."

"What about Zach?"

"Jamal's wife, Annie, will stay here with Zach for a few

hours." His face grew serious. "I know we're coming at this whole thing backward and sideways, but now that we've kissed and fought and made up and agreed to be friends and are raising a young child together and sharing our deepest secrets…well, I think it's time for us to have a first date, don't you?"

She chuckled at the absurdity of the relationship he'd just outlined. "Yeah, I guess that would be the logical next step in this entirely illogical relationship."

But a date? A *real* date? That would make this relationship a lot more serious. A lot more real. It would move them a giant step forward, and she wasn't sure she was ready for what that might mean.

Blake put his hand on her cheek and she leaned into it without thinking. It was just the natural thing to do. She closed her eyes as he bent to kiss her softly. He whispered her name, and the kiss quickly deepened to something meaningful and special and intimate. This kiss wasn't about their physical attraction, it was about something *more*, and she knew he felt it, too. It carried a promise of what was to come. He pulled away with a look of frustrated regret and whispered in her ear.

"Wear something pretty tomorrow." And he was gone, calling Zach to dinner as he left the kitchen. She leaned back against the counter, touching her lips with her fingertips. Tomorrow she was going to have a first date with a man who already knew her better than any other.

The following evening, as promised, they were seated together at a small table near the windows in Galantè. He'd asked her to wear something nice, so she'd pulled out a long velvet skirt Mel had sent her last winter. It was dark peacock blue, and flared just enough to dance around her ankles when she walked. The matching satin blouse was styled like a man's oxford shirt, and she'd tied it casually at the waist.

Blake was devilishly handsome in his dark suit and red tie. The flickering candlelight accentuated the strong lines of his face as well as the deep cleft in his chin. He was watching her in obvious amusement.

"What?" She wiped steak sauce from the corner of her mouth with her napkin.

"I'm just wondering where you put it all. Do you have a hollow leg I don't know about?" He was admiring her for *eating*. Terrific. Their waitress swooped in to whisk their dinner plates away and ask if they wanted dessert. Blake nodded.

"We'll share a caramel lava cake, Sarah. And bring two cappuccinos, please."

"Of course, Mr. Randall." And then she was gone. Amanda looked out at the peaceful lake shimmering in the moonlight, shadowed by mountains. "How did you get here?"

"What do you mean?"

"You own hotels in Barbados, Miami, Bali, Las Vegas. What brought you to a little blue-collar town in upstate New York?"

Blake followed her gaze toward the lake, his voice soft and low. "I'm really not sure. One of my advisors saw the resort on the market and did some recon on the viability of putting a casino here. It would be difficult, but not impossible. I liked the idea of something this close to Manhattan. Halcyon was on the market, too, and I figured we'd need the extra land, so I bought a castle."

"How did you get in the resort business in the first place? Were you following your father's footsteps?"

"Hell, no. My great-grandfather started a commercial real estate business—office buildings, mostly—and my grandfather grew it into an empire in New York and New

Jersey." Blake emptied the second bottle of cabernet into their wineglasses and took a sip. "My grandfather died the same year I graduated college. I insisted on taking my portion of the inheritance in cash instead of joining the business, because I knew my father would run it into the ground. Father only agreed because he figured I'd fail and come crawling back."

"But you didn't." She felt a jolt of pride that he had risen to the challenge at such a young age.

"No, I didn't. I bought a struggling hotel in Miami and turned it around. And things just progressed from there. I bought a couple more hotels. I bought the land in Bali where I'm building a resort. And, of course, Gallant Lake."

Sarah brought their dessert to the table, an impressive tower of chocolate cake and caramel sauce topped with whipped cream, nutmeg under a cage of spun sugar.

"What's next?" Amanda asked, picking up her spoon.

"I'm looking at Europe. And I need to do something with this place, just in case the Gallant Lake Preservation Society, or anyone else for that matter, keeps me from building my casino."

She returned his grin. "Julie and I were talking about that last week. This would be a terrific venue for destination weddings, especially if you used Halcyon. It's so close to the city, and…"

"Use Halcyon?" He sat back and looked at her with interest.

She grinned at his confusion. "The house would be a perfect setting for a wedding. Rent out the lawn for outdoor ceremonies and have the receptions out there under tents or here at the resort. You could even rent out the house itself for weddings. That grand staircase would make an amazing entrance for a bride."

"You've really given this some thought."

"I was trying to come up with options to convince you not to tear down the resort."

He was silent, then shook his head.

"I don't want Halcyon to be part of the resort. I want it to be my home."

"I thought you didn't want a home?"

He gave her a crooked grin. The one that always made her heart beat faster. "Zach needs it. And I think I do, too. I'm not worried about the resort. It's smaller than my other properties, but I like the idea of a boutique hotel just outside the city. Between the spa and the new golf course, it'll do just fine."

"Even if you don't get your casino?"

"Is the idea of a casino that could generate hundreds of jobs really that awful?"

"Not awful. Just misguided."

He stood with a chuckle and reached for her hand. "Come on." He rested his hand lightly on her waist and headed for the kitchen. "I want to make a quick check on the wedding reception going on tonight."

The kitchen was a noisy madhouse of activity, but the chef saw them the minute they entered. Dario ignored his employer and rushed up to Amanda, giving her a big kiss on each cheek.

"Eh! My *bambolina*! How are you tonight, *bella mia*? You look so beautiful!"

She laughed and gave him a hug.

"Dario, *mi angelo bello*," she said, "the filet mignon was fantastic. You have to teach me how to make that cognac sauce." He just laughed and shook his finger at her. She knew how tightly the chef protected his recipes. He turned to Blake.

"Signor Randall, you have a treasure in Miss Amanda and your little boy. They make my life brighter here in Gallant Lake."

Blake just nodded, his eyes dark with emotion. "Yes, Dario, they brighten my life, too."

She felt her cheeks flushing. As they walked away, Blake leaned over and spoke softly into her ear.

"My dear Miss Lowery, you seem to have completely charmed my staff. Whatever is your secret?"

She gave him a playful laugh. "I think it's the magic of Halcyon, Mr. Randall."

"Still waiting for Madeleine's ghost to appear up there?"

"What makes you think I haven't already seen her?"

They both laughed. He'd think she was crazy, but sometimes she wondered if there might be something to the legend of Halcyon. What else explained how she and Zach and Blake ended up together in Gallant Lake?

They walked through the kitchen to the long hallway leading to the ballroom, and they could hear the wedding band finishing up a popular line dance. After a smattering of applause, the music slowed. The singer had a beautiful voice, and the song was one of Amanda's favorites.

Blake pulled her close and she tensed out of habit. With her issues about intimacy, slow dancing had never been her thing. He spoke softly, his lips brushing her ear.

"I told you this was a date." His fingers started to move gently across her back, and she began to relax. He started to hum to the music. "What song is this?"

"It's the theme song from one of those silly vampire movies. It's probably the best thing to come from them."

He chuckled. "That's rich coming from a woman who believes in ghosts, don't you think?"

Blake gave her a gentle squeeze, resting his cheek on top of her head and pressing her closer.

Her fear whispered to her from the shadows. What if Blake's feelings for her were just mixed up with the excitement of the house and his new relationship with Zach? If she gave her trust to Blake and he betrayed her, it would break her. She silently prayed that he was different from all the other men in her life.

She finally sighed and focused on the sultry rhythm of the music, letting the warmth of his body push away all fears as they danced together.

Chapter Fifteen

Blake watched Amanda stare pensively into the fire. They'd walked back up to the house in silence after their hallway dance at the resort. Zach was asleep, and Annie said he'd been no problem at all. So Amanda wasn't worried about that. Which left only one thing for her to worry about. *Him.*

"Hey," he said. She swept her eyelashes up and sent him a piercing look. God, her blue eyes slayed him every time. "What's wrong?"

"What do you mean?" Her innocent expression didn't fool him for a minute.

"You seem distracted. What's on your mind?"

She looked down again without answering, staring into the fire. He heard distant music, probably from the wedding reception down the hill.

"Is that piano music coming all the way from the resort?"

Amanda gave him a soft, knowing smile. "Maybe it's courtesy of that ghost you don't believe in."

He knew she was a romantic, but he never thought she was delusional. "Are you telling me you think Madeleine Pendleton is playing a ghostly piano in my house?"

"Maybe she likes music." She caught his expression and laughed softly. "I know it sounds crazy, but sometimes I wonder, you know? The legend had to start somewhere."

The tension on her face earlier was gone as she stared calmly into the fire, which was now crackling merrily. Her profile, with her mane of hair pulled up on top of her head in a messy knot of curls, looked like a Grecian sculpture. Her entire body seemed relaxed and at peace.

If a haunted Halcyon had that effect on her, then he was okay with a haunted Halcyon. If she wanted him to believe in ghosts, then by God, he believed in ghosts. It was that simple. But he wasn't ready to admit it out loud.

"Yeah, the legend came from people who believe in fairy tales. Just because it's a castle doesn't mean it's enchanted."

"Who knows?" Amanda shrugged. "Maybe Madeleine's happy that Halcyon is becoming a home for you and Zach."

"And you." He said the words more forcefully than he'd intended, and she looked at him in surprise.

"Whatever happened to taking things a step at a time?"

He stood and pulled her up with him. "I swear I'm doing my best with the one-step-at-a-time thing. You're already living here at Halcyon." He pressed his lips to her forehead. "I'm not ready to let you go. Not when I'm just learning who you are. You amaze me every freaking day, Amanda, and I don't want to lose you."

Her hands rested lightly on his chest. "You see me *whole*, Blake. I've never seen myself that way. Not since…" Her eyes clouded. "I was broken for so long. But when I'm with you, I feel complete. I'm not afraid. I can't describe it but—"

He silenced her with a kiss. A long, slow, tender kiss. He took his time getting into her mouth and he heard a trembling moan coming from her throat as he explored her. His hands moved down her body and he pulled her close. She didn't pull away this time. He lifted his head and stared into those blue oceans. She whispered that magic word.

"Yes."

That was all he needed to hear. He sat her on the arm of a chair and held up his hand so she knew to wait. She watched in obvious amusement as he rushed to secure the doors and arm the alarm system. Then he led her upstairs to his suite. She hadn't said a word downstairs while he scrambled around. And she still wasn't speaking. Any worries that she was changing her mind vanished when she stopped by the bed and began unbuttoning her blouse.

She reached back to unfasten her skirt after discarding the top. He started to unbutton his shirt, finally yanking it over his head in frantic frustration when her skirt dropped to the floor in a billowing pile of blue-green velvet. He stared at her alabaster skin and all those marvelous curves wrapped in black lace. How could one petite body have that many rounded invitations to please come explore?

His staring must have made her uncomfortable, because she started to raise her hands to cover herself. He stepped forward with an urgent "No" escaping his lips. "The day we met, you said this house was magnificent. But it's not the house. It's you. *You're* the magnificent one, Amanda. Let me drink you in." His voice was raw with desire.

She dropped her hands to her sides, locking her eyes on his as he reached for her. His eyes were going to be her lifeline. He could see that now. It was his job to make sure she felt safe. He held her gaze calmly. He pulled the pins from her hair, brushing it back over her shoulders as it fell.

Flickers of panic danced across her eyes, but they were gone as quickly as they appeared. If he just moved slowly and kept his eyes on hers, they'd be fine. The only problem was he didn't want to go slow. He wanted to devour every inch of her, but he knew he couldn't. Not tonight. His thumbs brushed across her bra and her lips parted with a shuddering sigh. He reached behind her slowly and unhooked the bra, and she let it drop to the floor. His eyes left hers briefly to glance toward the two perfectly rounded breasts now in his hands. His thumbs moved back and forth, and she made a strangled sound deep in her throat. One hand slid lower across her stomach, and she trembled beneath his fingers. But her eyes were fixed on his, and she was trusting him. She groaned as his fingers moved across the slick softness between her legs.

"Blake…" She breathed his name, and he felt his heart catching fire with want of her.

She hissed when his fingers found their target. She didn't look away. Didn't close her eyes. Just stared at him and made the most wonderful little mewling noises in her throat as he explored her. With a small cry, her knees buckled and he caught her up in his arms, laying her on the bed. He finished undressing and crawled on top of her, catching her gaze again. She was nervous, but she nodded, giving him permission. He kissed her deeply, then started trailing kisses down her neck and across shoulders, glimpsing back up at her face after every other kiss. Her eyes followed him intently. She whimpered softly as he kissed her breasts and teased the tips with his tongue, then his teeth. He started sliding lower with his kisses when she spoke.

"Blake…please… I need you."

That was all he needed to hear. There would be time for exploring later. He grabbed at his nightstand for a condom, then came back over her. She lifted her body up toward his, and he let out a loud groan as he sank slowly into her. Kissing her softly, he watched her eyes grow wide, then fade into blissful, unfocused distraction. Their bodies started moving together. He felt so very absolutely *perfect* inside of her.

This is where he was meant to be. She rocked against him and he pressed into her more firmly, more demanding. There was only one moment when she got tense, and it was when he got distracted watching where their bodies were connected instead of looking at her face. He looked into her eyes and smiled.

"It's me, sweetheart. It's *me* making love to you."

She relaxed again, and they both picked up the pace. He felt her tightening and trembling beneath him. She started whispering his name over and over, and the sound drove him wild.

"It's okay, baby. It's okay to let go."

And she did. She exploded. She opened her mouth to scream and he dropped his mouth over hers to own all of her orgasm before joining her.

Amanda felt like she'd just shattered into a million pieces. So *this* was what it meant to truly make love. She'd had no idea she could feel so powerful and wise and womanly until she felt him coming undone inside of her body. She flexed her fingers against his back and he groaned. He lifted his head from beside hers and propped himself up on one elbow to look down at her. She giggled at the sight of his black hair standing on end.

"Laughter isn't exactly how a man wants to be greeted after mind-blowing sex," he growled at her. But his eyes showed nothing but amusement and heat. Lots of heat. And he'd said "mind-blowing." She grinned.

"You have such terrible bed head." She reached up to run her fingers through his dark curls. He closed his eyes at her touch, and she brought her hand down to his cheek. He leaned into it and sighed.

"I'm still trying to put my *brain* back together, much less my hair. That was... I don't know...*incredible* doesn't even come close to describing it."

"It was my first." She blushed as she said the words. His eyes snapped open, and she wished she'd never said anything.

"Your first?"

"You know...the first time I really...um...finished..."

A lazy smile slid across his face. "I'm honored. How was it?"

She giggled again. "I think you know how it was." Then she turned serious. "Thank you, Blake."

"Oh, hell no, I'm the one who should be down on my knees giving thanks to you, Amanda. It's never, *ever* been that good." He rolled slowly off her to rest on his side and remove the condom, then kissed her softly on the lips. "I want to keep you in my bed forever."

Her breath caught in her throat.

Forever.

"Blake…"

"Shh. Talk later. Not now. Right now I need to sleep, baby. Stay here and sleep with me." He pulled her into his arms and she closed her eyes, feeling safe and at peace.

When Amanda woke, the sun was shining brightly through the windows. She was alone in Blake's bed. She closed her eyes tightly.

She'd made love with Blake Randall. Her client. Zach's uncle. Her "friend." Her date. The man she couldn't imagine living without. She was falling for him, and hard.

The door to the suite opened and he walked in, carrying two mugs of coffee. His hair was damp from a shower, and he was wearing jeans and a plaid shirt with the sleeves rolled up. He looked good enough to eat. She blushed at the thought and pulled the sheets up higher to cover herself, which made him laugh.

"A little late for modesty, don't you think? Your robe is there at the foot of the bed, but feel free to stay as you are." He set a mug on the nightstand.

"I overslept. Zach. Breakfast."

She couldn't form whole sentences in his presence. Blake sat in the big chair by the fireplace, looking annoyingly smug.

"Zach's down at the game room at the resort. Jamal's keeping an eye on him. For some reason, you were in a very deep slumber this morning." Blake laughed when she blushed. "Don't be embarrassed, sweetheart. I managed to feed my nephew breakfast all by myself."

She sat on the edge of the bed, pulled on her robe and reached for the coffee. A dusting of cinnamon covered the white foam at the top of the mug. "And then you trotted into the kitchen and whipped up a cup of Dario's cappuccino? Come clean, Blake. You took Zach to the café at the resort."

He tipped his head back and laughed out loud. She loved the sound of his laugh. She loved *him.*

Wait. *What?*

She looked at him in shock, but fortunately he was still looking at the ceiling as he laughed. Oh, God. She was in love with Blake Randall. The man who abandoned his nephew. The man threatening to build a casino on Gallant Lake. The guy who didn't believe in love. The man who captured her body last night, and now her heart. Was there any chance for this to end well?

"Okay, I confess I didn't *cook* breakfast, but at least I made sure he ate." He noticed her distraction. "Amanda? What's wrong?" She forced herself to smile at him as she shrugged.

He moved to the edge of the bed, cupping her chin in his hand and leaning close to her face. "No regrets. Okay?" He dropped a kiss on her lips. "We'll figure this out."

Her body began to sing as a pulse of energy shot through her. She looked into his eyes. Those eyes that held her safely last night. Those eyes she trusted.

He studied her face. "If you keep looking at me like that, you'll never get out of this bed. And right now I have to go talk to someone in town about some land I'm interested in. I'll be back later. Are you okay?"

Land? The casino. *Damn it.*

"Still working on the casino plan?"

He stopped her with another kiss. "No, sweetheart. This place has become hallowed ground to me. No one's building anything here. No one." A shadow crossed his face for just a moment, then he grinned again. It was a sweet, child-like grin that charmed her completely. "You've ruined my good business sense, girl. Gallant Lake Resort stays whole. Halcyon is my home. My nephew's going to public school. And I have a brave, bewitching woman in my bed."

No casino. Zach in public school. Her in his bed. She threw her arms around his neck and kissed him. He groaned and turned, pressing her back against the bed, returning the kiss. He bit her lower lip and rested his forehead on hers. "I'm not kidding, Amanda. I'll keep you in bed all day long, and then again all night. We'll starve, but we'll die happy. Is that what you want?"

"Yes. But not the dying part." She giggled, then sighed into his neck as he hugged her. "You make me happy, Blake Randall. Scary happy." He lifted his head.

"Scary happy. Yeah, I guess that captures it, doesn't it?" He kissed her quickly, then sat up and rose to his feet. "Drink your coffee and get dressed, lazybones. I'll only be gone for an hour or so, and I promised Zach we'd go fishing."

Chapter Sixteen

She didn't join the boys for their fishing trip in the small aluminum boat. Instead, she curled up in one of the Adirondack chairs by the shore with a romance novel she'd borrowed from Julie. It was almost November, but the sun shone bright and warm. She tried in vain to keep her attention on the book in her hands and not on the incredible sex she'd had with Blake last night.

It was more than sex, of course. She was in love with him. Fingers of panic traced a path up her spine.

After an hour or so, the two fishermen returned to the dock, empty-handed but laughing. Blake surprised her by giving her a warm kiss right in front of Zach. Her face burned, but Zach just smiled and looked away. She frowned at Blake in disapproval, and he laughed.

"It's getting chilly out here, Miss Amanda. Why don't you come inside and I'll pour us both some wine?"

Blake and Zach were laughing upstairs when she came into the house, and another piece of her heart fractured. That voice of fear started whispering again. How long could their little fantasy family life last? Was Blake really ready for a home and a family? Could life here at Halcyon satisfy him for more than a few weeks? He still had an international business empire to run, so he'd have to travel a lot, leaving them behind.

She wanted to believe it could work. Because she was completely and utterly in love with the man. There was no sense in denying it. She just had to figure out exactly what that meant for her heart. And for her future. He walked up behind her as she stood in the living room staring out at the lake. He wrapped one arm around her stomach and pulled her back against him, sliding a glass of wine into her hand as he kissed the top of her head.

"You're thinking too much again."

How did he always know? He squeezed her and answered her unspoken question.

"It's in your shoulders, in your face, in your silence."

"I'm just wondering if we're kidding ourselves here." She hadn't really intended to speak her fears out loud. But there it was. He turned her in his arms.

"Kidding ourselves in what way?"

She sighed and blinked away. "It's like we've been living in a bubble. What will happen to Zach if something happens between us, Blake?"

"Happens, how?"

"We're giving him the illusion that we've become this instant family, and he'll be crushed if that falls apart." She didn't mention that she'd be crushed, too. "He's already been through so much. Are we doing the right thing for him? I mean, it's all fun and games while we sit here in Gallant Lake, but you'll be leaving again, and how appealing is this place going to be to you when the snow starts to fly and you're walking the beaches in Barbados or wherever?"

"What are you talking about?" He stepped back. "What have I done that makes you think I haven't been honest with you?"

She couldn't think of one thing. "Nothing."

"Then what the hell, Amanda?"

"Look, I know how you were raised. I know how driven you are. I know what you think about romance. Are you saying you've become a totally different person in the past few weeks?"

"Yes."

She gasped at how quickly he answered.

His eyes were steady as he held her gaze.

"Yes. I've changed. Haven't you?"

She looked down and thought for a moment. After all, she'd trusted him with her body, when she hadn't been able to do that with any man.

"Yes. I guess I have. But maybe we should take a step back." When would she stop living in fear? Why couldn't she trust him with her heart?

Love is like fool's gold, Amanda. Love is an illusion. A trick. A flicker of a moment that's not worth the resulting trouble.

She slowly opened her eyes the next morning, trying to get her bearings. She turned to look at the source of radiating heat behind her, knowing he was the reason she'd slept so soundly. Good Lord, he was gorgeous.

Blake's face was soft in slumber, but still sexy. His hair fell down over one eye haphazardly, and his lips were curled into an almost-smile, as if he'd just sighed in contentment. The sheets were down around his waist, so she got to peruse his broad chest, covered with dark curls. She couldn't help reaching out to trace her fingers down his sternum. His eyes snapped open when she touched him, and they were smoldering.

He reached his hand out and rested it on her cheek, giving her a crooked, sleepy grin. She immediately decided this was her favorite look on him. Rumpled, half-awake, aroused and in lo—

No! She gave herself a hard mental shake. He was not in love with her, regardless of her feelings for him. He was the guy who didn't believe in love. Didn't have time for it. Thought it was foolish. He could easily betray her, just like all the other men in her life had done. Frowning at her troubled expression, he stroked her bottom lip lightly with his thumb. He leaned in for a deep kiss, and she forgot what she was worrying about. He pulled her under his body without breaking contact with her lips. He traced kisses lightly down her neck and lifted the hem of her nightgown. He left her only long enough to get a condom from the nightstand, but even that was too long. She whispered his name.

"I'm here. I'm here, beautiful. I'll always be here…"

She decided to believe him a while longer and lost herself to the sensation of him filling her completely. She arched into him and closed her eyes, focusing only on the wonder of Blake making soft, sweet love to her. Her pulse began to race. She whispered his name over and over, and he growled as he became more aggressive. She wasn't afraid. In fact, she was eager. She dug her nails into his back and cried his name one last time as her body fell apart. He joined her wordlessly, groaning as he fell onto her, breathing hard.

Finally he spoke. "Best. Alarm clock. Ever."

She giggled into his ear. "Speaking of alarm clocks, Zach will be up soon, and if he comes looking for me…"

"How can you talk about *Zach* after we just set the sheets on fire? Let me just enjoy the moment, will you?" He chuckled and bit her lightly on the shoulder. "Besides, I can't move right now, even if the entire village of Gallant Lake came into this room. Even if Madeleine Pendleton herself joined us. I'm not moving."

She tightened her arms around him. He might break her heart someday. But until then, he was hers. He moved his weight off her and pulled her close. She nuzzled his chest and kissed him there.

"Just stay with me a few more minutes," he sighed. "Let me hold you." His breathing changed, and she knew he'd fallen asleep. She snuggled into him, but if she closed her eyes she'd never get Zach off to school. And she certainly didn't want him to walk in and catch them together in bed. She slid carefully out from under the covers and left Blake sleeping there.

He didn't come downstairs until after Zach left. She couldn't stop the laughter that bubbled up when he walked into the kitchen, looking so very pleased with himself.

"And here we go with the laughter after sex again." He held his hands to his chest in mock offense. "I'm going to get a complex."

"Sorry." She slid a mug of coffee across the island to him. "You just look so totally… I don't know…satisfied? Like a Cheshire cat."

"Satisfied is definitely how I'm feeling this morning. I didn't even feel you leave the bed. Is Zach off to school?"

"Of course. You're the only lazybones this morning." She reached for the paper bag on the counter, knowing Blake liked a simple breakfast. "Bagel?"

He nodded and she split the bagel and dropped it into the toaster. Her phone started ringing in her back pocket.

She did a little victory dance when the call ended, then had to explain it when she saw Blake's surprise.

"Your desk is ready! There's a guy in town who builds furniture, and I talked him into refinishing that antique desk I found in the attic." The heavily carved mahogany desk had been buried under boxes and drop cloths when she'd gone exploring up there. As soon as she uncovered it, she knew it would be perfect for Blake's office. "This project is almost done!"

Was it just her, or had an awkward silence fallen like a giant wet blanket over the kitchen? Blake shrugged, ate the last of his bagel and grabbed his travel mug of coffee. "Sounds great, babe."

So apparently it *was* just Amanda who felt the end racing at them. At her. He started to walk past, then stopped and gave her a fierce hug and kiss.

"Relax. The house is wrapping up, but you and I are nowhere *near* done. I told you I want your help with the resorts, and I've got plans, baby."

The corner of Blake's mouth tipped up into a crooked grin. "I need to go make some calls, but let's go into town for pizza when Zach gets home. We'll have a family night, okay?"

The words were right there on her lips when he kissed her and walked away. She *wanted* to tell him how much she loved him. Soon.

Blake's best friend let out a long, low whistle on the other end of the phone.

"Let me get this straight—your interior designer pretended to be someone else to get the job. And instead of firing her, you're…dating?"

Blake didn't answer. Amanda was walking down to the lakeshore with a warm sweater draped over her shoulders. He'd lost track of the conversation when she stopped to look back at the house. He doubted she could see him standing at the living room windows, but her shoulders straightened nonetheless. Halcyon was working its magic on her once again. He couldn't claim to understand it, but he knew she got strength from this pink castle.

"Blake? You still with me?"

Andy McCormack's voice interrupted his thoughts. "Yeah, man. Sorry. I was watching my girl walking outside."

"She must be something pretty special to pierce *your* armor."

"She's tough, Andy. Strong. Beautiful."

Andy laughed. "Oh, man, you're a goner!"

They'd been best friends since meeting at Harvard and were investors in each other's companies. Andy's company, McCormack Security, provided bodyguards, security systems and planning to companies and celebrities all over the world. Jamal had worked for Andy before coming to head up security at Gallant Lake.

Blake settled back in his chair. Amanda was walking along the shore now. She bent to pick up a stone, sending it skipping across the smooth surface of the lake.

"Okay, clearly you're not ready to talk about your new girl. What did the preservation society say when you told them you scrapped the casino plans? Have things calmed down any?"

The episodes of vandalism were ticking up in frequency and intensity, although the official members of the group claimed they had nothing to do with it.

"I haven't told them yet. I have some investors that aren't too happy about it, so I want to be sure I smooth those feathers before it goes public. And I need to have answers for the locals who *wanted* those jobs. I'll have to convince them we can create new jobs by renovating the resort and getting businesses to improve downtown Gallant Lake to draw in more people."

"And your family? What are they going to say when you bring her to Christmas dinner?"

Blake scoffed. "As if I'd sit down for Christmas dinner with any of them. They were never officially part of the casino. Father wanted too big a piece of the pie, so we never signed a deal. I'm not sure Nathan knows that, though." His brother seemed to assume the casino was a family project, if only because it was located in New York. But *assuming* was never a good business practice. Blake didn't want to discuss his family, though, and he knew the one topic Andy was always ready to talk about these days—his new fiancée.

"You still planning a Barbados wedding? Speaking of which, when do I get to meet the woman crazy enough to agree to marry you?" His friend met a feisty Southern girl while on vacation a few months ago, and Andy fell like a ton of bricks. He'd popped the question before Blake had a chance to meet her.

"Barbados next spring. Caroline's coming to the Builders Ball in New York. Are you bringing Amanda?"

Damn. He hadn't even thought about the annual must-attend event for every real estate investor on the East Coast. Would Amanda want to be in that coldhearted pack of overachieving snobs? Would it trigger a panic attack?

"I'm not sure." He cleared his throat and changed the subject again. "I still can't believe you're getting married, Andy."

"Believe it, my friend. I've never been happier. And it seems to me like you've got it pretty bad for this Amanda woman."

Blake shook his head. Yeah, he had it bad, all right. But marriage? It was way too soon to be going there, even if Andy and Caroline had gotten engaged barely six weeks after meeting. He ignored the comment and finished up the conversation. He wasn't ready to discuss his feelings for Amanda yet. Not even with his best friend. Not until he'd sorted them out for himself.

Blake leaned against the doorway to the living room the following Sunday evening and smiled. Amanda and Zachary were on the sofa together, watching a very loud movie about cars that transformed into alien robots. There was a bowl of popcorn between them, and they were giggling as they snuggled under a soft wool blanket.

Andy was right—Amanda had pierced his well-worn armor somehow. Torn down his carefully built wall. Thoroughly trashed his No Surprises Lifestyle. His goals had swung sharply from business success at all costs to keeping her happy and safe every day of her life.

And she'd done it without even breaking a sweat. First she agitated him to his breaking point and beyond, then she reeled him in for the kill with her brutal honesty and wisdom. He was in awe of her. She'd trusted her body to him in spite of her past, in spite of her fears. And now he wanted nothing more than to be with her every moment. He'd protect her with everything he had.

His stomach twisted. Relationships had always been a losing proposition for him. They were never worth the energy invested. Sure, people tossed around the *L* word like it meant something, but he'd learned differently time and time again. Why even pretend it was real? Look at the disastrous track record his family had in relationships. It was like they were cursed.

That old argument, the one he'd been clinging to for so long, suddenly sounded hollow. It was different with Amanda. There was a glimmer of something inside of him that had simply never existed until she came waltzing into his house. Was it hope?

Zach threw a piece of popcorn at Amanda and she caught it in her mouth, making the boy laugh. Tiffany's little boy. Zachary was Blake's chance to do things right. To make up for the way he let his sister down. His parents should have loved her better, damn it. If no one else, *they* should have loved their beautiful baby girl. He'd tried to love her enough for everyone, but he couldn't do it. It was too late for him to save Tiffany, but it wasn't too late for Zach. The kid had his mother's sense of humor. Her laugh. Her heart. He'd taken care of Amanda while Blake was halfway around the world being a jackass.

Warmth blossomed inside of him, as if he could actually feel his heart growing. He thought of that Christmas cartoon character whose heart grew so much with love that it burst right out of his chest. Yeah, this woman had done something to him, all right. It was a mind-boggling turn of events. He'd teased her earlier about remodeling him along with the house, and in truth, she'd done just that.

She looked up and saw him standing there, then smiled and tilted her head questioningly. He pushed away from the wall and walked over, sitting on the floor in front of her and Zach. He handed her one of the wineglasses he'd been carrying. She massaged the top of his head absently with her fingertips as the good robots started defeating the bad robots on screen. He leaned his head back against her knee and sighed.

This is what love felt like. He was in love with her. He was in love with the woman who challenged him and changed him and made him whole. He was in love with Amanda Lowery.

He was standing at the edge of a cliff, and the drop was shrouded in fog. Would he fly if he stepped off? Would he crash to the earth? It didn't matter. His heart had already leaped, so he was going to have to follow. Life as he'd known it was over. And he was okay with that.

Chapter Seventeen

Blake was later than usual getting to the office the next morning, and he was feeling pretty damned good about it. He was late because Amanda insisted he drive Zach to school. She insisted because Zach missed the bus. Zach missed the bus because they all overslept. They overslept because he'd woken Amanda sometime before dawn with a kiss in a place she'd never been kissed before. Yeah—totally worth being late. Over the past few days, he'd discovered sharing a bed with Amanda was worth pretty much anything.

Her sharp intake of breath when she'd woken had been quickly replaced with soft moans of pleasure while he'd explored every inch of her. The sun had been just beginning to rise when they'd finally dozed off in a tangle of arms and legs. By the time they'd woken again, there'd been no way Zach was catching the bus. She'd pretended to be upset, but he was pretty sure that was more embarrassment than anything else; as if a ten-year-old was going to guess what made Uncle Blake and Miss Amanda so very sleepy and smiley.

A soft knock at his office door brought him back to the here and now. He waved Julie in.

"Mr. Randall…"

"Julie, you're one of Amanda's closest friends. I think you can call me 'Blake' and still maintain our professional relationship during working hours."

Her brows lifted in surprise.

"I think so, too, Blake. Thank you. I just wanted to remind

you about the conference call. I've got it set up on your line, and the Miami management staff is standing by."

"Hmm? Oh, of course. I almost forgot." He was the one who'd scheduled the call to discuss the upcoming celebrity wedding in Miami. Even after the call started, he couldn't stop thinking about how Amanda looked in the moonlight last night, golden hair flamed out against the pillows as she whispered his name.

When he heard a sharp knock on his closed office door a few hours later, he figured it was Julie again. He couldn't have been more surprised, or more disappointed, at who opened the door when he called out.

His father and brother walked in without bothering to greet him. Nathan's eyes narrowed as he looked around the large office, taking in every custom detail as well as the panoramic view of Gallant Lake and the mountains beyond it through the windows that lined one wall. There was a reason Nathan had never been invited to the resort, and this was it. For all of his own personal wealth, Nathan was openly jealous of Blake's self-made success. Blake had broken free of their father's influence, and Nathan never had the backbone to do the same. Their father glanced around the room dismissively, clearly unimpressed.

Blake felt a sharp pain in his temple at the sight of his so-called family standing in his private office. The headache prompted a blunt question.

"What the hell are you two doing here?"

He didn't doubt for a minute that they were here to make trouble. His father took one of the small chairs in front of Blake's desk. Nathan stood by the windows, hands in his pockets, and barely acknowledged Blake's presence. But he gave away his weakness when his eyes kept darting to their father for validation. It was sad, really.

He might be five years older than Blake, but Nathan was clueless if he thought he was ever going to win respect from their father. First, Edwin Randall's respect was meaning-less, because the man was clueless. Second, he was too self-absorbed to acknowledge anyone else's accomplish-ments, even those of his own sons.

"Father. Nathan." Blake nodded in their general direc-tion. "Let me rephrase in case you didn't understand the first time. Kindly explain your presence on my property."

His father harrumphed. "We're here to discuss the casino. You brought this investment proposal to us, and I'm not liking the rumors I'm hearing. This type of gamesmanship is beneath us all, son."

Blake just shook his head. "It was a proposal. Not a done deal. No signatures."

Nathan finally joined the conversation, taking a seat next to their father.

"Rumor has it you're backing out of the casino plans, even though you nearly have the votes you need in Albany. We did our homework after you brought the idea to us. If you're really out, then we're in. We want to buy the resort, but if you won't sell, we're prepared to build a casino else-where in town."

Randall men rarely laughed, which was probably why Nathan and his father looked so stunned when Blake started to. Loudly. And for a good long time.

His father sputtered for a minute, then stood, trying and failing to appear patriarchal. "If the rumors are just a smoke screen and you're still planning on building the casino, you'd better plan on having us as partners, son. If not, we'll build our own."

Blake stopped chuckling and rose to his feet. They stared hard into each other's eyes until his father's gaze finally broke away in defeat.

"Good luck with that, gentlemen."

Nathan jumped to his feet, placing his hands on Blake's

desk and leaning forward with a scowl. He was doing his best to look and sound menacing.

"You can't stop us. The community wants the jobs. You'll cut us in, or we'll just set up shop on the other side of town."

"Really?" Blake casually stacked some papers on his desk, as if he was bored with the conversation. "I happen to know who owns the land on the other side of town, and he's not interested in selling."

Father looked confused, but Nathan's thin smile showed no signs of surprise.

"So it's true. *You're* the one buying up all the property around here. You think you're so clever, convincing everyone you're the guy in the white hat. Setting up house in that ostentatious castle. Sending Zachary to the local school. Screwing your designer."

Blake's pretense of nonchalance ended at those final three words. His hands curled into fists, crumpling paper as they did. Nathan blanched, but kept talking.

"Yes, we know all about your little girlfriend. Did you know Amanda Lowery lost her last job because there were rumors she was committing fraud? She was unemployed and nearly homeless when she set her hooks into you. And you want that gold digger raising Zachary?" Nathan's confidence was building again, his smile thin and threatening. "I wonder what a family court judge would think of your choices for Zachary? Maybe Michaela and I should seek custody, just to protect the poor boy. Think about that before you make any decisions about Gallant Lake, little brother."

Blake met Nathan's pale-eyed stare without blinking. His body might be frozen in place, but in his mind, he was pounding his brother's face into a bloody pulp. And maybe someday he'd do just that. But not today. It would be a show of weakness, and he wouldn't give them the pleasure. He could deal with Nathan and Michaela. They were serpents with teeth, but without venom.

"Stay away from my family, Nathan. You and Father both. Get the hell out of my resort. Stay the hell out of Gallant Lake, and stop wasting your breath on empty threats." He leaned forward and felt a jolt of satisfaction when Nathan backed away. "Don't you ever so much as *speak* Amanda's or Tiffany's names in front of me again. You've never been fit to lick the dirt off the bottom of their shoes."

He walked out of his own office, ignoring his brother's shouted vows to destroy him.

There was only one person capable of doing that, and she was sitting in a pink castle at the top of the hill.

Amanda was full of restless energy after breakfast. The workers were pounding away in the office, and that crew always made her uptight. Sure enough, there was Russ hunched over the table saw by the windows, as if he was trying to make his large form look smaller. As usual, he glanced up at her and glowered when he made eye contact. He always seemed so angry. He'd been friends with the guy Bobby fired for ranting about the casino, so it made sense that he was just as opposed to it and the Randall family. But he didn't seem to mind taking their money. She walked out into the main hall, telling herself she was being paranoid.

Maybe it was the conversation she'd had with Zach's teacher yesterday. She'd gone in for a conference, and noticed some anti-casino pamphlets on the corner of his desk. Thinking of Blake's promise that the resort would stay as is, she'd told Bruce he didn't need to print any more flyers or signs. She'd told him she'd heard a very reliable rumor that the casino plans were dead. But Bruce had been skeptical.

"No offense, Amanda," he'd said, "but it's hard to believe that when Blake Randall is still buying up property all over the county. I don't think he can be trusted. He just closed on the Maguire farm last week."

She hadn't argued, since Blake said the news of the casino being stopped wasn't official yet. There could be a dozen reasons why he'd be buying property, if he even *was*. It wouldn't be the first time some wild rumor about him had been spread around town. But she couldn't shake the conversation.

She had no reason in the world to be so edgy after the way Blake had woken her in the wee hours of the morning. Good Lord, what that man could do with his mouth! She blushed, even though no one was around. Sizzling sex was no excuse for sleeping that late. Or maybe it was. She ran her fingers back and forth on the mantel, lost in thoughts of what she might do to him tonight to return the favor...

"Oh, my God!" Julie laughed as she walked into the room. "I want some of what you've been having. You look positively dreamy eyed. Am I too late for lunch?"

Amanda cringed at being caught in a sexy daydream.

"Hi, Jules, I didn't hear you come in."

"Sorry if I startled you, but one of Bobby's guys left the door open. We're still on, right?"

"Yes, of course. I've got lunch set up in the solarium."

"Do I even need to guess who's got you so distracted this morning?" Julie grinned as she sat down and took a sandwich from the platter. "And just so you know, Blake's sporting a very similar postcoital glow."

"Julie!" She couldn't help but laugh. "Be quiet! I don't want the workers hearing about my coital *anything*. God, I can't believe I'm so transparent."

"Honey, you and I are friends. Of course I notice when you get all dewy-eyed and glowy. Things are getting serious?"

A familiar panic climbed her spine. Were *they* getting serious? Or was it just *her*? She took a few bites of her sandwich while her mind tried to make sense of things. She and Blake were sleeping together, living together, raising Zach together, but...so far he'd only talked about her *working* for him in the future. Nothing about what their relationship might be.

"I don't know, Julie. I'm so confused right now. It's not easy for me to trust anyone, even Blake, with my heart. I hate it, but my mind is always looking for what's going to go wrong, no matter how good things are." She took a sip of tea. "Christmas is less than two months away, and I don't know what his plans are. Will I still be here?"

Julie laughed. "My guess is a solid yes to that question. He's nuts for you. He asked me to confirm two tickets for the Builders Ball gala in Manhattan this weekend, and I'm *sure* he's planning on taking you."

It was the first she'd heard of anything called a "Builders Ball" *or* plans for the weekend. Amanda thought about what Bruce said. "Do you know anything about Blake buying land for the casino?"

Julie's eyes went wide. "That was an unexpected change of subject. I know he's met with some Realtors, but I got the impression he was backing off on the casino plans. Why?"

She told Julie about her conversation with Bruce Hoffman. She told her what Blake said about not changing the resort. But he never actually said he wasn't building a casino *somewhere*.

A rough laugh startled both women. Russ was standing at the entrance to the solarium, a smirk on his unshaven face. His clothes were rumpled, as usual, and Amanda could smell the stale scent of cigarette smoke from where she was sitting. He spoke before she could question why he was there.

"You still don't get it, do you? Randall's out to own the whole town. The whole damned *county*. He's snapping up everything that goes on the market. Pretty soon there won't be anyone left to fight him on that damned casino." He gave her a malevolent glare. "Unless someone stops him."

"Russ!" Bobby came up behind him. "What the hell are you doing in here? I told you to work on the trim in the office, which is that way. Don't let me catch you bothering anyone again."

Russ held his hands up, mumbled an apology and walked away. Bobby looked at the two women.

"What was he saying to you? The guy's worked with me before, but his attitude lately sucks. I can tell him to go…"

Amanda shook her head.

"You're almost done here, Bobby, and you need all hands on deck. It's fine." She gave him a smile. "But thanks for watching out for us."

Amanda and Julie stared at each other over the table after Bobby left. Blake said Gallant Lake was hallowed ground. Was he only talking about the resort?

"Julie, do you think he'd build a casino somewhere else in town and claim he'd kept his word?"

Julie ran her fingers up and down the handle of her teacup, frowning. "I *want* to say no. And I really can't believe he'd do that. But…" She looked over to Amanda. "His father and brother came to the resort today to meet with Blake. They were just going in when I left. They didn't look very happy, but…"

Blake never had anything good to say about his father and brother, but they *were* real estate developers. And they were family.

"Bruce and Russ both said he's buying land…"

"Well, we can check that." Julie sat back in her chair. "I help Bobby with his building permits, so I know my way around the county's website. I can pull the tax records online. If Blake's buying land, we'll know it, but I'm sure it's all just a crazy rumor."

She might be right, but it was a rumor that tapped into

Amanda's greatest fear—that everything in Gallant Lake was an illusion. That Blake couldn't be trusted. That he could betray her the same way all the other men in her life had done. Her stepfather. Jimmy Waldron. David Franklin. The creep who attacked her in New York.

There was a drumbeat hammering in her heart, warning her to think before reacting. That Blake *wasn't* like the others. That she didn't know everything. That she was jumping to conclusions. That she had no right to judge.

"Amanda? Tell me what you're thinking."

She looked up at the ceiling and blinked away tears. "I know I'm too quick to believe the worst, but I'm terrified that loving Blake gives him the power to really hurt me. That might just be a hurt I can't recover from." She met Julie's worried look. "I *am* in love with him."

"That's pretty easy to see. I think he's falling in love with you, too. The way he looks at you gives me goose bumps. He's been a different man since you arrived."

Was it possible he felt the same way she did? A flush of heat swept from her toes to her scalp as her heart whispered, *I told you so.* She took a deep breath and noticed the light fragrance of roses in the room. One of the random things she'd always blamed on Madeleine, but there had to be a logical reason the room always smelled like flowers. She stood, then answered Julie's questioning gaze.

"I'm going to grab my laptop. I'll be right back."

"Are you sure you want to do this?" Julie hedged.

Amanda closed her eyes in resignation. "I need to know."

Chapter Eighteen

Twenty pages of tax property records were stacked on the round table in front of Amanda. She'd printed the property records after Julie found them all. Blake's name was on every one of them.

"Hey." Blake's deep voice made her jump. He was standing just inside the solarium, rubbing the back of his neck absently. Lines of tension radiated from the corners of his eyes. He looked as on edge as she felt.

She stood slowly, her heart racing. She wanted to run into his arms. She frowned. She had to be strong enough to do what she *needed* to do, not what she *wanted* to do. She had to protect her heart. She rested her hands on the tax papers.

"Are you building a casino here?"

He rolled his eyes. "Not you, too. Why would you even ask me that question after I told you I wasn't?"

"Why won't you *answer*? You're buying land all over town, Blake. And outside of town, all over the county. Twenty different properties." She held up the papers and shook them. "Why do that if you aren't building the casino?"

He stepped forward, his mouth falling open.

"You pulled tax records on me? You've gathered the evidence and convicted me before you even asked a single question. What the hell, Amanda?"

He's right. He's right. He's right.

Her heart hammered out the mantra, but she was too determined to turn back now. She had to be sure. She had to have answers, no matter how much it hurt. "You still haven't answered my question."

He was standing across the table from her now, and she watched a parade of emotions cross his face. Hurt. Fury. Sadness. That drumbeat in her heart grew louder, begging her to stop.

"No, I'm *not* building a casino—here or anywhere. But I've told you that already, haven't I?"

"Then why are you buying up every parcel of land that's available? Houses. Farms. Businesses. Acreage. Why?"

His fingers curled tightly, then slowly released, as if he was trying to curb his anger. He muttered something to himself, then took a deep breath and met her eyes.

"It's not what it looks like." He gestured to the papers now scattered across the table where she'd dropped them.

"It's not what it looks like…" she echoed.

Slow down. Slow down. Slow down…

It was too late to stop the words she was thinking from spilling out. "In my experience, when a man says that, it's usually *exactly* what it looks like."

His shoulders dropped. "Damn it, Amanda, have I ever given you a reason to doubt me? Do you really think I'm anything like Franklin or whomever else from your past you think I'm channeling? This is *me*."

She wanted to believe him, but fear whispered to her from the edges of the darkness closing in on her. She turned away and moved to the window.

"Were your father and brother here because of the casino?"

"Yes, but not…"

She faced him again, unable to stop the question before blurting it out. "Are you going into the city this weekend? Alone?"

Because he certainly hadn't invited *her*. Blake's eyes closed slowly, and she could almost see him counting to himself, trying to control his reaction. After a long, tense pause, he opened those eyes just as slowly.

"If you're going to turn into a jealous mistress every time someone—"

"A mistress? Did you just call me a *mistress*?"

"You know that's not what I meant."

"Do I?"

He stared at her a long moment, then sighed. "Well, if you don't, then what the hell are we doing together?"

Her heart wanted this to stop. *She* wanted to stop. She wanted to stop hurting him. She wanted to stop destroying whatever they'd been building together at Halcyon. But she was no good at this. No good at trusting.

"So tell me about this Builders Ball. Who are you planning to take?"

Blake leaned forward and slammed his hands down on the table with so much force the property records went flying in different directions. They fluttered down to the tile floor like the dead leaves falling off the autumn trees outside.

"Are you kidding me? I was going to take *you*, but that feels like a really bad idea right now. In fact, the only thing that feels like a good idea is me getting the hell out of here so we don't do any more damage than we already have."

She knew it. He was always going to leave her. Her terror made her next words come out in an angry hiss.

"Well, don't let me stop you. Go ahead and leave! Go plan your big casino and all those wonderful jobs you talked about. Go back to your real life and your fancy balls and all your traveling. You were never going to stay here anyway, were you?"

He spread his arms wide in an angry gesture.

"Now you're just looking for ways to keep this ridiculous argument going. This is the kind of bullshit I hate. The stupid games. The petty jealousy. The verbal traps.

I get enough of this crap from my family, and I sure as hell don't need it from you."

He turned away, then spun back again, as if he was having the same kind of internal battle she was. His shoulders dropped in resignation.

"Amanda, I don't even know what to say to you right now. After last night. After this weekend. After I…" He stopped and his expression hardened. "If you can't trust me, if you think so little of me…if you'll fall for every whispered rumor…then what the hell are we doing here?"

Anger and hurt built in the silence until it shimmered in the air between them.

And still she couldn't stop talking. She had some visceral need to be the one to push them apart, as if she could protect herself that way. As if it wasn't already too late.

"What are we doing? Apparently…nothing."

She watched the shutters close behind his eyes. His emotionless face scared her much more than his anger had.

"I'm going to leave before one of us says something unforgivable. And we're getting pretty goddamned close to that right now." His voice was flat, but his words still felt like knives. "God*damn* relationships. I'll never learn."

He stared at the floor for a long beat, then turned away. The pain in her chest was so intense that her hand rose to cover it. A cloud must have passed over the house, because the light from the windows dimmed, and the room turned sharply colder. When she looked back to the doorway, Blake was gone.

His name escaped her lips in a whisper. She rushed to the door, but by the time she reached the front steps, his black SUV was already spinning its tires on the way down the driveway.

Chapter Nineteen

Every passing hour made Amanda feel worse. It was Thursday afternoon, and Blake hadn't called or texted since he left in a cloud of dust on Monday, although he did talk to Zach every day. She knew he was in New York because Zach told her as much, but she didn't know when, or even *if*, he was coming back to Halcyon. And it was all her fault.

Julie kept offering to stop by, but Amanda needed to be alone. She wanted to wallow in her pain and she didn't want anyone trying to talk her out of it. She deserved this. She paced the house endlessly, trying to understand what had happened. What she'd done. Why she'd done it. Whether or not she'd been right. And whether or not it could be fixed.

As usual, she ended up in Blake's office. The room was almost done. A dark Persian rug covered the hardwood floors. One long wall was lined with mahogany bookcases stretching to the high ceiling. An old-fashioned library ladder on wheels would be the final touch, giving access to the highest shelves. They just needed to finish the trim work and install the rail the ladder would slide on, and the room would be complete.

The desk had been delivered yesterday. The antique from Halcyon's attic still held a few secrets. The refinisher found several hidden compartments and false drawer bottoms. Most opened easily with spring mechanisms, but there was one, in the back of the lower drawer, that was locked up tight. A filigreed lock showed where a tiny key would fit. Everyone agreed it would be a shame to risk destroying something so delicately made. For now, it would remain sealed.

She ran her fingers over the carved edges of the desk, wishing it was Blake she was touching. With a sigh, she set her phone on the speaker dock on the corner of the desk and started her newest playlist—a repeating cycle of heartbreak.

The curtains swayed behind her as if someone walked past them. Maybe Halcyon's lovesick ghost was nearby.

"Madeleine, you're wasting your time with Blake and me. It's hopeless."

"Miss Amanda? Who are you talking to? Is Uncle Blake on the phone?"

Zachary stood in the doorway, head tipped to the side, looking at her strangely.

"Um...no. No one's on the phone. I was just talking to myself. I do that sometimes. Pretty silly, huh?"

He nodded, but didn't seem convinced. "When is Uncle Blake coming home? Why is he staying in New York this week?"

She wanted to scream to the rafters that *she* was the reason Blake wasn't with them. That she had hurt him and pushed him away, and she didn't know when he might be back. But instead, she smiled warmly and tried to reassure a young boy who had no idea that the two adults in his life had made such a monumental mess of things.

"I hope he'll be home next week. He has something to do in the city this weekend." She tried to distract Zach. "Are the boys coming over to swim today?"

Zach's new friends at school had enjoyed the indoor pool at the resort several times in the past few weeks. He was still enrolled in the Gallant Lake Elementary School as Zachary Lowery, but his closest friends now knew his real name, and that he actually lived in the castle on the hill. They were enjoying the perks of being friends with the resort owner's nephew.

"We're not swimming today. Maybe tomorrow." He shrugged, still staring at her curiously. "Did you and Uncle Blake have a fight?"

This boy was depending on them and saw them as a couple. As a family. *His* family. He deserved better than to worry about the adults in his life arguing on a regular basis.

"We had a…disagreement, Zach. Nothing for you to worry about." She hoped that was true.

"I heard you yelling the other day about all the places Uncle Blake is buying. Why did that make you so mad?"

Amanda gestured to the chair in front of the desk. "Have a seat, Zach." He sat in the chair and waited, with that wise-beyond-his-years expression she loved so much. She loved this boy. She loved his uncle.

"Your uncle and I are having a disagreement about something he wants to build here in Gallant Lake."

"The gambling place?"

She wasn't surprised he'd heard about it, probably in school.

"Yes, the casino."

"But he doesn't want to build it anymore. He told me so."

A pulse of hope made her sit straighter, followed quickly by a jolt of panic. Had she been wrong about everything? "When did he tell you that, Zach?"

"When we were fishing. He said he used to want to build a big place that would give lots of people jobs—" Amanda started to roll her eyes, but Zach kept talking "—but he decided it was more important to…pre…present…pres…"

"Preserve?" she prompted him, feeling her heart start to pick up speed.

"Yeah! He said he wants to preserve Gallant Lake. He said he was going to keep Gallant Lake safe from Uncle Nathan and Grandfather."

Maybe Zach had misunderstood his uncle. If not, she'd

chased Blake away over nothing. "Are you sure he didn't say he wanted to protect the *casino* from them?"

He gave her that exasperated look only a child can give an adult and get away with, as if she'd just said the stupidest thing. Then he shook his head.

"No, Miss Amanda. He said he's buying up everything for sale so Uncle Nathan and Grandfather *can't* buy it. He said they can't build anything without land. He said it was costing him a bunch of money, but it was worth it to keep Halcyon safe for his family. For you and me."

"Me and you?" The words were barely a whisper. Family. They were a family. Blake had been fighting to protect them, and she'd rewarded him by throwing accusations at him.

"Yeah." There was that condescending look again. "He said this is our home now—you, me and him. And he told me a man's job is to keep his home safe for the people he loves."

Her racing heart skidded to a stop. Blake wasn't buying land for the reason she'd accused him of. He was buying it to protect Gallant Lake. She'd been such a fool.

For the people he loves…

"Miss Amanda, are you okay?"

She blinked back fresh tears and did her best to reassure Zach. "Yes, honey. I think I just might be. Come here and give me a hug, then go do your homework, okay?"

He groaned, but did as she asked, running out of the room and leaping to slap his hand against the top of the doorway with boyish enthusiasm. She leaned back in the chair in stunned silence for a very long time, trying to absorb what Zach had just told her. She couldn't stop thinking about what Blake had done, and how she'd repaid him by jumping to conclusions and refusing to trust him.

Her heart beat out a steady tattoo of *I told you so. I told you so. I told you so.*

He'd left her. She'd accused him of lying, and all along he'd been trying to build a safe home for them here. He'd never once given her a reason to doubt him, but she just couldn't help herself. She dropped her head into her hands and wept at the damage her fear had created.

The evening passed in a fog. If Zach noticed her distraction at dinner, he didn't let on. He talked about school and his friends and wanting to learn how to play golf and wondering if his uncle would teach him. They watched a movie together after dinner, then she sent him up to bed. She found herself back in Blake's office, pacing the floor, trying to figure out how she could fix this. She was drawn to the enormous desk again, as if it might hold a secret answer for her.

She pulled out the lower right drawer, staring at the locked compartment. Elaborate brass filigree surrounded the tiny round hole for a key. The filigree looked familiar, and she knelt to get a closer look. As her fingers traced the unusual design of interlocking circles, she remembered where she'd seen that design before. She sat back on her heels.

It was *impossible*. It had to be impossible. Talking to a ghost she laughingly *chose* to believe in was one thing, but to think everything was set in motion back in August when she bought an antique evening purse…it was impossible. She ran up the staircase to the yellow bedroom. The delicate beaded purse she'd bought in Gallant Lake in August was sitting in the closet, wrapped in tissue paper. She unsnapped it and reached inside, pulling out a tiny key with a filigree top that matched the design around the lock in the desk exactly.

The key to Otis's desk.

In Madeleine's purse.

Back down in the office, she wasn't at all surprised when

the tiny key slid into the lock perfectly. There was a barely perceptible click when she turned it, and the front of the compartment fell forward.

The grayed papers inside looked fragile, and she reached for them gingerly. It was a stack of letters, tied together with a pale blue ribbon. Each letter was tucked carefully into an envelope, addressed to Otis Pendleton in Manhattan. These were Madeleine's letters to her husband, carefully protected all these years. Amanda removed them from the drawer and noticed a familiar scent. She lifted them to her face. Roses. Madeleine had sprinkled her letters with rosewater.

She untied the ribbon and spread the letters across the desk. They spanned nearly three decades, from the beginning of the Pendletons' marriage to the very end of it. It felt voyeuristic to read these intimate letters from a hundred years ago, but there was no way she could resist. "Here we go, Madeleine. Let's see what you have to say."

Amanda read for endless hours, eventually moving to an easy chair close to the fire with a glass of wine. The letters were sweetly written in the language of another time. The depth of love in Madeleine's words made her heart ache.

September 18, 1903

My darling Otis,
There are weeks when I curse this arrangement we have made ourselves prisoner to. I adore this insane pink palace you built for me, but to live here alone for days on end is torture of the highest degree. You, my dearest love, are in the noisy metropolis alone (how I pray that you are alone!). Yes, you will tell me 'tis foolish to fret like this, but as the nights grow longer and colder, I spend more time walking the halls of Halcyon with Doubt as my only companion.

I worry that you'll forget me, and that some other woman might just capture the heart and body I claim as mine...

October 27, 1903

Oh, Sweetest One,
You were right to scold me so fiercely last weekend.
That dark disease of jealousy drove me nearly mad.
I would never betray you—I'd rather die. I know I
will be true as surely as I know that I am breathing.
So how could I believe that your love is somehow less
than mine? How could I insult you in that manner?
Oh, how I hated to hear those words from your lips,
because their truth seared my heart. Thank you for
tolerating my silly fears, and for reassuring me yet
again that you love me, and only me...

January 16, 1904

...I believe I had more pleasure from the giving of
your Christmas gift than you had in receiving it, my
love. The look in your eyes when I told you I was car-
rying your child is something I will treasure all my
life. To think that the passion we share so wantonly
in our bedroom has brought forth this blessing! Yes,
I blush to think of it, but I am insanely proud of it, as
well. It is intoxicating to think that your warm body
against mine could produce life. I love you, dearest,
and you will be a marvelous father...

July 22, 1917

Sweetest love,
The simmering, sultry days of midsummer are upon

us. I've found these early hours on the balcony to be my favorite time. I like to lean on the warm walls of Halcyon and think long and often useless thoughts. I sit here and pretend that Emily is alive. Our darling fifth and surely final child, taken from us so cruelly. She was so tiny at birth, but how she fought to stay with us. But even the magic of Halcyon could not keep her from God's waiting embrace. I miss her so! Otis, Jr., Andrew, Michael and little Tabitha need us, so survive we must. Yes, I am stricken with grief, but I need to feel your sure hands on my body once again. Come home to me, darling. We can survive whatever life flings in our path, as long as we are together...

June 7, 1929

My darling, I cannot believe that we have now held four weddings here at Halcyon! And wasn't Tabby the most beautiful bride last Sunday? You may have noticed your silly wife could not stop crying throughout the ceremony. I watched her come down those stairs in my own wedding dress, and was swept away to our wedding day so many years ago. You are still the one and only love of my life, Otis, and I am amazed every day at the joy you bring to me. This house is a testimony to that love, and I see you and feel you in every stone. We have built a magical place here, my darling, and we have been happier than surely any mortal deserves...

September 21, 1929

...If only I were there to hold you today, my love. I know it had to be beyond painful to dismiss your own brother, but I say "good riddance" to him. He

*was a horrid business partner and a worse brother.
The crash of the London markets proves you were
right to be concerned over his rash investments. I am
confident you can recover from whatever damage he
has done to the firm with his foolhardy decisions...*

October 25, 1929

*...I know that times are looking desperately dark and
dire, my love. It has been many years since you chose
to stay in the city to work over the weekend instead
of coming home to my waiting arms. I understand,
but it pains me nonetheless. I may just come to the
city and fetch you myself! Regardless of how this all
turns, we have each other, and we have Halcyon. And
frankly, dearest one, even if we lose Halcyon, it will
stand here for someone else. If you and I end our days
in a shanty, I know that a new love story will eventually begin at this beloved castle. Some other fortunate
couple will realize that after everything we mortals
fill our lives with, the only thing that matters is love...*

When the sun rose over Gallant Lake, Amanda's chair
was surrounded with fragile letters scattered across the
floor. She'd dozed a few times during the night, but most
of it had been spent reading. She'd laughed and cried right
along with Madeleine and Otis as they worked at building
the kind of grand love affair that lasted far beyond their own
lives. The letters contained the legacy of Halcyon. They
were a lesson in love and trust. Madeleine was speaking
to her, and she got the message loud and clear. Love was
worth fighting for. Trust isn't always easy, but it's necessary, and it has to be mutual.

She would never betray Blake. How on earth had she
ever thought he could betray her? She'd let her fears and

doubts sabotage her chance at happiness, but she could choose to change that. Loving Blake opened up a future that included laughter and arguments and making up and working together to get through whatever challenges came their way. It was the life she wanted. More than *anything.* And she was willing to fight for it. She *had* to fight for it. She had to fight for them. She and Blake would bring love back to Halcyon.

She pulled her phone from her pocket, desperate to hear Blake's voice. To ask him to forgive her. To tell him she trusted him. The phone sat in her hand for a long time, but she couldn't bring herself to do it. A phone call wasn't enough. She needed to see him. She needed to be looking straight into his dark brown eyes when she told him she was in love with him.

An idea started to warm within her. She couldn't stop smiling while she hustled Zach off to school. As soon as he stepped on the bus, she grabbed her phone again. Her first call went to Julie, then to Jamal.

Amanda plowed ahead before she lost her nerve. "I know you work for Blake, but I need help with something, and Julie said you knew a friend of Blake's who could help us. But I need you *not* to tell Blake about it. Can you do that?"

Jamal was silent for a moment. "In all honesty, Amanda, that depends on what you're talking about."

"I want to surprise him. A *good* surprise. I want to go to this Builders Ball thing, and I need your help to get there without Blake knowing. We had a fight, and I was wrong, and I need to go. I need to see him."

There was silence on the line, and she knew Jamal was struggling between his job duties and his desire to help. Finally he sighed. "It's a very exclusive event, Amanda. You can't just show up at the door. You need to show an invitation, and it's tomorrow night."

Her heart started to fall. Julie said the tickets were in Blake's name.

"Look," Jamal finally said, "my former boss, Andy Mc-Cormack, is Mr. Randall's friend. I'm sure Andy's going to the ball. He could get you a ticket. Let me give you his number. If Andy is cool with it, then I'm in."

Chapter Twenty

By noon that same day, the plan was in place. Andy Mc-Cormack was skeptical when she called and introduced herself and her plan. He pointed out that surprises weren't exactly Blake's favorite thing, and this could backfire on all of them. But then he speculated that it might be time for Blake to break free of his No Surprises Lifestyle.

"I've learned life can bring nice surprises in unexpected places," Andy said as a woman giggled in the background. "Blake told me he was going to set up his home base in Gallant Lake. Blake doesn't do home bases. He mentioned this pretty designer who'd turned his world upside down. I'd like him to find the kind of happiness I've found, and I have a hunch you might just be the girl to give it to him. So yes, Amanda, I'll make sure there's a seat for you at our table, which is also Blake's table."

"Oh, Andy, I can't thank you enough. What can you tell me about this party?"

"The event started back at the turn of the last century, when New York City was building up to the sky. The builders, bankers and architects started a foundation to help the less fortunate, and the ball was their major fund-raiser. I'm sure it had a more dignified name originally, but for decades now it's just been the Builders Ball. It's become a massive charity event, raising millions of dollars in just one night. It's very formal. Think black tie times ten. This will be my Caroline's first Builders Ball, too, so you can keep each other company." A woman spoke in the background and Andy laughed. "Caroline says she's wearing a chocolate-colored gown, so you can't wear brown if you're sitting with us... Ow!" More voices in the background. "How the hell was I supposed to know you were kidding? Damn, woman..." More muffled conversation behind a covered phone. Then he was back, and laughing. "Okay, my bride-to-be wants me to tell you we're reserving you a suite at the hotel where the ball is being held so you can get ready there. She can't wait to meet you. She's only talked to Blake once by phone, and she thought he was kind of an asshole. Your willingness to go through all this trouble to surprise him has her reconsidering her assessment. We'll see you there."

She thanked him again and ended the call. Julie had already offered to stay at the house with Zach. It was Friday. The ball was *tomorrow*. She couldn't just show up in an off-the-rack dress and costume jewelry, or she'd embarrass him. She needed a fairy godmother. Or three. She picked up the phone again.

"Mel? I need a fashion miracle, and I need it in twenty-four hours. We'll need Bree's help, too. And Nora. Are you up for a challenge? Good. Here's what's happening..."

Blake looked out over the New York skyline from the penthouse suite of his hotel. The sun was settling low in the afternoon sky. He was going to make his appearance at the gala, shake all the right hands, meet Andy's fiancée, and bolt right after the meal. He was driving home to Halcyon tonight.

He couldn't wait any longer. Amanda was convinced that he'd lied to her about the casino. As angry as he'd been, he understood why her trust was so fragile. Raped at sixteen. Betrayed by a lying, cheating boss. Attacked on the streets of New York. She had a right to be nervous and skeptical. But he wasn't used to having someone doubt him the way she did, and he'd handled it badly.

She didn't trust him because she didn't know how much he loved her. And she didn't know how much he loved her because he hadn't *told* her.

He was in love with the woman, and that's all there was to it. She was the center of his universe. Everything else revolved around that golden-haired woman and his nephew. All that love circling between the three of them and they'd never once discussed it. But tonight he was driving to Halcyon, dropping to his knees and begging her to love him back.

He sipped whiskey from the glass he was holding. If only he knew what the hell she was up to right now. Jamal and Julie had been oddly unavailable since yesterday. Blake called the resort for Jamal three times today to find out if he had any news on some minor vandalism that had been happening around the resort, and Julie kept saying he "just stepped out." Then Jamal would call right back on his cell phone. It was weird. Blake didn't like weird. Blake liked predictable.

He pulled out his phone and called Julie. She'd been his eyes and ears this past week, letting him know that Amanda was okay. She sounded breathless and surprised by his call.

"Blake! Shouldn't you be at your party?"

"I'm heading out shortly." He heard a video game battle going on in the background, and Zach was laughing. "Are you at Halcyon?"

"Oh...yes... I...uh...just stopped by for dinner."

"Is Amanda right there?" The thought of her standing close enough to Julie to take the phone made his heart pound. Maybe he should skip the damned gala and drive home now. Maybe he should talk to her and tell her how he felt.

"Amanda? Oh...uh...no. She's upstairs. She's...um... taking a shower."

"At dinnertime?"

"Yes. She was…working outside this afternoon. She got…um…sweaty."

"What are you having for dinner?"

"Oh, we had pizza at the café…" Before he could question why they had pizza when she'd just said she was at the house for dinner, Julie rushed to correct herself, laughing nervously. "I mean, we had pizza for *lunch*! We were at the café for *lunch*. Not dinner. I think Amanda's making…meat loaf…or something. I'm not really sure, but I know it'll be great."

"Okay." Blake frowned. Things were definitely weird at Gallant Lake. "Is Jamal still down at the office? I was going to give him a call."

"No!" Julie's voice was unusually loud. "I mean…he was going home early tonight. I think he's taking Annie out to dinner for some special occasion or something, so he didn't want to be bothered with calls."

That didn't sound like anything Jamal would ever say. He was always on call. But maybe it was his anniversary or something. Blake rubbed the back of his neck and tried to dismiss his annoyance as he ended the confusing conversation. Julie sounded oddly relieved.

What the hell was going on?

Chapter Twenty-One

Amanda took a deep, shaky breath. What on earth was she doing here in Manhattan? Blake hated surprises, and she was about to show up uninvited. As his date. She shuddered. What if he was with someone else? It was a ridiculous thought, but still. What *would* she do if she walked in and he was there with someone else? She'd die on the spot, that's what she'd do. But she wasn't going to worry about it. She just had to focus on getting ready and finding enough courage to go up to the ballroom.

"Amanda? Are you there?"

Her iPad was propped up on the dresser, and Mel's video call was just coming in. Before Amanda could say anything, another window popped open on the screen. "Amanda? It's Bree, darling. Are you there?"

She jumped in front of the tablet and grinned at her cousins.

"I'm here, girls, and I'm ready for you to make me look fabulous!"

They both applauded, Mel from Miami and Bree from Los Angeles.

Bree responded first. "Oh, sweetie, you already look fabulous! Raquel's been busy, hasn't she?"

Her cousins had pulled out all the stops for her tonight. Mel had called her couture designer friend and a jeweler who owed her a favor. Reality TV star Bree had sent the best hair and makeup artist in the entertainment industry, Raquel Dubois.

Raquel had been hard at work for over an hour, and

Amanda's makeup was flawless. Her hair was piled high on her head. She was wearing a black bustier studded with crystals, and a black lace thong that left little to the imagination. Mel gave her a wolf whistle.

"You look amazing. Go just like that."

They all laughed.

"Girls, I love everything you've done, and I'll owe you forever. But I need your help. I can't decide on a dress, and I'm running out of time. I don't know which one sends the right message."

Bree lifted a glass of wine to her lips. "Well, Mandy, show us the options."

Amanda picked up the tablet and aimed it at the wardrobe rack in her room. "I've narrowed it down to these three. The tight black strapless one, the dark red ball gown with the low, low neckline and no back, or the blue silk with all the draping and the side slit."

"The next question," Mel said, "is what exactly *are* you trying to say? What's your goal here? Make him jealous? Make him sorry? Make him want to jump your bones on the dinner table? What?"

Amanda set the iPad on the dresser and stood in front of it.

"I want to be the woman he loves."

Bree set her wineglass down quickly while Mel coughed.

"Okay, then." It was Bree. "Go with the blue. And, Raquel?"

The beautician stepped into the picture. "Yes, Miss Mathews?"

"Let her hair down. Glue some of those little crystals in it, but just a few. Enough to look dew kissed, but no more. Like you did for Carrie's hair at last month's awards show. And tone down the makeup for a more natural look."

They sorted out her jewelry from the pile of jewelry boxes, settling on a diamond choker, simple drop earrings and a wide gold bracelet studded with tiny diamonds. Mel asked about shoes.

"Black, silver or gold?" Amanda held up one of each.

"The black ones," Bree said. "Bags?"

"I'm carrying that antique bag I bought with Mel in Gallant Lake."

Mel laughed. "That will be perfect!" She had no idea *how* perfect. She had no idea that it was Madeleine Pendleton's cocktail bag. Or that the key they'd all laughed about had unlocked secrets from a century ago.

Amanda felt tears threatening as Raquel unpinned her hair, then pulled some narrow strands back from the side of her face to clip in the back. Large curls fell down over her shoulders. Raquel grabbed a tissue and handed it to her so she could carefully blot under her eyes.

"Don't you dare cry!" Bree called out. "Don't cry until Tall, Dark and Handsome has a chance to see you..."

Another video call rang in. It was Nora, the Atlanta socialite. "Hi, y'all! What did I miss? Oh, my God, Amanda! You look like a movie star! But you still look like *you*. Where's the dress?"

"Hang on and you'll see..." Amanda stepped away from the webcam and into the cobalt blue dress, which hugged her figure in all the right places. When she stepped back in front of the camera, all three cousins squealed together.

"That's it!"

"Oh, my God, you look like a water nymph!"

"Gorgeous!"

She spun in front of them, then caught her reflection in the mirror on the wall. She didn't recognize the elegant woman staring back at her. She'd never worn a fifty-thousand-dollar dress before. And she'd certainly never worn a quarter million in borrowed diamonds. She brushed a strand of hair behind her ear and forced her shoulders back. She could do this. She *had* to do this.

Her phone chirped with a text. It was Caroline Patterson, Andy's fiancée. Just arrived in the ballroom. We're at table four. I'm in dark brown velvet. Blake isn't here yet.

Amanda typed a response. On my way. Wearing blue. She glanced back to the iPad and waved to her cousins.

"This is it, girls. Wish me luck!" She blew them a kiss and pressed the button on the tablet as they all waved and shouted their love to her. Jamal was waiting outside her room, dressed in a tux, and his eyebrows shot to his hairline when he saw her.

"You look stunning, Amanda."

"Thank you, Jamal. Let's hope Blake thinks so."

The ballroom was a glittering wonderland. Table four was on the far side of the dance floor. A laughing brunette was standing there in a skintight brown dress, with auburn hair piled high on her head. Next to her was a tall man with reddish-blond hair and striking blue eyes. The brunette saw Amanda as she was walking across the dance floor and smiled warmly, nudging the good-looking man at her side.

"You must be Amanda! I'm Caroline." She had a soft Southern drawl. "Oh, my God, you look amazing." Caroline gave her a quick squeeze. "This is my fiancé, Andy. He and Blake go way back, and he's been sweating bullets all day about helping you with this little surprise. I hope you know what you're doing."

Amanda shook Andy's hand. "I hope so, too." She barely whispered the words. She was having serious second thoughts. This could go wrong in so many ways. Andy stepped away to speak with two gentlemen who'd called his name. Caroline leaned close, and her accent seemed to thicken.

"If you're trying to knock his socks off, that dress will do it for sure."

Amanda looked at the other woman. "I need him to know how much I love him."

Caroline whistled softly. "You haven't told him how you feel? Well, honey, this is one hell of a place to do it. Andy says the crowd here can be pretty intense. The current and former mayors are here, and the governor is the guest speaker. You've got some balls, girl, if you know what I mean."

A sheen of sweat covered Amanda's skin. If this plan backfired, it would be very public. And it would break her heart. She tried to shake off the clawing panic. "How long have you and Andy been engaged?"

"Only about a month. We're hoping to have the wedding at Blake's Barbados resort next spring. Andy would be happy dashing to Vegas this weekend for a quickie I-do. But I'm my momma's only child, and she wants a real wedding with all the trappings. How can I say no to her?"

Amanda stopped listening somewhere around "dashing to Vegas."

That was the moment Blake walked into the ballroom.

He was alone, which was an enormous relief. He looked tired. Or maybe worried? He shook some man's hand, then turned and looked up. His eyes locked on hers. He froze, and so did she.

"Holy beefcake, Amanda, is that him?" Caroline hissed into her ear.

Amanda could only nod in response.

"No wonder you want him to love you. And look at how he's looking at you… I could melt just from the residual heat over here."

Amanda tried to read all the expressions that ran across Blake's face. Shock. A quick smile. Confusion. Worry. His gaze drifted from her face down the length of her gown and back again. The corner of his mouth slid into a crooked grin. She knew that look. Caroline was right. It was pure molten desire. He started across the floor toward her. A smiling man reached for his hand, but Blake brushed him aside without slowing a beat. His eyes never left hers. Caroline stepped back with a gasp as Blake approached.

Amanda braced herself, forgetting to breathe. Who needed oxygen when she had Blake? He stopped abruptly in front of her, his chest nearly touching her upturned chin. His hands clasped both sides of her face, his face so close that she could feel his breath coming hot and quick. His expression was so intense, so raw, that she almost couldn't bear to look at him. She didn't know how long they stood like that until she heard Andy's voice.

"Make your move, Randall, or walk away. You're turning into the floor show."

People nearby were watching them with surprised curiosity. And still Amanda and Blake stared at each other. His voice was thick with emotion when he finally spoke.

"You tell me you love me, Amanda Lowery." His voice cracked. "Tell me you love me, damn it, because I sure as hell love you."

Relief washed over her.

"I love you." She barely had the words out before his mouth fell on hers, bruising her lips and forcing her teeth apart. His tongue pushed deep, and her hands moved up the front of his tuxedo until her fingers found the lapels and grabbed them.

"Jesus, get a room..." It was Andy again. "Have some dignity, man."

Blake pulled away and Amanda groaned when his lips left hers. They were definitely the center of attention now. She stepped back, her face burning, but he didn't let her go far, keeping his hand tightly on her hip. He held his other hand out to Andy.

"I take it you had something to do with this?"

Andy laughed. "You had me worried right up to that smokin' kiss, my friend. I know you don't like surprises, but Amanda can be very persuasive." Andy pulled Caroline forward. "And this is the girl that made *me* lose all my common sense. Caroline, this is Blake Randall."

Blake released Amanda to put his arms around Caroline. "Great to meet you. He's a lucky guy. Are you still looking at Barbados for the wedding?"

She nodded, looking up at him with a bit of awe. Andy started to grumble.

"Okay, okay, hands off my girl. You've got your own now."

"Yes, I do." He smiled down at her as she moved back to his side. "I do, indeed. Champagne, baby?" He placed a kiss on her forehead. "I'll be right back. You still have some explaining to do."

She grinned as he turned away with a nod to Jamal, who looked relieved. Andy was introducing Caroline to another couple, so she took the opportunity to glance around the ballroom. This was definitely a top-shelf crowd. Her borrowed diamonds had nothing on what some of the women were wearing.

She was supremely grateful for the gown, which was on par with the rest of the expensive dresses in the room. There were plenty of familiar faces from the news and gossip pages among the guests. She spotted Blake standing in line for cocktails near the windows and breathed a sigh of relief. He loved her.

The meal was a blur of rich food and loud laughter. Their table was easily the rowdiest in the ballroom, with Andy and Blake ragging on each other relentlessly. They were like a couple of frat boys, and Amanda loved hearing them tell stories about each other. She and Caroline became fast friends, and the conversation never waned. When the music started, they were the first two couples on the dance floor.

After several songs, Andy offered to switch partners. It was a little odd to feel someone else's hands on her, but she trusted this sun-tanned man with the deep blue eyes.

"Are you okay, Amanda? You seem nervous." His voice was lighter than Blake's, but intense, as if he was ready to leap into battle at any moment.

"I'm fine. I used to have issues about being touched by strangers, but I don't think of you as a stranger. You and Blake are more like brothers than friends, which sort of makes you family."

"I'm an only child, and Blake may as well be, so yes, we are like brothers." He grinned down at her. Blake was dancing nearby with Caroline, but only had eyes for Amanda.

"Thanks for everything you did to make tonight happen."

He gave her a light squeeze, then spun her toward Blake. "You're welcome." He glanced at Blake. "You did good, my friend. She's a keeper."

Blake released Caroline into Andy's arms. "You too, man. We rock."

The two women rolled their eyes in unison as their men laughed.

Jamal was on his phone when they returned to their table, and he didn't look happy. He pulled Blake aside, and Amanda saw Blake's face pale. She went to his side.

"What is it?"

He took her hand, his face grim. "Trouble at the resort. There was a fire at the old clubhouse." The clubhouse was an older building that had been temporarily pulled back into action while the golf course was being expanded and renovated. Blake had shown her the plans for a brand-new structure that would be built on the edge of the lake.

"Was anyone hurt?"

"No, it was after dark when it started." His frown deepened. "They think it was arson."

Amanda stared at him in dismay. The protesters had been a nuisance, but Julie told her things had taken a more aggressive turn recently. Julie had been confronted right on Main Street in town. Jamal said the number of threatening emails and phone calls coming to the resort had jumped sharply. That Russ guy said something about "stopping" Blake. But *arson*? What if they came to the house? She reached for Blake.

"Zach...he and Julie are alone at Halcyon. If someone tries to go to the house..."

Blake pulled her in close and kissed the top of her head.

"We're leaving for Halcyon now. Jamal went to get the car. Zach and Julie are fine. No one's been near the house, and extra security is setting up as we speak."

She followed him out the door without another word.

Amanda was curled up under Blake's arm in the limousine. He pulled her closer and buried his face in her hair. God, he loved the scent of her. He loved the feel of her in his arms. The way she'd laughed as they were dancing.

"You know," he said softly, "right up until the end, that was the best Builders Ball ever. I still can't quite believe you're here."

She chuckled against his chest. "Your reputation for hating surprises had everyone sweating. Andy was afraid it was going to backfire. And poor Jamal was sure he was losing his job."

"And yet you managed to convince them to do it. I definitely need to find a place for you in my company. You're quite the negotiator." He reached down and tipped her chin up so he could see her face. "What made you do all of this? Showing up here... What changed?"

"I learned I was wrong. You were telling the truth about not building the casino. You bought the land to protect Gallant Lake."

He frowned and dropped his hand from her face. He didn't want to renew their argument, but... "But I'd already told you I wasn't building the casino."

She pushed herself upright and stared straight into

his eyes. "I know. And I know it hurt you when I didn't believe you. I'm so sorry about that. More sorry than you can imagine." She dropped her head, and he had to listen closely to hear her next words. "You're nothing like all the men who've betrayed me. I knew that in my heart, but I still..." She looked up, her face crestfallen. "But I still doubted. I was afraid to believe what we had was real. That it could last. That you could possibly feel the same way."

He placed a gentle kiss on her lips, then her nose, then her forehead as she rested her head on his shoulder again. They'd both made so many foolish mistakes. "I'm sorry, too. I lost my temper and stomped away like a spoiled kid. I'd just come off a confrontation with my father and brother, and I took it all out on you. Instead of fighting for us, I walked away. I promise never to do that again."

She lifted her head and stared at him for a long minute. Headlights moved past them outside, flickering across her face. She gave him a crooked grin.

"A friend gave me some really good advice this week."

"Yeah? What advice was that?"

"Well, first she made me understand that I shouldn't expect your feelings to be any less than mine. If I would never betray *you*, then it was cruel to think that you could betray *me*. Then she told me that 'after everything we mortals fill our lives with, the only thing that matters is love.' After hearing that, I realized I had to make sure you knew how much I loved you."

He took a deep breath to slow his pounding heart. "Smart friend. Who was she?"

"Hmm? Oh, I don't think you've met her..."

With a quick move, he scooped her up and set her across his lap. He needed her in his arms. Forever.

"Careful!" she yelped as she adjusted her dress. "All of this stuff is borrowed, so don't tear the dress. I turn into a pumpkin at midnight."

He ran his hands down the bodice of the dark blue gown. "I like this dress. I think we'll buy it." He held up her hand so the bracelet twinkled in the reflection of the headlights of cars around them. "I like this, too. Let's keep it. The rest we can take care of tomorrow. And don't worry, I won't let anyone turn you into a pumpkin or anything else, Mandy."

"Mandy? I don't think you've called me that before." She tipped her head to the side and grinned at him.

"Isn't that what your family calls you?"

"Sometimes. It's a nickname Nora started. I like how it sounds on your lips."

"Okay, then. *Mandy*, snuggle into me and get some rest. We've got another hour or so before we're home."

She obliged with a sigh. "Our home. It's a dream come true, Blake."

"*You're* the dream come true, sweetheart." He kissed the top of her head and waited until her steady breathing told him she was asleep. Then he lowered the window dividing the back of the limousine from the front. Jamal was behind the wheel.

"Any news?" Blake asked quietly.

Jamal shook his head. "Deputy Sheriff Adams is running the official investigation. No one suspicious has been near the house or the resort. Tim and Bobby are both camping out on sofas at Halcyon tonight while Julie and Zach are asleep. Plus we have the usual staff outside. There are a couple construction guys coming in on Monday to wrap things up, and then they're done, so we won't have to worry about that traffic in and out."

Blake pressed a thoughtful kiss on the top of Amanda's sleeping head. He needed to put out a statement this week about canceling the casino plans. He'd only held off because he wanted to have an alternative to present to appease both his investors and the people hoping for jobs.

He glanced down at Amanda again. This wasn't about

business and investors anymore. This was about protecting the people he loved. The situation seemed to be under as much control as possible at this point.

So why did he still feel so uneasy?

Chapter Twenty-Two

Amanda welcomed Sunday morning with a cup of coffee
on the balcony outside the master suite at Halcyon. Someone
was walking through the trees. She held her breath until she
recognized Tim from the security team. There were people
guarding Halcyon night and day now, keeping any possible
troublemakers away. The Gallant Lake Preservation Society
was cooperating with the investigation, insisting they had
nothing to do with the recent acts of vandalism and arson.

"Hey, you." Blake's deep voice made her skin heat up.
She turned to the doorway and grinned.

"Hey, yourself. Good morning." He draped his arm over
her shoulders and kissed her temple. She tipped her face up
and he dropped a chaste kiss on her lips. They were relaxed
with each other at last. Comfortable. No longer trying to
prove anything. It was a revelation to her that she could be
this thoroughly content.

He nibbled her bottom lip and grumbled. "You're daydreaming while I'm kissing you. Am I boring you?"

"I'm daydreaming about how much I love you." She felt
him smile against her mouth.

"Well, in that case, I'll allow it."

He raised his head and noticed the coffee she was still
clutching.

"And you didn't spill a drop. I'm impressed with your
focus, Miss Lowery." His sable eyes met hers. "What are
you planning to tackle today?"

"I want to draw up plans for the guest rooms on the
second floor. Are you up for some real construction? I'm

thinking of knocking down a few walls to make larger rooms. It's not like we really need twelve bedrooms, and those rooms are so small."

He nodded. "Make all the plans you want, but wait until after the holidays to tear things apart, okay?"

"Which holiday? Thanksgiving is only a couple weeks away."

Blake gave her a squeeze. "I don't think even you could get a renovation done by Thanksgiving. I was referring to Christmas."

"Why? Does Santa have big plans?" Christmas had never been a very happy time for her since her dad died. And Zach—his mom died last Christmas. Maybe it *was* time to make new memories.

He laughed. "Yeah, something like that." He looked like he was keeping a secret. What was he up to? And what on earth would she ever give him for Christmas?

She kissed his cheek playfully. "Don't forget that Zach has a birthday party to go to this afternoon. He's really excited about it."

"How could I possibly forget? It's all he's talked about. A party at the arcade in the next town, complete with laser tag. It's every ten-year-old's dream."

She saw just a brief shadow cross his face, and she knew he was thinking about all the rowdy birthday parties he never had as a child. She rested her palm against his cheek. "Zach's birthday is next spring, and we'll make sure he has the wildest birthday party ever seen in Gallant Lake. And Uncle Blake will be able to ride the ponies and play laser tag and dress up like a pirate and be just like all the other little kids."

He laughed out loud and pulled her tightly into his arms. "I'm going to hold you to that, Miss Amanda."

She knew they were in for a long night as soon as Zach got home from the party. He'd clearly had way too much ice cream, along with who knows what other junk food. He'd been laughing when he'd arrived home, but she could almost see the greenish tinge to his skin. He rubbed his stomach absently while he watched television with her and Blake.

It was no surprise when she heard her name being called in the middle of the night. Blake barely registered her exit from their bed, rolling over with a grunt. She pulled her bathrobe tight and trotted down the hall, finding Zach on his knees in his bathroom. It wasn't a pretty sight. *Welcome to parenthood, Amanda.* She soaked a washcloth in cold water and held it against his forehead as he threw up. She rubbed his back and cooed words of comfort to him for two hours, until he finally seemed to have purged all the garbage from his system. He begged her not to leave, so she curled up with him in his bed where they both drifted into an exhausted sleep.

That's where Blake found them Monday morning. She woke when he pressed his lips to her temple. Zach was still sound asleep. She looked from the clock to Zach's pale face and knew there was no way he was making it to school today. She put her finger to her lips to silence Blake and slid out of bed gently. Once they were out in the hall, he spoke.

"I woke up and you were gone. What happened?"

"All that junk food caught up with him in the middle of the night. I didn't want to wake you. I know you have that conference today." Blake had scheduled a video conference with the resort managers to discuss how best to restructure the chain of command so that he could operate the company with fewer personal visits to the resorts. He was releasing some of his tight control, and she knew that wasn't easy for him. He grinned down at her and brushed her hair behind her ear.

"Thanks, babe. I promise I'll make it up to you. Are they finishing up in the office today?"

"Yes. They just need to put up the last of the crown molding. One last chance for me to climb a ladder…"

He arched a brow at her, and she thought for the thousandth time how lucky she was to fall in love with such a gorgeous man. He was dressed for business today, in a dark suit and gleaming white dress shirt. His black hair curled over the collar, and she couldn't resist putting her fingers in it.

She pulled his head lower. "I'm just teasing you. Go have your meeting. I'll see you later." The kiss was lingering and sweet.

"Take good care of our patient." He winked at her before turning away. Bobby and his crew were hammering away downstairs, so she headed to the suite to shower and dress before she went down to the main floor.

Zach was awake by the time she'd dressed, and she ordered him to stay in his room, promising to deliver a light breakfast.

"It's hard to believe it's the same house, Bobby." She stood in the main hall a few hours later and looked around. Her sketches had come to life, and so had Halcyon.

"You were the brains of the operation, Amanda. I just supplied the muscle." Bobby grinned at her. "I know you want to start the second-floor demolition, but Blake said it will have to wait until after the holidays." She shook her head. She knew he wanted to give Zach a wonderful Christmas, and figured he was planning something big.

She and Bobby hugged and she waved goodbye to the workers as they filed out. She fixed a cup of soup for Zach's lunch and was just heading toward the stairs with it when she heard the front door open. She turned, expecting to see Blake, or maybe Bobby. But it was Russ, the one who'd said Blake needed to be stopped. Her stomach dropped.

She started to ask what he was doing there, but her words froze in her throat when he turned to lock the front door.

He'd probably walked right past security, since he'd been working on the house. He was only a few feet away, and when he turned back to face her, the malice and madness were clear in his eyes. In his left hand was a red container of gasoline. In his right hand was a gun, and it was aimed straight at her.

RUN!

The warning voice screamed in her head, but she couldn't move. It wasn't a panic attack that rendered her motionless. It was the thought of Zach upstairs. She blinked and tried to focus, setting the soup on an end table with trembling hands.

"I... I don't understand." She moved away from the stairs toward the center of the room. She didn't want him leaving the main floor. "What do you want, Russ? What are you doing?"

"I want your boyfriend to leave my town alone. To leave my family alone." He moved closer. She started to step back and he raised the gun. She froze. The scent of stale cigarette smoke assaulted her senses, and she placed a hand over her roiling stomach. His gray eyes were narrow and cold.

"Y-your family?" Amanda stuttered.

"Randall bought out my parents' farm. And my uncle's place, too. Been in the family for decades. Those places should have come to my cousins and me, not some New York City developer. What the hell does he want with it all? Those are worthless pieces of land to anyone other than us."

Blake had been buying land all around Gallant Lake to keep his family from developing it. But he was only buying what was already for sale.

"Didn't your family have the farms for sale?"

The man scoffed. "Sure, there were for-sale signs up, but no one was gonna buy them. No one wanted to buy *anything* in Gallant Lake until Randall showed up and started all his big casino talk. Eventually my parents would have died and it would come to us. Now we have *nothing*. And it's not just us. Other guys have had their inheritances robbed from them, too. We decided to fight back."

"But…your families *wanted* to sell, and got fair market value…"

"We needed that land! It was *ours*! And Randall *took* it from us! Now I'm gonna take something from him." He looked around the hall.

Think, Amanda! This is no time for panic…

"Look, Blake's not building the casino anymore," she managed to say as her mind raced. "He changed his mind…"

"Yeah, I heard that rumor, too, but I don't believe it. And he still owns the land I need to make a living."

"You made your living off the farm? Then why did your parents—"

"They didn't *know* what we were growing back on the hill. They didn't know what we were cooking in the barn on Harrison's old place. And now it's all gone, thanks to your big man from the city. And it's time for some payback."

This wasn't about the casino. Blake probably had no idea he'd stepped in the middle of some small-town drug ring in his attempt to save Gallant Lake.

She concentrated on keeping her breathing slow and steady. A sheen of sweat blossomed across her skin. Russ stepped closer, but she forced herself to stand her ground and look him in the eye. She was tired of being afraid. She was done with it. If she was going to die here, she was going to do it without showing fear.

"You'll go to prison for this."

He looked around the room. "Nah. By the time they see the old place going up in flames, I'll be long gone."

He was going to set fire to Halcyon. With her and Zach inside. She had to think of some way out of this. She had to stop him.

"That's a terrible idea. Even if Blake leaves, he still owns your land. You still lose."

"I figure he'll be more than happy to dump that land, just to get out of town and be done with it. And we've got partners ready to snap it up." Russ gestured toward the stairs with the handgun.

"Come on. We'll start upstairs, where they'll find your body. Then I'll burn my way down and walk away."

"Miss Amanda? I'm hungry…"

Zach stood at the turn of the staircase. He looked from her to Russ in confusion. His eyes went wide when he saw the gun. Russ stared up at Zach. He moved to point the gun toward the boy with a thin, frightening smirk.

"Amanda?" Zach's voice was high and thin. A surge of adrenaline coursed through Amanda's body as she shouted. At the same time, she leaped toward Russ.

"Zach! *Run!*"

Russ's attention snapped back to her and he struck her on the side of her head with the butt of the gun. Everything went black for a moment. She staggered but stayed on her feet.

"Run, Zach!"

His footsteps pounded up the stairs. There was a back staircase he could use to escape, or even the small elevator. He had options from upstairs if she just gave him some time. She clawed at Russ and he hit her again. She fell to her knees, but got back up, fueled by anger and desperation. She put herself between him and the staircase. He gave her a look of contempt and roughly pushed her aside as he headed to the stairs.

"What a tragedy that a woman and boy died together in the fire."

Blake would never survive losing them both.

She had to fight. She grabbed at Russ and held on to his shirt, slowing his progress as he put his foot on the stairs. They wrestled like that all the way to the third floor. When she and Russ both tumbled into the hallway on the third floor, she started to beg.

"Please! He's just a boy!"

"Yeah. *Randall's* boy." He held the gun up to the side of her head and she held her breath. "I'll find him easier without you swattin' at me the whole time."

The silence was heavy and tense, broken only by her ragged breathing. The cold barrel of the gun pressed against her temple. This was it. She imagined she could hear the trigger starting to move, and she offered a silent prayer that Zach would get to Blake somehow and be safe.

A door shut loudly inside Zach's room, making them both flinch. Russ's head snapped around, and he shoved her to the floor. "I'm going to finish that brat before he gets out of here."

He ran down the hall and kicked open the door to Zach's room, ignoring Amanda's screams for him to stop. She was hot on his heels. The bedroom was empty. The bathroom door was open but it was empty, too. She watched, gasping for breath, as Russ stood in the center of the room, spinning wildly to point the barrel of his gun from door to door. He stopped when he faced the closet.

With a sinking heart, Amanda realized the same thing Russ did. The closet was the only place to hide in this room. Zach had to be in there. She leaped toward the closet door as Russ raised the gun and pulled the trigger. Again. And again.

The roar was deafening, and the shock of the sound seemed to suspend time somehow. Amanda was vividly aware of her body flying horizontally in front of the closet door. She felt the first bullet slice into her left arm. The pain was sharp and clean, like a razor's cut. But the pain of the next strike was different. The bullet struck her abdomen, just right of center, and the burning was so intense she knew she had to be dying. She could hear her own screams as if they were coming from somewhere far away. All she could see was red when she hit the floor. She felt the warmth and wetness of her own blood on her fingers. She couldn't move, paralyzed with shock and pain.

Russ stepped over her to open the closet door. She turned her head. She wanted Zach to know he wasn't going to die alone.

But the closet was empty. Her eyes closed in relief. She was the one who would die alone. That was okay. As long as Zachary lived. Relief washed over her. Another door slammed somewhere inside the house. Was it Zach? Russ was already running into the hall.

She gritted her teeth and forced herself to her feet, with her right hand clutching her bleeding abdomen. She made it around the corner of the hallway before her legs betrayed her and she collapsed against the wall, sliding to the floor. She screamed Zach's name one last time, but the sound barely escaped her dry lips. She watched the action as if through the wrong end of a telescope, out of focus and far, far away. Russ was running for the stairs.

And then he was just…gone.

Men were shouting somewhere. Blake called her name, but she couldn't answer. Her world was growing darker, and so much colder. Jamal was saying they "had him." More pounding steps, then Blake was holding her.

"Amanda!" His voice shook, then he shouted loudly. "She's been shot! Get an ambulance!" His trembling lips settled softly on her forehead and he began to plead as he rocked her in his arms. "Don't leave me, baby. Help is coming. Please stay with me…"

"Zach?" It took the last of her strength to whisper the name.

"He's safe. He came to get me. Amanda… Amanda? Oh, God…no…" His voice cracked as everything she knew faded to blackness and silence.

Chapter Twenty-Three

Blake had always adored Amanda's petite build, but not now. Not when it made her look so tiny and fragile in the hospital bed. She was ghostly pale, with tubes and wires everywhere around her. Her long hair was pulled to one side and cascaded over her shoulder in a golden ponytail, having been lovingly brushed and secured by Nora.

Her cousins had arrived yesterday, and were holding their vigil in the waiting room, taking turns sitting with Blake. But once in a while they gave him time alone with her. Time to grieve and pray and plead with whomever was in charge upstairs to give him more time with the woman he loved. He made promises. Vowed to change. Vowed to make peace with his family if that's what it took to bring her back. Give up his businesses. Become a missionary in Africa.

He'd do anything.

Anything.

ANYTHING.

He rested his forehead on the back of her hand, which he was clutching tightly in his own. A large hand settled on his shoulder. He looked up to find Andy standing at his side. Caroline was behind him, tears brimming in her eyes. Could it be that just a few days ago they were all laughing together at the Builders Ball? Andy stared at Amanda, clenching his jaw so tightly that a muscle in his cheek twitched. It was Caroline who spoke first.

"She's strong, Blake. So strong. I could see it the minute I met her."

Andy gave his shoulder a squeeze.

"Thanks, guys." His voice sounded foreign to his own ears, raspy from exhaustion and tears.

"Julie's got the resort under control," Andy said quietly. "The business is fine." The video conference had ended abruptly when Zach ran screaming into the conference room. That was two days ago. Two days that felt like a lifetime.

"What do you need, Blake?" Caroline's voice was soft.

That was easy to answer. There was only one thing.

"I need her to wake up. She lost so much blood…" He reached up and touched his fingers to Amanda's still face.

"Give her body time to heal," Andy said. "She'll come back. Don't give up." He sat in a nearby chair and pulled Caroline down onto his knee. "The bastard who did this is in jail?"

"Right now he's in the hospital, but he's headed to jail after that."

"Why is he in the hospital?"

"He fell down the stairs. Cracked his skull and broke his leg." Blake looked at Amanda. "He keeps insisting someone pushed him, but Amanda was nowhere near the stairs when I got there."

Blake lifted her hand and kissed it. None of it mattered right now. He just wanted her to wake up for him. He wanted her back.

Andy continued softly. "Dan Adams told me they found a meth lab Russ and his cousins were running. It was quite an operation. He'll be in jail a long time, Blake."

"I don't give a damn about him right now. I just want her back. I want her back…"

He dropped his head to her hand again and sighed. He was vaguely aware that Andy and Caroline were still sitting there, silent sentinels and loyal friends. He was so dog-tired his whole body ached from it. It wasn't just lack of sleep. It was anger and grief and worry that were draining him.

He wanted his girl back.

Amanda's thoughts were dark and murky. Fragments of awareness fought to come together, but they couldn't quite get there. She wanted to open her eyes, but they wouldn't cooperate. She wanted to beg for something to drink, but her dry lips were just as uncooperative and would not move. Once in a while she heard sounds, but nothing that made sense. Words came through in bits and pieces, and if more than one person spoke, the voices blended together into an annoying, foreign-sounding mess. She heard Blake's voice once, and it sounded like he was…what? Begging? Praying? She thought she felt tears on her hand, but she couldn't move it, couldn't open her eyes, didn't know whose tears they were. She had no sense of time, and didn't know if she'd been trapped in this darkness for hours or days. There was a distant, pounding ache in her side that presented a constant backbeat to her thoughts. Sometimes she wanted to cry from the pain, but even her tears refused to follow orders.

And then, as if on command from some other power, her eyes swept open. She blinked quickly and tried to assess where she was. A machine was beeping quietly next to her. The room was dark, with only one soft light over the bed. She slowly turned her head. She was in a hospital room. The pain in her side was no longer in the background. It was sharp and insistent.

Everything came back to her in a rush. She'd been shot. She took a deep breath and reveled in the feeling of air moving in and out of her lungs. She was alive. She was *alive*.

"Blake, she's awake…" A woman's whispered words caught her attention. There was a sudden movement at her side, and Blake's beautiful, wonderful, handsome face appeared directly over hers. He looked so tired. His eyes were tense, and there were deep, dark bags under them. His hair was a mess, and his skin was pale. But love shone from him like a warm blanket, and she grinned up at him.

"Wow." Her voice cracked. "Do I look as bad as you do?"

He took a sharp breath, clearly unprepared for humor. Then he slowly returned her smile.

"You look perfect, baby." He dropped a kiss on her forehead and stayed there for a moment, trembling lips pressed to her skin, as if he was trying to compose himself. "You look absolutely perfect. You came back to me."

"Zach's okay?"

He smiled against her skin. "Zach's fine."

His lips brushed against hers reverently, their noses touching. Caroline and Andy stood, and Caroline winked at Amanda. "We'll give you some time alone, and let the others know you're awake."

And they were gone. Blake gave her a much-needed sip of water, then sat back in his chair and held her hand. He ran kisses across her palm and down to her wrist, pressing his lips on her pulse point.

"For two days, I've been kissing this spot over and over, just to feel your heartbeat. I thought I'd lost you…" His voice cracked, and she lifted her fingers to touch his face.

"Tell me what happened. How did Zach escape? What happened to…that man?"

"You should rest…"

"I need to know." Her voice was stronger now. She had to put the pieces together in her head.

He sat back and looked over his shoulder. "Andy will try to give us privacy, but your cousins will only wait so long…"

Her cousins were here? She narrowed her eyes. He was trying to distract her.

"Then you'd better start talking. I need to put my memories in order, Blake. There are too many holes, and nothing makes sense."

"Okay, okay." He started talking quickly, as if the memories were no fun for him. "Zach ran to his room after he saw you downstairs. When he ran into the bedroom, he saw a small panel open next to the fireplace that he'd never noticed before. Talk about perfect timing. It was a secret passageway that had been built into the house, with a hidden stairway.

"He started down the stairs, then he heard you and Garrity fighting." He noticed her look of confusion and explained, "Russ Garrity. The son of a bitch who tried to kill you."

She remembered now. "It was all about drugs, Blake. Not the casino. Drugs..."

"I know, babe. The sheriff knows, too. Russ and his cousins are looking at serious time."

"What happened with Zach?"

"He turned back. He was going to try to save you." Amanda closed her eyes in horror at the thought. "He insists that's when he heard his mother's voice, as if she were standing right next to him, telling him to find me fast. He ran down to the resort, screaming bloody murder about a man with a gun." Blake's face paled even more.

"I barely remember racing up to Halcyon. Jamal and I unlocked the front door as gunfire rang out. A piece of me died right then. We came in to the sound of more shots, and I heard you screaming. It was a beautiful sound, because at least I knew you were alive. We ran up the stairs, and found Garrity halfway down the staircase. Jamal grabbed the gun while I ran up and found you in the hall..." His voice trailed off. She could only imagine what he saw. He took a breath and continued. "There was so much blood. The blood loss is what nearly killed you." He clutched her hand and brushed his lips across her knuckles. "The bullet grazed your liver. But it also nicked an artery, and when you forced yourself to move, the bleeding..."

"We heard a door slam. Maybe it was you and Jamal coming in." She smiled. "Or maybe it was a ghost."

"Yeah, right. Would have been nice if our so-called ghost showed up *before* you got shot."

"I thought it was Zach. I tried to save him, but I collapsed before I could do anything." Amanda's eyes closed for a moment, overwhelmed at the thought of how close they came to disaster.

"Amanda, please don't close your eyes. Look at me. I've waited two days to see those beautiful blue eyes of yours."

She blinked away the tears that threatened to fall. She knew he hadn't left her side. She reached out to him with her left hand and winced at the jolt of pain she felt.

"That's just a flesh wound on your arm. It'll heal in no time."

But something else caught her attention and she didn't register what he was saying. There was a ring sparkling on her left hand. It was a glittering canary diamond in a pillow setting, surrounded with small white diamonds, all supported in a lacy platinum setting that fit her small hand perfectly. Blake lifted a shoulder when she met his loving eyes.

"It's a golden diamond for my golden girl. I was going to propose this weekend at Halcyon. I figured we could have a Christmas wedding. When I wasn't sure..." His face darkened, and he looked as if he were in physical pain. He swallowed hard. "I wanted you to be wearing it, you know? In case something happened." He took a deep breath and said the next part quickly. "If you died, I wanted to be sure you were mine. I wanted you to be my fiancée before you left me..." Her heart pounded so loudly she thought he'd hear it. She couldn't imagine what he'd gone through while she was unconscious. He seemed lost in somber thought, then he looked up and gave her a boyish grin.

"I think I knew we'd be together from that first day when I caught you breaking into my house. You were so beautiful and so full of…life. When I watched you sleeping in my bed that day, I thought I'd stepped into a fairy tale."

She laughed, and grimaced at the pain it caused. "I didn't break in. The door was wide-open."

"Whatever." He chuckled. "Even when you drove me crazy and challenged me and flat out defied me…even then, I just couldn't stay away from you. I know this sounds sappy, but I was the moth to your flame." She rolled her eyes, but he kept going. "I'm *serious*. You didn't hesitate to call me out when I was being an idiot, or when I was being a coward, or when I was in denial. I told you I didn't believe in love, and you made me see what a lie that was. You rebuilt me, Amanda, from the ground up. I thought I hated surprises, but you've surprised me at every turn. I want to spend the rest of my life looking forward to the next surprise you have in store, whether it's orange chandeliers…"

"Paprika," she protested softly. She felt a tear escape the corner of her eye and roll down her cheek.

"…or little boys on my doorstep that you won't let me discard. You told me once that I saw you whole. Well, you *made* me whole, my love. The ghosts from our pasts can't hurt us anymore." He got up from the chair and gave her a soft kiss. "And the ghosts from Halcyon's past are on our side. Marry me, Amanda. Marry me."

A rising hum of voices was building outside the door to her room. He dropped to one knee at the side of her bed, still holding her hand.

"Say 'yes' before we're invaded by all the other people who love you."

"Blake, from the first moment you touched me, you've made me feel safe. I know I fought you and panicked and occasionally tried to chase you away—" he smiled at that "—but you kept insisting what we had was right and true. And it was. It *is*. I'm done with being afraid. Life is waiting for us both, Blake, and I can't imagine facing it without you. I love you, and—"

His mouth was on hers before she could finish. Insistent, tender, passionate and protective. Everything that *he* was, that's what his kiss was. There was love there. There was security there. And as she parted her lips with a sigh of surrender, she knew without a doubt there would be arguments and laughter and passion and challenges and common enemies and many, many friends in their future. There would be babies for sure, and there would be Halcyon. But most important was the love they shared. Her right hand rose and twisted in his curling black hair. He growled as she tugged him closer. He was hers. She was his. No more secrets. No more fear. Only love.

They were barely aware of the door to the room pushing open. Nora stepped in, then raised her hand to silence the group behind her. Julie held Zach's shoulders tightly to keep him from dashing forward. With her were Mel, Bree, Andy, Caroline and, yes, even Dario, weeping loudly into his handkerchief. They stopped en masse and waited for the kiss to finally end before flooding into the room to welcome Amanda back to the world of the living.

Epilogue

December 29

Blake fidgeted with the collar of his gray morning suit. Damn Amanda for insisting on the formality. And damn him for not being able to say no to her. Zachary shifted at his side, and dug his fingers under the collar of his own matching suit. Blake winked at him, but Zach just rolled his eyes.

"How much longer, Dad?"

He was Blake's best man, clutching two wedding rings tightly in his hand. Blake and Amanda began the adoption process last month, with Zach's blessing. He'd never had a father, and he got such a kick out of calling Blake "Dad." That was nothing compared to what Blake felt every time he heard it. The boy needed security and stability, and he'd have that as their son. Amanda had no intention of replacing Tiffany, and she'd insisted he call her "Aunt Amanda." But Zach argued that once she married his *dad*, then she'd be his mom. His second mom.

Andy hovered nearby, laughing with Caroline about something. He was probably gloating over the fact *he* didn't have to wear a silly tux. A small crowd was gathered in Halcyon's main hall, which had been transformed into a Christmas wonderland. The tree stretched to the high ceiling at one end of the room, covered with hundreds of twinkling lights. The ornaments were all colors and shapes. Amanda wanted a giant, old-fashioned tree, and she got it. Their gifts had all been opened on Christmas morning, then whisked out of sight in preparation for the wedding.

Pine boughs were wrapped through the chandeliers and draped across every surface downstairs. Amanda chose an ivory and pink color theme for the wedding, and Halcyon was glowing like a candy confection. The marble fireplace had been transformed into an altar, complete with a large brass cross Amanda found in the attic. Ivory and pink roses fell in a beribboned blanket from the mantel to the floor. A string quartet was set up in front of the tree, playing a soft medley of Christmas music and love songs.

Blake caught a movement on the stairs and turned as Amanda's cousins came down the steps in one giggling mass of pink silk and ivory velvet. Amanda wanted to keep things small and refused to choose only one cousin to be an attendant, so the three of them were dubbed "the women in charge." Bree coordinated the decor and logistics, Mel helped create the gown, and Nora worked with Dario on the menu. The three women had been upstairs helping the bride with last-minute preparations.

Bree nodded to the quartet, and they stopped playing. People moved to take their seats near the makeshift altar. A man in a black tuxedo sat at the new grand piano that had been Blake's Christmas gift to Amanda. With a gesture from Bree, the guests stood and turned to face the staircase. The pianist paused, then played the Vangelis hymn Amanda had chosen. Blake rested his hand on Zach's shoulder. The moment had arrived, and not a moment too soon. No one else in this room had any idea how fortuitous their short engagement had proven to be.

Julie stepped into view on the stairs. Her hair was pinned demurely behind each ear with jeweled clips. The pale pink gown showed off her freckled skin. She beamed at Zach before turning her smile to Blake as she moved to stand across from them.

The entire room sighed when Amanda rounded the corner of the staircase. Her hair was piled high on her head, with a few tendrils curling down her back. She held a small spray of pink and ivory roses. When they'd found Madeleine's old wedding gown in the attic, Amanda immediately sent it to Mel to be used as part of her own gown, and Mel's designer friend had worked wonders. The century-old hand-beaded Irish lace was draped and gathered over a cream satin sheath that hugged Amanda's curves perfectly. She looked like a vision from a very grown-up fairy tale as she walked toward Blake. The neckline draped low, highlighting breasts that threatened to overflow the satin bodice. Was it possible they were already getting bigger?

There was amusement in her eyes when he looked back to her face. She knew he'd been checking her out, and she certainly knew why. They grinned at each other like a couple of lovestruck teenagers, shy and adoring. She rested her hand in his and they turned to the pastor. Blake had a hard time focusing on the words being said, because he couldn't take his eyes off his beautiful bride.

He was in love. Forever love. The kind of love that songs were written about. The kind of love he'd never believed in until Amanda Lowery walked into his house and his life. He was one lucky bastard.

Amanda went to their suite to freshen up after the wedding meal. She was tired, and she'd had a rough morning before she started to get ready for the ceremony. But she was also blissfully happy. She headed back down the stairs. *Blissful*. There was a word she rarely thought of, much less used. But it was perfect for what she was feeling today. Sure, she still felt a little green around the gills, and throwing up every morning was no fun with her wound still healing. But the doctor had assured them there was nothing to worry about.

She was Mrs. Blake Randall. It was hard to remember what her life had been like before she met him. They were new people now, and they were building a new family here in Halcyon. She rounded the final turn of the staircase and stopped to gaze fondly at the people gathered for the wedding celebration. A DJ was playing music, and people were dancing in the living room, which had been cleared of most of its furniture for the occasion. The cake had been cut, the flowers had been tossed, the garter had been thrown. Now she could relax and enjoy the festivities.

Blake stood talking to Julie and Bobby near the Christmas tree. This was an intimate gathering of friends and associates. Other than Amanda's cousins, there were no family members here. Her mom was terrified of flying, and they'd promised to visit her in Kansas soon. Blake's family wasn't even an option. Despite that, or maybe because of it, the hall was bursting with love.

Her husband smiled across the hall at her when she caught his eye. Unconsciously, her hand traveled to her stomach, and he followed the movement. He looked back to her face, his smile deepening. He knew exactly what was growing there—his Christmas present. They hadn't told anyone—it was too soon, and it was a bit awkward with the wedding and all. But at nine weeks, her morning sickness was beginning to fade and her body was adjusting to the new life beginning deep in her womb. Her doctor was confident the pregnancy would proceed without complication.

It had been a shock to receive the news in the hospital that she was expecting. Amanda kept insisting it was impossible, but the doctor pointed out that even the best birth control methods failed sometimes. Madeleine Tiffany Randall had survived the shooting and seemed to be thriving.

Blake teased Amanda about the name choice, asking if she intended to name the baby Otis if it was a boy. But she knew this was a girl. It was *their* little girl. Zach's new sister.

Their little Maddy. She walked down a few more steps and glanced toward the fireplace, where several clusters of guests were talking. As one group moved away, she noticed two women standing together near the rose-covered mantel. They made a curious pair.

The older woman had golden hair, pulled into a bun that rested low on her neck. She was wearing an elegant blue satin gown that looked straight out of a silent Hollywood movie from the 1920s. The younger woman had long ebony hair, braided and intertwined with colorful ribbons. Her flowing dress was gathered under her breasts with another ribbon. She looked bohemian, free-spirited and very contemporary. The two women turned together to face her, and Amanda stopped breathing, bringing her hand to her throat. The young woman had Blake's dark sable eyes, flecked with gold. She smiled, and Amanda recognized Zach in her open, trusting grin. The older woman dipped her head in her direction. Amanda had seen her before, of course, in the picture that hung in the upstairs hallway. It was a photograph of Madeleine Pendleton that was dated 1925.

"Amanda? Are you okay?" Blake was suddenly at her side on the stairs. "You look a little pale. Is our daughter dancing the tarantella again?" She looked up into his laughing eyes. He insisted her morning sickness was due to his healthy offspring dancing in her tummy, even though the baby was barely bigger than a kidney bean at this point.

"I just saw…" She glanced to the fireplace. The women were gone. Maybe she'd imagined it. Or maybe Madeleine and Tiffany showed up to give their blessing to this happy family.

"You saw what, baby?"

She went on tiptoe to place a kiss on Blake's lips. "I saw the future, sweetheart," she said to her husband. "And it's going to be wonderful."

"I don't doubt it. Not for one minute." He took her hand and walked her down the remaining stairs.

"Come dance with me, Mrs. Randall."

"Forever, Mr. Randall."

And she did.

* * * * *

COMING SOON!

We really hope you enjoyed reading this book. If you're looking for more romance, be sure to head to the shops when new books are available on

Thursday 26th December

To see which titles are coming soon, please visit

millsandboon.co.uk/nextmonth

MILLS & BOON

Coming next month

CRAZY ABOUT HER IMPOSSIBLE BOSS
Ally Blake

There was no way he wasn't fully aware she stood behind him. The man's ability to read a room was legendary. He noticed changes in temperature, pulse, breathing, tone of voice the way other people noticed being kicked in the shin.

Yet still Lucinda took a selfish moment to drink him in before making herself officially known.

For Angus Wolfe's profile was a study in staggering male beauty.

The man was all chiselled angles. Sharp jaw close shaven. Hair darkly curling and a mite overlong. Reading glasses he refused to admit he needed to wear did nothing to soften the impact of the most formidable pair of dark hazel eyes that had ever been seen.

Even the tendons in his neck were a sight to behold.

Then he shifted. Slowly. Like a big cat stretching in the sun. The lines of his charcoal suit moved with him, cut as they were to make the most of his...everything. Each one cost more than she'd spent on her car. She knew. She paid his bills.

Then she spotted his socks. Peeking out from the top of his custom-made dress shoes she saw the merest hint of a wolf motif. She'd given him those socks for Christmas.

Her heart gave a little flutter, releasing a gossamer

thread of lust that wafted from throat to belly to places less mentionable.

She squished the thing. Fast.

Angus Wolfe might be able to read a room, but if anyone dared claim that Lucinda Starling - his long-time Executive Assistant, his right-hand woman, his not-so-secret weapon – was a teeny tiny little bit in love with him, he'd have laughed till he split a kidney.

Either she kept her cards closer to her chest than she realised, or he had a blind spot when it came to her. The fact that he had no clue was a gift. And she planned to keep it that way…

Continue reading
CRAZY ABOUT HER IMPOSSIBLE BOSS
Ally Blake

Available next month
www.millsandboon.co.uk

MILLS & BOON
MEDICAL
Pulse-Racing Passion

Set your pulse racing with dedicated, delectable doctors in the high-pressure world of medicine, where emotions run high and passion, comfort and love are the best medicine.

MILLS & BOON

THE HEART OF ROMANCE

A ROMANCE FOR EVERY KIND OF READER

MODERN
Prepare to be swept off your feet by sophisticated, sexy and seductive heroes, in some of the world's most glamourous and romantic locations, where power and passion collide.
8 stories per month.

HISTORICAL
Escape with historical heroes from time gone by. Whether your passion is for wicked Regency Rakes, muscled Vikings or rugged Highlanders, awaken the romance of the past.
6 stories per month.

MEDICAL
Set your pulse racing with dedicated, delectable doctors in the high-pressure world of medicine, where emotions run high and passion, comfort and love are the best medicine.
6 stories per month.

True Love
Celebrate true love with tender stories of heartfelt romance, from the rush of falling in love to the joy a new baby can bring, and a focus on the emotional heart of a relationship.
8 stories per month.

Desire
Indulge in secrets and scandal, intense drama and plenty of sizzlin hot action with powerful and passionate heroes who have it all: wealth, status, good looks...everything but the right woman.
6 stories per month.

HEROES
Experience all the excitement of a gripping thriller, with an intense romance at its heart. Resourceful, true-to-life women and strong, fearless men face danger and desire - a killer combination!
8 stories per month.

DARE
Sensual love stories featuring smart, sassy heroines you'd want as a best friend, and compelling intense heroes who are worthy of them.
4 stories per month.

To see which titles are coming soon, please visit

millsandboon.co.uk/nextmonth